STRAIGHT OUTTA DODGE CITY

T0119461

BAEN BOOKS edited by DAVID BOOP

Straight Outta Tombstone
Straight Outta Deadwood
Straight Outta Dodge City

STRAIGHT OUTTA DODGE CITY

Edited by
DAVID BOOP

STRAIGHT OUTTA DODGE CITY

Straight Outta Dodge City copyright © 2020 by David Boop

Additional Copyright Information:
Foreword copyright © 2019 by David Boop; "The Hoodoo Man and the Midnight Train" copyright © 2019 by Joe R. Lansdale; "As Long as Grass Shall Grow" copyright © 2019 by Mercedes Lackey; "A Simple Pine Box" copyright © 2019 by James Van Pelt; "Fang for Fang, Fire for Blood" copyright © 2019 by Ava Morgan; "Junior & Me" copyright © 2019 by Harry Turtledove; "The Dead Can't Die Twice" copyright © 2019 by Samantha Lee Howe; "The Adventures of Rabbi Shlomo Jones and the Half-Baked Kid" copyright © 2019 by Eytan Kollin; "*Rara Lupus*" copyright © 2019 by Julie Frost; "Stealing Thunder from the Gods" copyright © 2019 by Kim Mainord; "Kachina" copyright © 2019 by James A. Moore; "Finding Home" copyright © 2019 by Phyllis Irene Radford; "The Murder of the Rag Doll Kid" copyright © 2019 by David Boop; "Hell-Bent" copyright © 2019 by Tex Thompson; "Ghost Men of Sunrise Mesa" copyright © 2019 by Jonathan Maberry.

A Baen Books Original

Baen Publishing Enterprises
P.O. Box 1403
Riverdale, NY 10471
www.baen.com

ISBN: 978-1-9821-2436-6

Cover art by Dominic Harman

First printing, February 2020

Distributed by Simon & Schuster
1230 Avenue of the Americas
New York, NY 10020

Library of Congress Cataloging-in-Publication Data

Names: Boop, David, editor.
Title: Straight outta Dodge City / edited by David Boop.
Other titles: Straight out of Dodge City
Description: Riverdale, NY : Baen, [2020] | "A Baen Books original."
Identifiers: LCCN 2019048645 | ISBN 9781982124366 (paperback)
Subjects: LCSH: Western stories.
Classification: LCC PS648.W4 S76313 2020 | DDC 813/.087408—dc23
LC record available at https://lccn.loc.gov/2019048645

Pages by Joy Freeman (www.pagesbyjoy.com)
Printed in the United States of America
10 9 8 7 6 5 4 3 2 1

To the Daves (Summers and Riley)
This is all y'all's fault, you know?

CONTENTS

FOREWORD

David Boop

Many things that bring us joy in our lives came about by happy accidents. Coca-Cola, for example, started out as a headache medicine and, instead, became our remedy for sleepiness, the "solution" for cleaning pennies, and go-to for children who want to burp loudly, thus annoying their parents and grossing out their younger siblings. Thank you, Coke!

I never set out to write or edit weird westerns. I came by it quite by accident. I wanted to write mysteries. Specifically, amateur sleuth mysteries. I hoped to be the next Dick Francis, my favorite at the time. Even though I was a voracious reader of science fiction and fantasy, I considered them beyond my reach. How could I ever compete with Alan Dean Foster or Jack L. Chalker? And westerns? I hadn't even considered them...yet.

In an attempt to break in as a mystery writer, this being 'bout 2003, I regularly searched for mystery publications and contests. The *Tony Hillerman Mystery Short Story Contest* required a western-themed mystery. On the surface, this seemed easy. Westerns are just a blend of tropes, right? White Hat. Outlaw. Murder. How hard could it be?

There have been many examples of that type of western writing out there, but good westerns, the type that stick with you, are far from cliché. Movies like *Unforgiven, Tombstone, 3:10 to Yuma,* and *Silverado.* Fiction such as *The Assassination of Jesse James by the Coward Robert Ford, The Ox-Bow Incident* (both turned into great movies), or the short story collection *Bad Dirt* by Annie Proulx (author of *Brokeback Mountain*). These are all examples of westerns that defied formula.

And yet, I have never done anything the easy way. Thinking I could set myself apart from other contestants, I dreamed up a story about an outlaw who wakes up dead and, as a ghost, has to solve his own murder. I bet no one had ever thought of that: a ghost solving his own murder! (He says naively.)

William Ragsdale, once a lawman, lives in the desert outside the Arizona town he once terrorized. Unmolested for many years, he's murdered by someone holding a grudge. As he passes through the town, looking for clues, the "Rag Doll Kid" must face his own sins as he looks for final redemption.

Print. Send. Wait.

Whether it was that the supernatural aspect was too much, or that there were waaay better-written stories submitted, "The Murder of the Rag Doll Kid," did not achieve any recognition. As disappointment washed over me, I wondered if I would ever break into the industry I longed to be a part of? The answer was...

Sort of.

The story was rescued by a small indie spec-fic magazine called *Tales of the Talisman* shortly after losing in the contest.

Let me digress for a moment.

I get it. As a reader, you only have so much time in a day/week/month/year for reading, and you want to make sure every story you set aside time for is gold. Maybe you stick with only the well-known magazines, like *Asimov's* or *Analog*, but, in doing so, you miss an opportunity to discover the next big name. There are many famous authors who got their first sale in a micropress 'zine. There are whole magazines dedicated strictly to the genre you love. Like cross-genre detectives? Try *Occult Detective Quarterly*. If slipstream fantasy and horror is your thing, *Three-Lobed Burning Eye* is for you. Want more weird westerns? Try *Beneath Ceaseless Skies*.

All you have to do is look and you will find.

Tales of the Talisman (originally *Hadrosaur Tales*) was the passion project of writer/editor David Lee Summers (whose story, "Fountains of Blood," you might have read in *Straight Outta Tombstone*). It ran for twenty years and published short stories by the likes of Neal Asher, Beth Cato, and Marsheila Rockwell.

I happened to be at a convention with Mr. Summers, and I bemoaned my loss in the Hillerman contest. Curious, Dave asked for the plot of the Rag Doll Kid. After I explained, he said, "Well, that sounds like the type of thing I publish. I love weird westerns. Let me look at it."

"*Weird* westerns?" I asked, "What's that?"

"Any western crossed with another genre. By adding a ghost, you wrote a paranormal western, or . . . weird western."

He definitely knew more about it than I did, so I sent the story to him. He liked it enough to publish it. He gave me my first check as a semi-pro author. This was a huge deal! With that sale, I learned I could submit and sell my work—something I wasn't sure of before that. *And* this all happened with a genre I hadn't known I was writing in. Happy accidents, right?

It should have occurred to me though. I'd grown up with *The Wild Wild West* reruns and TV movies, and loved shows like *The Adventures of Brisco County, Jr.* I read Jonah Hex comics and watched *The Valley of Gwangi* and other cross-genre western serials on Saturday afternoons. My geek cred was there, but I hadn't considered these types of westerns anything but westerns.

[Baen has allowed me to include an updated version of "The Murder of the Rag Doll Kid" in this volume, for your potential enjoyment.]

A funny thing happened right after my first weird western hit the stands. I got an email from another editor asking if I would write *him* a weird western story for his indie press.

David B. Riley is editor of *Science Fiction Trails Magazine*, a long running cross-genre publication that has gone through many incarnations over the years. At one point, it had become *Steampunk Trails*, then *Story Emporium*, and finally back to SFT. "Grismel Guffyfeld's Quickdrawatorium" involved an alien presence setting up a virtual reality game to see who was the fastest gun in the galaxy. I continued to write more tall tales set in Drowned Horse, Arizona, and these would form the basis of my *Drowned Horse Chronicle*, of which twenty-some stories have been published to date. I've come to know the genre intimately as I've read the other stories I share anthologies with. My experience is partially why Baen trusted me to present you with three volumes of fantastic westerns. (Thank you, Toni!)

So, why tell you all of this? You were, most likely, drawn by the names on the cover and hoped to immerse yourself in their vision of an alternate world infused with dinosaur gunfighters and alien-altered werewolves. Maybe you longed for zombies, and ghosts of the past, and demons attacking Dodge City? Certainly, my origin story was not what you signed up for. But I do have a point (thanks for waiting).

If you are a writer like me—and many of you are—somebody will be the first to believe in your words. David Lee Summers not only published my first weird western story, but also my first science fiction story. David B. Riley has published more of my weird western and steampunk stories than anyone else, and I will continue to send him those stories as long as he is willing to look at them. They both believed in me, even when my craft wasn't smooth and my endings weak.

And I've tried to honor their belief by paying it forward myself.

I've always looked for new voices, authors hitting their heads on the semi-pro ceiling for a long time, and then giving them a chance to prove they're worth reading, too. You'll find them in all three volumes of the *Straight Outta* series.

They deserve the same chance to be read that the Davids gave me.

Sadly, *Tales of the Talisman* and the *Tony Hillerman Mystery Short Story Contest* are no more. Summers continues to publish novels, many of them weird westerns, through Hadrosaur Press, and Anne Hillerman continues on with her father's traditions over at WordHarvest Press. Fortunately, though, *Science Fiction Trails* lives on! Another *Drowned Horse Chronicle* appeared in their pages recently, as of this writing. I recommend you give them a read, *and*, if you fancy yourself a weird western writer accidently or on purpose, it's a good magazine to get started with. Riley will do right by y'all.

Let me end with this dedication.

To David B. Riley and David Lee Summers.

I owe you both so much for leading me through the world of weird westerns. You've had patience with me, as I've struggled to get the story right. You've supported me as an author and as a person. We've laughed together and grieved together. Your faith in me is why there are these three volumes of weird western tales. You are great writers, editors, mentors, and friends.

I dedicate this anthology to you.

Thank You!

DB 02/16/19

STRAIGHT OUTTA DODGE CITY

The Hoodoo Man and the Midnight Train

Joe R. Lansdale

There's people don't believe in booger stories, as my grandma used to call them, but that don't mean there isn't strange stuff out there in them dark woods or, for that matter, on the streets in town, out there on a buggy ride down to the river for a picnic, or coming through the woods spitting black smoke and carrying hell and damnation with it.

Thing is, once you know the world has a sliced sky from which things leak, well, you can't never lay down at night without your protections.

I work in a gun shop and I live there too, but it isn't just any gun shop. Zachary, who prefers to be called Zach, repairs and even makes guns, but he's got another kind of job that don't always pay and sometimes does, depending. But it's a job he will take on either way in the end. If he tries to dicker and fails to get some money out of the deal, he just sighs and goes on with it.

Zach had owed a hundred good deeds on account of a bad thing he did, and on the day the old man came in, his black skin graying, his black suit graying, as well, thinning too, a wide-brimmed black hat on his head with a white feather in it, I seen Zach perk up. Zach had done ninety-nine good deeds and still owed one more. That was the only way he could get rid of the baggage. He thought that old man might be the last deed needed for him to get shed of his little problem.

Now, when I say good deeds, I don't mean help an old lady

across the street so she don't get run over by wild horses. A thing like that is damn sure a nice thing to do, but it don't go on the ledger, so to speak. It's got to be bigger than that. Something real special.

I guess Zach's around fifty or so, though I have heard people comment on how he seems to stay at an age and not move away from it. Zach is a stout man with a gleam in his eye, and his skin is dark as the bottom of a well, and always shiny, like he just ran a race in the hot sunshine. He's always bent forward a little, like he's considering tying his shoe. If he wore shoes.

Zach not only makes and repairs guns, he can shoot them right smart, as well, and has a fast draw. And then, of course, there are all the magic books and talismans. He knows that stuff. That's his side business, and all the business he does, he does well.

I was sold to him when I was young by my folks who didn't want me. They were going through town with a traveling medicine wagon. They sold a few bottles of this and that. All of which my mama made, and nearly all of them a mixture of water and whisky and berry juice, but nothing that would do anything for you but make you slightly drunk and loosen your bowels.

Cure-all my folks called it, but it didn't cure much. I didn't miss them any. My pa beat me, and mama didn't love me enough to even hit me. I don't know it for a fact, but I heard they was hung from an oak tree for selling something that made a child get sick and die. Mama probably put the wrong berry juice in a bottle or some such when she was drunk. She could be a bad drunk. It was the parents of that child and some townsfolks that did them in. It wasn't the law, but it was justice, no doubt.

Zach had been good to me. He was teaching me a trade, two trades, like he had. I got three meals a day, and I had a bed in the back of the shop. It was set on top of a pentagram, surrounded by all the protections Zach had made for me. Blue bottles full of dead flies and horny-toad guts, crosses, silver doodads, and a salt circle around the inner circle of chalk that made up the outside part of the pentagram.

Early on, I wondered if there was any sense to all that stuff, until I woke up and seen sitting there in the dark, all around that chalk and salt circle, a series of squatting toad-like things. It was frightening, but I knew then that it was the circle and all that other stuff that kept them out. During the day I didn't have to worry, Zach told me, but at night, if I wanted something like water or a good book to read, a fresh candle for my night table, I needed to bring it in before the dark got deep and the clock beat twelve. Straight-up midnight was the time the demon door opened and the things came out in search of those that were involved in the hoodoo.

I told Zach I didn't never have to do that before he took me in, and he said, "I know, but them demons want me, and now they want you, or anything to do with me and you. You want a girlfriend, have your fun, but don't never fall in love, 'cause you can't have it, not really. You love someone, you're bringing them into something slimy and dangerous, and, once you're in the life, it takes something really special and goddamn biblical to get out of it." He said there were days when he hated having pulled me into all these dark shenanigans.

I told him I was glad to have been rescued, and that Mama and Pa were a lot worse than the demons, because wasn't no spells and diagrams that could keep them out, and besides, he had educated me some. I could read and write and do my ciphers, and I was learning the gunsmith trade, as well as that other trade of his.

I know I'm wandering, but I think for you to understand it better, you got to know Zach's circumstances, about them good deeds. You see, I was good deed number fourteen of the one hundred he owed. I've seen him do all the others up to where he is now. I helped him do quite a few.

He told me once that he had gotten as far as ninety-eight good deeds once, then messed up by doing something bad, and had to start over, and when he did, the baggage got heavier. When I say baggage, I ain't talking about no grip, or a tow sack full of possibles.

In the back of the shop there's a long hallway, and off the hallway are two rooms, one on the left, one on the right. I'm off to the left, and Zach is off to the right. But at the end of the hallway, hanging on the wall, is a big old mirror made of silver, and it's shiny as a baby's ass all greased with lotion. The mirror is framed in Hawthorn wood painted red with hogs blood and grave clay, and the painted wood is treated with hoss apple juice.

When Zach enters the hall, if even the light is bad, you can see him and me in the mirror, but you can also see the baggage, and no matter how many times I see it, even expecting it, it gets to me, makes my bones tremble inside of me like an old house rotting its lumber.

It looks a little like an old woman, and she's got her arms around Zach's neck, and her legs wrapped around his middle, and her head rises just above Zach's. Her face is long and she has a possum jaw, with a lot of jagged teeth in it, and once a month she smells so bad Zach can hardly stand it. Just once a month, and on that day he doesn't work, just rides off in the country and lives with the stink, which when the morning breaks and the sun gets warm, goes away, like a visiting in-law you don't care for.

He can do whatever he would do without her on his back, but she's there, in dark spirit he says, and he can feel her arms around his neck and her legs and feet around his waist, and he can always feel her hot breath on the back of his neck, and on that stink day, he says it's the breath that nearly kills him, 'cause it reeks like a feed lot for cattle. She's his baggage for killing a child to save his own. Both children died, his and the one he sacrificed to the dark ones. I don't know much more than that, but let me ask you, would you kill a child to save your own? You can bet my folks wouldn't have done a thing to save me or any other child either. They sold me for thirty dollars and was glad to get shed of me.

I was telling you about the man that came in, all dressed in fading black, and the first thing he sees is me, working on some leather, designing a holster for a pistol, using the pattern laid out for me by Zach.

I didn't really need the pattern anymore, but I liked to keep it near, just as a way of feeling like I always had it in case I needed it. Working on the guns, well, that's a different story, especially some of the guns Zach worked on, and certainly the ones he made to his own design. I liked him nearby to make sure I was doing that kind of business right.

"Boy," the old man says, "maybe you ought to leave the room. I got to talk to this man here."

"He doesn't leave the room," Zach said, his hands on the glass-top counter that held a number of Colts and Remington pistols. "He's my apprentice. Name is James."

"What is he? A high yella?"

"I suppose you could call him that. I call him James."

The man nodded. "All right then, but I got the kind of business to talk about that you pull out of a deep dark sack."

"I understand that kind of business, and so does the boy."

The old man nodded again.

"I been trying to find someone for years to help me do what I got to do, 'cause there's someone stolen and riding a kind of train that don't never let a passenger off. They say you're the man I need. A hoodoo man."

"Go on," Zach said.

"I heard rumor of you from an old man out in West Texas. Thing is, the whole thing that happened to me happened here in this very town, and now I'm back in it. I find that strange, that I didn't know you were here all along."

"Fate makes circles," Zach said. "I keep a low profile on the hoodoo business, and you got to be in the hoodoo to know who I am and where I am. In the hoodoo, like you. But, I don't work for free."

The man came closer to the counter, opened his coat, took out a small bag and set it on the counter in front of Zach, and said, "That there is silver dust. It's what I can pay you. It's worth a lot."

Zach pulled the draw string loose and pinched some of the dust and worked it with his thumb and forefinger, and let it fall back in the bag.

"All right," Zach said. "Tell me about it."

Zach locked the door and turned the sign to CLOSED, and we went into the back room and sat at the table where me and him eat. I got out the bottle and poured them both little glasses full of a dark whisky.

They took their sips, and I sat silent, and then the wrecked old man said, "Some years ago, right here in this town, I made a mistake. I wanted to be rich and powerful, and, well, there was a woman, and she was a fine-looking woman, dark, dark skin, with a heart like a lump of coal. Name was Consuela. Skin like black velvet, long legged and high breasted, but she had a gleam in her eye they made you weak."

"I know who Consuela was," Zach said. "We had what you might call a rivalry. Before her house burned down with her in it."

"Again, I had no idea there were two hoodoo masters in town."

"You don't really master the hoodoo. It masters you."

"True enough. Consuela had me do things for her, bad things. I stole and killed for her. She had spells, you see, and she needed certain things and certain events to make those spells happen. Items and sacrifice. She used them spells to help me along with money and for a long time magnificent health, 'cause that was before the hoodoo was in me. She owned my pecker, owned my soul. I dressed nice, had money in my wallet and fine clothes, of which these I'm wearing are remnants, but there were restrictions and prices to pay. One was, she kept me in her sight. Didn't want me to let on what I knew, I suppose, but mostly she kept me like a pet. All that I was missing was a collar and a bowl on the floor.

"Got so the only time I could get away from her was when I was on one of her errands. It's hard for me to talk about those errands, because sometimes they were bad errands. Really bad. I really don't want to talk about that.

"Then come a day I'm on my own at night, and I'd done a thing so bad I was sick, and I couldn't make myself go back to Consuela, not right then. I went to the café just to have some place to go where the light was bright and the voices in the room weren't demonic whispers.

"There was this young woman worked at the café. She was petite, soft looking as a puppy, skin the color of coffee with a splash of cream. Not as wildly beautiful as Consuela, but she was certainly pretty. I went there every chance I got, just to be in the warmth and the light, to smell fresh coffee and frying eggs and bacon. But mostly, I went there for her.

"When things were slow in the café, she would pause and talk to me. I learned she lost her parents to a fever, lost everyone she ever loved in one way or another, and yet, she was cheerful, positive, and I could feel the meanness I had in me, that Consuela had encouraged, easing out of me, like a snake going away from the chicken house.

"Her name was Jenny. She liked a simple life, and I decided I could like one too. I had to get rid of Consuela. I figured the best way to break her hold on me was to kill her. I thought I was most likely able to do that when she slept. You see, at night we slept in a bed inside a circle drawn on the floor, with diagrams—"

"We know all about that," Zach said.

"Why I come to you. You got a reputation for knowing your

business. When Consuela was asleep, and I was lying in the bed next to her, I eased over to the side of the bed and pulled the hammer out from under it, where I had placed it earlier in the day, and hit her in the head. She could keep those demons out, but she couldn't keep me out. I hit her and hit her until her skull and wicked brain were nothing but a splash on the sheets. And these demons that were all around us, they cackled.

"I waited until morning, when the cock crowed, and the demons around the bed became mist and wafted away. I got out of bed and fell to my knees, weak from fear and guilt and excitement. I'd broken the hold she had on me. I cleaned myself up and waited until Jenny was at work. I was thinking me and her could go away together. It might take some time to convince her, but I was determined. That's how much I loved her. You seem perturbed."

The old man had noticed that Zach's expression had changed and that he had cupped his hands together and let them rest on his chest. He seemed to be holding something inside of himself.

"You're blaming Consuela for the very things you wanted," Zach said. "She didn't make you do nothing. You did bad things on your own to get money and power, and now you want to lay it at her feet, justify what you done. You weren't under any kind of spell, because if you were, you wouldn't have been able to plan killing her, or even want to."

The old man nodded slowly, the feather on his hat bobbing like a big white finger. "Yeah. I can't disagree with that. That doesn't change the fact that she was evil and killing her was a good thing. Shall I go on with my story?"

Zach nodded.

"When morning came, I felt weak. It wasn't like I had slept. I ended up going into the front room to lay down on a pallet. Woke up and it was near dark, checked the big clock in the hall. It wasn't long before midnight. That's how much what I had done had taken out of me. I had slept the entire day and part of the night away.

"I realized, of course, that the demons would soon be out. I had to get back in that bed with Consuela's corpse so I could be protected by the charms and the pentagram. I was in the hoodoo life, a minor hoodoo man, but minor or major, the results would have been the same. These days I make my own pentagram and lay out the protection. It's second nature now. But right then, I didn't have the time. Not that I slept that much with her body in the bed, and after me sleeping all day, I was wide awake. The sheets were bloodstained, her brains splattered about, all of it beginning to stink. And I swear, her dead body twitched in the bed all of the night.

"Still, next morning, I felt happy, just as free and happy as I could be. I cleaned up, fixed me some food, and then I began to feel like I was carrying something heavy on my back."

"You're toting the baggage," Zach said.

The old man nodded.

"I can see its reflection in pools of clear water, and in things that are silver. It looks a little like Consuela. In one way it's heavy, and in another it's not."

"Your baggage is different from mine, but it's still baggage," Zach said. "And it's soul weight, not weight by the pound."

"I know that now, but that day and that night, I was figuring it out, consulting the tomes Consuela had, the books she never let me look in, only allowing me to read the pages she chose, teaching me little spells and having me run her errands, but never teaching me the big things.

"I boarded up the room where Consuela lay, took all the protections into the front room and drew a new pentagram and set myself a fresh pallet inside of it. Next night I could hear a lot of pounding and ripping in that other room. The demons were having their way with her body. Doing whatever they do. That night I started going back to the café to see Jenny."

"You had killed a woman with a hammer, and you went to courting?"

"Consuela was a monster. I had rid the world of her. I wanted a new life, a better one. One without murder and spells. Is that so bad?"

Zach didn't reply, but he sighed heavily.

"After a couple weeks and a lot of sweet talk, I convinced her to walk with me down by the river. She brought a blanket, and we sat on it and looked out at the water. Soon we were kissing, and then we did what men and women do. We hadn't no more than made love, than I felt that baggage on my back grow heavy. I had a moment of joy, and that seemed to make the baggage grow heavy.

"We hadn't no more than gotten dressed than I heard it. A little toot at first, then a long low whistle coming from the north, heading in our direction. Jenny heard it too, said, 'There aren't any trains near here.'

"But there was. We could hear it, and then we could see its smoke rising up above the forest, floating into the moonlight. It was coming closer. The whistle grew louder, the smoke grew thicker, and my courage grew smaller. I didn't know it right then, but I know it now. It was the Midnight Train."

I saw Zach stiffen.

"Then we saw the tracks. One moment they weren't there, then they were. Not on any bridge mind you, they lay right on the water, and ended at our feet. There was a split in the woods and the split was shiny like a polished coin, and then we could see the train. It had one big ol' red light in front, and the smoke it was puffing had turned thick and dark. We were frozen to the spot. It looked as if that train was going to run right over us, and wasn't a thing we could do about it.

"Jenny took my arm and squeezed it. Instinctively we knew there wasn't any reason to run. It would catch us. The train stopped. No metal screeching, no sliding. The engine stopped right where the tracks ended. There was a hiss of stinking steam, and the cool air crackled against the hot engine.

"Then a door on the side of the train opened up, and some steps was rolled out. A little creature so white you'd have thought it was made of snow, bounced down the steps and landed on the ground and looked at me and Jenny. It looked like a huge white frog, but kind of human too. Its mouth cracked wide, and it was toothless, all pink gums, showing bright in the moonlight.

"Then another one of them toads hopped down. This one was black as a raven's wing, and it had a mouthful of shiny teeth, pointed and long. It looked like it could have chewed its way through an angle of iron.

"Then both them things turned their heads and looked up at the open doorway, like they were scared. First there was a boot, hanging in midair. Blood red, and tipped at the toes with shadow. Then there was a leg stuck in the boot, clothed in white pants with thin black stripes. As the boot put a heel on the top step, another boot and leg appeared, and the owner of the boots and pants stepped into view, ducking its head to come out of that door on the train. He wore a big white hat with a thin black band around it. He was eight foot tall if he was an inch. I could feel that burden on my back swell and grow heavy on my soul.

"This tall man, pale of face with the corners of his mouth

upturned, like he might break into smile, came to stand on the ground by the train, the toad-things on either side of him. He looked at us. His eyes were dead looking. You could barely see his moonlit pupils through the milky covering over them, but now and then in that rich moonlight, you could see red shadows move in the whites of those big, dead eyes. He had on a long, white duster and his hands were big and his fingers long and many knuckled. He lifted one hand, extended a finger and pointed right at Jenny. Then he turned his hand over and wiggled his finger for her to come to him. Jenny clutched my arm harder, and the tall man smiled. It was a smile where the edges of his lips slid up to touch his earlobes, widening so that I could see some blocky white teeth like tombstones and a thin, forked pink tongue that licked at the air like a snake.

"The train had come for Jenny, but the taking of her was to punish me for what I had done to Consuela. Her hex reached out beyond her death to make sure I stayed unhappy.

"Jenny says, 'Pray. Pray to Jesus.' But I knew there wasn't any Jesus that could help us. That's when the tall, white man pushed that duster back with his long-fingered hands, and I could see on his hips, in snow-white holsters, two big ol' pistols. He kept that horrible smile on his face, linked his fingers, flexed, popped them so loud, both me and Jenny jumped. He pointed at Jenny again and nodded toward the train.

"Now the windows, which had been foggy, cleared, and what I saw through them windows I can't explain. It was full of passengers and they were screaming and howling, had their faces pressed against the windows. They looked as if they had been boiled, fried, and generally shit on. I looked at the tall man, and he cocked his hands above his guns, and though I was wearing a pistol and wasn't a bad hand with a gun, I knew right then I couldn't beat him, and if even I could, my bullets wouldn't do a thing to him. It was obvious to me that I either had to draw and lose, or give up Jenny.

"I can't tell you how ashamed I am, which is why I have come to you, to repair as best I can what I did. I put my hand on Jenny's back and pushed her toward him, said, 'Take her.'

"Jenny stumbled forward, looked back at me. I can still see her face, the expression of betrayal. Not long before, I had held her in my arms and we had made love, and now I was passing her on to an eternity of torment. She didn't say anything. Not a word, didn't make a sound. Don't think she could. The hopping men came and grabbed her arms, lifted her and carried her onto that horrible train. And then I heard her scream. It was a scream that made the short hairs on my neck stand up, made the goose bumps on my arms ripple and my stomach rumble with fear.

"That tall man, he got on the train too, and the steps went up with a snap. He leaned out from the door, and he cackled at me, and the sound of it was like having your flesh cut open with a crosscut saw. The train coughed smoke, and when it did, an open space near the engine lit up with a white light. I could see inside that gap, and the Engineer was there with his oversized engineer hat and baggy coveralls. He was little more than bones stretched over wet, dark flesh, and he and the Fireman, I suppose the other man would be called that, were feeding screaming, struggling bodies bound up in guts and skin and long weaves of hair, straight into the blazing fire box. When they went in, you could hear them scream, and then their screams became as one and turned into the sound of the train's whistle. The train coughed, and it began to back up, and then in no way I can explain, I was no longer looking at the engine, but at the caboose. Away that train went along those tracks, and as it went the tracks disappeared behind it. The woods swallowed the train, but for a moment I could hear it toot its whistle, and I could see smoke above the tree line. Then the whistle stopped screaming, and the smoke was gone. There was only the moonlight tipping the trees with hats of silver.

"Everything outside that bubble we had been in set itself free. You could feel it in the wind and in the way the trees weaved a bit in the breeze. Where before the world was silent, you could now hear night birds sing, frogs bleat, and crickets chirp.

"The train was gone, and Jenny was gone, and there I stood, the weight on my back heavier than even moments before. A coward in moonlight and shadow.

"I ran away quick, didn't go back down there, next day or the day after. Didn't want the train to come back. I had Consuela's books of magic, some she had written herself in her own crabbed handwriting. Heavy of heart, and heavier of soul, I began to read them carefully. I started thinking maybe I could get Jenny off that train, get that burden off my back. But if the answer was in those books, I didn't find it.

"I decided I had to search out someone who could help me, not knowing the very person who could was right here in this town, near where it all happened. I packed up my goods and Consuela's books and all her money, which was considerable, loaded it all in a wagon drawn by two strong horses. I quested for years, looking for help, and now, here I am, looking at you, asking you to help me for a bag of silver. I'm getting old now, and if I die with this thing on my back, well, no telling where I'll end up, but I know this much, it isn't good. Jenny's on that train, and it's all my fault."

When the story was finished, we all sat there quietly.

It was the old man that broke the ice.

"Will you assist me? Help me rescue Jenny?"

Zach pooched his lips the way he does when he's thinking hard on something. He let the old man's question hang in the air awhile. Finally, he spoke.

"Go back to wherever you're staying, and let me marinate on this thing. Come see me tomorrow when the sun's dying, and I'll tell you what I will or will not do. But let me explain to you what you're up against. It's not just the Midnight Train, but the Dueling Man and his minions you got to deal with. And let me tell you, the Dueling Man is made up of more bad deeds than either of us have seen. He works for the Engineer. He could go bear hunting with harsh language and wipe his ass with an angry badger, and that doesn't even begin to explain what he is and how he is. Go away for now."

That old man got up slow, like he had to build himself bone by bone to stand up, and then he dragged out of there like there was a ball and chain on his foot.

I looked at Zach. "Well?"

"I don't know. He's blaming this Consuela for everything he's ever done, and he mentioned murder as some of the things he done. I'm thinking he did it for himself, as well. That he earned his burden more than Consuela gave it to him. Her death was just the final act that put that weight on his soul."

"But what about Jenny?" I said.

Zach didn't answer.

☆ ☆ ☆

That day, I did all the work that was to be done, except some fine touch-ups on a gun being made for a gambling man. It was going to have some etchings on the hilt, and Zach had to do that. He had the talent, and he had the steady hand.

Zach sat in the hallway in a padded chair in front of the long mirror and looked at himself and that baggage on his back. He had a stand by his chair, and had a lamp on it and some hoodoo books. I looked in on him a couple times, brought him a cup of coffee and a piece of ham and bread about noon. He took it from me without comment, continued to look at himself and his baggage in the mirror. The thing in the mirror looked at me, and when it did, it made me feel cold from the top of my head all the way down to the heels of my feet. I got out of there pretty quick, left Zach to his considerations.

It was late afternoon of the next day when the bell over the door clanked, and the old man came in and walked over to me. I got up and told Zach he had arrived. Zach sighed deep, rose and followed me into the main part of the shop.

"Your decision?" said the old man.

"I've studied on it. I have to build you a gun, a special gun to use against the Dueling Man. I'll have to make some special ammunition for you too. Come back in a week's time, and I'll have it ready."

The old man tipped his hat and went away. Zach looked at me. "This is going to require a lot of black coffee."

The days passed by so slow you would have thought they was crippled.

I did the work Zach asked me to do, as well as kept making coffee, because once he got started on that gun he didn't sleep much, and with all that coffee, how could he?

Among the jobs I did for him was pack some powder and a specific shot inside the casings for the pistol's ammunition. Those were big ol' bullets when they were finished. Fifty calibers, and for a pistol! But here's the odd thing, they was as light as if they was made of air and a prayer.

Zach had some metal to use for making pistols and such, but this metal he had he got out of an old trunk in the back, and the long barrel of the pistol was made of a steel so blue it made a clear spring day look dull. You could see your reflection in it.

Zach looked into it with me, and I could see the baggage on his back, that horrible face. That told me there was silver in the bluing. That barrel was light in a similar way as the ammunition. The hilt was made of Hawthorne wood, painted black with a paint made of ashes and drops of frog blood and glue. When the gun was finished, it looked right smart the way it gleamed in the sunlight coming through the window.

Zach let me handle it. It was the best-balanced pistol I had ever held, single action, 'cause Zach said it was a more steady shot when cocked and aimed.

I gave Zach the holster I had been working on, made of gold-dyed leather, the dye some concoction of Zach's. He heated an iron in the fire from the wood stove and burned designs into the leather. Those designs were swirls and little figures that Zach said were spells and such. I took his word for it.

He loaded the gun, shoved it in the holster, had me put it away. When I carried it to place inside the trunk where he kept his most important stuff, that gun seemed alive in my hand. I thought I could hear it whisper.

Zach had finished his work two days early, and when he was done, he went to bed and stayed there through dark and light without waking for two whole days.

Come the morning of the day the old man was to come, Zach got up and had me heat some water and fill a number-ten tub. He stripped down and got in it and soaked in a lot of soapy suds.

When he finished bathing, he got dressed. Put on black pants and a black shirt and a black hat with linked silver Conchos for a hat band. He wore a bolo tie with black strings and silver tips, and the clutch of the tie was silver and in the shape of a scorpion. He pulled on black boots fresh polished with silver-tip toes. He had me fetch the holster and pistol. I brought it to him, and he sat behind the counter on a stool and read a dime novel while waiting for the old man to come. He had me pull down the shades and lock the door and turn the sign to say CLOSED.

We sat there all day, Zach reading dime novels, and sometimes reading from the big hoodoo books he had, or from clutches of loose notes.

It was nearly dark when there was a tap on the door. I looked at Zach, and he nodded. I opened the door to the sound of the overhead bell clanging. It was the old man, dressed as he always was, like Zach, in black, except for that tall white feather. He was bent over more than before and walked like his feet was tied together. He was old the day he first came into the shop, but today, he was much older.

"I have the gun," Zach said.

Zach lifted the holstered pistol up and put it on the counter. The pistol had the smell of gun oil about it, but there was something else, a tinge of something long dead; just a whiff, but it was there.

The old man spoke, sweat popping out all over his face. "I want to get Jenny off that train, but I've gotten old, and I'm not that good a gun hand anymore. I appreciate the gun, and I'm sure it's worth all the dust I paid you... But can I ask you to handle it? To be my surrogate?"

Zach smiled, made a kind of gurgle that might have been a laugh, and said, "I expected just this. I can tell a man that wants to do something he's afraid to do and wants someone else to do it for him the moment I talk to them."

"If I were younger—"

"When you were younger you let the Dueling Man take Jenny. You killed a woman who, though she may have had it coming, you were in the deep hoodoo with before. The power, the money, the black magic. I know what kind of draw Consuela had. I was in her arms once. Does that surprise you? Her price was too high for me. But not you. Then you wanted out, and you wanted something clean and innocent to make you feel clean, so you took up with Jenny and let the doo-doo from the hoodoo rub off on her."

"I was young then."

"We all been young," Zach said. "But, that's not enough of an excuse. Not for what you said you done. You got guilt on you, and shame, and that's at least a good thing. It's the only reason I'm helping you. You feel remorse for what you've done and have thought about it for years. As for Jenny, I don't know her, but she's an innocent soul, and I want to get her off that train. So, let's cut the bull and get down to brass tacks and good ammunition."

Zach looked at me. "I going to have to depend on you for something, son. And it's a big thing."

"Just tell me what you want," I said, and I sounded a lot

braver than what I felt, having heard about the Dueling Man and the Midnight Train.

"When, and if, I dispatch the Dueling Man, there will be the two demons. The frog-like things he's been talking about. I'll try to deal with them. Meantime, you gather up all the courage you have, because it will take it, and you get on that train and you yell, 'Miss Jenny, I'm a hoodoo man, and I've come for you.'"

"But I'm not a hoodoo man," I said.

"Yes, you are. You've worked for me, and I'm going to put a spell in your pocket. It's not a strong one. There ain't much in the way of strong when it comes to the Midnight Train, 'cause you might have to face the Engineer. He gets you, all bets are off. Your ass is good and got. The good thing though is the Engineer lets the others handle the bad business most of the time, but if he should decide to handle it himself, you get off that train quick as you can.

"That little spell I'll put in your pocket, it'll make it so if someone on the train tries to grab you, they'll not be able to. But it's not a long-lasting spell. Some of those on the train will be wailing and begging for you to take them with you. You won't have the ability to take anyone off the train except the one you call out to. When you call out for Jenny, she'll come to you. She may not look just right. In fact, she will look terrible. You take her hand, and that will give her the protection you got. But that sucks on the protective spell, and you'll have even less time than before.

"Get her and you run for the door, any door that'll get you off that train. Even if it's moving, you jump, you jump as hard and far as you can, and have Jenny jump with you. She gets off the train, she'll be the Jenny that was put on that train all those many years ago.

"Course, if I can't beat the Dueling Man, then you run like your ass is on fire and don't never even think for a moment about getting on that train. I'll be done for, me and my baggage will get on that train, and we'll ride and ride and ride. We succeed, then I'm free of my baggage."

"What about me," the old man said, "will I be free?"

"That remains to be seen," Zach said. "I don't like you. I got nothing for you except to help Miss Jenny. Where she is, that's on you. And just to make myself understood, if you get out there and decide to run, like you did before, I'll shoot you. That way, with the baggage you got, I can assure you of a long train ride."

"Should I actually go with you?" the old man said. "Maybe, being old like I am, decrepit, I ought to stay here until you get back. I might make things worse."

Zach laughed loud enough to tremble the rafters.

"Oh no you don't. You're going."

We had some ham and bread, and Zach let the old man take a shot of whisky, but Zach didn't have none. He had coffee instead, and when he finished with it, he said, "We'll go down early and take the lay of the land. I suggest we go to the place where you and Jenny encountered the train. Might as well make this whole thing full circle."

We played some cards as the night grew rich, and then we packed up some folding stools and a basket with more of that damn ham and bread in it. Zach went and wrapped his mirror in a black cloth and brought it out and put it with the other stuff.

"What you need that for?" the old man asked.

"I hope it'll give me an edge."

We didn't bother with horses. It wasn't that far away, and Zach said if we all got killed, or worse, taken on the train, we didn't want to leave the horses out there all alone.

That kind of talk made me nervous.

Zach had the old man carry the basket of ham and bread. I had the folding stools under my arm, and Zach carried the cloth-covered mirror, which is a really light tote. He, of course, wore the big gun on his hip.

It wasn't a long walk. You were in town one moment, and then you weren't. Before you knew it, you was traveling along a moonlit trail in the woods, on down to the river. You could hear it gurgling before you could see it.

When we got to the river, Zach said to the old man, "Where were you when the train came?"

"Almost right here. Maybe a little closer to the river."

It was a full moon night, and it was near bright as day, and the moon's reflection in the water made it look as if it was floating on the river. The water and the trees looked to be frosted.

Zach got out his big turnip watch and popped the cover on it and looked at the time in the silver moonlight.

"We are two hours ahead of time. Good."

I unfolded the stools as Zach set the mirror so that it stood upright, but with the cloth still over it. The old man placed the basket on the ground and sat down heavily on one of the stools.

I won't lie to you. I was as nervous as a long-tailed cat in a room full of rocking chairs, and the old man, well, I think he was starting to wish maybe all those years he shouldn't have been planning to come back here and set Jenny free. And maybe it wasn't so much about Jenny, as it was getting rid of the baggage before he died. I figured that was what his look out was for. Get her off that train and lose that baggage.

Zach gave me a little bag and told me to put it in my pocket, that it was my protection. I took it and did just that, but I'll tell you, the idea that there might be anything in that little bag that would spare me from what was on that train was hard to grasp.

"What about me?" the old man said.

"You don't get a bag," Zach said. "You got to depend on me."

Zach ate some more of the ham and bread, but me, I was too nervous to eat, and so was the old man. We sat there watching the river, the woods, and the big ol' moon, waiting for the tick of midnight, which came slow. The minutes weren't in any hurry that night, and seemed each of them was an hour long.

Finally, Zach got out his watch again, looked at it, said, "Won't be long now."

Short time after he said that the air turned chill, and we heard a kind of chugging, a long way off, but the sound was growing closer. There was a long high lonesome whistle and a series of toots. It sounded like a train, and at the same time it didn't.

Black smoke appeared above the moon-tipped trees, and a rolling white mist moved between the trees and blew over the river. When the mist faded there were tracks lying right on top of the river, and running on through a gauzy silver split in the woods. Then, here come that train. You could see the cow catcher in front, black and shiny as Cain's sin, and the one big light of the train was like a burning red eye. The whistle blew long and hard, and the air went still as an oil painting, and there was a bright cold glow around us for some distance, and outside of that glow I could see bats frozen in flight. Time had stopped out there, but we were inside the spell of the train and what it carried.

The train chugged on across the river, and the engine passed us close enough that the wind from it blew off the old man's hat.

He didn't try to chase it down. He may not have even known he'd lost it, so intent was he on that strange, black train.

The train stopped with part of it on the tracks stretching across the river, but with a lot of it on the river bank. The engine was right next to us. You could hear the train crackle as the hot engine was being cooled by the air. We was still on our stools, but now we stood up, and I could see that the old man was trembling like a naked man in a snow storm. Zach seemed remarkably calm. He pushed his coat back so that the hilt of the hoodoo gun showed. He took a deep breath.

Then came a snapping sound, like a big bone breaking, and a door on the side of the train sprang open. Down came some steps. They just flopped right out of the train and expanded, with the bottom step lying flat out on the ground.

Something moved inside the doorway, and then it leaped out, not bothering with the steps. It was a kind of black frog, I think, and yet, it looked somewhat like a man, bent low and held up by its squatty legs. Its hands were in front of it, and the thing was rubbing them together like a fat man ready for lunch. It had a mouthful of long, sharp teeth.

Another one of those things sprang into view, pale and larger than the other, more upright. It didn't have no teeth at all, just pink gums the way the old man had described them.

A boot stuck out of the doorway, rested heavy on the top step. A leg grew up from the boot, and then another boot came out of the train, and a leg grew up inside of that, and then above the legs the air darkened and took the shape of a man dressed all in white, except for black stripes on his pants. He wore a snow-white hat and had on a long white duster. He smiled. It was how the old man had described. The tops of his lips nearly touched his ears, and that mouth was like an open doorway to somewhere you didn't want to go. It was filled with teeth that made you think of murder and cannibals. The man's eyes—if it was a man—had a dead look, but in the whites of his eyes were little red shadows. They flickered and crawled. His forked tongue lashed out and whipped back inside his mouth like a snake discovering the weather was bad.

It was the Dueling Man, of course.

The Dueling Man turned his head from side to side, as if trying to figure us, and then he pushed his duster back on both sides, and you could see his guns, and they were just as the old man had described them.

Zach stepped so that he was centered with the man, and when he did he said, "Move the mirror up beside me, son. Now!"

I did just that. The mirror was so light and easy to handle I managed it in instants.

The Dueling Man's expression hadn't changed. He wiggled his long fingers and the whites of his eyes were no longer white with red shadows flicking around the edges. They had turned completely blood red. The frog-things squatted on either side of him.

"Take the cloth off the mirror," Zach said.

I whipped it off, and when I did, the Dueling Man's head pivoted slightly to take in his reflection in that silver mirror. I looked at that reflection. It was of a handsome man in the Dueling Man's clothes, not nearly as tall, normal teeth. Fact was, he was quite handsome in that reflection. Squatting beside him was a sad-looking naked man on one side, and an even sadder-looking naked woman on the other side of him. Tears fat as rain drops began to run down their faces.

I glanced at them, back to the mirror. The handsome reflection of the Dueling Man drooped, and he rested his hands on the hilts of his pistols like he was all worn out. He sagged inside his duster and white clothes. His unique boots looked worn and scuffed, and as I watched his white suit frayed and became covered in dust that made the cloth gray. The brim of his hat lost its snap and wilted.

The wide, ear-licking smile on the Dueling Man's face closed slowly, and he just stood there, looking at his reflection in the mirror, thinking on who he had been before he became a slave to the train and the Engineer. I felt sure that's what the reflection was. Who he had been.

In that instant Zach drew.

It was a cheater's way to do it, but it was still the right way to do it. The Dueling Man, distracted by who he once was, hesitated, and that's when Zach's pistol cracked. A hole about the size of the tip of my thumb spotted him between the eyes and you could hear what had been in his head splattering out behind him.

His long legs wiggled and then they collapsed inside his boots and all of him, clothes and flesh, went into those boots and the white hat fell down on top.

The demons came for Zach.

The old man looked as if he might run.

"Hold up," I said.

"I got him," Zach said, and even as those demons rushed forward, he whipped the gun over his shoulder and shot the old man right in the chest, without even looking.

The old man crumpled, ended up on his knees. He held his hand to his chest and fell forward, his face in the dirt.

"Consider that an extra good deed," Zach said as he shot one of the demons solid in the head, and then shot the other. It was all so fast and so calm you would have thought Zach wasn't doing nothing more than out target shooting.

The demons collapsed onto the river bank and the next instant they were gone to dust. The train fired up, and I bolted for the steps, hit them with a leap and was inside the train just as the steps clapped up behind me and the door slammed shut.

The train's corridor ran left and right, and I was in a kind of gap between them. I could see all the way up to the open engine, and I could see the Engineer with his big engineer's hat on and his dirty overalls, his flesh all taught, the bones in his face breaking through in spots. I swear he had an extra set of arms that lifted up out of his overalls. He and the Fireman, who was short and stout and dark from soot, sweat-licked from the fire in the engine, was loading gut-wrapped bodies into the fire.

They stared at me, but neither moved toward me. They kept loading those bodies, working to get that train to run. If it did, and I couldn't get off before my protection went thin, then I would be trapped.

I took a deep breath and turned in the other direction, started through the cars. The seats were full and the people in them, if you can call them that, were coming out of them. They were blistered and scarred and their hair was in patches. They all reached out for me, but soon as they touched me the spell in my pocket coated them with fire.

They leapt back and the flames went away. I moved on through the box car, yelling, "Miss Jenny, I am a hoodoo man, and I've come for you."

A man and a woman stood up from a seat and moved into the aisle in front of me. At first, they were just two scab-covered monsters, like all the rest, and then one of them called my name and I knew immediately who they were.

My mother and father. I won't lie to you, hate them as I did, I was sad to think of where they ended up. Somewhere along the line, they'd gotten in the hoodoo and, when they was killed, they took the train ride. I felt my heart melt. But pretty soon, it was solid again. What they wanted wasn't me, it was a way off that train. Zach was my family. Not them.

By then, the train was chugging and moving and rocking, and it was hot in there. It was as if the heat was lessened by that charm in my pocket, but I could feel it pushing at the air around me. I was starting to grow weak.

I kind of closed my eyes and forced myself between my mother and father, remembering how my father had beat me with a strop, and my mother had cheered him on. They reached out to touch me as I passed, and their hands flamed. They screamed and stepped back into their row.

"Miss Jenny!" I called out again and again.

Then, as I entered the next boxcar, a little figure came out of one of the seats and staggered toward me. I could see that she was female, but her boiled skin flapped off her face and her neck was broken so that her head was on her shoulder. She was naked, but it wasn't an exciting kind of naked. It was the kind that made your stomach churn and your brain deny.

She said to me in a voice that bubbled as if she was swallowing lava, "I am Jenny."

I hesitated, but finally stuck out my hand. She took it. No flames came off of me and jumped on her. It was Jenny all right. I turned and started pulling her after me as I ran back through the box cars.

We hadn't gone far when I seen the old man that had hired Zach. He had been hoodooed onto the train, and his baggage was full grown now, weighting him down so much he was nearly bent double. He lifted an eye and looked up at me. The baggage, a filthy old woman that I knew was Consuela, grinned rotten teeth at me.

"Help me," he said.

"You earned your place," I said, and pushed by him and the thing on his back. I yanked at Jenny's hand and glanced back at her, saw her head was straight now. The flesh on her face was flapping back into place and her skin was turning to its former coffee and cream color that the old man had described.

We came to the doorway and the steps. I opened the door with my free hand, kicked the steps out.

When I looked up the Engineer was hustling from his place up front, coming along the floor like a spider, using those extra arms to launch him forward. His engineer hat tilted to one side, but it stayed on his head.

Behind him, in the engine room the Fireman's face turned soft, and he yelled in a voice that coughed out in smoke. "Run! Run for all you're worth!"

There wasn't really anyplace to run, but there was the open door now and the night outside, the moonlight.

I said to Jenny, "Jump."

I stood Jenny in front of me and gave her a bit of a push, and she jumped. I stepped onto the top step, coiled my legs and leaped, just as the Engineer grabbed my boot, and it come off in his hand.

I went tumbling, and it was like I'd never stop. Down a grassy hill and into a wad of briars and brush. I hit something hard then and I was out.

When I awoke, my head was in Jenny's lap. She was put back together, so to speak. Her features were smooth and beautiful, and her skin looked like chocolate there in the moonlight. She was stroking my forehead. Tears were running down her cheeks.

"You got me off that awful train, away from that awful place."

I sat up slowly and looked around. There wasn't no train tracks and no train, and I had no idea where we was.

After I got to my feet and looked around, placed the moon, which was beginning to slide down behind the trees, I knew the direction to go. I was all cut up from the briars and such, but Jenny had pulled me out of them, and wiped me off with the folds of her dress, staining it with my blood. I had nothing worse than a missing boot and a slight limp that was going away even as we walked. Jenny had hit ahead of the briars and wasn't cut up at all. Her blue dress was ripped a little and there were pieces of weeds and cockleburs in her hair, but she looked fine.

We finally managed to get to where Zach was. He had covered the mirror and was sitting on one of the stools eating some ham and bread.

Except for the Dueling Man's boots and his hat on top of

them, there was nothing left of him. The body of the old man was there, but I knew his soul was on that train with his baggage, riding on and on for a bleak eternity. And I knew too, from the way Zach was smiling, his baggage was gone.

"Hello there," Zach said.

Jenny stayed on with us, which suited me fine. She didn't have any connection to her old life. The café she had worked at, and the people there, were long gone. I found me and her kind of suited one another.

Since I didn't have no baggage on me, I felt I could have a life, a relationship, not like before when I was linked to Zach. You see, after that night, I was done with the hoodoo in any shape or form.

I quit working at the gun shop too. Zach insisted. He wrapped the hoodoo gun up and put it away.

Me and Jenny was hitched by the justice of the peace, got a place of our own. In our little home, no demons came out after midnight, and I could get up and have a glass of water or go to the outhouse anytime I pleased.

One day, when I went to visit Zach, just to see how he was, not to get involved in anything, he and everything in the shop was gone.

A man down at the livery told me Zach bought a wagon, hitched his horses to them, and that was the last he had seen of him. But Zach had left me something, figuring I'd come to the livery to ask about him, since a wagon would have to be rented or purchased to haul off all that was in the shop.

What Zach left me was a wooden box.

"It don't have no key," said the man at the livery.

I took it home and used a chisel to pry it open. Inside was the bag of silver the old man had given Zach. In the bottom of the box was a note.

SO YOU AND JENNY DON'T HAVE TO WORRY NONE.

Well, so far, me and Jenny don't have no worries, but now and again I think about Zach and wonder where he is, and if he's still gunsmithing, or if he might be back heavy in the hoodoo business again.

As Long as Grass Shall Grow

Mercedes Lackey

They called this part of Oklahoma Territory the "Cherokee Outlet," because it was supposed to give the Cherokee, whose tribal reservation lay to the east of it, a way to get to their traditional hunting grounds. Andy Falk figured they probably did use it for that, but they also leased it to cattle ranchers for grazing and, normally in April, that would be all you would see out here—cattle and whatever wild critters shared the land with them.

But this was not a normal April, and the cattle had been forced to share the southern boundary of the Outlet with a strange and motley assortment of human beings, riding and driving beasts and contraptions that stretched for miles along the northern border of what was called the "Unassigned Lands"—a parcel of territory that had not been assigned to any particular tribe when so many thousands of unfortunate Indians had been ripped from their homelands and sent marching out here to be "resettled." In Andy's opinion, that was a far-too polite word for what it had been, which was unvarnished theft. Members of what were called the "Five Civilized Tribes" in particular had "assimilated" in the East on their ancestral homelands, made farms and prospered in the image of whites, in the belief—as white men had assured them—that if they imitated white men, they should have the same privileges and protection of the law as white men.

That had been a lie, of course. As soon as white men wanted those lands, white men got them, and Five Civilized Tribes got

25

rounded up and marched westward, with only as much as they could carry in their wagons or on their backs.

Andy sighed, looking eastward, and thought about those promises.

Andy had no intention of joining in any successive land thefts after this one. In fact, he wouldn't be here now if it hadn't been for an accident and a promise of his own.

A promise that had been made two weeks ago, when he had been in the town of Caldwell in Kansas, with no more intention of participating in this venture than he had of flying.

Andy Falk of Milwaukee, Wisconsin, would still have been at home in Wisconsin instead of this—at least to him—unseasonable heat of Kansas, if he had not been sent to find someone.

The love of his life, the clever and witty Elsa Baumgartner (she of the flaxen hair, merry blue eyes, and rosy cheeks) and her family had not heard from her father, Heinrich, for weeks, and they were worried. He was a land surveyor, and like dozens of others, he'd taken work with the federal government to survey and lay out 160-acre parcels in the Unassigned Lands of Indian Territory in advance of the Land Run that was to take place in April. The work should have been done; Heinrich Baumgartner should have been home, or at least have sent a letter if he'd been delayed. And Andy reckoned that volunteering to find the head of the household would put him farther up in the list of potential suitors in Elsa's eyes than he was now, which was just short of the middle. So he saddled his horse, Prinz, and headed south.

To be sure, Andy had never been further south than Chicago, but he considered that he was well prepared for Kansas, having read several stories for boys about the Wild West by Karl May in *Der Gute Kammerad*.

Andy, and Elsa, and all of Elsa's family were, of course, German, and had immigrated to Milwaukee and the colony of Germans there. But no one ever took Andy for anything but an American, because Andy had a secret.

Andy Falk—born Andreas—was an Elemental Master, a master of Earth Magic and its Elementals and, as an Elemental Master, he could summon a local Elemental to teach him any local language overnight. The Elemental he had summoned his first night in New York City had not only taught him American

English, but taught it to him with the local accent, a fact that always made him chuckle.

But he very quickly discovered that Karl May's stories had left him woefully unprepared for Kansas *and* his "eastern" accent made him a target for sharpsters, at least until he bought himself a revolver and wore it openly.

Fortunately, he knew how to use it.

Andy was a stubborn fellow, and his dogged persistence paid off. He traced Baumgartner like a hunting hound until he came to the border town of Caldwell, a town that had swelled to some fifty thousand people in anticipation of the Land Run. And that was where he found the surveyor, exhausted from lack of sleep, in an army-issue two-man tent at the edge of town, tending to a fellow surveyor who was deathly sick with cholera. He had not contacted his family because he had not dared leave his partner's side long enough to send a wire or a letter. No one here wanted to help him. Their minds were fixed on Harrison's Hoss Race.

"Get some sleep," Andy said, forcefully. Heinrich was too exhausted and grateful to argue. He stumbled to the other side of the sheet dividing the tent into two living spaces, fell onto the cot and was snoring in less than a minute. Andy turned his attention to the cholera-stricken surveyor.

Outside the tent, the air was so thick with the dust churned up by the fifty thousand or so people that had taken over this town that it was impossible to keep anything clean. There wasn't enough food or water, and Baumgartner must have used his connections with the Army to get both, though the food was hard biscuit and the water looked like sludge.

First, he called on his powers to purify the bucket of water beside the bed; like much of the water in this town, it was more mud than water. He made the silt in it gather all the contamination, then solidified the particles of tainted earth into a rock-hard ball that he lifted out and rolled out the door of the tent. Getting a dipper full of the now sparkling water, he held up the stricken man's head and put it to his lips while he assessed the man's condition.

Earth Masters were often doctors, but Andy was no physician, and to his dismay he quickly realized there was nothing much he could do to help the poor man, even with his powers.

He could try and strengthen the surveyor, but in the condition the he was in now, that would be of limited help. Andy himself just didn't know enough about medicine and the human body to purge the disease out of the poor man.

So once he had lent all the strength the man could take in, all he could do was what Heinrich had been doing. Apply damp cloths to the man's forehead, give him water and watch over him as the daylight faded and sunset turned to night. Just before it got too dark to see, he lit the lamp sitting on a small crate next to the man's cot, and turned to see that the fellow was awake, his eyes, bright with fever, fixed on Andy.

He expected the man to ask who he was, or where Heinrich had gone. But instead, the cracked lips parted, and what issued from them, in a harsh whisper, were the words, "You are an Elemental Master."

Andy started. "Yes—" he blurted. "But—"

"I am—an Earth Master." The man gripped his wrist with surprising strength. "Listen. This is important. You must—go on the Land Run. Go for me."

"I can't—" Andy began.

"*You must.* There is a section—must be protected—" The man shook with the effort of speaking. "Notebook. In vest."

Andy extracted the notebook from the man's vest pocket. Written down were explicit instructions on how to find a particular section in the eastern panhandle of the Unassigned Lands. "Go there—claim it—protect it. Promise!"

Andy feared what would happen if he *didn't* promise, and so he gave his word, and the surveyor settled back satisfied, and soon drifted back into feverish sleep. Andy tucked the notebook in his own vest pocket and thought nothing more of it. Instead, he again did what little he could to bolster the surveyor's strength in hopes the fellow would manage to fight off the disease himself with support. In the morning, refreshed by a good twelve hours of rest, Heinrich took over, and it was Andy's turn to bolt some of his provisions, and fall into the cot.

But by the time he awoke, the poor fellow was dead. Heinrich was just overseeing the undertaker as the body was removed. "A gut fellow you are, Andy," Heinrich said sadly. "I vill vire my vife, den I must see Hardesty's vife in Chicago and bring her der sad news und her husband's body. I vill see you in Milwaukee."

And Andy could only nod, knowing that if he *did* get back to Milwaukee, it would be long after Heinrich returned.

Andy pondered all this as he readied Prinz for the dash. He'd done what he could to prepare; Heinrich had left behind the bulk of the dead surveyor's goods and gear, telling him to take what he needed, so he had appropriated the clean cotton shirt and canvas trousers as being much more appropriate for the conditions than his woolen suit. There had still been army biscuits enough for several days, which Heinrich evidently had been subsisting on since his friend fell ill; Andy had taken this, the man's two canteens, a canvas shelter, a couple blankets, and his long rifle and ammunition. The rest he had packed up and left in the care of the owner of the General Store, with the understanding that he was to hold it until Andy or Heinrich came to claim it.

Four days before the Run, the soldiers guarding the Unassigned Lands had allowed those waiting on the Kansas border to cross the Cherokee Outlet and assemble on the northern border. Following the instructions in the notebook, Andy had worked his way to the eastern panhandle of the area, until he was due north of the section he was supposed to find, a spot divided into two equal halves, north and south, by a waterway the surveyor had noted as "Lagoon Creek." There he planted Prinz right on the line being maintained by the soldiers, and waited with the rest.

To stake a claim, he, like all the others, had a two-foot-long wooden stake carved with his initials and entry on it. He had to get to the center of the section he was looking for, find the surveyor's stake and land description, replace it with his own, return to the land office with it, and register his claim.

This was the only part of the mission he was certain of; as long as a "sooner" hadn't snuck in ahead of the appointed time and claimed the prize, Prinz could, and would, outrun and outlast every other horse he could see from where he sat. Not only was Prinz from a long line of hardy warhorses, able to carry a man in heavy armor all day, he came from a long line of fleet hunters. He had the speed, strength and stamina most of these other horses lacked.

And he had Andy's Earth Magic to replenish his energy and keep him fortified.

"President Harrison's *Hoss* Race" was what they were calling it, although besides horses, there was every sort of vehicle imaginable here, wagons, buggies, carts, and every sort of animal and none. Some hardy individuals evidently intended to make a run for their stake on foot. There were even a couple of high-wheeler bicycles, although Andy could not imagine how they thought they were going to negotiate the land he sensed in front of him now, crossed with hidden ravines and other obstacles.

That was another advantage he had as an Earth Master. Every inch of the land in front of him was as clear to him as if he himself had surveyed it. He knew were the ravines were that could break a horse's neck—where creeks of slippery stones were hidden—where there were gopher burrows that would break a horse's leg. Many horses would probably die or be hurt in this race. Prinz would not be one of them.

"It's going to be a beautiful day, isn't it, Earth Master?"

Andy jumped, as startled by the melodious feminine voice at his stirrup as he was by being addressed for the second time as an Earth Master. He looked down.

And Elsa fled from his mind as quickly as if she had never existed at all.

The woman at his stirrup had straight, brown hair done in a practical knot at the nape of her neck, not Elsa's flowing golden curls. She had brown eyes, not Elsa's cornflower blue. Her face was thin and a little sunburned, and another man might have called it "plain." She held the reins of a rangy roan mare, her tack was worn, and her faded calico dress and white bonnet looked to have plenty of wear on them. But Andy thought he had never seen a woman so *alive,* her eyes dancing with good humor, her mouth curved in a slight smile, as if she knew amusing secrets. Beside her, Elsa was just a china doll.

He had heard of love at first sight, especially among Elemental Masters, but he had never believed in it.

Until now. He felt terrified and elated, all at the same time. Every nerve in his body tingled, as if he was about to be struck by lightning. His mind was incredibly clear, and yet he could not get a single word out. He stared, and tried to breathe.

"Alice Brown, Air Master," she said, with a tiny bob of a curtsey, just enough to make a joke of the gesture.

"Andy Falk," he replied, managing to get his wits about him.

"You do know," she continued, as if they had known each other for years, "that only a head of a household can stake a claim."

His heart plummeted. He had *not* known that! What—

"If you get your claim, I'll marry you," she continued, electrifying him all over again. She patted the shoulder of the mare next to her. "If you want. Daisy and I may not be able to outrun most of these nags, but we can follow you, and I can guard the claim while you make the run to the registry."

"Why would you do that?" he asked, after gulping down astonishment. This was surely too good to be true. There had to be a catch. Had she enchanted him somehow?

And yet, he could not detect any deceit in her, and he was usually good at picking out the sharpsters, even when they were women.

"Because I haven't a cent to my name that's not with me, and that purse is too thin to live on for very long," she said frankly. "My folks are both dead of fever. My brother got married and his wife made his life hell until he sent me packing with a lot less than the half of the inheritance my parents left me. I need a place to live and food to eat, and I ain't afraid of hard work. We're both Elemental Masters, so we ought to get along all right, and if we don't, well, a hundred sixty acres can make two farms, easy." She had gone pale while she talked, as if she was now afraid of her boldness, afraid he'd think badly of her, afraid he'd think of her as some kind of hussy, or that she meant to cheat him somehow. "I may be no prize, but where else are you going to find a wife who's another Master?"

Now, he could have said he didn't need a wife, but that would have been a lie, and it wasn't a good idea for magicians to lie, as their lies all too often came true in the worst way. He could have said that he *had* a girl, but that would have been a half lie, for he was only one of half a dozen suitors, and anyway, after one look at Alice, Elsa had been driven clean out of his head. He could have said he didn't *want* a wife, but that was as big a lie as the first two. And anyway, his mouth blurted, "Done!" before his head had gotten through half of those thoughts.

But then he added, for the sake of getting everything out in the open, "I've made a promise to a dead Master. I've got a map to a stake, but it's on land he pledged me to protect, and I don't know why. It may be worthless. It may be dangerous. But a promise is a promise, and I aim to keep it."

"Then I'll help you," said Alice, and then there was nothing more to say, because it was coming on noon, and it was time to fill Prinz full of as much sustaining magic as the horse could hold. Prinz was used to this, and held rock steady while Andy reached deep into the earth, brought up its power, and passed it into his mount. He just finished as the nearest trooper began riding his horse back and forth, restlessly, peering to the west, where presumably the signal to let the race begin would come from. Alice mounted Daisy and backed her a little way out of the line; wisely, he thought, because when the shot came to send them on their way, the front of the line was going to be a dangerous place. She wasn't the only person to do so; the cautious and those who intended to remain behind were doing the same, and the wavering line on the border separated into two.

Andy bent down over Prinz's neck. Prinz, the veteran of many a race, knew what this meant, and Andy felt the stallion gathering himself for a racing start.

Andy felt, rather than saw, the line at the very limit of his vision jerk forward, and at that moment, the trooper in front of them shot his pistol straight up in the air.

Prinz threw himself forward with a tremendous leap, trusting to Andy to feel out the ground in front of them, and getting himself a nose length in front of any other horse in their part of the line. Around him, behind him, it was utter chaos, the thunder of horses' hooves on the ground, the clatter of wheels and the clashing of wagon chains. The horses all surged forward, some of them already tangling with others and going down with screams of fear and pain, taking their riders with them. Wagons careened wildly forward, and some were wrecked immediately. Behind them, the screams of horses and men and women pierced the cloud of dust that arose. But Andy could take no thought for them. He extended his senses, into the ground before him, and into Prinz, warning him of gopher holes, hidden rocks, uneven ground. Prinz surged into the lead with Andy's help and guidance and, in fifteen minutes, they were far ahead of the pack.

But Andy didn't rein him in. He could run for hours like this, with his strength bolstered, and he would have to. The claim Andy had been told to make was a good hour from the border at Prinz's top speed. He kept feeding Prinz with energy, and kept a lookout for the landmarks the surveyor had left in his notebook. Here a dry creek bed. There a creek with a trickle of water in it. There a particular clump of three trees. There weren't a lot of such landmarks; this was not the fertile land of Wisconsin. This was a harder soil, and his Earth senses told him it didn't see water nearly as often. It would take a special sort of farming, and even then, there would always be danger of losing everything to drought. Drought came often here, the land told him. That was why the trees here had deep taproots, and only grew where water flowed all year long.

He *felt* the claim before he saw it, which he had not expected. His Earth sense stretched nearly a mile in front of him, and the difference, the *specialness* spoke to him. At that point the trees of the bottomlands of Lagoon Creek were little more than a dark mist on the horizon. And then he knew why had to protect it.

It was sacred land, deep in the heart of that section. Land where once gods had walked, and might walk still.

Andy was a Christian, but he was also no fool. He knew very well that there were other gods, and that they still had power. Why else would the God of Moses have said, "Thou shalt not have other gods *before* me"? To his mind, that implied there were plenty of other gods, and that it was perfectly all right to give them honor in their own place, as long as Jehovah took precedence.

He didn't have long to think about this, however, as his final landmark, a lightning-blasted tree that had been drawn with exquisite detail in the notebook came into view. He aimed Prinz for it. If a sooner hadn't managed to hide out here and run in to claim it, he was far enough ahead of the pack it should be his.

And his heart leapt as his Earth senses coursed ahead of him, and he realized this was some of the best land he had felt yet on his ride. If he could stake it, claim it, and protect it—he could also farm it.

Prinz plunged through the woods—and these actually *were* woods, more trees than he was used to seeing here—and he wrenched his attention away from his Earth senses and to his ordinary ones. The section marker should be down here, in this rich bottom land, just before the creek itself.

There! He spotted the two-foot-tall stake, surveyor's papers fluttering at the top. It hadn't been claimed yet!

He pulled Prinz to a sudden stop, the stallion's feet slipping and skidding on the lush prairie grass beneath the trees, tumbled from his saddle, and seized the stake with both hands. He wrenched it out of the earth, ignoring the splinters in his palms, pulled his own stake out of his saddlebag and—grabbing a hand-sized stone from beside the hole where it had been—hammered it home. And only when the claiming stake and the papers attached to it were safely in his saddlebag did he breathe again.

And then he lost his breath all over again, as an Indian rose up out of the grass, long rifle trained on his head.

He was an old man, but Andy didn't doubt for a moment that his hand was steady and sight keen. His head had been shaved except for a stiff crest of hair, like the crest on a roman helmet, to which an eagle feather had been attached. His chest and arms were bare, his neck adorned with strings of beads and a round pearl-shell ornament. He wore a breechcloth and leggings of deerskin. And Andy had no idea which of several tribes hereabouts he could have come from—but he had no doubt that the man was here to protect this land.

Last night he'd done his best to commune with the elementals of this place, asking them to give him all the human languages hereabouts that they knew. So he took a deep breath, held up his hands to show they were empty of weapons, and tried Cherokee.

"I am here to protect this place, not claim it," he said.

Nothing.

He tried Caddo. Then Sac and Fox. Then Osage. Then Kaw. Still no reaction. And he began to grow desperate.

And then, suddenly, as he groped for the words from yet another tribe, the old man—laughed.

"I wish that you could see your own face, white-skin," the old man said around laughter, in perfect English. "I thought I had better ease your mind before you pissed yourself."

Andy nearly fainted with relief.

"Where is Hardesty?" the Indian asked, moving forward through the waist-high grass with an ease and grace that belied his age. "I was expecting him, not you."

"Dead. He got cholera from bad water on the other side of the border, and I got there too late to save him," Andy replied sadly. "I'm very sorry."

The old man grounded the stock of his rifle and sighed. "I'm sorry too, and for his wife. He was a good man. I did not know him long, but everything I learned of him told me he was a very good man, as well as a fine Medicine Chief of Earth, as you are."

"And you are also a Medicine Chief." This much Andy was sure of; he felt the power radiating from the man.

"The last of my band," he replied. "And the last to guard their resting place and the dancing floor of our gods. Hardesty pledged he would do the same."

"And he sent me in his place." Andy fished the notebook out of his vest and handed it to the old man who looked through it. "I'm Andy Falk, and I promised to claim this land and protect your sacred ground."

"I am Red Hawk." The old man held out his hand to Andy, who shook it, not at all surprised to discover the man had a powerful grip. "We now have a problem before us. There are those coming who will try to steal this place from us before we can register the claim."

Andy felt his insides clench up. He had been hoping that with all the troopers out here claim jumpers would be taken care of. But he had no doubt that Red Hawk was right. "Then we will—" he began, and then heard the galloping sound of hooves.

Before he could react with alarm, though, he saw the sort of Air Elementals *he* was used to—three little half-naked girls with butterfly wings—come zipping toward him through the treetops. *That would be Alice,* he thought, and turned to see Red Hawk staring at the Sylphs with his eyes wide and jaw slightly dropped.

Alice came trotting toward them through the trees on her horse—spotted Red Hawk, and pulled up her mare short.

Red Hawk recovered himself before she could bolt or reach for a weapon, as the three Sylphs hovered above her, looking from him to her and back again, uncertainly. "Do you know this woman, Earth Chief?" he asked.

Andy shook off his own bemusement. "Alice Brown, this is Red Hawk. He is the local equivalent of a Master. Red Hawk, this is Alice Brown, another kind of Medicine Chief."

"Ah." Red Hawk eyed the Sylphs again. "These—flying maidens are not something I have seen."

"They came with my mother's mother when she came from across the ocean," Alice told him, losing her wariness. Then she turned to Andy. "The rest aren't far behind me. They spread out quite a bit, and I am sure many of them stopped at the first unclaimed stake they found, but it won't be long before you—"

"—we," he said firmly.

The tense anxiety faded a little and she smiled. "*We* have to fight off the claim jumpers."

"No," Red Hawk said firmly. "You are not fighting off claim jumpers. This man and I will. You are going to take his horse, which is faster than yours, and ride to the place where claims are made."

"Registration office," said Andy, nodding, although his qualms assailed him. What if she registered the claim in her own name? What if she sold it to someone else? His heart said to trust her, but his mind—

"You think I'm not as good a fighter as you?" Alice shot back, her eyes flashing.

Red Hawk raised an eyebrow. "I think nothing of the kind. I think that I would be shot trying to register a claim. I think that you are the smaller of the two pale-skins, and the horse will carry you faster. And I think before you go, I should bind you as mates so that you may truly say that you are registering for him."

Alice flushed a bright crimson, but Andy couldn't tell if it was from embarrassment at her mistake, or because Red Hawk had said he was going to marry them.

All he could think was that he was having a little trouble breathing now.

"Come down," Red Hawk commanded. "This will take little time."

Alice dismounted and held the reins of her horse in her left hand. Red Hawk took her right, Andy's right, and bound them together with a rawhide thong he took from the belt holding his breechcloth, chanting something in his own language as he did so. Andy's flesh tingled where it touched hers, and he couldn't look away from her eyes.

Then, on the last word, *something* flashed between them. It was definitely magic, but more than that. It was as if the world turned inside out for a moment, and when it settled again, everything settled into a pattern that felt *absolutely right* in some indefinable way.

"There," Red Hawk said, matter-of-factly, when he was done. "You are mated." He unbound their hands and tucked the thong away. "Now, woman, *go*. The sooner you arrive, the better."

"Leave everything but one of the canteens," Andy said as she handed him the reins of her mare and mounted Prinz. "The lighter you travel, the better. Water Prinz, but not too much."

She nodded, tossed down the saddlebags and one of the canteens and trotted the stallion to the creek. She let him drink almost exactly as much as Andy would have, then pulled his head up, turned it in the direction of the registry office, and urged him into a canter. In moments, she was gone.

"What weapons have we?" Red Hawk asked, practically.

"Your rifle and mine. My revolver." He checked Daisy's saddlebags. "Alice's revolver." He pulled out a holstered Colt and an ammunition belt. While neither were new, they looked significantly newer than Daisy's tack. He checked to make sure it was unloaded, spun the cylinder, checked the action. All in good working order and recently cleaned. Satisfied, he loaded it and handed it and the belt to Red Hawk.

Then he got his own rifle and revolver, loaded both, and looked to the Indian expectantly. Red Hawk made a careful survey of the area around them with narrowed eyes. "I knew whoever was in the race would have to be coming from the north," he said, finally. "Claim jumpers could be coming from anywhere."

"That's true," Andy replied. "But they'll have to come *here*, looking for the survey stake, and to stake their own claim." He looked around as well. "I'll stay out in the open, at the stake. You go into hiding. They'll concentrate on me, and if they won't see reason—"

Red Hawk nodded. He faded back into the undergrowth, and in a moment, was gone.

Andy cleared ground near the stake and made a small fire. While he waited, he finally got a chance to look over this land he had claimed.

The first thing he noticed was that the trees were not going to be good enough to make a conventional wooden house out of. Many were cottonwood, which was notoriously poor for almost every purpose except kindling and shade, and his Earth senses told him the others were mostly of a sort of oak that was full of knots and twisted grain. Clearly, he would need to find some other way to build a house.

But there was water here, and decent land for growing things. He thought he remembered something about the natives here making large, multifamily lodges, somehow—

Then he heard the sound of a horse's hooves, coming out of the west. He stood up, rifle held down at his side, but ready to be brought up at a moment's notice, and waited.

At the sight of him, the rider abruptly pulled up his horse. They stared at each other for a long moment. Andy didn't like what he saw. He brought the rifle up, just a little more.

"This's my claim," the man stated.

"My stake says otherwise," Andy replied, as the man took his right hand off the reins, and held it near his holstered revolver.

"Reckon you can get a shot off afore I can?" Beneath his bowler, the man had hard eyes in a face that seemed set in a perpetual snarl. Andy lifted the rifle enough to take a shot.

"Reckon I can," he stated. "And I reckon I'll kill your horse with it. You'll have a hard time aiming with your nag going down under you. Then if I feel kindly, I'll let you walk out, if you can walk. And if I don't, the second shot will be at close range between your eyes."

Could he do that? He didn't know, actually. He'd never shot anything bigger than a jackrabbit.

But this man didn't know that, and Andy hoped that the calm way he stated his position would convince him that Andy could, and would.

The man's eyes widened with shock, then narrowed with anger. Without another word, he reined his horse around and galloped off, spurring it roughly.

"He'll be back," came Red Hawk's voice drifting out of the trees. "And he will bring more."

Andy sighed. "I was afraid of that. Maybe if I find a good tree to—"

"Lend me your power," Red Hawk demanded. "We are not far from the gods' dancing ground. There may be something I can do."

If Andy knew which direction the claim jumpers would be coming from, he could soften the earth enough to turn it into something like quicksand—

"Let me do something else first," he said, and backed away from the stake, putting his back to a grove of trees. Kneeling down, he put one hand on the ground and let his power flow into it, until the entire area around the stake was as soft as waterlogged mud. He'd positioned himself so the claim jumpers would *have* to cross that stretch in order to get to him, no matter which direction they came from.

"Good! Good!" Red Hawk exclaimed, at his elbow. "Very good! If you have power left—"

He held out his hand to the native, who clasped his wrist; he did the same, and he let the remainder of his magic flow into the old man. It was not an inconsiderable amount. "You are the Master here," he said, simply. "Tell me what to do."

"Wait for them, as you planned," Red Hawk said. "And fear nothing. I will take the mare to safety."

With his back to the grove of trees, he set his rifle within reach and unholstered his Colt, and waited.

He wondered where Alice was. He wondered how long she would have to wait in line. Those who had decided to grab the first available parcels, no matter how poor, would be at the office first, but surely she would be in the pack of those who—

He heard hoofbeats again, but just a single horse. Too fast to be Alice, who could not have gotten registered this quickly. He waited. Through the trees came a Federal Trooper, who, on seeing him, pulled up his horse short of the danger zone.

"That your claim stake?" he called, tugging on his hat by way of a neutral "hello" and to show his gun hand was empty.

"Yes, sir, it is. Sent my wife to the registry office with the survey stake." Those words, "my wife," put an electric thrill up his spine. "Just had one claim jumper I ran off, and I'm expecting more."

The trooper looked around. "Not surprised. Good land." He looked back at Andy. "We're spread mighty thin out here, and things are known to happen. You do what you have to do, son. I'll check back on you soon as I can. Just make sure I don't have to tell your wife she's a widow. If you disappear and someone else is holding your stake, that'll be all I can do." And with that, he turned and rode off again.

Well, that gave him tacit permission to do more than shoot a warning bullet. He just hoped it wouldn't come to that—hoped Red Hawk had something up his nonexistent sleeve.

More time passed. The shadows cast by the trees moved slowly across the open stretch in front of him. He took time for a sip of water from his canteen; his stomach was too knotted to try gnawing on one of those ration biscuits. "You need water, Red Hawk?" he called.

"I am well," came the reply, although he could not have told *where* it came from for the life of him.

Then, finally, the sound he was waiting for carried over the buzz and whirs of insects and the different calls of unfamiliar birds. Hoofbeats. Many.

He braced himself. And through the brush they came. Seven of them, all of them armed, all of them with guns in their hands, and all at the canter. *"There he is!"* shouted one, and they all spurred their tired horses into a gallop, clearly intending to rush him and cut him down in the proverbial hail of bullets.

And that was when their horses hit the softened earth.

He'd basically turned it to powder to a depth of about four feet in a stretch twenty feet long and six feet wide. As he'd expected, when the horses hit it, the powdered earth erupted in a cloud of blinding, choking dust. What he *hadn't* expected was that the front halves of the horses would plunge in while the rear remained on solid ground.

With screams of fear and pain, the horses somersaulted into the trench, sending their riders flying.

A couple of guns went off, and he ducked, but none of the whizzing bullets came near him. The dust rose in a great cloud as horses continued to flail and scream and choke in the trench. He heard at least one man's screams that were suddenly cut off. And coughing. He felt a little sick, yet filled with relief—

But the relief vanished, as he heard more hoofbeats coming from his right. He turned, and saw a dozen more men also with guns out, who reigned in their horses and stopped short of danger.

The leader—the man he had first run off—narrowed his eyes and lifted his lip. "That's a mighty slick trick you pulled there, stranger," he snarled. "Too bad you ain't gonna live to appreciate how clever you was."

"This is just one stake," he said, knowing that there wasn't anything more in his budget of magic, and that not even he and Red Hawk together could win against a dozen men. "There's plenty more unclaimed land up and down this creek. Why contest me for this piece?"

The man sat back in his saddle, smirking, sure now that he had the upper hand. "I already got the rest of this creek staked, and I aim to have all of it. This's the best land nearest where the railroad's coming. Creek never runs dry. I'll be gettin' top dollar for this land, and I aim to ride out of here a rich man. Now, if you've got two hundred dollars in gold on ya, I *might* forgive ya for killin' my boys, and sell an acre or two back to ya."

Andy had heard plenty about men like this one—speculators who had bribed the surveyors to show them the best stakes. And even if Andy had money, he had no doubt the man would just kill him and rob him. There was nothing to stop him. The trooper had warned him of just that.

"No gold?" The leader laughed. "Well, that's too bad. I'd have been inclined to let you start running, but not after you ambushed my men. Now yer just a bug, and I aim to squash ya."

Half of the men raised their guns and sighted on him.

And that was when the giant spider rose up from behind the trees to his left, a strange, sharp odor wafting from it.

The horses whipped their heads around, caught sight of it, reared, and tried to bolt. Seven escaped, their horses running with such terror that not all the sawing at their bits in the world was going to keep them from running until they either stopped out of exhaustion or killed themselves and their riders. Four of the men were thrown, one hitting the ground headfirst with a *crack* that told Andy he wasn't getting up again. The leader kept his seat, but looked up at the giant spider head gazing down at him and screamed.

And then the spider's whole body dipped, seizing the claim jumper in mandibles the size of his arm and bit. The leader went limp. As Andy watched in horrified fascination, the body suddenly bloated until all the seams on the man's clothing popped. And then, just as suddenly, it shrunk to skin and bones.

The spider dropped the dry carcass into Andy's dust trench, then dipped and picked up the first man that had been thrown but was still alive, and repeated her actions. She did this two more times. The dead man she unceremoniously nudged into the trench with the end of one leg.

Then she looked down at Andy.

Fear nothing, Red Hawk had said. So Andy stood his ground, though he shook like a leaf in the wind, and looked up into those strange eyes.

"*You have chosen the guardian well, my son*," said an odd, sweet, gentle voice that came from that head.

"Thank you, Grandmother Spider," replied Red Hawk, who had suddenly appeared at Andy's side. "He was not my first choice, but I think he is the better of the two."

"*Please make the land solid again, Guardian*," said Grandmother

Spider, and to Andy's astonishment, she shrank, and power flowed from her into him. He knelt and touched his hand to the ground, asking all the dust to settle back down and become solid earth again. The air cleared, and the screaming of the injured beasts stopped, and there was nothing but silence.

And the spider was now roughly his height, and they stood eye to eye. *"I am Grandmother Spider,"* she repeated. *"All things come to my web, and break their necks therein. You will be the land's Guardian when Red Hawk walks the paths of his ancestors. But before he does, he will teach you of us, of Bear and Cougar, of Beaver and Hawk, of Eagle and of me. And you and your children, and your children's children will keep our dancing ground safe, as long as grass shall grow. You may call on us at need."*

"Yes, Grandmother Spider. As long as grass shall grow," he said, a little breathless, understanding now that these were the American equivalent of the Greater Elementals he knew, but had never actually seen. Grandmother Spider was obviously Earth, Beaver—water, Eagle and Hawk—air . . .

His head spun a little. You did not *summon* the Greater Elementals. They were, in effect, gods. The ones that you *could* honor, as long as you kept Jehovah first. And this one had come to help Red Hawk.

And him.

"The honor is too great, Grandmother Spider," he stammered.

A silvery laugh came from the creature. *"I will determine whether or not it is an honor, child."* And then, she shrank and shrank until she was the size of a silver dollar, and ran off into the grass.

Alice returned at midday the next day, looking tired, but satisfied. Clearly she had gotten Prinz fed and watered somehow, as he looked in fine fettle and ready for another run. As they ran to meet her, she swung herself off Prinz and pulled papers out of her dress pocket. "Here are—" she began, when Andy enveloped her in his arms and kissed her.

When they were both breathless, he finally broke it off. She could only look up at him, unable to speak for a moment.

"There is a lot to tell you," he said. "But the most important is—welcome home, wife."

A Simple Pine Box

James Van Pelt

Emmanuel Sprig set up his wagon on the busiest street, Bennett Avenue, hoping that it had been a tragic week in Cripple Creek. Picturesque mountains surrounded the mining town on all sides, but he only paid attention to men coming from the bank, women carrying parasols, and well-dressed pedestrians. He'd heard the mines overflowed with gold here. People had money. Sprig blocked the wheels, paid a boy his last dollar to stable the horses, then flopped his billboards over the wagon's side.

"Sprig's Professional Photography, Specializing in Family and Memorial Portraiture."

He whistled as he set up a table. Traveling agreed with him, he figured. Ever since he'd found the fancy coffin, he'd been feeling better. His back quit aching. The raspy scratch in his throat cleared up. Even his sore tooth had faded. Sleeping in its padded interior did him well. Better than sleeping on the ground.

Street dust coated his jacket, and he wanted a drink. He looked longingly at the saloon a few steps away, but he'd need paying customers before he could go in, and if he didn't collect deposits for portrait sessions to take place in the next few days, he'd be begging door to door for table scraps.

A pert woman in a calico dress stepped off the boardwalk and marched toward him.

"I am the widow Mrs. Molly Armundson," she said, putting out her hand. "My neighbor's son, Timkins, passed a couple days ago. Can I arrange a sitting with you?" She carried a covered basket that smelled of fresh-baked bread. "I'd like to give her an image to remember him by. His mother is my friend, and since my husband died, leaving me comfortably situated, I want to do this for her." She coughed primly into her hand. Color high in her cheeks hinted that she might have a touch of fever herself. Illness was endemic in the mining towns.

"I'm sorry for her loss, ma'am. How old was the boy?" She might have been thirty, a businesslike and pragmatic presence, like many mountain women. Her dress was clean, and her skin glowed in the morning light. Sprig suddenly felt particularly unwashed and grubby.

"Timkins just turned two. A tiny thing. The shits got him."

"Of course. It's a tragedy. I haven't found a studio quite yet." He'd seen a hotel when he came into town with southern facing windows. He bet their lobby would be a fine, well-lit room. "I will have to make arrangements, or do you have a preferred location?"

"Our houses are nearby. Timkins so loved the tree between my house and his that I think his mother would want to remember him there."

"Of course, that would be best."

She took a step back as if to go, then reached into her basket. "You look like you've been some time between meals. Would you like a bun? They're just out of the oven."

He took it and bowed. "You are a Christian saint, for sure."

By sunset, Sprig had scheduled four other sessions, three for children who'd died in a spate of fever and intestinal distress in the last week, and one formal sitting for a finely dressed lady who had promised to send a remembrance to her fiancé in the East. His money bag jingled pleasantly. Enough for room, drink, bath and shave. Nothing like a good dose of scarlet fever, mumps or rubella for business. Of course, a mining accident could be just as lucrative. Grieving widows would dig deep to pay for a portrait of their deceased. Either way, Sprig profited. Memorial portraits made up two thirds of his business.

He folded the signs back into the wagon. He swept the canvas off the gleaming coffin. Whoever built it surely loved fine wood-work. His face peered back at him from the buffed varnish. The interior was just as fancy: a quilted, padded bottom would give the dead the most comfortable bed they might ever sleep in. For an extra dollar, Sprig offered to pose the deceased within it; a coffin that elegant reflected well on the family.

☆   ☆   ☆

Traveling from town to town frightened Sprig more than he liked to admit. Maps were poor, and a miner's directions for getting to the next camp were worse. Often he found that the road he followed led to an abandoned shaft or a dead-end canyon. Once, he spent a night next to a cemetery filled with weathered crosses. Another time he'd been stuck with nothing to eat for four days beside a long, steep trail no wider than his wagon while he worked to repair the axle. Everywhere he went, he found evidence of the gold rush: rusted mining equipment, broken wagons, claims signs and survey stakes. Sometimes he'd meet lone prospectors. Often times they were eccentric, irascible, unstable men who seemed more at home with the rocks and a gold pan than with human beings.

Nothing surprised him, but he worried that anything could kill him. Bears crossed his path. A mountain lion skirted his campfire as he sat tending the flame one night—a huge cat whose shoulders were higher than Sprig's head. Dangerous men might ambush him.

He found the coffin at the end of one of those exhausting days.

The two mules who pulled his wagon kicked at each other until one went lame; a stream where he'd hoped to replenish his water was yellow with mine tailings, and he'd developed a deep cough that rattled the top of his head. The setting sun told him he wouldn't reach Florrisant before nightfall. He'd heard the town had two churches, which meant it had at least six saloons.

The wagon turned on the trail into a clearing among the pines. It was an odd kind of clearing, though. Fifty-foot-tall trees leaned away from the center, their branches scorched. Some had fallen. Bushes and grass had burned to black ash, and in the clearing's center, broken metal shards, some several feet across, jutted up from the raw earth. He picked up a thin sheet of it as big as a cabin door that weighed much less than he expected.

Maybe the clearing had been where miners stored dynamite or gunpowder. The explosion must have been tremendous. Sprig wondered if what had happened there was more than just dynamite. A wagon loaded with nitroglycerine might cause this kind of destruction, but what fool would drive a load with the unstable substance over a road this rough?

The coffin lay on its side at the crater's edge. It was the only identifiable object in the debris. He righted it. Six feet long. Two feet wide and deep. Silk padded sides and bottom. His hands tingled when he touched it, but the sensation quickly faded. Like the metal pieces he'd examined, it weighed much less than it looked like it should. He bucked it into the wagon easily. That night, he slept in it for the first time—the padding was so much more inviting than the rough ground. The stars shone crisply. They always hung like shimmering diamonds, but that night they seemed benign and unexpectedly beautiful. He slept easily for the first time in the mountains alone, and when he woke in the morning, his cough had faded to just a tickle at the back of his throat. By midday, he realized that he was not on the road to Florissant and had to backtrack. The clearing was still there, but the metal he'd examined the day before was gone. He stared at the ashy spot for some time, trying to understand what had happened before moving on. After a second night in the coffin, the cough disappeared completely. He woke unaccountably happy, and the coffin turned into a money maker in Florrisant, when he charged extra to pose mangled miners, gut-shot gamblers and disease-killed babies in it.

At midnight in the Cripple Creek boarding house, he still couldn't sleep, although the bed was deep and soft. For weeks, he'd been sleeping in the coffin as he traveled from mining camp to mountain town, fighting to move his wagon over rocky and washed out roads, and now that he lay in a real bed, he missed the hard wood against his elbows. Nights passed pleasantly in the solid box. It kept the wind out, and he didn't worry about snakes. Now, despite how much he'd looked forward to it, the boarding-house room seemed too spacious. Someone in the next room snored enthusiastically, and he imagined the mattress crawled with bed bugs and lice.

When he staggered down the stairs for breakfast the next morning, he'd hardly slept, and the familiar throbbing in his back had returned. His humor didn't revive until he'd had a third cup of coffee and a second heaping of biscuits under gravy. Sprig cooked poorly on the trail. The well-prepared meal was a treat. The boarding-house owners were as unlikely a couple as Sprig had ever met—the husband looked to be eighty if he was a day, a bald head fringed with gray—and the wife might have been nineteen if Sprig was generous. Her voice rose whenever she talked to her husband, who must have been hard of hearing. Sprig wondered if they'd like a portrait. The old man didn't appear to have many days left on this Earth. What he did have, though, was a work shed with a sink in back that would serve as a place for Sprig to develop his exposures.

The widow Armundson waited for him on her porch, a small bundle in her arms. A matronly woman sat in a chair beside her, with a defeated and distracted look in her eyes. Sprig carried his tripod and camera under one arm, and the rest of his equipment in a heavy valise in the other hand. The early morning clouds had cleared away, so he had plenty of light to work with. "You said he had a favorite tree?"

"Molly, I told you there ain't no need," said the sitting woman. Molly put her hand on the woman's shoulder.

The blanket fell away from Timkins' face. Despite its closed eyes, no one would mistake Timkins' repose as sleep. Sprig wondered if the "couple days ago" Mrs. Armundson indicated wasn't closer to a week. "Your boy's angelic," he said. "Many mothers prefer to be holding their child for the portrait."

Mrs. Armundson glanced at the grieving woman, and her expression told Sprig no.

"Or we could surround him with his toys by the tree."

The woman said more to herself than to them, "I brought out his crib. Carried it over two mountain passes. It's the same crib I had when I was a baby. My mother gave it to me before she passed."

"That will be perfect."

Sprig arranged Timkins in the crib under the tree, careful not to squeeze the child. The body felt like it might be oozy. Thirty minutes later, after making several exposures, they were done.

During the session, Mrs. Armundson coughed and coughed. Her petite frame shook from it. Sprig looked at her with concern after one long session. "I'm fine," she said weakly. "Mountain air doesn't agree with me."

He didn't believe her. In the lungs like that, it could be pneumonia or whooping cough. His own throat felt scratchy again. If his symptoms went as they did the last time, he'd sound as bad as her in a day or so. "A tablespoon of honey in a shot glass with whiskey might feel good, ma'am. Always works for me."

"It might at that," she said.

The next three sessions were in the mortuary, a grand, two-story structure with a beautiful hearse parked in the front. Dr. Livingston Johnson owned the establishment, and seemed much more concerned with polishing the beautiful wood-and-glass carriage than caring for the dead, who were dumped unsympathetically under a tarp on the floor in the back. "I only have one table," the balding undertaker explained. Sprig helped him dress the first cadaver, a young miner whose skull had been partly caved in by a support timber that snapped directly over his head. "See," said the mortician, "we turn him like this, so the pillow shields the injury."

Sprig nodded. "Perhaps we can use my display coffin for the photograph. It is more stylish than your wares." He pointed to the wooden coffins stacked in the back of the preparation room.

"A simple pine box is all these men can afford, sir."

"I know, but for the photograph, they will look the way their loved ones hoped in their final moment on Earth. A tasteful flower arrangement beside them, or their favorite possession nearby will do the mourners more good than you can imagine." Of course, when he placed the deceased in the deluxe coffin, the extra dollar filled Sprig's pockets that much faster.

One man Sprig posed with a Brady stand, a set of rods and hooks that held the corpse up and the head straight. The man's rifle leaned against him, as if he was holding it from a hunting trip. Sprig thought the photograph would turn out well. The flash impressed the undertaker most.

"Magnesium powder and potassium chlorate," said Sprig. "Sorry about the smoke." He coughed and cleared his throat.

The other two men went into Sprig's coffin.

"That is a beauty," said the undertaker when Sprig wheeled it in. "Never seen woodwork like that."

With the window and back door open, fully lighting the room, the wood's sheen showed to its best advantage.

"Can't see the joints at all," said the undertaker, running his hand around the corner. He drew his hand back quickly, then laughed. "I thought it vibrated when I touched it. Darnedest thing."

Sprig placed a bible on the corpse's chest and rested his hand on it. "Bodies are always better once they're arranged."

The undertaker handed Sprig a bouquet of flowers held together with lace. "Damned if you aren't right. That's Elliot Dareus. Cut his leg working the buckets in the Mount Rosa mine. The wound festered and the leg swelled up like a watermelon. Died before they could amputate. I swear he looks healthier now than he did a month ago."

The dead man's face seemed to have relaxed under the powder the undertaker had applied.

Sprig fought down the urge to cough as he placed the flowers and then made sure his camera was properly situated and primed. "It's a magic box, that one is." The flash filled the room with smoke again.

Sprig loaded a kettle of hot tea and a pot of vegetable soup, both wrapped in towels, a jar of honey, and a whiskey flask into a basket he borrowed from the boarding house. Before he set out for the widow Armundson's house, he assured the young landlady that he would return everything.

She answered the door with a blanket wrapped around her shoulders, looking miserable. Her hands shook, holding the blanket against her chest. He imagined he could feel the fever radiating from her.

"Mr. Sprig, what can I do for you?"

He held up the basket smelling of vegetable soup and tea. "I thought that was a true kindness you did for Timkins's mother. If you're still feeling poorly, I could do a kindness for you."

She opened the door wider for him. "If that's boardinghouse soup in the basket, you surely can. I don't have the energy to cook tonight."

Her house was bigger inside than the front made it appear, and the furniture was store bought.

"My husband did very well in the mines before the accident," she explained.

"How long ago, if you don't mind my asking?" Sprig balanced a saucer on his knee while sipping tea laced with whiskey from a delicate china cup.

"Eighteen months come September." She breathed shallowly and with what looked like some pain, although more relaxed since she'd downed three shot glasses filled with whiskey and honey. "Do you think another dose of your elixir would help?" she said. "I don't know if it will cure me, but dying wouldn't feel nearly as bad."

"Certainly." He carefully measured a tablespoon of honey into the small glass, then topped it with the liquor.

A few minutes later, her chin settled to her chest and her breath whistled softly. The lone lantern she had directed him to light cast a wavering illumination on her face, a soft, buttery patina that made her both tragic and noble. Her house truly loomed around her. As they talked, she evoked the nights she'd spent since her husband died, reading in her empty house, dealing with grief and then emerging from it to help her friends, working with the city planners to make Cripple Creek a great town. Molly sounded like a force to admire, but no one likes to be sick alone. Even the strong can be brought down.

Sprig rearranged the blanket so that it covered her neck, and slipped out the front door.

The sun had set. Light streamed from the hotel on Bennett Avenue, and men's loud voices from the saloons broke the mountain silence, but Sprig didn't waver. He ran past the saloons, past the dry goods and barbershop, and didn't stop until he reached the mortuary.

"I need my coffin," he explained to the undertaker as he rushed to the back room.

Holding the long box over his head like a man portaging a canoe, Sprig returned to Molly's house. The single lantern sputtered, nearly out of oil. Sprig didn't know where she stored her oil, so he worked quickly, putting the coffin on the drawing room floor, carefully picking up Mrs. Armundson, and then laying her inside. He pulled the blanket around her, and before the lantern flickered out, he was sure she looked as if each inhalation was easier.

He pulled a chair with a high back and upholstered arms next to her, and when the light winked off, settled in for the night.

"What on Earth?" cried the widow Armundson.

Sprig blinked against the morning light coming through the drawing room windows. The woman sat in the coffin. "What is this, Mr. Sprig? Have you been here all night?" She sounded more puzzled than upset.

"I'm sorry, ma'am. I don't want you to think badly of me, but I believe that coffin has medicinal qualities, like healing waters. I hoped that it would help you to feel better." Even though she didn't appear angry, her reaction horrified him. He hadn't thought about how she would respond in the morning.

She clambered out of the box, pulling the blanket with her. "This is entirely improper. You must leave, and take this... this contraption with you."

Sprig stood the coffin on one end. "Really, I believed it might relieve your symptoms."

"Out." She pointed to the door. "And don't let anyone see you leaving. I have a reputation to uphold."

Sprig trudged back toward the boardinghouse, dragging the coffin behind him. It wasn't until he'd gone a couple blocks before a thought occurred to him. The widow Armundson didn't cough once as she tossed him from the house. In fact, for a woman who'd drunk way too much the night before, and was sick to boot, she'd sounded remarkably vigorous.

He picked the coffin up, raised it over his head as he had the night before, and whistled the rest of the way to the boardinghouse. His first sitting for the day wasn't until noon. He could get three or four hours sleep himself, if the boardinghouse owners didn't think it too odd that he did it in the coffin in the work shed. If the coffin worked as he thought it would, he could rid himself of his pesky sore throat and painful bark. He was pretty sure that despite what he'd said to the undertaker, the coffin was not magic. It felt more like the workings of a machine. Maybe the box wasn't made of wood at all. It was too light. It was too well constructed. The coffin buzzed like Edison's electrical contrivances that filled the news.

Sprig finished the day's work by late afternoon. The memorial portraits for the passed infants that he'd scheduled on the first day in town went quickly. Babies presented less of a problem to pose. The biggest challenge was dealing with the families who were filled with unreasonable requests. "Can you make my Lonnie smile?" "Jasmine loved her doll. Her hair should be done in the same style." And, "I have seen photographs that have been colored as in real life. Can you give me such a photograph?" He had to explain repeatedly that hand coloring a print was beyond his skills.

Still he finished the baby pictures with time to spare. The "lady" who said she wanted to send a photograph to her fiancé presented a different problem. Sprig arranged to shoot her in the hotel's lobby where the slanting light poured through the huge windows, using their elegant furniture for the image. The challenge was that the woman began undressing as soon as Sprig closed the doors for privacy.

"He's my beloved," she exclaimed as Sprig blustered that he didn't take those kinds of pictures. He averted his face while holding out her jacket. "Only he will see the photograph," she said.

After Sprig convinced her to cover herself adequately, he finished the session, but she insisted on poses with leaning and postures and come-hither expressions that might set a minister's blood boiling.

Mrs. Armundson waited for him outside the lobby door. She wore a different calico dress from the one she had when he met her, and all traces of her cough and fever were gone. "I may have treated you unfairly this morning," she said without preamble. "It would please me mightily if you would drop by my house for dinner tonight."

Sprig didn't have a chance to answer before she turned and exited the hotel.

As he worked at the boardinghouse shed, his face ached from smiling. He could develop and print the day's images before cleaning up for the widow Armundson. Much of his work had to be done in the dark, but he'd made so many images over the years that the lack of light did not bother him. He was surprised, though, when he finished and inspected the prints, that night had fallen. The yard behind the shed was nearly as dark as the shed itself.

So, when he stepped from the shed, the light that suddenly streamed from the heavens blinded him. The three tall figures who descended in the light didn't speak as they entered the shed and emerged with the coffin. Sprig's limbs were paralyzed.

Clearly, though, the device was theirs. Sprig strained to look up, to see the light's source, but his muscles ignored his efforts. He groaned in an effort to move. If they took it now, how could he keep Mrs. Armundson well? Would his own aches return?

His foot twitched, and Sprig leaned toward them, raising his hand maybe an inch against the invisible bonds. That was enough. Unbalanced now, he fell, like a doll posed into one position, striking his cheek against the ground. He could feel his face swelling as momentum rolled him to his side, still as rigid as a statue, tears streaming from the sudden pain.

The figure who was not holding one end of the coffin paused and looked at Sprig. Through the tears, Sprig couldn't read an expression, if there was one. The face didn't look right—eyes too far apart, mouth too small, no lips—but the tall creature paused.

Sprig gasped out, "I need it."

Whether the creature understood him, Sprig didn't know, but it knelt, hovered its hand over his cheek that warmed as if in the sun. The air buzzed and the heat spread down his neck and through his limbs like heated molasses.

Except that he couldn't move, he'd never felt so fine, so whole.

Then the figure stood and turned away.

Sprig watched them float up from the ground with his coffin between them. When the light flicked off, he relaxed, released from whatever had held him. The sky appeared empty except for the hard-edged stars, and not even a wind whispered to indicate that anything had occurred.

An hour later, wearing a suit he'd borrowed from the landlord, Sprig sat at Mrs. Armundson's table. She laughed often and clearly didn't know what to make of his story.

"The coffin, though, it is really gone?" She offered him a slice of cake.

"Yes, ma'am. I believe they were the proper owners. It wasn't a simple pine box at all."

She refilled his wine glass. "Too bad. I haven't felt this healthy since my husband died."

"Me neither." He touched her hand. "Perhaps you would accompany me for a short stroll? We could admire the night sky."

She dimpled when she smiled, an indescribably appealing expression by candlelight that Sprig knew he'd never be able to photograph. The best way to preserve the image would be to remember it.

"Only," she said, "if you agree from now on to call me Molly. And what shall I call you?"

He smiled. A lady had never given him permission to be so familiar. Sprig rose and offered his arm. "My friends call me Emmanuel."

Fang for Fang, Fire for Blood

Ava Morgan

"Resist the devil, and he will flee from you."
James 4:7, Holy Bible

Apex, Kansas, 1880

Restaurant owner Cora Bishop slung her gaze out the window to the dusty street and eyed the white sheet draped over the lifeless body of twenty year-old Jedidiah Hamilton. A small crowd gathered outside her establishment to gaze in horror as the undertaker loaded the body onto a mule-drawn wagon. Preacher Hamilton, Jedidiah's father, staggered behind the wagon in a daze and put his face in his ebony hands. Poor man.

A sharp creak made Cora's head turn. The double doors to the restaurant flung open, and in shuffled the two farmhands Tim and Morrison, who brought Jedidiah's body back to town fifteen minutes ago. The handful of customers inside gawked as the men walked by the first set of wooden tables. Cora recognized the sorrowful weariness that weighed down their eyelids and formed grim lines across their dark-skinned brows. "Come sit at the counter," she bade them, while giving a firm look to her other customers to stay where they were. One by one, they reluctantly returned to their meals.

Cora wiped the counter clean of bread crumbs and soup splatters before setting two glasses down. "This meal is on the house, gentlemen."

"Just somethin' to drink, please," said Tim. He wore a tan hat. "Make it strong and make it a double."

"Only the saloon serves liquor."

"We'll go there next. A cool glass of water, then," Morrison requested. He spoke to his friend while Cora got the pitcher and poured for them. "Bad way for a preacher's son to die. Neck ripped clean open."

Cora's bones chilled as she overheard them. She didn't mean to eavesdrop. Her hearing was simply better than most.

Tim drained his water glass. While she refilled it, he said, "Wolves must've done it. They need to be shot."

"Got to catch them first."

"Wolves?" Cora spoke, her voice soft.

Both men appeared to notice her for the first time. "Yes, missus, er, Miss Cora." Tim lowered his eyes, gripped his glass, and stared at his reflection on the water's surface. "Jed said yesterday he was going to a surveyor's camp five miles further west. He thought they were with the railroad and wanted to find work."

"I was out this morning looking for one of my calves that wandered off," said Morrison. "I found him dead on the side of the road. Throat wide open but not a drop of blood anywhere."

A shiver ran along Cora's nerves. The same shiver appeared to jump across to Tim next. "Hush, Morrison." He practically hissed between his teeth. "It's too gruesome for women to hear."

Morrison took a faded handkerchief from his shirt pocket and mopped his brow. "Sorry, Miss Cora."

They thought her female nature was why she appeared visibly upset. Cora didn't correct him. It was easier for them to think so. "It's all right. Go on."

"I went and got Tim to help me bring Jed to town. Jed should've preached like his pappy wanted instead of looking for another job."

She filled Morrison's empty glass. "You both should eat. If you don't have the appetite now, at least take some bread and beef with you when you go."

Tim nodded his appreciation. "It's mighty sweet of you."

She gave a polite smile and turned to go into the kitchen to get more soup for the other customers. She heard Tim scold his friend again. "Why couldn't you be quiet? You know her husband died the same way Jed did."

Cora's chest ached. Her husband Samuel had been deceased

for two years, but what she heard and saw today made the pain of grief return. They left Georgia to start a new life in Kansas. Cora and her husband struggled to find steady work in the newly emancipated South. Samuel had heard of the great Pap Singleton, whose bold, fiery speeches called for poor black men and women to leave the South, to seek employment and true freedom out on the Western frontier. When Samuel came to her, dark eyes bright with excitement and conviction, and told her he wanted to do this, Cora felt her heart stir. She agreed that they should set out for Apex, one of the black free-towns in Kansas.

Yet Samuel didn't make it to Apex. She always thought his manner of death was...unnatural. When they were on their way to Kansas, he left camp outside of Savannah one morning to go wash himself by the river. He didn't come back. Cora found his body several miles downstream, his throat gouged as though he were attacked by a wild animal, yet nary a single drop of blood on his person or on the ground. His body had been drained of all blood. He never got to see the free "Promised Land" she and other black people were told awaited them west of the Mississippi.

Another shiver started to form. She suppressed it. Whatever killed her husband two years ago in Georgia was back in her life and preying on other folks in their settlement.

She had to get answers tonight.

Cora waited until the close of business day. She helped Mrs. Jenkins, her business partner and restaurant co-owner, clean the tables and floors. The older widow extended a wrinkled hand to pat her shoulder. "Don't you let yourself get upset by what you saw today." The woman's voice was gentle and motherly.

"I can't help it, Mrs. Jenkins. It made me think of Samuel."

"But this is different, child. Jedidiah shouldn't have gone from town with no rifle to defend himself. Folks know there's coyotes and wolves in the hills."

Cora didn't think it was different. However, she didn't want to keep talking and risk alarming the eighty-year-old woman. "See you in the morning, Mrs. Jenkins." She embraced her friend and left the restaurant.

She stepped outside to see other establishments also beginning to close their doors for the day. She headed further down Main Street to pay a visit to Sheriff Grisham. He might be able to help her.

Cora found the door to the sheriff's office ajar. She heard him talking to a man inside. Their tones were hushed and laced with tension. She gave a polite knock on the door before entering. "Good afternoon." Immediately, both men ceased talking and gaped at her when she walked in. "May I speak with you, Sheriff?"

She recognized the other man as Mr. Harold, the editor of *The Apex Weekly*, the town's newspaper. The sheriff nodded to him. The man tipped his hat to Cora before leaving the office. He closed the door behind him.

"What can I do for you, Miss Cora?" Sheriff Grisham leaned back in his chair and put his feet up on the desk.

Cora had a hunch he was showing out for her, trying to act calm and relaxed when only a moment ago, he and Mr. Harold sounded more skittish than two sparrows caught in a thorn brier. "I want to speak to you about Jedidiah Hamilton."

The sheriff sighed. "The town's getting ready to bury him in a few days. Can it wait?"

"I'm afraid not. Sheriff, I heard about the manner in which he died."

"Then you shouldn't have been listening to gossip. Preacher Hamilton spoke about that last Sunday, but I didn't see you in church."

"Are you saying his throat wasn't ripped open, then?" She fixed her stare on the sheriff. She wasn't going to let him dance around the subject.

He moved his eyes toward the window and appeared to be studying the sunset. "It looked like a wolf got him. Should've been carrying his rifle."

"Sheriff, I have reason to believe it was more than a wolf."

He narrowed his eyes and shifted them on her again. "More? What do you mean, more? A pack of wolves instead of just one?"

Cora looked down at the desk. "I don't know. I must say, though, I have seen another man fall victim to that kind of attack. A tear in the throat, loss of blood, but no blood in sight."

"Only Lord knows the minds of widows."

She lifted her head. "I beg your pardon?"

"You heard me." The sheriff took his feet down from the desk. "You're still grieving your husband's death. You think the same thing happens to every other man who dies in the wild."

She couldn't believe his sudden charged outburst. "Sheriff,

this is the only the second time I have heard about a man who lost his life in a similar way that my Samuel lost his."

"This isn't...wasn't Samuel this time."

The louder Sheriff Grisham's voice rose, the more he gave off an aroma. Cora smelled the pungency mixed with his sweat. "You're scared, aren't you?"

He fell silent. Then his mouth clamped down in a hard line. "Go home, Cora."

"Do you know what's out there? Has anyone else been to the surveyor camp?"

"No. Jedidiah is barely cold and here you are, trying to spook folks 'bout how your husband died the same way. Go home and let the town bury its dead."

Cora felt her hands curling into fists. She had to control her anger. No sense in trading harsh words with the sheriff. He was a man running scared. She turned and marched out of the office.

Sheriff Grisham was right about one thing. For now, it was good to go home. She needed to think about some things.

Hours later, when the last storefront lantern went dark on Main Street, Cora slipped out of her house and into the night. The light wool of her husband's trousers rustled on her legs as she hurried through the empty streets and past the wooden sign with the town's name staked into the hard-packed earth. She went west to the surveyor's camp, according to John's directions.

To her eyes, both the dirt road and trampled grass were visible as if it were early evening, not a quarter past ten. She remembered what she told her mother the first time her abilities appeared when she was eleven, some eighteen years ago. *Sometimes the night looks like day to me and Tamsy, Mama.*

Don't tell no one, Mama had whispered a warning while Cora and her little sister Tamsy were huddled in the shack they shared with two other slave families on the Georgia plantation. Tamsy slept on the ground, her skinny feet sticking out of the moth-eaten gunny square she used for a blanket. Moonlight streamed through a patch of sod on the wall and cast its silvery beam on Mama's black skin, making her round, unlined face take on a light all its own. Then Mama frowned, creating ridges on her forehead. *Don't tell no one of your ancestors' secret, or I'll lose you both.*

Cora never told another soul how she could see or hear real

well, or how she could make her body change and do things other folks couldn't. She didn't even tell her husband while he was still living. Samuel, Mama, and Tamsy were all gone now, leaving her alone with the secret.

A twig snapped. Cora crouched down in the tall grass. The howl of a lone wolf carried in the air. She peered through the grass at a yellow light coming from a campfire up ahead. Her nostrils tingled with the smell of burning wood chips and raw meat. Three tents formed a line behind the campfire.

Cora heard another twig break in half under a boot. The person wasn't far behind her. She sniffed and smelled two different kinds of sweat. The person wasn't alone.

She waited until someone cocked a rifle. "Get up out of the grass." His drawl was Southern and drunken. "Do it show and slow them hands."

Cora didn't think he'd like it if she told him he got his words backwards, so she stayed quiet and complied, rising slowly to her full height. She kept her hands up. A light flashed in her face. She squeezed her eyes shut before opening them to see the face of a bearded white man. He held a kerosene lantern.

"It's one of them from the Negro settlement a few miles east." He pressed his face in close. Cora saw what remained of his dinner stuck in his long beard. "This one's a she, but dressed like a man." He lowered the lantern. "What you doing out here, missy?"

"I saw the light from your campfire. I must've got turned around."

"You sure did." He held out his other hand as if he were going to give her a good push to send her in the right direction.

"Wait, Boone," said the man's drunken friend. "He might want to see her, help her get back."

Who was *he*? Cora wondered. She wanted to get into the camp. She made her voice higher in pitch and slipped a blank, naive look over her face. "If a gentleman can help me, I'd appreciate it."

"He's a gentleman." Boone led the way to the camp with his lantern.

Foul air hung in the atmosphere like the hot breath of a foul suitor, eager to descend in an undesired advance. Cora could barely breathe. She coughed as the sickly sweet smell of decaying raw meat carried on the humid wind, mixed with campfire smoke.

She expected to see more railroad surveyors, either tending

to the fire or cooking food. Nobody except her and the two men moved through the camp. They led her to the row of tents. Firelight did a slow dance across their stained canvases. Some stains were light brown, possibly from dirt. Others were darker in color, reminding her of the rust color of dried blood.

Boone stopped in front of the largest tent, situated in the middle. Cora rubbed the back of her neck where her skin prickled. Boone lifted the flap of the tent. "Sir, there's a woman out here."

Cora noticed how quickly his voice fell into a low mutter. She strained to hear the rest.

"...says she's lost..."

She heard a deep-voiced murmur in reply, yet was unable to make out the exact words. Then she realized the words weren't being spoken in English. She glanced at the man with the rifle. He had a look of understanding on his face while he listened to Boone and the mysterious man inside speak.

"Drazek says come in," Boone said to her, his words coming at her in plain English.

Candlelight illuminated from the opening in the tent flap. Cora's fingertips itched as though something sharp wanted to come out through her skin. She stepped past Boone and went through. The tent flap fell behind her, causing candlelight to flicker across worn leather volumes stacked within an open fancy brown-gold valise.

"Come closer, dear lady. I'm told you are lost." The fellow's pleasant words took on a peculiar life of their own, filling the room and surrounding Cora. She heard Englishmen before, and a German once, but this man's accent was entirely foreign to her ears.

She followed the light to find two sturdy candles burning on a table next to an empty plate and a glass half-filled with dark liquid. Seated was a man in a grey coat. His black hair was pulled in severe fashion from his face. Shadows moved over his pale skin and the sharp, asymmetrical lines of his features.

"My name is Abel Drazek. I'm a frequent visitor to your country. My men and I are here to see if the land is fit for a new railroad."

One of those Old World investors. Cora used to hear the wealthier patrons in her restaurant talk about them. According to what the patrons said, the investors put money in American steam engines and hotels because they were running out of moneymaking opportunities in their own countries. "I'm Cora." She said her first name and nothing else until he spoke again.

"They tell me you're lost, Cora."

She nodded. Inside Drazek's tent, she almost choked on the stifling air. "I lost my direction home. I don't like the sound of those wolves out there."

"They are disturbing," he agreed. Drazek's chair scraped the ground when he stood. Almost six and a half feet tall, his head missed the tent ceiling by an inch. "I was told they attack men. That's why I hired Boone and Roy as field guides."

Cora watched the light reflect in his eyes where the pupils should be. "The wolves got a man yesterday. Killed him."

"How ghastly." Drazek tilted his head, the way Cora saw crows do when they sat on the town signpost and stared at weary people on a hot day. "I find the American wilderness particularly vicious, animal and human inhabitants alike." He gave a tiny shrug. "Ah, well, the railroad will civilize things."

A loud crash came from outside.

"Wait here." Drazek went around the table so fast the candles hardly had time to flicker from the breeze he stirred up. He left her in the tent.

Cora went to the valise on the floor and opened the first book, a volume with a rust-red cover. Its pages smelled of dust and mildew from water damage. Symbols decorated the pages, strange symbols with six and eight sides, the kind she imagined Preacher Hamilton wouldn't approve of. Her neck tingled while she studied the foreign handwritten words next to the symbols.

She glanced at the tent flap before opening another volume. Black ink smeared along the edges of the pages. She turned to one and saw an illustration that snatched the breath from her lungs.

It showed two male figures, one on the ground and another crouching over him. The man on his back had eyes that bulged in an expression of horror. The second wore a wolf skin over his head and arms. He grinned over the first with long, sharp teeth and a torn object dripping from his mouth. Cora looked closer and realized it was a piece of the other man's throat.

Footsteps approached the tent. She placed the books in the valise and stood just as Drazek returned. Her heart pounded in the space of time between him entering and presenting her with a smile.

"Apologies. Roy knocked over a supply crate." His smile never reached his eyes. He stared at her for a moment longer than was considered polite before breaking his gaze. "Boone and Roy will escort you to the main road."

An invisible weight pressed on her shoulders. She felt like the entire tent would collapse on her at any moment. "Thank you, Mr. Drazek." She made her way to the front of the tent, where she had to walk by him to get outside. A man his size, one would expect to give off plenty of heat. She sensed only a chill as she slipped past.

The two guides waited. Roy still had his rifle. He appeared to have sobered since she went into Drazek's tent. He pointed the barrel up in the air. "Can't be too careful at night," he said.

Cora walked with them away from the camp. She looked over her shoulder. The light inside Drazek's tent had gone out.

She counted her steps as she walked in silence. On the thirty-third step, she heard the rough scrape of Roy's calloused finger as it began to slide towards the trigger. Her fingertips itched before her claws shot through her skin. Cora whipped around and flung the firearm from his grip.

Roy growled. Cora thought he was going to rush at her. Instead, he paused for a brief moment. In the span of seconds, she saw his eyes take on a yellow glow. His jaw, once clean shaven, began to fill with heavy, dense hair, thick like animal fur. His neck widened and became corded with muscle. She heard bones snap and joints crack as his shoulders reshaped within his shirt, stretching the front of the fabric. Buttons snapped off and the collar ripped away to reveal more fur sprouting along his chest. He was changing. Into what, Cora didn't know, but she couldn't let him finish.

She raked her own claws across his face, tearing into his elongated snout. He staggered back. She used her strength and the force of his momentum to shove him to the ground. A snap and a sharp crack resounded. He didn't rise again.

Boone came at her next. In her struggle with Roy, she missed his transformation. He loped toward her on all fours, a man-wolf with tufts of fur sticking out from a contorted frame. Flaps of skin hung from his arm and one side of his head. Cora felt her own teeth lengthen and sharpen in her mouth as he closed in.

Her hand came down in a slashing motion. Her claws

penetrated flesh and muscle. Warm liquid splattered her cheek. He fell at her feet.

"I knew you weren't just a simple woman. Your scent is familiar. I've smelled it on another person before."

At the sound of Drazek's voice, Cora looked up from Boone's body and scanned the surroundings. The camp behind her was quiet and still. Tall grass swayed ever so slightly. Air stirred at her back. She turned as iron-hard hands clamped on her arms.

"You went through my books. Did you think I was a simple-minded man, Cora, to believe you were lost?" Drazek spoke low and threatening in her ear.

She twisted in his grip. "You're not a man. You're a devil." She struggled to get free. His strength was beyond hers at that moment. "You killed Jedidiah Hamilton."

Moonlight revealed fangs in Drazek's mouth. "The foolish youth came into my camp, uninvited. He saw my men in the middle of their transformation. He thought he would try to pray and cast the devil out of us." He stopped talking to issue a hard laugh. "We couldn't allow him to tell anyone what he saw here. His blood renewed us."

Cora inched her head away from his. "Did you kill my husband in Savannah, too?"

"The one whose scent remains in your clothes? I recall he tried to fight back, told me to stay away from his wife. He was stronger than he looked." He dug his fingers into her shoulder. She cried out as his sharp nails penetrated her jacket and pierced her skin. Her stomach clenched in fear and disgust as he lowered his mouth to the wound and lapped at the blood with his tongue. He drew his head back and groaned, eyes closed in ungodly ecstasy, a ring of red around his lips. "Now I see why he fought so hard to protect you. I taste the power hidden within you. Generations of it."

"My husband didn't know about my power. He protected me because he loved me."

Drazek opened his eyes again. "But your power made him strong, too, because he was so close to you. Tell me its origins."

She stared into soulless black pools in a face as waxen as the moon. "No."

"Aid me, Cora, and I won't kill you. I've been watching your town. All I want is more blood from the people there."

"Why Apex?"

"When I drank the blood from your husband, and from that boy's, I was able to face the sun, if only for a few minutes. It's because of the dark skin they share. I can draw that strength from their blood to sustain me. But your blood is even more powerful. Why are you different?"

Incensed, Cora felt the change beginning in her muscles. Her tongue thinned and lengthened. "I don't know why I'm different, but I do know you can't have Apex," she said before her voice could produce little more than a reptilian hiss.

She succeeded in extricating herself from his hold. Pebbly soil dug into her foot as one of her long, scaled appendages had burst through the toe of her boot.

Fabric seams ripped as her body grew and expanded. Scales erupted on her arms as the clothes tore away. She couldn't remember the transformation ever being that fast.

She hissed again as her tail dropped to the ground. Now she could see over the few trees in the area. Cora swung her long neck to view Drazek standing ten feet below her, his monstrous face agape.

She acted swiftly while he remained transfixed. She lashed him with her tail and put the full force of her weight behind it. He slammed face first to the ground. It should've killed him, or at least broken most of the bones in his body.

He pushed up using the strength of his arms. He lifted his head, eyes gleaming vengeance while blackish red blood ran down his face in ribbons. He turned and raced for his tent.

Those books he kept in his valise. Was he running to get them? Was there something about those strange words and symbols inside that he could use to harm her?

Resist the devil. Cora remembered the words from the Bible. She couldn't let this creature who fed on the lifeblood of men continue to feast.

Drazek returned with the red book in hand. She opened her mouth and lowered her head, intending to crush his bones between her teeth. Instead, something hot grew in her belly and boiled its way up her throat. She knew what was coming next. Before, she always held back. This time, she unleashed the flames.

Drazek's slanted eyes became round. As the candlelight in his tent once made light show in his eyes, the fire from Cora's throat now filled their black spaces. He screamed once as his head and body became engulfed.

Cora backed away as he did a staggered run toward the camp. He fell against a stack of crates. His body, bathed in flames, set them alight. Drazek ceased to move shortly thereafter.

The flames rolled over him and begin their climb along the tents. Cora watched the camp burn to the ground. Her body slowly changed back into a woman.

Never let them know who you are. Cora learned from her mama that they'd descended from a tribe that once lived near the Gambia River in West Africa. Until she discovered her own abilities, she thought tales of her people's shapeshifting powers were just stories to entertain children. Some ancestors had the ability. Some did not. Her ancestors called her transformation the *Ninki Nanka*, a river dragon.

Folks in this land would call her a devil.

She watched the flames crawl in her direction. She gazed at them in disbelief. Mama was right. Nobody should know what she could turn herself into. They weren't ready. She vowed to protect the people of Apex, but continue to keep her secret.

With trembling hands, she removed the clothes from Roy's body and put them on. She turned east in the direction for home.

The next morning, Cora went into the restaurant to work as usual. Patrons came in for breakfast. She heard them whisper about Jedidiah's upcoming funeral service. She kept her head down and helped Mrs. Jenkins cook and serve the food.

A short while later, in the afternoon, Sheriff Grisham came in. He approached the counter and ordered a plate of potatoes and chicken. Cora set the food down in front of him. He still smelled like sweat, but there was less fear mixed with it today.

"I came to see you. Thought you should know about something," he mumbled, while shoving a forkful of potato in his mouth.

She poured him a cup of water and waited for him to finish chewing.

"I saw smoke on the horizon this morning. My deputy and me rode out to find where it was coming from. We saw the surveyor camp, or what was left of it." He speared a chunk of chicken. "It looked like a man died there. We found a couple dead wolves, too. Their bones were all twisted up and bent out of shape. Fire probably did that."

Cora said nothing.

"Anyway, we now know it was the wolves that got Jedidiah because they tried to go after the man in the camp, too."

"What do you think caused the man's death, Sheriff?"

"Looks like he was trying to run away from the wolves. There were some busted crates around him, so he must have fallen over them. We found broken glass from a kerosene lamp. He must have dropped it when he ran and started the fire."

She nodded along. "That makes sense."

The sheriff stopped chewing and gave her a patriarchal frown. "Of course it makes sense. I told you it was just some ornery wolves roaming the hills."

"Well, I'm glad they won't be bothering anyone else."

Sheriff Grisham finished the rest of his food. "Poor Jedidiah. It's sad, but there ain't nothing we can do about it now. Just like we can't go back and do anything about your husband. Try to move on, Cora."

"I'll do my best."

"I believe you will. You got that spitfire in you. A bit too much of it, sometimes." He wiped his mouth on the back of his sleeve before he stood. He reached into his back pocket and put some coins on the table. "Good afternoon, Miss Cora."

"Good day, Sheriff." She masked a smile as he turned to leave. Once he departed, she set to wiping the crumbs away from where he ate at the counter.

She was relieved to finally solve the mystery surrounding her husband's death, and grateful to be able to protect the citizens of Apex from a predator. But there could be more people out there like Drazek, bloodthirsty devil-men who wanted to prey upon the innocent.

Well, if they were out there, she had plenty more fire deep within her belly to give them a very warm welcome to hell.

Junior & Me

Harry Turtledove

Listen, you yellow-bellied son of a green-yolked egg, this is how it happened. And if you don't like it, well, we can just step outside where Junior and me'll chew your snout off for you.

This here was down in the Red River bottoms, sixteen—no, seventeen—years ago now. I was down on my luck. I guess you could say so. The dancing girl in Dodge City I'd got sweet on, she laughed in my face. She was after somebody who'd keep her in a style she wanted to get used to. She had somebody in mind, too, and it weren't me.

I could have killed him. Not, I *wanted* to kill him. I *could* have killed him, easy as you please. He was fresh out of the shell, practically—a kid from the East who kept books at the bank and for the grocery store. He didn't know what she was, any more'n he knew about knives and eight-shooters. All he knew was, he liked the curve of her haunches.

If I did kill him, I might've done him a favor. Caught up in her web, he'd have had a demon of a time biting free. He wouldn't be the same afterwards, neither. You never are.

But Sssue—that was her name, Sssue—wouldn't've given me a tumble even with him gone, not the way I was then. I had trouble buying my own firewater, let alone anything a dancing girl with big dreams might want. If he got dead, Sssue would've latched on to the next fella like him she ran across.

I had sense enough to see that, even if it took longer'n it should have. Soon as I did, I got out of Dodge. No, I didn't know where I was going. North, south, east, west? I didn't care, long as I got the hells out of there. I headed south on account of . . . on account of I did.

That's how I ended up going toward the Red River country. Dumb luck, and I still wonder sometimes if it was good or bad. But I didn't know about any of that. All I knew was, I needed to get gone.

You've seen how, when you get a tenth of a daytenth outside of a town, the air starts smelling sweet again? You get away from the stinks of all the people and critters packed too tight together. You get away from sour smoke and stirred-up dust and everything else. The world starts tasting the way it must have right after the gods hatched it. You get used to the way a town smells, but you don't hardly ever get to where you like it.

I was free. I told myself I was, anyways. I just about made myself believe it. Whether it was true or not, it made the feathers on my crest come up for a spell.

Of course, lots of times free means free to starve. Yeah, I didn't owe a soul any silver, much less gold. A good thing, too, 'cause I didn't have hardly any silver, much less gold. Sssue had it straight when she saw I wasn't rich and likely never would be.

Little birds hopped in the grass to either side of the trail. They cocked their heads as I ambled past. Some of them flew away, just to stay on the safe side. Things like me ate things like them when we got the chance. Somewhere down deep in their little birdbrains, they knew it.

I started panting. It was warm and sticky, the way it gets when you're heading south from Dodge. When I came to a stream, three or four turtles jumped off rocks and into the water. Like the birds, they didn't trust me. Like the birds, they had their reasons.

Before I crossed, I gave that stream my own once-over. The turtles that splashed away were little, no bigger'n my hand with the claws all spread. But you don't want to find a snapper with your foot while you're wading, not if you care to keep that foot in one piece.

"Ahhh!" I hissed in pleasure when I came up on the far bank. The water drying on my scales cooled me off for a little while. It felt mighty fine.

A line of great shadows swept across the plain, sliding straight toward me. One passed plumb over me. I didn't like that, not even a little, and made a sign with my thumb and first finger to turn aside the dark omen. People say you're liable to die soon if a huzzard's shadow catches you. Huzzards eat carrion, so you can see why folks talk that way. I didn't exactly believe it, but I didn't exactly *not* believe it, neither.

One of the huzzards let out that croak they make. Hearing it didn't make me feel any easier. I scowled after their flight line. On they glided, not caring about me at all. Why should they? A huzzard's wings are wide as five or six people lying snout to foot. We're big enough for them to notice, but there's not enough meat on one of us for a flight to get excited about.

So they soared on, and I kept on. I crossed another creek. This time, I kept a closer eye on the turtles. But they kept an eye on me, too. I didn't get to grab one. Pretty soon, I'd start feeling the empty in my belly. Thinking about that made me imagine I felt it before I really did.

I was panting hard when it got to midday. The sun was hot, and my shadow puddled under me like it was trying to hide. I wouldn't've minded lying up for a spell, but I couldn't find anywhere to do it.

That's about when I heard a clatter behind me. When I turned around, the southbound stage was gaining on me. Four overworked drosaws hauled the coach full of folks who didn't care to use their own hind legs to get where they were going. I might've taken it myself if I could've paid the fare.

The drosaws rolled their eyes when they got close. They can smell that things like me eat things like them. That's why hardly anybody rides 'em, you know. They just won't put up with it. The harnessing keeps 'em far enough away from the coach to get too worked up about it. Most of the time, it does.

Got me a surprise when the coach stopped alongside me. The driver leaned my way and said, "Ha! Thought that was you, Rekek. Had enough of Dodge, have you?"

"Oh, you might say so, Havv," I answered. "But what's it to you?" If he wanted to laugh at me because of Sssue, I was gonna climb up there and bite chunks off him. *That'd* fill my belly, all right.

But he didn't. He said, "You see, I don't got nobody riding blunderbuss for me. Gafk, he came down sick this mornin'. You want to ride along in case we run into trouble, you can do that. You'll get his wages 'til we come to Newtown."

"Which Newtown?" I asked. I must've gone through a dozen places by that name, some of 'em tin pot, others good sized.

"On the Red River," Havv said. "You know that's the route we run."

When I thought about it, I did. I didn't want to do much thinking, though. I didn't much want to wash up in that Newtown, either. Not that anybody there wanted me dead or anything, but it wasn't where I'd aimed for.

But so what? Riding instead of walking, more silver in my pouch afterwards? "I'm your man," I said, and scrambled up alongside him. Folks always said I was a natural-hatched fool. I reckon they knew what they were talking about. Now I do, too. I was proud of myself then.

Yeah, a fool.

The blunderbuss Havv handed me had more range and more oomph than an eight-shooter, but not a whole hells of a lot. It'd faze the little raptors or the natives, maybe even the middle raptors. A ranno'd laugh at it. If a ranno came after the stage, we'd've all jumped out and run for it. You do that and you hope the ranno goes for the drosaws, not the people. You hope it doesn't have smaller killers skulking along behind, too. Otherwise, the huzzards will circle down and take care of the raptors' leavings.

We didn't see any rannos that day. Hardly any raptors, either, little or middle. The big hornfaces and the drosaws' wild cousins, they've been hunted in those parts till they're right scarce. You'd almost reckon you was back East.

Almost, but not quite. We didn't get to Cycadia till most of a daytenth after sundown. One of the drosaws got itself a limp, and Havv had to slow down so it could keep the pace. The passengers grumbled.

They cussed up a storm, to tell the truth.

Havv listened for a while. Then he lost his temper, or made like he did. "I'm doin' the best I can, dad gum it!" he hollered. "You can shut up in there, or you can git out an' walk!"

Nobody got out. Havv's mouth dropped open. The nictitating membrane slid across his left eye, the one toward me. He had the whip on the passengers, same as he did on the drosaws, and he enjoyed it.

He handed me some smoked meat. I gnawed on it. It needed

some gnawing. He passed me a flask. I took a good knock. That went down a sight easier'n the meat.

Before the sunlight died altogether, he struck a match against a square of slate and got a paraffin lantern going. The light it threw was thin and orange. "Hard to make like it's daylight," I said.

"You do what you can, is all," Havv said, and he wasn't wrong.

I hate the dark. Everybody does. Bad things happen then. The nasty, hairy critters sneak out from wherever they hide and make trouble. Or if they don't, you keep expecting they will, and that's just as bad.

Something howled, out beyond the lantern's small circle. The hairy critters don't see so real good; they make noise to warn others they're around. The drosaws didn't like it a bit, especially the half-lame one.

For all their snorting and honking, though, they kept plugging along. One of them let go of the trace with its hand for a spell, but the length of wood was lashed to its forearm, too, so that didn't do it any good. It got a grip again and soldiered on.

When the dark really slammed down, I said to Havv, "Give me one of your matches, will you?"

"Here you go." He handed me a match and the slate. "What you want it for?"

I struck it, then took the last cigar out of my pouch and stuck it in my jaws. It was so dark even with the lamp, the match's flare near blinded me for a bit. I puffed, got the cigar going, and sucked in smoke. It eased the nighttime jitters a bit. If I coughed, then I coughed, is all.

I thought so, anyways. Havv said, "Nasty habit you got there, Rekek. Stinks—and it's bad for your wind, too."

"How about you let me fuss over all that?" I said.

He clucked like a broody hen, tear my tail off if he didn't. "I'd've known you'd went native, like, I would've let you keep walking back there."

Yeah, the natives've been smoking burnweed forever and a day. It's always grown here, far as anybody knows. But I never saw anything wrong with it, really. I like the smell, no matter how Havv grumbled. I like the way it relaxes you. And they say burnweed'll kill you if you use it long enough, but how long is that? Chances are something else'll get you first.

Something out of the prairie wanted to get us. Out at the

edge of the lanternlight, out where I couldn't see much but a shape skulking along on all fours, two eyes glowed green, not red like people's eyes and raptors' and drosaws'. Horrible and unnatural, I thought. Way it seemed to me was, the nasty fur thing wanted to make a run at a drosaw, likely the lame one, who was on that side. But it didn't have the size or the nerve. It yowled and disappeared into the black, one more ghost I hoped I never saw again.

"Reckon it's gone?" Havv wasn't griping about the cigar any more.

"Hope so," I said. "If it'd hung around much longer, I was gonna let fly with the old blunderbuss."

"If you didn't do it on your own, I'd've told you to. I hate them things."

"Who doesn't? They make the feathers stand up all down my backbone and my tail," I said. "Whatever god hatched 'em from the World Egg must've been havin' herself a bad day."

Havv looked at me. "A World Egger, are you? Me, I've always leaned towards Out of the Sky."

We knocked the gods back and forth like smashpins till the drosaws finally hauled us into Cycadia. The town has a spring that never fails. Explorers and trappers and hornface herders liked that. The cycads growing all around the spring gave the place its name. It's smaller than Dodge, but it's more peaceful. Not a bad town at all.

People stumbled out of the stage and staggered toward the hotel. They'd been cooped up as long as anybody could stand. Havv and me, we got the drosaws to the stable and made sure they were seen to. Then we made for the hotel our own selves.

Naturally, it was full up by the time we walked in. The old lady behind the counter said she'd push tables together in the dining room and find us blankets, but she'd have to charge us for a regular room. I hefted the blunderbuss. Havv took out his eight-shooter and looked at it. Didn't point it anywhere near the old lady. Made her thoughtful just the same.

All of a sudden, price came down by half. "I'll see what's in the kitchen, too," she said. "On the house." So we got a place to sleep and fried chicken—pretty good even if it had gone cold—for cheap. Havv shelled out for everything, and got hisself a receipt from the old lady. Sooner or later, the stage company'd pay him back.

"Later, I bet," he said as we wrapped ourselves up in the blankets and tried to get comfy on the tabletops. "They're so tight, they don't even shit."

"That's how you get to run a company," I said, not that I knew the first thing about it.

Not far from us, a lantern burned low. Nobody likes true dark. True dark still belongs to the little hairy things. Some rustles and scrabbles said they might come out in spite of the lantern. I was too worn to care. I closed my eyes. Unless a varmint walked over me, I aimed to sleep till sunup.

And what I aimed at, I hit.

Havv got even with the passengers for snaffling all the rooms ahead of us. He banged on their doors as soon as the sun woke him and me, most of a daytenth before we were supposed to head out of Cycadia. Some of 'em cussed him, but he didn't care a bit. They had to be awake to cuss him, and awake was how he got 'em.

The stablehands gave us a fresh drosaw team. Some papers for Havv to sign, on account of ours that hurt its foot—they couldn't use that one for a replacement till it healed up. He signed. Why not? He was doing it for the company.

Some of the passengers were still sore at him when they got back on the coach. Some were sore at me, too. Did I help with the door banging? Oh, maybe a bit. I didn't fancy sleeping on tables, neither. All that grumpy rolled off us like water off your scales. Nothing much they could do about it 'cept haul their own baggage while they walked.

Off we rolled. The drosaws started kicking up dust right away. I hissed and snorted. My nictitating membranes did what they could, flicking bits of grit out of my eyes. Say what you will, dust is better than mud. Slogging through mud up to your cloaca? If you've ever done it—and who hasn't?—you know how awful that is.

Flies buzzed around. The drosaws' hides twitched. They didn't have feathers to flick bugs away. Mine started working double time. Scales are tough, sure, but some of those bloodsuckers have mouths that'll punch through iron thick as your thumbclaw. Sure feels that way when they punch into you, anyhow.

We kept on south across the plains. A small herd of wild

hornfaces grazed off in the distance. We left them alone, and we were lucky enough that they did the same with us. They were more worried about some middle raptors prowling around. They started to go into a horn circle to stand 'em off. You always wonder how they know to do that. Not like they could learn it in school or anything.

More huzzards spiraled overhead. These were way higher up than the ones I'd seen the day before. The white of their under-wings looked small against the blue. Any time a huzzard's wings seem small, you know it's a long ways off.

They slid across the sky toward the hornfaces and the rap-tors. Huzzards aren't stupid. Matter of fact, they're pretty damn smart, especially when it comes to vittles. They saw there might be some dead meat left over for 'em in a little while.

We went on rolling along. Every so often, a drosaw or two would pause to graze a bit, pulling up some trailside grass and grinding it in that battery of teeth they have. Long as they didn't linger, Havv let 'em do it. He knew you get more out of critters in good shape than from peaked beasts you whipped along till they dropped.

Farther south we went, warmer and muggier the weather got. More and more cycads and palms sprouted alongside streams. Thunderheads started piling up. Havv's tongue flicked in and out—he didn't like that one bit better'n I did.

"Rain, rain, go away," I said. Yeah, if there's anything worse than plowing through mud in a heavy stage on narrow wheels, fry me if I know what it might be.

The huzzards liked the weather fine. They ride the winds around those clouds like you wouldn't believe. I swear by the gods, when they get winds like that they reckon they're overgrown buzzbirds. You'd pay money to watch 'em, but I didn't have to. They were just up there for free.

"Ain't that somethin', Havv?" I pointed up to them cavorting.

"Somethin'. Yeah." But he didn't hardly look. He paid atten-tion to the trail and to the drosaws and to whatever spots ahead might be dangerous. That was as much as he had room for inside himself. What I'm telling you is, he made a damn fine driver, old Havv did.

Sharp as his brainclaws were, though, I spotted trouble first. I mean, the huzzards did. One heartbeat, they were flinging themselves around in the sky the way they had been, gallivanting all around for the sport of it. The next, they all started winging off to the east fast as they could go—and huzzards go pretty good, let me tell you.

They don't spook like that on a whim. They don't go after food that hard, either—not like they have to chase it. No, something they saw wasn't right. I clicked the blunderbuss to half-cock, just in case. "Maybe you should get your eight-shooter handy, Havv," I said. "Something wrong off to westward."

He'd been minding the drosaws, the way a driver should. But his pupils went from slits to big black circles when he saw the huzzards flying off. "Shove a stick up my cloaca if you ain't right," he said, and shifted the reins to his right hand so he could shoot with his left.

He tried to get more speed from the team without picking up the whip. He didn't have three hands, any more than anyone else does. Even with the whip, I don't reckon he could've done enough. Robbers or natives were going to do what they could any which way.

I worried about the natives more than robbers. Robbers'd take what they wanted and then leave us alone unless our fightback riled 'em too much. Natives wouldn't leave us anything. They were after what we had, and they were after our meat. They hate us even more than they fear us.

Look at it through their eyes and you can't hardly blame 'em. Over the past few hundred years, we've pushed 'em back from the coast almost all the way to the Rockies. They had bronze and crossbows when we got here, but not iron and gunpowder. They fought again and again. They lost again and again. And they sickened and died like nobody's business. That thinned out big tracts of land.

They ain't like us—the natives, I mean. Oh, some of 'em know our lingo, even if they talk funny. And some of 'em raise their tails in salute to our gods. But they ain't really like people. Shorter, squatter, feathers in funny places, hides brown instead of green.

Everybody knows that. Not everybody knows or believes they can't breed with real people, any more than rannos can with raptors. They smell wrong, so you don't want to cross tails with their womenfolk to begin with. No matter what you hear, they don't want anything to do with ours, neither. "I'd sooner screw a drosaw," one of 'em told me once, and I didn't even bite him, on account of I felt the same way.

And they're sneaky. By the Eggshell, they're sneaky! They've learned they can't lick us straight up, so they don't fight straight up. I looked in the direction the huzzards came from, but I didn't spy anything out of the way. If I hadn't had a thing or three to do with natives before, I would've wondered if I was imagining things.

Like I said, I didn't spy anything out of the way—and then I did. Four or five natives popped up out of nowhere all sudden like and rushed the stage. I know—not out of nowhere. The gods-damned rotten eggs must've been there all along. They must've been, but I didn't spot 'em. And I have me some practice spottin' 'em, too. I'd be gnawed bones if I didn't.

Havv let out a holler, "You passengers with pistols, now's the time to use 'em! Try not to shoot each other, hear?"

Just then, a crossbow bolt hissed by in front of my snout, too fast for my eyes to cross. Took *that* native out of the brawl for a bit. A crossbow'll kill you as dead as an eight-shooter will, but you can't load it up again near as quick.

One of the natives had an old musket he'd begged or bought or stolen from somebody who should've known better than to let him get his scaly fingers on it. He stopped to fire, but he didn't shoot straight. He stayed stopped, too; a muzzle-loader's almost as much fun to ready for another shot as a crossbow is. I knew that too well—my blunderbuss worked the same way. I'd likely have one shot, and I'd need to make it count.

Havv started banging away then, and so did two passengers. The drosaws went crazy. They don't know what shooting's all about, but they know they don't like it. Then one of them crumpled up with a crossbow bold in the short ribs. If the natives got one more, the team wouldn't be worth turds. They knew it as well as I did, too.

"Oh, gods!" Havv bawled. "There's more on the other side of us!" He fired that way, once, twice.

The natives on my side were just about to the stage. If they couldn't shoot us, they'd tear us to pieces with their teeth and claws. I gave 'em the blunderbuss. I hate flintlocks, I purely do. Click, hiss, then *bang!* half a heartbeat later. If you're lucky. If you don't misfire.

I got my *bang!* I wouldn't be spinning this yarn if I didn't. Kick damn near busted my shoulder. You don't hardly aim a blunderbuss. You put in a charge and fill the barrel half full of shot or junk or whatever you've got. The muzzle flares, to make sure the stuff goes every which way when it flies out.

I knocked over two. One took a lot of the charge square in the chest—wasn't much left of him from the middle up. The other thrashed for a bit before he lay still, but lay still he did. That's about as much as you can hope for from a blunderbuss.

And fry me if Havv didn't reach out with another blunderbuss as soon as I let fly with the first. How? I don't know how, consarn it. Maybe he really did have three hands. I pointed the piece at the natives. They took off running like middle raptors—which they ain't so far from, you ask me. A passenger winged one with a pistol shot. Only made the stinker run faster.

"Hoped they'd lowtail it," Havv said, "That one ain't loaded."

"Remind me I never should ought to game with you," I said. His bluff paid off, though, so I couldn't cuss him the way I wanted to. The natives on his side of the stage had had themselves a bellyful, too, and ran away like their pals. We were safe. Compared to how we'd been a little while before, anyways.

While Havv got the team under control, I borrowed his eight-shooter and went back to make sure the native who hadn't got all chewed up wasn't playing mammal and getting ready to do something nasty and sneaky. You got to check every single time.

But this one was a goner. Some junk had gone in through an eye. The thrashing? Didn't matter a copper's worth.

Something moved by the other carcass, though. The feathers on my back twitched. That native, he should've been *dead*. Wasn't enough of him left to be alive, not any more. But his leg kept twitching irregardless.

No, not *his* leg. *Hers.* When the natives raid, sometimes they all raid. If a gal's got a hatchling, she'll tie it to her leg to keep it out of mischief and go with the rest.

A shot rang out behind me—Havv, putting the wounded drosaw out of its pain. I wondered if I should smash in the little fella's head. I didn't feel bad about killing his mama. She would've done the same to me, and given the hatchling my liver to eat. She would've had some herself, too. But slaughter someone just out of the egg? Call me thin-shelled, but I couldn't stomach it.

"Let me have a chunk of that drosaw meat," I said.

"You don't want to eat none of her, Rekek. Nasty stuff," Havv said.

"Not for me. For Junior here." I held up the hatchling. I named him, too, though I didn't know it yet.

Havv hissed. "Don't keep that little monster! Good gods, bite off its head and get things over with." A couple of passengers peering out the window shouted the same thing, only louder and filthier.

Well, that just made me mad. You don't want to rile me—I reckon you found that out your own self, didn't you? I kind of aimed the second blunderbuss at the stage. Stupid passengers didn't know it wasn't loaded. They shut up right smart. You bet they did.

"I'll hang on to him awhile, see what he turns into," I told Havv. "If he tries biting my tail off or starts stealing or whatever the hells, I'll cut him loose. If he don't... I got no hatchlings of my own that I know about."

"You're crazier'n a hornface that's been eating locoweed," Havv said, but he cut me a nice chunk of drosaw kidney. I fed it to the baby native. Junior gulped it straight down. I gave him more. He ate that, too. Then he licked my hand. When I bent down over him, he sniffed my snout. Then he licked it, same as with my hand. Then he bared his little needle teeth to show he was happy.

Our hatchlings act the same way. They got to know who'll feed 'em, and it ain't like they can talk or understand straight out of the egg. To Junior, I was his new mama. He was so little, he'd never recollect the one who laid his egg.

Anyways, that's how I came by him, and he's been with me ever since. Yeah, he talks a bit mushy. He can't help it. But he's a better person than most ordinary folks I know, and we get on fine. If you want to say one more stupid thing about it, we gods-damned well *will* take you outside and teach you manners. Ain't that right, Junior?

See? He said, "Right." You followed him good, didn't you? *Didn't* you, stranger? Yeah, I figured you did.

The Dead Can't Die Twice

Samantha Lee Howe

Sheriff Deane worked the gun free from the corpse's cold dead hand, breaking two of the man's fingers in the process.

The barrel was warm to the touch, as though it had recently been fired. It was a double-action pistol, .38 caliber Colt Lightning.

As he held it, Deane started to feel uncomfortable. There was a familiarity. As though it had once belonged to him. The feeling grew stronger the longer he held the gun. This was not his weapon of choice, and so the sensation confused him.

"He's been dead for at least twenty-four hours," said Doc Stewart, breaking into Deane's thoughts.

They'd found him just outside of town. A stranger to these parts. Six foot tall and fair haired—Deane knew everyone in the town and the surrounding ranches and none fit this man's description.

"A foreigner maybe?" asked Stewart.

"Maybe..."

With a strange reluctance, Deane placed the gun, along with the man's clothing, money and pocket watch in a wooden box and marked it as belonging to the corpse. It was a relief to put the weapon down.

"If he ain't, we'll soon have a relative coming for this..." Deane said.

As if he had predicted the future, a tentative knock announced the arrival of a visitor to the sheriff's office. Deane opened the door and found a petite woman standing on the dusty wooden decking outside.

"Miss Lacie?" he said. "What can I do for you?"

"I heard a body was brought in, Sheriff..."

"Yes, but..."

"I think it's my brother..."

Deane stepped back and allowed Lacie to enter.

"May I see the body?" Lacie asked.

"Ma'am?" Stewart said. He appeared to be as surprised as Deane to see her there.

Miss Lacie was the schoolmistress, a spinster almost thirty years old, who barely spoke to anyone other than her students. She was meek and somewhat fragile in appearance with nothing alike in coloring to the dead man.

"We didn't know you had a brother..." Deane said.

"He only arrived a couple of days ago," she said. "He disappeared soon after... I thought maybe he'd gone again. Then I heard about the body you brought in."

Stewart pulled back the sheet covering the dead man. Lacie looked at the face; hers was as rigid as the corpse's.

"It's him," she confirmed. Then she retrieved a handkerchief from her reticule and dabbed at her dry eyes.

Deane didn't know how to react.

"How did he die?" Lacie asked.

"Looks like natural causes..." Stewart informed her. "Was he sick?"

Lacie shook her head, "Never a day in all his life." Lacie dabbed her eyes again. "May I take his possessions now?"

Deane experienced that weird sensation again. This time he recognized it as apprehension. Lacie's request was not extraordinary, but it was sudden. As though this was why she'd really come. Deane wondered if it was the money—a substantial amount had been found in the man's pockets—or the gun. He assumed it was the former as he had never seen Lacie with a gun, though many women carried them around town.

He asked her to sign a chit on which he listed every item.

Lacie took the watch first.

"Belonged to our father..." she commented. It was solid silver; an expensive piece.

When it came to the gun, Lacie picked it up with her

handkerchief as though she were afraid she'd catch something just by touching it. Then she dropped it into her reticule. She took the money from the box, as well.

"You can burn the clothes," she said. "Or give them to someone."

She turned then and headed to the door.

"What about the body?" asked Deane.

Lacie paused by the door, then, as though it were an after-thought she said, "I'll get the undertaker to collect him."

She left, closing the door behind her. There was barely a creak as her light frame walked on the wooden deck outside.

Deane found himself watching her. She crossed the street and paused at the grain supply store, glancing in the window, where she waved at the owner's small boy—one of her pupils. Then she strode confidently onward toward the undertaker's workshops.

"Odd," he murmured. Stewart had covered the body by the time he turned around. "You really think this was natural causes?"

Stewart shrugged. "What else? No wounds..."

"Then why was he holding the gun?"

Stewart said nothing.

Deane walked back to the body and pulled the cloth from the man's face as though he expected to find the frozen emotionless expression changed. His refusal to accept simple explanations was what made him the best sheriff the small town had ever had, but the doctor was certain there was nothing to find. Yes, the man's death was unusual. But people died all the time out here. Starvation and dehydration being the worst offenders. Anything could have happened on the outskirts of town. Maybe he'd been bitten by a rattlesnake...

"She didn't tell us his name..." Deane realized.

The door opened again and Kyle Banks, the undertaker, stepped into the office.

"Miss Lacie sent me," he said. "This him?"

"Yup," said Stewart. "She tell you his name?"

"Henry," answered Banks. He checked the body over. "I'll bring the cart." He left Deane and Stewart alone again with the corpse. When he returned, the three men carried the body out to the funeral cart.

"She wants it done before sundown," Banks told them.

A quick burial wasn't anything unusual. The desert heat soon

caused the bodies to stink and disease was rife. They dropped
Henry's body into a cheap coffin on top of the cart and Banks
jumped onto the back. He placed a lid on top of the crate and
nailed it down.

The saloon was busy as always. This was a mining town, rapidly growing with more settlers arriving weekly. After long days
working their claim, the settlers needed to unwind and spend
some of that gold they so proudly mined.

Deane ordered a whisky and took a seat by the window,
looking out onto the street. Dusk had come up quickly while
Deane thought about Henry's body in the pauper's casket, deep
in the ground as the dry earth clattered down over it—shovel by
shovel. He wondered if Miss Lacie had paid the few coins for the
drunken sot of a pastor to say some words over her brother, or
whether she had stood alone as the sun set, but for Banks and
his gravedigger, solemnly burying the coffin.

He didn't have to ponder this question long as the pastor
came in, his hand grasping the newly earned coin that would
go a long way to feeding his drink habit.

Deane knew everyone in the saloon, even the girls, not that
any of them bothered with him. They knew better than that.
A dutiful husband—God-fearing despite how drunk he saw the
pastor get—Deane held his pride on remaining a good man. But
Deane was off duty now, and a shot of whisky always settled him
after an unexplainable death. His deputy, Felix, would be in the
office all night, ready to deal with anything that may happen.
Deane knew that not much would, and Felix would sleep in one
of the cells until morning. After which, he'd stagger back home
to his wife when his shift was over.

Since Deane had taken over, and run off any of the "wrong
sorts," the town had been a safe and happy place to live. They'd
acquired new families over the years, and the population had
grown in size and respectability. Deane wanted to keep it that
way. That was why he didn't like finding the body of a stranger,
dead on the outskirts of town.

Deane sipped his whisky. The liquor burned his throat, but
he was hardy to it. He'd been drinking since he was twelve years
old. Now at the age of thirty, Deane drank very little.

And, Alice would be waiting for him.

They'd met in Kansas City and Deane had loved Alice right away. It had been a short courtship, and her aunt had given him permission to ask for her hand. They wed quickly and their son, Petey, came along in the first year. There'd been no other children since, but it didn't worry Deane or Alice.

Deane finished his drink, and picking up his hat, he left the saloon as the music grew louder. The hour was late; soon would be that time of night when the God-fearing forgot religion, and the prostitutes had their pick of customers. Deane needed none of it.

He untied his horse and walked it back towards the stables at the end of the main street. Inside the barn, he stabled the horse before a trough of fresh water and some hay to distract the animal while he brushed it down. Then he left the stables and headed into the back alleys toward his own home.

As Deane turned off the main street, he heard the distinct crack of a gunshot down a side street. He hurried towards the sound, and that's when he learnt that things had truly changed in his small, sleepy, safe town.

Miss Lacie lay in a pool of her own blood. Her eyes were sightless and Deane knew by the hole in her chest, no sawbones could save her. Deane knelt by the body trying to make sense of what he saw. Why would anyone shoot the mild-mannered schoolmistress? The death made no sense and shocked him, even though he'd seen many a murder during his time as sheriff.

Others came running as he examined the woman's body.

"Sheriff!" yelled a terrified voice from the house just two doors away. "There's a gun here. On my doorstep!"

The house belonged to an old watchmaker and his wife—long since retired when his eyesight failed him. The couple led a quiet life, as anyone should in Deane's town.

The .38 caliber Colt Lightning that Lacie had taken that morning sat on the porch. Deane picked the gun up and stuffed it into the back of his belt.

"Did you see anything?" Deane asked.

"No, sir! We were abed when we heard the shot..."

"Someone call for Doc Stewart," said a man in the gathering crowd.

The doctor arrived, and Lacie's body was placed on the same gurney that had carried her brother earlier that day.

Deane found Felix sleepy-eyed in the office. The sight of the body coming in brought the deputy to his feet.

"I heard shots," said Deane. "Found her dead soon after."

"You didn't see anyone?" asked Felix.

Deane shook his head. "Whoever did it slipped away as quiet as a mouse."

The raucous harmony of the night was ruined for all concerned. There was a killer loose in town and, since no strangers had rode in recently, suspicion would eventually fall on one of their own. It was not a prospect that Deane relished.

They buried Lacie in the graveyard beside her brother the next day, but not before Doc Stewart dug a .38 slug out of her chest.

Deane suspected that her brother's gun had been used to do the deed, but it was unclear why anyone would want to kill the quiet spinster. To confirm his suspicions, he examined the extracted slug, and noted the scoring on the side of the cartridge.

"I'll need to fire this thing to make a comparison," Deane told Stewart but for some reason Deane never did. Instead he locked the gun up and neither he, nor Stewart discussed it again.

After that though, Deane decided to make it his mission to find out more about the schoolmistress, and her brother.

He started with Mrs. Fairbanks from the church council.

"I heard about the shooting," Mrs. Fairbanks said when she opened the door to Deane. "Who'd want to do an awful thing like that to Miss Lacie?"

"That's what we're trying to determine," Deane said. "You were on the committee that hired her ... what do you know of where she hailed from?"

"She said she'd come from Glenwood Springs," Mrs. Fairbanks said. "She didn't talk much about herself though. More about the stuff she'd be able to teach the children. She was a regular at church on Sunday, and we never had a whiff of scandal. My son liked her, too. She was a good teacher. We'll be hard pushed to find another like her."

Deane thanked Mrs. Fairbanks and left. No scandal, law abiding, it was just the information he had expected to hear, but he was disappointed that there wasn't more to go on.

Still ... *Glenwood* ... That was a week's hard riding away.

In his office, Deane found his wife Alice and his son Petey waiting for him.

"Can I leave Petey here for a while?" Alice said. "He's underfoot now that school is off, and I have the laundry to do..."

"Sit down over there, buddy," Deane said to his son. The boy took a seat at Felix's desk, and Alice gave him a slate and chalk to practice his numbers on. She kissed Petey on the head, came to Deane and did the same before leaving.

Deane sat down at his own desk and began to write up a report about the death of Miss Lacie, but there was so little he could say that it barely filled half a page.

He looked out at Main Street and let his mind wander as he watched the occupants of the town going about their daily business. There was the pastor's wife carrying a basket full of groceries; old Dougal walking his decrepit dog up and down the street until the dog was as confused as the old guy was about his way home. A young prostitute called Celeste, up early considering the night in the saloon she must have had, was coming out of the apothecary shop clutching a bottle of something. Then there was Mikey Craven...

Deane blinked. Mikey was an odd boy, fourteen years old, with only his widowed mother to keep him on the straight and narrow. But he wasn't a bad sort, Deane knew that. Just had a tendency to find trouble. Like when he stole the apples from Mrs. Fairbanks's tree—the boy had said they were windfall, but Mrs. Fairbanks said she saw him pick them. Deane had punished the boy—a night in a cell had taught him he didn't want to get himself in any real trouble.

Now as Deane watched the boy moving through town he knew something was up. Mikey's eyes were wild, darting all over the street as his head turned this way and that. His face was pinched and snarling, like a jackal. He looked... feral.

Deane got out of his chair and walked up to the window. He watched Mikey go, and then saw him dart down the back, around the saloon.

"Stay here..." he said to Petey. The boy didn't look up as he continued practicing his numbers.

Deane left his office and walked down the street toward the saloon. Then he dipped behind the building just as Mikey had.

He didn't see the boy at first. He was standing in the shadows as though he didn't want to be seen. But a subtle movement, a shift from one foot to the other, gave the boy's location away with a small creak.

"What you doing here, son?" Deane asked, startling Mikey.

"Nothing, Sheriff. Just avoiding the sun is all," said Mikey but he was twitchy and appeared guilty, though Deane didn't know of what.

"Come out here, and let me get a look at you." Mikey's eyes widened, and Deane had the feeling the boy feared something. "What's with you?"

Mikey stared at him as though he were seeing a ghost.

"Sheriff...I...done nothin' wrong..."

"Then what you hiding from, boy?"

"Sheriff...why you pulling your gun on me...?"

Mikey's eyes bulged as he stared at Deane.

"What you talkin'...?"

Deane looked down at his hand, and there he found the Colt Lightning. It was warm in his palm—like the first time he picked it up. It terrified him though he didn't know why. He relaxed his finger off the trigger and looked down the barrel; flicking it open he counted the bullets inside. There were four remaining.

"Get outta here," he told Mikey, and the boy ran back toward the high street.

Deane stuck the gun in his belt. Where was his own gun? His holster hung empty, and he never went anywhere without it. When had he last touched the weapon? Unnerved, Deane wondered why he had Henry's Colt. Why had he drawn it?

He went back to his office. Petey was still sitting at the desk writing on his slate as though he hadn't noticed Deane leaving at all. Deane opened the safe and found *his* iron inside. Deane shook his head. He must have been so tired that the previous night, when he thought he'd stowed the Colt, he had placed his own gun inside instead.

Deane took out his gun and holstered it. Then he placed the Colt firmly inside the safe. There was not likely to be anyone claiming the gun, but Deane didn't want to touch it ever again.

A short time later Alice came by to take Petey back home with her.

"I sure do hope they get us another school teacher soon," she said.

Deane watched his wife and son leave. He wondered about how bad Petey must have been that morning in order for Alice to bring him to the office. The boy had sat quiet and had not bothered Deane even with the simplest request. Frowning, Deane locked up the office and followed Alice and Petey down the main street. He crossed the road to the other side and stood in the shadow of the apothecary's doorway. At a distance, he saw his wife talking to the grocer as he swept the dust from his front step. Then he saw the man touch Alice's hand. It was a quick, sly and intimate gesture. Deane slipped farther back into the shadows. He watched as Alice cast a glance up the street towards his office—expressing, perhaps, a moment of guilt?

Alice walked on, and Deane continued to follow. He had never had any cause to doubt her and didn't know how to react to the sensation of suspicion and jealousy. Surely, this was all in his mind. He couldn't have seen what he had just seen. He had to be misreading things.

He passed by the grocer shop and glanced at the owner—Daniel Hooley, a widower of not more than a year. Hooley glanced up from his sweeping and frowned when he found Deane watching him.

"Sheriff..." he said giving a nervous nod.

Deane nodded back and then followed Alice and Petey all the way home. When he got to his house, he saw bed linen and clothing hanging wet on the washing line out front, the bright hot sun bleaching the cotton white. Deane knew that Alice had to have been washing when she said she was, but there was a deep-rooted nagging doubt now about her and Hooley.

"Daddy, what you doing home?" asked Petey.

Alice turned and saw Deane behind them. An imperceptible flush colored her cheeks.

"Thought you'd be busy today, trying to find who killed Miss Lacie," she said.

"I'm busy right enough," he said. "Just wanted to check on you and Petey. Things ain't right around here..."

Alice frowned. "You don't think we're in danger?"

"Until we find the culprit, no one is safe," Deane said. "Stay indoors and don't stray beyond what's necessity."

Alice hurried inside with Petey. Deane stared at the door long after it closed. Then he turned away and walked back to his office. Hooley was inside the store stacking his shelves with new stock. Deane didn't go in, and Hooley didn't notice as he passed. If he had, Hooley might have seen the tightness of Deane's jaw and the hard set of his eyes.

A loud knocking on his front door brought Deane from a deep sleep. He staggered from his bed in his long johns, and lit the lantern on the dresser.

"What's that?" said Alice. She was sitting upright in the bed by the time the light filled the room. Her eyes were wide and scared.

Deane picked up his gun from the table at the side of the bed, then he took the lamp and went downstairs leaving Alice once more in the dark.

The hammering on the door continued.

"Who is it?" Deane said.

"It's me. Felix! There's been another one, sheriff..."

Deane opened the door to his deputy looking scared and tired. Two nights of no sleep would do that to a man.

"Who is it?" Deane asked.

"Daniel Hooley. The grocer. Someone shot him clean through the head."

A loud gasp behind him caused Deane to spin around. The lamplight spilled over his wife's terrified face. She looked as though she were about to collapse with shock.

"That poor man..." she stammered. "And after his wife, Andrea, died in childbirth..."

Deane's face went blank as he turned back to Felix. "Where's the body?"

"It was a .38 bullet..." Doc Stewart said. He dropped the crumpled metal down onto Deane's desk. "Just like Miss Lacie. This was lodged in the man's brain."

"So someone else has a gun like this one," said Deane, "'cuz Lacie's gun is locked up inside my safe."

"In the safe?" Felix asked, puzzled.

"Yeah."

"I went in there for spare ammo. I didn't see it," Felix said.

Deane opened the safe, and all three men peered inside.

"See," said Deane. "There it is."

He reached in and picked up the weapon. It *was* the Colt that had belonged to Lacie's brother Henry.

"I guess I mustn't've noticed it," said Felix.

The metal of the gun felt uncomfortably warm in Deane's hand. Out of habit, he flipped the barrel open and counted the bullets. There were only three.

He placed the gun back in the safe and closed it, saying nothing of his findings to the doctor or his deputy. Instead, he dismissed what he'd seen, believing he must have miscounted the bullets earlier.

"I have to get back to my wife," Deane said.

Alice looked like she'd been crying when Deane returned to the house.

"What's goin' on?" she asked. "Why're nice people suddenly dying?"

"Who said the grocer was nice?" Deane asked.

"Well... he didn't... there was never anyone with a bad word about him or Andrea..."

"Go to bed," Deane said.

Alice scurried away, though she wasn't usually one to take orders from anyone. Deane couldn't help noticing how affected she was by Hooley's death.

Was that all his imagination? Or had Alice and Hooley been more than acquaintances?

In their bedroom Deane stripped back down to his long johns and slipped under the sheets.

"How well did you know him?"

"No more'n anyone else," Alice said.

Deane didn't believe her. But, if there had been something forming between them, that no longer mattered. Daniel Hooley was dead, and he wouldn't be coming back from the grave any more than any other corpse.

The next morning Alice was her normal self, and she hummed a little tune while making breakfast.

Deane ate the usual grits this time with crispy bacon (usually only served him on a Sunday).

"Thought you deserved that," said Alice.

After breakfast, Deane put on his gunbelt and holstered his gun. The metal felt uncommonly hot and, as he raised the weapon up to examine it, he found the .38 Colt Lightning in his hand instead of his usual Smith and Wesson.

Startled, he shoved the weapon into his holster before Alice saw it. Then he kissed his wife on the cheek and hurried out.

It was early, and Main Street was empty as Deane walked along it. His heels brought up puffs of dust as he walked. Felix had sent a telegram late last night to Hooley's only brother. The grocer's store was closed and would remain so until Hooley's relative arrived to either reopen it or to sell it on.

In the office, Felix slept soundly in the empty cell. Deane didn't wake him. Instead he opened up the safe. There he found his own gun again, and he quickly switched it with the Colt. He didn't look inside to see how many bullets remained.

A few hours later the pastor's wife came in.

"My husband didn't come home last night. I think he was down by the saloon. And maybe... with one of them floosies..."

"Don't excite yourself," Deane told her. "Sure, he drinks. But he's never shown any interest in the girls."

Deane left her in the office with some hot coffee. Then he went to the saloon. He walked in and straight upstairs, knocking on each of the girl's rooms before poking his head inside. The pastor wasn't there.

"Anyone see him last night?" he asked the bartender.

"He didn't come by..." said the man as he dusted and polished the glasses for the day.

As he pushed open the doors, Deane came face to face with Banks, the undertaker.

"I found the pastor," Banks said. "Down in the cemetery."

"Another .38?" Deane asked as Doc Stewart examined the pastor's body.

The doctor nodded. "He's been dead since the early hours. The stiffening is just setting in."

Deane didn't know what to say. He couldn't understand why anyone would kill the pastor. There had to be a connection between all of the victims. But the only thing he could determine was the type of weapon used.

When the undertaker took the pastor's body away, Deane stood alone once more in his office. He opened the safe and took out the Colt. The gun felt hotter than ever in his hands. He opened the barrel and found, without surprise, that only two bullets remained.

I'm losing my mind, he thought.

No one had access to the gun but him and his deputy. He knew that Felix was not involved: The weapon kept appearing in Deane's own holster around his own waist. But why?

Instead of returning the gun to the safe, Deane placed it in his holster. He wanted no more deaths in his town. He would keep the weapon with him that day, thus ensure that no one else could use it. Or, if the culprit was desperate enough, he may even try to take it from the sheriff, in which case Deane would catch him.

Daniel Hooley's brother, Ethan, arrived later that day. Daniel's body was already in the ground and so after visiting the grave, Ethan made his way to the sheriff's office.

Deane was sipping coffee and eating cake that Alice had packed with his lunch.

"Do you know who did this?" Ethan asked.

"We are still investigating," said Deane. "Perhaps you could tell me if your brother had any enemies?"

Ethan grew quiet a moment. Then he said, "At his last town he made himself too familiar with other men's wives... Eventually the scandal forced him and Andrea to leave. I thought he'd learned his lesson."

Deane looked away from Ethan, out the window and to the street.

"There's been no scandal here that I've heard," he said.

"No? I guess it must be somethin' else," said Ethan.

Ethan went to open up the grocery store.

"It'll be business as usual," Ethan promised. "I've been looking to settle somewhere hereabouts anyways."

"What you doin'?" Alice said.

Deane woke. Alice had lit the lamp and was staring at him. His wife looked scared, as though she'd seen a ghost and not her husband standing at the foot of the bed.

"How'd I...?"

"I heard somethin'," she said. "Then I woke and found you... just standin' there."

His hand burned. Deane looked down, finding the Colt

clutched in his grasp. His finger poised over the trigger and the hammer pulled back as though ready to fire. Alarmed, he put the gun down on the dresser. His hand trembled.

"I wanna ask you somethin'," he said turning to look at Alice.

"What?"

Alice shrank back. She looked frail and small, almost child-like. Deane felt guilty that he had scared her so much.

"What is it?" she asked again.

"Hooley..."

Alice frowned. "What about him?"

"He ever...get *friendly* with you?"

"Hooley was a flirt. But he did that to all the women..."

"Did you *like* it?" Deane asked.

"No. It made me feel...uncomfortable. I married you. I only want to *know* you."

Deane rubbed his hand over his brow. "I don't want any more deaths in my town, Alice."

"Come back to bed," his wife beckoned. "You're just stressed. And no surprise with a killer out there."

Deane came around the bed to his side. He sat down and swung his feet up onto the mattress.

"Jeez..." hissed Alice. "Your feet..."

Deane looked down and saw dust and muck on his bare feet. And bloody scratches on his ankles. He winced as he suddenly became aware of the stinging.

"What did you do?" asked Alice.

"Guess I musta walked outside," he reasoned. "In my sleep."

Alice got up and brought the wash bowl and jug around to Deane's side of the bed. She washed and dried his feet.

"It's gone. You can sleep now," she said.

Deane curled up in the bed and fell asleep as though nothing had happened.

Deane woke to more chaos and Felix, once again, banging on his door. This time the prostitute, Celeste, had been found dead. Not in the saloon, but out near the cemetery, in the center of a wild rose bush that the pastor's wife had planted some time back. Deane didn't need to ask what bullet the Doc had found in her. He already knew. Just as he knew that only one bullet remained in the gun he now carried in his holster.

Deane went to Main Street. He found Ethan already at the store. A fresh supply of fruit had come in. The housewives of the town had lined up to buy it.

"I need to talk to you," said Deane.

"Sure thing, Sheriff," said Ethan. "I'll call by when I finish serving these ladies." He smiled at the women with the same flirty expression his brother had once had. Deane didn't like it. He found his hand resting on the gun as he walked away from the store.

A little later, Ethan came to the office.

"Sit," ordered Deane.

Ethan sat by the sheriff's desk and looked at him benignly.

"What can I do for you, Sheriff?"

"I've been thinking. Your brother. He only lived here, about eighteen months..."

"That's correct, Sheriff."

"Where did he live before he came here?"

"Glenwood Springs."

"Glenwood? That's where Miss Lacie came from."

"Miss *Lacie*?"

"The schoolmistress. She arrived about six months ago. Along with the pastor and his wife. But before them, Celeste came to town."

"I don't understand..." said Ethan.

"Did you know any of them?"

Ethan frowned. "I knew a Lacie. Back in Glenwood. Lacie Holliday. She married Doc Holliday, a few days before his lungs packed in."

Deane asked Ethan to describe Lacie Holliday. The description sounded just like the dead teacher.

"What about Colin Dylan, the pastor?"

"Yeah...He gave Doc his last rites..."

Deane stroked the butt of the gun.

"He left 'cuz of scandal, too," Ethan said, though by then the explanation was unnecessary.

"How'd your brother fit into this?" Deane asked.

"Rumor was that Lacie married Doc because she knew he was dying and it helped deflect some of the suspicion Daniel's wife had of him and Lacie. By then, Andrea was pregnant. Daniel said they'd bought a store out this way, and she was happy to leave with him. Next thing I heard Andrea had died in childbirth."

"What about a whore called Celeste?"

Ethan shrugged. "I didn't know any women of that sort. But my brother may've."

Deane knew there had to be a connection, and he wanted the mystery wrapped up in a neat little bow. Daniel, Lacie, and the pastor were all connected to Doc Holliday. Deane, of course, had heard of the infamous Holliday's death. It had reached their town in a newspaper brought by a group of prospectors. The news of Holliday had made interesting gossip for a few days. Deane recalled this was where he'd heard the name Glenwood Springs before. It had been in that newspaper clipping. He thought he even had it still somewhere.

"Is that all, Sheriff?" Ethan said.

"There's a connection," Deane said as though speaking to himself. "I'm just not sure yet what it is."

Ethan left the sheriff's office, and Deane barely noticed. His fingers stroked the Colt's butt, over and over, feeling the heat of the weapon seeping into his hand.

What did it all mean?

Deane took the weapon out of the holster and looked in the chamber. He'd already known this, but had to confirm, that there was one bullet left.

Someone else in their little town probably hailed from Glenwood Springs.

Deane thought he knew everyone in the town, but he couldn't remember when they all arrived, or where they all came from.

And then, Deane realized, he hadn't mentioned the first victim to Ethan. Miss Lacie's brother Henry had to be somehow involved in this too.

He locked up the office and headed back to the store to take this up with Ethan, only to find the store had been closed early.

Later that day, Deane asked the pastor's widow, "Do you know of anyone else here who hailed from Glenwood Springs?"

"Glenwood? Why there?"

"It seems there was a connection. The people who died, including your husband, came here directly from there. So you must have known Miss Lacie and Mr. Hooley."

"I married Colin just before we moved here. We met in Wichita. He never said he knew anyone here already."

Deane questioned her further, but it was clear she didn't know anything of her husband's life in Colorado.

"Here's the town register, Sheriff," the woman said eventually. "It may have the information you're looking for."

Deane took the thick leather-bound book and opened it on the most recent page. There he saw the names and dates of each of the victims and as he'd already learnt, how they all arrived within months of each other and came from Glenwood Springs.

There wasn't anyone else who was new to the town or from Colorado.

Other than the pastor's drink problem, Deane hadn't heard any rumors about any of the victims before they died. But even Alice knew that Daniel Hooley had a wandering eye. If anyone suspected that Miss Lacie had been married to the famous robber and gambler, then it was never gossiped about. As far as Celeste was concerned, Deane could find no connection at all.

Then one of the girls from the saloon came to see him.

"Celeste was pregnant when she arrived here," the girl said. "It happens."

"What happened to the baby?" Deane asked.

"She took something to rid herself of it. She was sick for days. Doc Stewart had to be called. Then he gave her something that helped her pull round."

"I guess that's what you girls do all the time?" said Deane.

"The orphanage in Kansas has a few of mine. I don't hold with taking a life... Sometimes nature takes care of it on its own. But Celeste liked to take her potions."

"Where'd she get the stuff from?"

The girl glanced across the street to the apothecary shop.

"Did she know who the father was?" Deane said as the girl turned to go.

"Oh yes," said the girl. "She boasted about it. She'd been this gambler's girl back in Glenwood. Until he got sick in his lungs. She said before he died, he begged her to keep the kid. Said it was all he had left."

"Doc Holliday?" Deane surmised.

"You knew *already*?"

"Just a guess."

"He said he'd come for her if she killed his child. But he died even before she rid herself of it," said the girl. "Celeste once told me..." She trailed off.

"What?" said Deane.

"That, well, she thought she saw him sometimes…standing by the graveyard. But I thought it was the guilt. The baby is buried there you see. She was quite far on before she ended it. Had to birth it, dead as it was. Doc Stewart made her name it and give it a proper burial. He didn't know what she'd done though. Only Celeste knew. And me too… I guess he thought it was a stillbirth…"

Deane found the newspaper cutting in the top drawer of the dresser when he pulled out his clean shirt.

There was a picture of Doc Holliday. A death photo, taken as he lay in his open coffin. He looked peaceful. Deane recognized the man: It was Henry, the man Miss Lacie had said was her brother.

But it *couldn't* be the same man. The dead don't rise and die twice. Deane was confused and began to question his own sanity. He had to see that body again. Had to look into that dead face one more time. Surely his memory was playing tricks with him?

He pulled on his clothes and hurried to the undertaker's.

"We got to dig up Henry," he said.

Banks looked at the faded photograph in the newspaper clipping and paled. "That man was newly dead."

"Maybe Holliday had a twin?" Deane suggested.

At the graveside, Deane waited while the digger and undertaker shifted the earth. Soon, the box was hefted up out of the ground.

"It's light," said Banks. Then he levered the top open.

The coffin was empty.

"Grave robbers?" said Banks.

They pulled Lacie's grave up to see if she too was missing, but the body of the schoolmistress still lay there. Though now swollen with decay.

They put her back in the ground.

"Don't tell anyone about this," Deane said to Banks. "We don't want superstition and panic."

"There was a body in there when we put him in the ground," Banks said. "Though Miss Lacie was acting weird about it."

"What d'you mean?"

"She said, 'He shouldn't have come.' There was 'no place for him' among the living. I thought it was grief talking. But Pastor Dylan. He comforted her. Said he'd do the rites again if needed to 'keep him down.' Then she stuffed some money in his hand, and he did them three times over the grave. Along with a prayer I'd never heard before. Something about the dead not rising."

"Why didn't you tell me any of this sooner?" Deane said.

"I thought he was just feeding her superstition."

"There's more than superstition going on here," said Deane.

"In my experience the dead don't leave their graves," said Banks. "It's gotta be a living person doing this."

Deane went home, the Colt still in his holster. At least no one else had died that day. Maybe it was over? *One bullet left*, he thought as he reached his house.

Alice was bringing in the washing. Her golden hair shone in the sunlight. Petey played on the patch of grass they had for a garden.

"Hey!" said Alice. "How goes it, Sheriff?"

Deane smiled at her. She seemed happier these days. As though she were free of some awful threat. Yet Deane knew there was still a killer on the loose. At least until—and the thought was insane—the last bullet was used.

They passed a peaceful evening together. Alice darned Petey's trousers, scuffed open at the knees for the second time, and Deane poured himself a whisky.

Later when they went to bed, Alice initiated intercourse. She didn't usually, but Deane was happy to oblige.

Then, with the Colt still in his holster, Deane slept.

He opened his eyes onto another world. Where was he? *When* was he?

Alice—a little younger than when they first met—with a woman who looked a lot like her aunt, but Deane knew had to be her mother.

"You ain't marrying no gambler," said the woman now. "Your father would turn in his grave."

"Mamma, he has money. Lots of it. He promised to help with your debts. He wins all the time. Don't you understand? We'll want for nothing!"

"I won't agree Alice, and you're too young to do this without my consent."

The vision faded. *Then...*

"I could kill her..." Alice said.

She took his hand. Deane pulled her to him. He was confused, but glad to hold her.

"Did you hear me?" she said again. "I could *kill* my mother."

They were in a parlor. Deane couldn't recall ever being there before. The door on the other side of the room opened. The woman he'd seen earlier now came inside.

"What is he doing here? I told you..."

Alice reached around Deane and yanked the Colt from his gunbelt. In a split second, she pointed the weapon and fired.

"What have you done?" said Deane, leaping from his seat. He went to check on the woman. The bullet hole in the middle of her forehead confirmed her death. How had Alice been such a good shot? Deane had never seen her pick up a gun.

"Not me," she said, putting the weapon in his hands. "It was you..."

Men ran in then and, grabbing Deane, they yanked him around. Then he saw, reflected in the mirror above the fireplace, his white blond hair, tall lean frame. It was not his own image he saw now, but that of a young Doc Holliday. They pulled him from the house, and Alice shouted his guilt for all to hear.

Deane opened his eyes and found himself once more standing over the bed. Alice recoiled against the headboard.

"Why you looking at me like that?" she demanded. "What's wrong with you?"

The Colt Lightning held his grip as though the metal had melted around his hand. It burned.

"You killed your own mother," Deane said.

"What are you talking about?"

"I saw it. Through *his* eyes."

"You're not making any sense. Look at me. I'm your wife. I've never even held a gun..."

Deane's eyes cleared, and he saw Alice truly for the first time. For what she was and had always been.

"Gun? I didn't say how she died..."

"Look...I'm..."

"You set him up," said Deane. "You set up Doc Holliday."

Alice's face changed: She knew the ruse was up.

"I knew him as John... Others called him *Henry*... She, my mother, wouldn't let us be together..."

"You shot her. He took the blame. Now he's back, Alice. Back for revenge on all of you that caused him pain."

Alice burst into tears. "I didn't owe him anything. He was a coward."

"He was lucky to have friends in high places. They made the whole thing go away. But you, Alice. You went to live with your aunt in Kansas. He never forgave you. He thought you loved him, Alice. Just like I believed you loved me."

"I do..." she said. "Doc was a mistake."

He raised the Colt and aimed it at her head.

"You can't kill me," she said. "They'll string you up..."

"I'm not going to pull the trigger Alice, Doc is. Just like he did with all the others."

"Please. I'm your wife. What about Petey?"

Deane faltered. The gun in his hand felt less stable. Then his mind drifted out of his body.

He thought he heard Alice cry out. But then he was no longer there.

Deane straightened up. The sheriff had always stood well below six feet, now he towered over. His dark hair faded, becoming white blond.

"Doc!" Alice gasped.

The Colt fired. Alice's body jerked against the headboard. The heart in her chest burst as the .38 bullet burrowed in.

Doc saw her eyes glaze as the pain of death engulfed her and she slumped.

"Daddy?" cried Petey at the bedroom door. "Are you and Mamma in there?"

Petey opened the door, and saw his dead mother, and his father gone. There in his place was a tall blond stranger.

"It's all right, son," said Doc Holliday as he holstered his gun. "I'm out of bullets."

As Petey ran to his mother, Doc Holliday left the sheriff's house. He was revived for now and confident that he'd last a little longer in this body, just as he'd been able to use the previous one.

In time, this one would die, but his spirit would live on in another. After all, the dead can't die twice.

The Adventures of Rabbi Shlomo Jones and the Half-Baked Kid

Eytan Kollin

1877

Part 1
The Town of Last Drop

Shlomo Jones gave the mule a halfhearted threat followed by a halfhearted snapping of the reins. Neither were sufficient to get the exhausted animal to move one inch.

"Come on, Rivka," the dirty and exhausted man said. "The town is right over there." The not-so-recently arrived immigrant even pointed to the small ramshackle wooden town just about three miles away, nestled at the base of the Arizona hills. The mule looked back toward Shlomo and snorted. Shlomo sighed and looked at his wagon. It was an open wagon being nothing so much as a platform with two-foot wooden sides. It was just long enough and wide enough to carry a coffin, which it did. The coffin was old and battered, looking like it had been in the ground for a while before it was dug up and repurposed, which is exactly what had happened. Strapped on top of the coffin sat a steamer trunk and a carpetbag, secured with shipping cord.

With another sigh, Shlomo got off the hard wood seat and, even though his cramped legs did not want to walk an inch, his tuchus was glad. Walking and stretching at the same time, Shlomo went to the mule and gently took the bridle and stroked Rivka's muzzle twice before slowly walking forward, bridle in

103

hand. The mule paused for a second as if debating the value of being stubborn versus getting to town with a trough and maybe a stable with hay instead of dining on Arizona scrub grass in the 90-plus temperature. After a moment Rivka switched her ears and started walking forward.

Relieved to be finally moving, Shlomo welcomed the shade of his big black shtetl hat with the wide brim. Being wide-brimmed, it did an admirable job of keeping out the sun and the rain. It wasn't a cowboy hat in any sense of the word, but Shlomo kept it. It was free and so ugly few were likely to steal it. Plus, it belonged to his deceased brother, a gentle reminder of him. The rest of his clothes were various bits and pieces he'd picked up along the way. The Levi blue jeans came from a stint in the silver mines of the Comstock. His very comfortable cotton shirt had been won in a game of chance in which Shlomo had cheated more skillfully than his opponent. The boots had been acquired from the feet of a man who would never need them again. The only item of clothing he'd actually paid for was his full-length duster. It was a hearty brown color with a wide lapel. It reminded Shlomo of a pirate jacket he'd seen in a magazine on his first day in New York City. He'd liked it so much, the vagabond actually spent three weeks working in San Francisco to simply pay for it. A circumstance he had found singularly distasteful. Of course, needing to work hard and save money was only a problem he had *before* he discovered his "special" talent.

When Shlomo was a mile from the town, he opened the carpetbag atop the coffin and retrieved the Colt revolver from where he left it. If it was possible to scowl and smile at the exact same moment, Shlomo did so as he belted the gun to his waist and tied the holster to his thigh. With lightning speed, he took the gun from the holster, switched it from hand to hand, twirled it from hand to hand, and guided it back into the holster with such speed that the pistol almost bounced back out. He did this without an ounce of joy at his obvious talent. He let the duster drape over the gun.

As Shlomo led his wagon down the main—and effectively only—street in town, someone shouted his way, "Who's in the coffin?"

"No one," Shlomo replied and waited a beat before he added, "yet." This brought a laugh from the group of men waiting near the saloon. He took off his hat and gave the men a slight bow.

"Tell me gentlemen, is the stable a good place to quarter my mule, or should I just take Rivka out to the field and shoot her now?"

This elicited more laughter from the men before one of them said, "Go to Cletus, right on the edge of town. Just arrange the price before you hand over the bridle, and you'll be all right."

"Thank you, sir," Shlomo said with a deeper flourish of his old hat and made his way to the opposite side of town.

"Welcome to Last Drop, stranger," a man said as he came out of the stable. The man was tall and wiry, looking a bit like Ol' Abe Lincoln. Shlomo had only voted in one election in America, but he had voted for Lincoln. It was one of the few actions he had taken as a recent immigrant that he was truly proud of. But other than the build, the man bore no resemblance to the sixteenth president. Shlomo did not detect any burning light of intelligence from those dull eyes.

"Well, I don't want to be a stranger. My name is Shlomo, Shlomo Jones," He extended his hand. The man gave Shlomo a strong, squishy shake with his manure-stained hand.

"Good to meet ya, Slow-mo. I'm Cletus." He pointed a thumb to his chest.

"Actually it's Shlo-mo," Shlomo said, accenting each syllable.

"That's what I said," smiled Cletus. "Slow-mo."

Shlomo sighed. "That's it exactly. How much to stable my mule, Rivka, and my wagon for two or three days?"

"I can do it for fifty cents a day."

Shlomo sighed again. "I can manage two days on fifty cents a day. I will have to see about the third day though."

"Fair enough," Cletus said and held out his hand again which Shlomo shook. "Don't you worry none. I'll take good care of Rivka." Shlomo couldn't help but notice that the American had pronounced the mule's name perfectly. "She'll be brushed and fed, and I'll clean her hoofs too."

"That is most kind, but be careful on the hoofs. She is a bit . . . temperamental."

Cletus just smiled. "Ain't my first mule, Mr. Slow-Mo."

"I guess it ain't. Where is a good place to bed down?"

"The saloon's got some rooms, but they charge two-bit prices and it's a one-bit place."

"I guess it's the only place."

"Well other saloons tend to catch fire soon after opening," Cletus said innocently.

"That can happen if you're not careful," Shlomo judiciously agreed.

"Always good to be careful," Cletus said nodding.

Shlomo went to his little wagon and untied the top carpetbag and told Rivka, "You be nice for the stable master." He grabbed her by the jaw and looked into her eyes. "No nipping!"

Rivka tried to bite his hand.

There were at least fifteen armed men in the saloon at a time of day honest men should be working. That usually meant trouble.

"Well, that is the stupidest hat I have ever seen," a tall, fit man said from the bar.

Shlomo turned his eyes hat-ward. "It is true that my hat may not be the best hat in the world, but it was my brother's. So I'll keep it."

"You sound funny," said the man at the end of the bar with a slight southern accent. Shlomo noticed that all the other men in the bar waited. That was never a good sign. He decided to deal with this quickly.

"I should sound funny. I'm a Jewish man from Poland. I've been here for fourteen years. You think it would have gone away, but no, still I sound like a schnook from a shtetl. I was hoping the Army would give me English, like a Yankee, but no luck."

"You were in the Army?" a man asked from one of the tables, but from the glares he got from the other players, he probably regretted it instantly.

"Indeed I was. My brother and I fought with the New York volunteers. Not that we were from New York mind you. But to be fair, we did volunteer."

"Did you see any action?" asked another man.

Shlomo sauntered up to the bar and placed a quarter on the surface. "Mister, did I see action? Like you wouldn't believe. At Gettysburg, I was. My first battle." Shlomo grew silent as his mind went back to the battle. Some of the men also entered their own terrible memories.

"Your brother fight with you?" asked that man at the bar.

"His last battle," Shlomo gritted out.

"You're a Jew boy who fought for the damn Yankees," the man at the bar spat out, his southern accent becoming more pronounced.

Shlomo's eyes hardened as he smiled. "Yes, mister, I did fight for the damn Yankees. I started at Gettysburg, and there I was when Lee surrendered at Appomattox. And I voted for Father Abraham in between."

"You better hope you're better with a gun than you are picking a savior, you Jew son of a bitch," the man said, shifting his hip so his jacket fell away exposing his pistol on his hip.

Shlomo just smiled and, reaching over the bar grabbed a shot glass and bottle, poured himself a drink. "You know, mister, it is funny you should mention that." Shlomo took his shot of whiskey and coughed. "Oy! That is a good shot of whiskey. But we were talking about guns. You see in Poland, indeed in all of Europe, Jews aren't allowed to have guns. At least not in the parts I was in. But in America, Jews can have guns." Shlomo drew his gun so quickly, it appeared as by magic.

The man at the end of the bar who had barely twitched his shoulder was already looking down the barrel of Shlomo's gun. He froze, as did everyone else in the saloon. "Just to repeat, in Europe, Jews can't have guns," and with a loud slap the gun was back in his holster. The large southerner's eyes gaped at the seemingly impossible speed. "But in America, everyone can have a gun." And in a flash Shlomo's gun was back in his hand pointing in the general direction of the southerner who even with his head start only managed to have his hand on his gun's grip. "Even Jews," Shlomo finished in a voice that was no longer even remotely friendly. "So mister," Shlomo said putting his pistol back in its holster with exquisite sloth, "what you have to decide is, are we still having a discussion about guns and saviors, or is this something else?"

Slowly the southerner moved his hand away from his holster, and the room breathed a sigh of relief. "Where'd you learn to draw that fast," he finally asked.

"Just something I picked up after the Army."

One of the men at the table shouted out, "James, we should hire him to help out." More men shouted in agreement.

Shlomo looked at the James they spoke to, and took his second drink. "Help out with what, Mr. James?"

"We have a problem with a mine that's filled with gold."

"That sounds like a problem I would like to have. I worked in a silver mine, but never a gold mine. How bad can it be?"

"It would be great if not for the band of blood thirsty redskins that have taken it over. All mining has stopped, and they killed ten men this past month. The mining company hired us to deal with it, but we can't get at them in the mountains. We'd use artillery, but the mining company won't let us do that. They don't want the mine damaged." James spat.

Shlomo thought about it and smiled. "Mister, this just may be your lucky day. I don't think a fellow with a quick draw will be all that very useful in a battle. I was in a lot of them and, in most, quick wasn't as useful as keeping your head down and shooting at a compass point, if you know what I mean." About half the men in the room laughed in memory. "But it just so happens that I have an...ability—recently discovered I might add—that could be exactly what you need."

James looked at Shlomo suspiciously. "What sort of...ability?"

"Tell me, Mr. James. Have you ever heard of a golem?

Part 2
The Golem

Shlomo, James Beaumont, and three of his men walked back to Cletus's stable. Obviously, the men were "escorting" Shlomo, but they tried to be diplomatic about it. As they approached, Cletus brushed Rivka by the barn door.

"Cletus," said James, "could we have a little privacy?" He said it like a request, but it was clearly an order.

Cletus looked suspicious. "You not going to hurt Mr. Slow-Mo? He looks funny and speaks funny..."

"Mr. Cletus, I'm standing right here," protested Shlomo.

"...but he's good people," Cletus finished as if Shlomo had not spoken.

"That is kind of you to say, Mr. Cletus," Shlomo said. "But I'll be fine. Mr. James and me have a business arrangement to discuss."

"Well, I guess I'll be in the yard if you all need me. Come on, Rivka." Cletus led the mule to the far end of the yard—Shlomo knew his mule well enough to jump nimbly out of the way as she stomped at his foot as she went past.

"Show me what you can do, Jew boy."

Shlomo's hand flew to his gun but just froze there waiting.

James grumbled but finally added, "Mr. Jew boy."

Shlomo considered that enough, shrugged, and went to his wagon. "Gentlemen, if you could help me clear off the bags and get my coffin off the wagon, I'd appreciate it. Anywhere on the ground will do." The hired guns looked to James who nodded. They helped Shlomo clear off the wagon in short order. Shlomo went to open the coffin when James held up his hand.

"What's in there, Mr. Jew boy?"

"Dirt," answered Shlomo.

"Dirt?"

"Dirt," confirmed Shlomo.

"Just dirt?" James asked again sounding very confused.

Shlomo opened the coffin to reveal a coffin filled with light, dry, brown soil. "Not just dirt, Mr. James. It's the dirt from my brother's grave."

"You've been carting the dirt from your brother's grave from back East to all the way over the west?" James furrowed his brow, seemingly unable to grasp what Shlomo had said.

"Well, to be honest, not over the entire west. I don't know if you know this mister, but the US of A is a very big country. I don't know if it's as big as Russia, but it's pretty big."

James used his fingers to squeeze his eyes shut as he said his next words as if in near pain. "I don't care for your itinerary, Mr. Jew boy. Why the hell have you been carting this around?"

Shlomo looked at the men and smiled. Then he slapped his hands together and rubbed them briskly, then he raised them on either side of the coffin and began to speak. "*Baruch atah adonie*..." His hands started to glow.

Meanwhile, at the Knuckle Nugget Mine

Far off in the Knuckle Nugget gold mine, an Indian known only as Line Walker to the small group that he had protected, woke from his soundless and dreamless sleep with a scream.

When his followers asked him what was wrong he responded with, "There is still magic in this world." And then he promptly passed out again.

Back in the livery stable, Shlomo slumped to the ground in front of a mass of dirt shaped roughly like a man—in that it had something like legs, head, arms, torso—but really, it was just a lump of dirt formed to the barest, brutish shape of a man. The men informed him in colorful words that they'd had seen snowmen with far more definition.

"What the hell is that?" demanded James.

"That," a sweat-drenched and panting Shlomo explained, "is a golem."

"What can it do?" James tipped his hat back and looked up at the giant mound of human-shaped earth.

"Golem," Shlomo instructed, pointing at the three henchmen, "Don't hurt them, but take their guns."

"Screw you, Jew boy," the man closest to Shlomo said as he drew his gun and fired directly at Shlomo, who stood no more than four feet away. The golem moved his hand to block the bullet with incredible speed for a creature made of dirt. The gunman gulped loudly as the golem reached for him. That caused the other two to draw their guns and all three blasted the golem, who did not seem to care. With one swipe of his earthen arm, three guns were knocked from three hands. As the men screamed in pain and danced around blowing on their hands or putting them under their armpits, none made a move to stop the golem as he slowly bent over to gather up the guns and bring them to Shlomo. He dropped them at his master's feet.

"And he can do the same to the redskins?" asked a smiling James.

"Absolutely," assured Shlomo. "But, I should warn you there will be conditions."

"What sort of conditions?"

"First of all, he can't kill."

"Why the hell not?" James sounded like a man who just found out Christmas was cancelled.

"Well, I shouldn't say 'can't.' I'm sure he *could* kill, but I won't order him to do it. No way, mister. No how!"

"Again, I ask, why the hell not?"

"Because the legends of my ancestor Rabbi Loeb make it very clear that once a golem learns to kill, it will never stop."

"What the hell do you care if he won't kill you?" asked the earlier gunman, genuinely confused.

"Maybe he would kill me, mister. I sure as hell don't want to find out. No killing. That's final."

"Well, how is that going to help us?"

"Mr. James, you saw what he can do. He'll get those Indians out of the mine no problem. Knock 'em out for you, if that's what you want."

James rubbed his jaw in thought. "That'll do," he said. "You stack em up, and we'll just kill them after."

"I'm afraid not, Mr. James. The golem can't be involved in an action that will result in death. Isn't the Army rounding them up anyway? Let them have the Indians."

"The Army will just leave them to starve on a reservation. It'd be kinder just to kill them and be done with it." James seemed to fervently believe this. His men, still cradling their hands, managed to nod in agreement.

"I'm sure you're right, Mr. James. But nonetheless, if you want my golem you have to promise to bring them to the fort. Let the Army have them. What do you care? They will be out of the mine, after all."

James thought some more, smiled and said, "What the hell, Mr. Jones? The redskins can starve for all I care so long as we get them out of the mine. What other conditions you got?"

"I would like a thousand dollars in gold." Shlomo grinned knowingly. He had roped them in, now came the haggling, something he also excelled in. They settled on six hundred, a hundred more than he expected.

Twenty-four hours later, a hung-over Shlomo and James, along with the fifteen men in his gang, waited behind a low hill from the entrance to the Knuckle Nugget mine. Well, fourteen now. One man had poked his head above the slight rise and was rewarded with an arrow through his eye.

"Goddamn, you redskin sons of bitches!" James challenged.

Shlomo put a hand on James's shoulder. "Don't worry, Mr. James. That will be the last man to die today."

The dusty Jew went to the coffin and, clapping his hands together once more, began his blessing. When he was done, the golem rose as Shlomo fell to his knees. After a moment, he ordered his golem to stand on the rise and moved behind it. As he did so the golem was hit with many bullets and two more arrows, both of which stuck in his body.

"Listen if you would, you Indian people," Shlomo warned them. "If you fight my golem, he may not kill you, but he will beat the tar out of you and don't think that he wouldn't. He will. I'll be honest, he *won't* kill you, but you will still lose. You will still be thrown out of the mine, and you will be bloody and bruised when you go to that Army fort. I suspect the Army fort is not a nice place, but will it be nicer if you go there all broken and battered?"

In response, many more bullets bore into the golem with little effect, but one arrow flew between the armpit of the golem, a space barely bigger than the arrowhead itself and through the brim of Shlomo's old hat. "Oy Gevalt!" Shlomo shouted and scurried back over rise.

"So that's how Jew boys say 'holy shit,' huh?" James and his men hunkered down as not to repeat Shlomo's mistake.

Shlomo was about to give a detailed explanation of the subtle meanings of that most versatile of phrases, but decided then was not the time. Instead, he called to the golem. "Golem, go to the mine and knock out anyone who is fighting. Don't kill them!"

The golem went over the rise, and Shlomo waited a moment, sighed, drew his pistol, and followed. Luckily, no one took any shots at the scrawny Jew in the funny hat with the mountain of earth rumbling toward the mouth of the cave. The Indians had barricaded themselves behind three built-up areas of rock and dirt. Shlomo recognized that someone here had fought in the Civil War and not just on horseback. Shlomo dropped behind a pile of rocks barely big enough to hide behind, then poked his head above the rocks to watch the "battle" unfold.

The golem went to the first line of works ignoring every bullet and arrow. Shlomo only saw the upper body of the golem behind the barricade. Every couple of yards, he would hear a grunt, or a crack or a brief scream as the golem swept through the Indians' defenses.

After five were knocked out, the last two abandoned the line and ran for the second defensive line. One of them was a beautiful Indian woman who caused Shlomo's mouth go to dry. He was about to command the golem not to hurt her when several bullets ricocheted off rocks around her as she fled. James's gang quickly popped up and were taking pot shots like some weird carnival game. In a flash, Shlomo drew and fired his own gun above their heads yelling, "I said, NO KILLING!"

The men ducked back down and did not reappear. By the time Shlomo returned to the Battle of the Knuckle Nugget Mine, the golem had cleared most of the second line. The distracting Indian woman ran for the cave entrance.

"Golem," Shlomo shouted, "drag the knocked-out Indians to a pile near the cave entrance."

The golem did as instructed. Shlomo took the opportunity of a lull in the action to run to the side of the cave entrance and wait with his drawn pistol. Sure enough, the woman poked her head out and threw a stick of dynamite at the golem as he was walking away from the pile of Indians to get more. It landed at his feet. Shlomo shot above her, forcing her back into the cave.

The dynamite blew the golem's lower body clean off. Groans wafted from James's gang on the rise of the hill, while faint cheers and war whoops came from the cave. But after a moment, total silence fell over the battlefield as the remains of the golem vibrated and wind whooshed from all directions. As the wind increased, all the blown-up bits were blown back toward the golem's upper half. Faster the wind swirled, like an unnatural dust devil, and faster the pieces gathered. As the last of the wind died down, it revealed the once-more-intact golem. Without a moment's pause, the golem picked up where it'd left off, dragging the last two unconscious Indians to the cave entrance, as directed. Task finished, the golem waited for its next command.

Shlomo shouted into the cave. "Listen to me, Indian persons. You can't win. Please don't make me send him in after you. You surrender and you leave. Good at my word, no one has died yet. Don't make me go back on my word."

"We don't trust the word of white people," said a strong, angry and yet very feminine voice.

"What a coincidence. Neither do I. But you will *have* to trust me." Shlomo shrugged. "I'm the one with a golem."

After some heated words, a scraggle of women, children and elderly left the cave, about fifty in all.

"We'll wait for your warriors to wake up and then you must be on your way to the Army fort," Shlomo confirmed.

"This is our land," the very pretty, but very angry, Apache warrior woman called out while helping one of the oldest men Shlomo had ever seen keep to his feet. "Your promises are the same as every white man: lies." Shlomo was again impressed both at her beauty and her fury. He was less impressed that all the fury was directed at him.

"You're right about the lies, but this ain't your land anymore." James arrived on scene, producing a burning stick of dynamite for which he made to throw at the pile of knocked-out Indians.

"NO!" Shlomo grabbed at James's arm causing him to drop the dynamite at their feet. Both looked down and then at each other before scrambling up the hill as fast as they could. James kicked Shlomo, forcing him to tumble back toward the nearly finished wick. As he scurried for his life, Shlomo watched as more sticks of dynamite passed over his head to fall among the helpless Indians. "Golem, protect the Indians!" The first stick of dynamite exploded still too close to Shlomo. As the bomb made him deaf and the debris assaulted him, the world spun around him in a sickening way.

Shlomo lay in the dirt, semiconscious, watching the events unfold but unable to do anything about them.

The golem ran at James's gang. The men blasted at the golem with everything they had to no avail. The men were tossed around like ragdolls. Shlomo saw bones protruding out from skin, and "heard" wordless screams. The second set of dynamite went off, reducing the hapless Indian braves to so much meat. Pieces of blood and gore hit the golem, and it froze for a second.

Shlomo knew this moment. The golem had failed in its task and would now seek vengeance.

When it moved again, it grabbed the heads of the hired guns between its massive hands and squeezed. Their skulls popped like shattering crockery.

James screamed for his men to retreat, but not before grabbing Shlomo by the shoulders and dragging him away. The Indians fled back into the cave. Almost sullenly, the golem stood at the cave entrance protecting the Indians from the outside world.

Shlomo's last thought before succumbing to the dark was that it was a pity. Once an hour had passed, it would crumble back into a pile of dirt.

"Who's going to protect me?"

Part 3
Shlomo's Hanging

Shlomo woke up in a jail cell, his ears still ringing. He slowly got up and brought his hands to his aching head. Out loud, he said, "Lord, if you want I should be dead for all the bad choices I have made in my life, could you not find a quicker way?"

Then a rope was slung over his neck and tightened. "On the other hand, Lord don't listen to a schnook like me. We can take our time." He followed the length of it, all twelve feet, to find James Beaumont waiting outside his cell, a huge grin on his ugly face.

"Now don't go and be taking that Louisiana necktie off just yet, Jew boy," James Beaumont said, satisfaction in his voice. "It's there so you realize the importance of saying yes to my next request."

"You want, I should make another golem."

"Considering that your last one killed four of my men and, with the one the Indians killed, that makes five, yes. Yes, I do. That little fiasco of a battle cost me a third of my men, and the Indians are still in the mine."

Shlomo paled. "The golem killed. Oy, that is not good."

"You don't say. Popped their heads like grapes. So, you're gonna make another one and have him finish the job. Now that we know he can kill with no problem at all."

"Mr. James, a golem can always kill. That's why I can't make another one. That soil is tainted now. Who knows what will happen?"

"Who cares? Send it in to kill the redskins, and we'll ride like hell for an hour till it goes away, if you find that you can't control it."

"And if this one lasts more than an hour? What if it sticks around and decides to keep killing? My blessed ancestor supposedly faced such a golem, but he knew how to send it back. I don't."

"Fine, use different dirt."

"Mr. James, if I could use different dirt do you think I would be hauling that dirt around the country?"

"Don't care, Jew boy. If you bring it back, you live. If you don't, we hang you in front of the town for killing those five men. Lots of people in town are not happy with you siding with the Indians over white folk. We're just gonna kill the redskins anyway, even if we have to collapse the mine and dig the company a new entrance. They don't have any warriors left to speak of, so your golem will make short work of them."

"Mr. James, I'm not bringing him back. And it's not just to

protect the Indians. It's to protect *everyone* in a hundred miles of this place."

"Listen up, you Jew son of a bitch. The only one who will die if you don't—well besides the damn redskins—is you." James spat on Shlomo's face. "Think on that, you Christ-killing bastard!"

Shlomo left the spit where it was, not wiping it off. "Mr. James, I am far from the best person G-d almighty put on this Earth, but if I do what you ask..." Shlomo smiled sadly. "Well, that would make me just like you. I think it better to die."

James Beaumont seemed just as happy with that choice by the way he waved his pistol for Shlomo to move.

Shlomo shrugged and left the cell. He walked slowly, but steadily, giving a sad shake of his head every once in a while and generally attempting to look brave, but truly acting forlorn.

Truth was, Shlomo had a plan. It was stupid plan, but better than being hanged.

As he got to the door, he burst out of the knot of men escorting him and, in a flash of great speed, made it a good ten feet down the street before anyone could react. James, the first to his senses, put his foot down on the rope.

Shlomo's neck jerked at a painful angle as he flew in the air and crashed down on his back. The people in the street pointed and laughed at the crumpled weird little man.

"You dead yet?" James looked down at Shlomo, smirking.

"Not yet," Shlomo squeaked out in a barely heard rasp.

"Reckon, we can fix that." He turned to the gathering crowd. "It's time to hang this Jew son of a bitch!"

With cries of delight, the crowd dragged Shlomo to the center of town with festive glee.

"I'm down five men!" James proselytized. "Men who didn't have to die, so I am going to enjoy watching this freak of nature dance at the end of a rope."

Shlomo looked at the gallows. It wasn't one of those drop-floor fancy versions, but only a high beam between two posts. He shuddered.

Shlomo's fear fired James up. "You're right to be afraid," snarled James. "No quick drop for you. Y'all's gonna twitch for a long time!" The remainder of James's gang carried Shlomo to the gallows. They threw the rope over the high beam.

Shlomo grasped at the rope as they hoisted him into the air, until his legs dangled free before tying the rope to the support beam. Shlomo kicked and swayed as the rope constricted, cutting off his air. If he had known this would be his fate, he would have just lain on the stick of dynamite earlier and been done with it.

Through the cheers of the crowd, Shlomo swore he heard the bray of an enraged mule.

Rivka burst through the crowd sounding as furious as ever a mule sounded, and galloped right up to Shlomo who barely managed to stand on her back. If he balanced on his tippy toes he could relax the noose some. The scene became even more farcical; when someone in the crowd tried to get close enough to knock Shlomo off the mule, Rivka would kick and bite. This made balancing on the back of the spinning, screaming, biting mule a dance of such complexity as to make a prima ballerina despair. But somehow Shlomo stayed on.

After a few minutes of this, a bored and irate James drew Shlomo's revolver to shoot the mule dead. He froze, however, as the sound of a Winchester's retort filled the air.

Cletus stood at the edge of the crowd, pointing in the general direction of James, who then slowly put the pistol back. Cletus might not have been the best shot in town, Shlomo thought in his oxygen deprived brain, but it was tough to miss with a Winchester at that range.

"What are you doing, Cletus?" James asked in a conversational tone.

"Can't let you hurt Rivka there," Cletus said in the same tone. "Your beef is with Mr. Slow-Mo. You leave Rivka alone."

James sighed. Cletus may not be the smartest man in town, but Shlomo hoped he was one of the most stubborn.

"Fine. We'll just wait for the Jew boy to slip and die, and you can get the crazy mule afterwards."

"Works for me," Cletus agreed. He apologized to the slowly strangling man. "Sorry about that, Mr. Slow-Mo." Shlomo wanted to say he had no hard feelings, but then his feet slipped. He strangled there, desperately trying to find the mule's back. Rivka didn't help by not standing still long enough for Shlomo's feet to gain purchase.

"Well, this won't take nearly as long as I thought," said a delighted James. Again, his happiness was interrupted when three fire arrows flew through the air, one after another, all hitting the roofs of three different buildings. The desert dry wood needed little encouragement to catch fire and within moments, the town was filled with smoke. People rushed to fight the flames and barely noticed a fourth arrow slicing through the rope above Shlomo's neck.

He fell hard onto the spine of his mule, landing backward. He hit his testicles bringing forth a yelp and causing him to slump forward. With his face on the rump of his mule, Rivka took off like all the hounds of hell were after her.

Two men lifted weapons to shoot at Shlomo, but more arrows came from the edge of town killing both men. James's gang sought cover, but by the time they were ready to fight back, Shlomo waved goodbye from his hauling ass.

About a mile out of town, Rivka stopped, and Shlomo slumped off the mule, falling bonelessly to the ground. When he finally got the noose off his neck, he took a long shuddering breath. Footsteps approached, and he got ready to fight, only to discover the fierce Indian woman. Up close, she had to be one of the most beautiful women he had ever seen, and he had traveled through France on the way to America.

"I should want to thank you—and everyone with you—who saved my life."

Emotionlessly, she informed him, "There is no one else here. I did this on my own because the rest of the warriors are dead, thanks to you."

He started to croak out, "About that, I should want to apolo—"

Snarling, the woman smashed him across the head with her unstrung bow. As darkness took him, again, Rivka snorted her approval.

Part 4
Rabbi Shlomo Jones

Once more at the Knuckle Nugget Mine, Shlomo woke to an even bigger headache than the dynamite one from earlier. Actually, it was probably the same headache just worse. He couldn't get the strength to open his eyes.

A cup was pressed to his lips, and an older-sounding man said in perfect Yiddish, "Drink slowly, my son, but drink. It will help."

In desperation, Shlomo took a tiny sip of what had to be the vilest liquid he had ever sampled, and he had fought for the Union. But before he could spit it out, he noticed that his head ached slightly less immediately. Having to choose between horrible taste and unending pain, Shlomo thought about it a moment, gave a shuddering sigh and drank more.

By some miracle, he did not throw up and, by the time he was done drinking, his headache was almost entirely gone. "That is it, son," said the man.

When Shlomo opened his eyes, he did not see a rabbi or a fellow Jew, but the ancient Indian he had seen escaping from, and then fleeing back into, the mine earlier.

"You speak Yiddish?" Shlomo said in surprise.

"Not a word," said the ancient Indian in perfect Yiddish. "But you are hearing me in Yiddish? Crazy name for a language."

"So when I speak, you don't hear Yiddish?"

"I hear what I call 'the language of the people.' Catchy, huh?"

Shlomo had a million questions about that, but settled for, "Why am I in this cave?" When he noticed the hostile stares of the women and children around him, he added, "Why haven't you killed me yet?" Shlomo held up his hands. "Not that I am complaining, mister. I can assure you, I am done complaining. No more complaining for me! Every time I complain, I seem to get into a worse situation and, though that might SOUND like complaining, I can assure you it isn't." Shlomo raised his arm heavenward to accent his "not" complaining when the tittering of children and adults alike made him pause. He looked to his benefactor. "What is so funny?"

"You are, Jew Boy Slow-Mo. And thank you. These people have not laughed in a very long time."

"They are welcome, but please my name Shlomo. Shlomo Jones."

"I am Line Walker. Shlomo Jones. We must leave."

"I agree. I don't know how long I was knocked out . . ."

"Thirty-five minutes," answered the woman who had saved, and then knocked out Shlomo. She approached the fire with a grace and purpose that Shlomo found alluring and terrifying. The girls of his shtetl didn't look anything like this.

"Ah! Welcome, Dahteste." Line Walker took her hand.

"You woke up finally." She looked at Shlomo like he was something vile she had stepped in.

"And good he did," said Line Walker. "Have the farting dick people returned?"

"Yes, Line Walker."

"Wait," said Shlomo, "the farting what people?"

"We are close, Dahteste," Line Walker said. "One more sunset and the passage will reopen to my land. I can bring all the people that are left with me."

"Excuse me," said Shlomo raising a finger. "The farting what people?"

"The farting dick people," hissed Dahteste. "That is what he calls whites because they all hold penis like objects that make a loud noise. He says that it explains all anyone needs to know about white people."

"I'm not exactly considered a white person," Shlomo said trying not to be charming, while still trying to be charming.

"You look white to me," she scoffed.

"Shlomo Jones is not white," confirmed Line Walker. "Well, at least not white the way the other whites are."

"She does not seem to like me," Shlomo said to Line Walker conspiratorially.

"You *did* kill her father and brother," the old man responded the same way.

Shlomo looking stricken asked Dahteste, "I am so—"

Dahteste slapped Shlomo. "You do not get to apologize! That Earth Spirit you summoned knocked them out and dragged them into the open for those bastards to kill. That is your fault!"

"That was not supposed to happen. They were supposed to let you all go to the fort."

"And you believed them! You're either a liar or a fool!"

"I am not a liar!" Shlomo paused. "But maybe I'm a fool. I was a drunk, greedy fool who took their whiskey and their money and didn't care."

"That is not entirely true, Shlomo Jones," corrected Line Walker. "You cared enough to ask them not to kill us, but you did not care enough to make sure they wouldn't. I think there are many farting dick people like you. Caring people, but not caring enough."

Shlomo fell to his knees. "I killed those men." He started to bang his head on the sandy cave floor. "I killed those men. I killed them for money and booze. I can't undo that!"

Line Walker lifted Shlomo's head by the chin. "You can't undo that, but you can help those whom you have hurt."

"How?"

"You *must* summon another Earth Spirit to defend us," demanded Line Walker.

"I can only create a gol...summon an Earth Spirit once a day. The earliest I can create one will be this afternoon, near sunset. How long is that?"

"Seven hours," said Dahteste. "But the farting dick people will attack in less than an hour."

"I cannot help you," pleaded Shlomo.

"There is nothing you can do?" sighed the old man.

"He can, he just won't," spat Dahteste.

Shlomo pleaded to them to understand. "It is said if you try to create more than one in its time, you will only summon death to you. I tried it once when I was drunk and before I could utter a word I felt my life draining away. To do so would kill me."

"We are dead anyway. You with us."

Shlomo made as if to argue, but shrugged instead. "There is some truth to that." Then shook his head. "Even if I could make one before dying, I would need the dirt I had used before, and I can't."

Line Walker nodded his head in agreement. "You must not use that earth. It is tainted."

"Exactly, it is. Hey, how did you know?"

"I smelled it after you and the others left."

Shlomo tried not to picture that. "Without that earth, I cannot make a golem and *with* that earth, the golem will likely kill you as sure as protect you."

"Come with me." Line Walker got up and moved to the back of the cave.

Shlomo followed. "Isn't this supposed to be a gold mine? It seems much more like a cave."

"This section has no gold and was abandoned. Luckily, it is the only section we need."

"Wait. You only wanted to stay in the nongold part of the mine and for this they wanted to kill you?"

"The yellow metal makes the farting dick people evil," said Line Walker.

"Mister, you have no idea." Shlomo spotted a mound of red

clay that to Shlomo had a slight glow. A similar glow he had only seen from another pile of earth in his entire life.

Shlomo smiled. "Well, that's that. It was nice knowing you, Mr. Line Walker. You're the first Indian I have ever really talked with."

"I'm not really an Indian. My people left this world centuries ago. Long before the farting dick people ever showed up."

"They died?"

"Don't be silly. We just walked the ley lines to the spirit world."

"Oh, is that all," said Shlomo. "I will summon an Earth Spirit with this. And all it will cost me is my life. Well it's not like I was doing much with it anyways." He rubbed his hands together.

"Wait." Line Walker held up a hand. "What will you command the Earth Spirit to do?"

Shlomo smirked. "You want to know what to do, you pile of dirt," Shlomo yelled at the clay. "You will protect the innocent. That's what you will do!"

And with that, Shlomo Jones clapped his together and rubbed them before he said the words he had said many times before, but this time, he felt his very life ebb away. He began to fall when Line Walker caught him. As he did, both Line Walker and Shlomo glowed with a white light that turned into a multicolored pulsing strobe before spreading to the piled clay in front them. Shlomo continued his prayer/spell. His weakness left him and his words filled the cave, shaking the tunnel until dust rose and rocks fell. The same light poured from his eyes, and the cave disappeared in a blinding flash.

Shlomo awoke just inside the cave. Dahteste spoke to a large, very large and perfectly formed, red-skinned, blond-haired man who stood in front of her completely naked.

"Who the hell are you?" Shlomo said, immediately concerned and protective of Dahteste, despite the number of times she had hit him. The six-foot seven-inch giant was circumcised and *very* proportional. It intimidated him some.

"I don't know, Rabbi," the giant said in perfect Yiddish. "Who am I?"

"What's his name?" Shlomo asked Dahteste.

"How should I know?" she spat out looking out the mouth of the mine. "You're the one who created him. Well, you and Line Walker."

Shlomo looked to the giant again, then to Dahteste, then back to the giant. Blinking, he asked, "Golem?"

"Yes, Rabbi," the giant said innocently. "What is my name?"

"Names later," Dahteste said, pointing out the cave to the eight men setting up a twelve-pounder piece of artillery. "Fight now."

"Golem, go and disable that gun. Make it so the men can't fight, but don't kill them. Make it so they can walk when you're done. Outside of that, though..."

"He's going into battle, not church, Rabbi," Dahteste reminded him.

"I'm not a rabbi," Shlomo said vehemently. Before they could debate more, the golem had run from the cave and approached the overlook.

"Please G-d, I know I have no right to ask a thing of you after being the shnook I have been, but please let the hour be up *after* the golem is done saving these Indians."

Dahteste looked at Shlomo and considered his words. "You would use your prayer to save us?"

"I have to make up for what I did the best I can. Luckily, the golem will only need a minute or two, and we should be safe till your people can leave."

"Rabbi, you and Line Walker cast your spell over three hours ago."

And with a wild whoop, she flung herself out of the cave and toward the gunmen on the rise.

The red-skinned blond raced toward James's gang. Seven of the men tried to get the gun pointed at the golem, but as it got closer one man ran away. Shlomo recognized James Beaumont. So apparently did Dahteste, who changed her course to intercept the gang's leader. With a curse, and then an apology for cursing, Shlomo ran after Dahteste.

Out of the corner of his eye, Shlomo tracked the golem as it approached the field piece. He methodically grabbed each man by his right hand and squeezed. The men abandoned the field gun en masse. The gang routed, Shlomo concentrated on catching up to Dahteste and James Beaumont.

James and Dahteste disappeared over the rise and then came a gunshot. In seconds, he cleared the rise and found Dahteste holding her arm, blood pouring from her fingers. James aimed to take a second, killing shot.

"Hey," Shlomo shouted. "I'm glad your *verkachte* Confederacy died, and I'm glad I helped kill it!" That had the desired effect. James forgot Dahteste and snarled hungrily. Pointing with Shlomo's own gun, he said, "Die, Jew boy!"

Ignoring Dahteste was the last mistake Beaumont ever made, though, as with one fluid motion, she pulled a dagger from her boot and embedded it in the mercenary's neck.

Bewildered, James stared at the protruding knife, then at Dahteste's triumphant face. He dropped Shlomo's gun, and his body followed it to the ground.

Shlomo rushed back over the rise. He was not surprised to see the golem running toward him.

"Golem, stop!" The golem did so at once. "Go and check on the Indians in the cave. Make sure they are alright."

"But Rabbi, what about Dahteste and that still dangerous man?"

"First," sighed Shlomo, "I'm not a rabbi. Second, the man is no longer dangerous and thirdly, Dahteste is mostly fine. But keep the Indians safe. Check on them."

"Yes, Rabbi," the golem said and ran toward the cave.

Shlomo returned to Dahteste. "Are you all right?"

"It only grazed me," she assured him. "I have salves back at the cave."

"Good," said Shlomo. "Now go back to your people and, whatever you do, don't let the golem out till I have buried the body."

It was well past sundown before Shlomo had buried the unlamented remains of James Beaumont in an unmarked grave never to be found.

Part 5
The Half-Baked Kid

"You're not dead," Line Walker said in that still amazingly perfect Yiddish.

Line Walker stood next to a wall that contained a glowing circle of light. A woman walked through happily, a small girl waving to Shlomo from her mom's shoulder. He gave a small halfhearted wave back as the light enveloped them, and they vanished.

"It is a traveler's moon that I was waiting for," explained Line Walker. "Now that it is here, the door is open, and we can go.

It will be the last here for a long time, I think. I stuck around to thank you. You and your Earth Spirit saved us."

"I am so very glad, but how is it that I find myself alive?"

"As you summoned your Earth Spirit, I connected you with the energy that resides in all of this place. It is why I can go home from here. It sustained you, but such a gift comes at a price."

"A price I must pay before I could agree to it," argued Shlomo.

"It did save your life," countered Line Walker.

"Agreed," admitted Shlomo. "What is the price?"

"You have killed nine men through your actions who would not have died. Out in the world you will find nine innocents that you must save for your debt to be paid. You will save many more than nine before you are done, but you will know the nine when you see them. Help will be provided. The Great Spirit likes you, Shlomo Jones. But he teases you, as well."

"I am the Lord's chew toy," muttered Shlomo, deciding this night couldn't get any crazier. Line Walker waved while walking backward into the circle of light. In a flash of light, it disappeared.

Shlomo made his way out of the cave. The moon and stars shown so brightly that Shlomo had no trouble making out the perfectly chiseled, six-foot seven-inch red-skinned golem with blond hair.

Still completely naked.

"Hello, Rabbi Jones," the golem said. "It is an honor to meet you."

"I am *not* a rabbi," corrected Shlomo.

"But you *are* a rabbi," said the golem. "Who I am is a mystery to me."

"Who you are? More importantly, why are you still here? My golems only lasted an hour before."

The golem was the picture postcard of confused. "I have been alive for many hours."

"How?"

"Your magic combined with the native energy of the soil created this," Dahteste said as she came up to the duo, her arm now wrapped in a dressing. "You are yet another white man stealing what is ours to your advantage!"

"Dahteste? If you hate me, so much, why did you stay? It can't be to help me."

Dahteste looked away from him, but the disgust was evident.

"Line Walker said I was too filled with rage to walk between the worlds. I would get lost, and my soul would die in truly dark places, never to know light again."

"Ah-haa," Shlomo said, his finger in the air. "So you are not ready to travel. Many Jews were denied passage from Europe because they were ill. It is a thing. How can I help you get better?"

"Line Walker says I will have to truly forgive you for me to be able to return and join my people. I may even bring others with me, at that time. But in order for me to forgive you, I must see you truly suffer." She gave him an evil grin. "I can't wait to get started." Shlomo took a half step back. "Don't be foolish. Line Walker informed me *I* can't hurt you myself. I must help you find your nine innocents. But I can watch while others make you suffer."

She seemed wistful, Shlomo thought.

"What's my name, Rabbi," asked the golem interrupting.

"You look half-baked to me," said Dahteste. "Let's call you that."

"I like that," said the golem. Turning to Shlomo, he asked, "I am half-baked?"

"Are you sure you want you should be known as half-baked, kid?" questioned Shlomo.

"The Half-Baked Kid," the golem tried out the name. "I like that, Rabbi. Thank you. I am The Half-Baked Kid,"

"Fine, but I am not going to call you that all the time. Your first name can be Chaim. Why not? You're alive, are you not? But what am I going to do with you?"

"Well, you may want to put clothes on him. Not that I mind him like this, but you might find it hard to explain." She gave Chaim an appreciative smile.

"Oy," said Shlomo. "I need a drink."

"What's a drink?" asked Chaim.

"I will be glad to show you all about drinks, later," Shlomo said. "First we need to go back to town and get my wagon, my mule and you," he said, *not* looking at the naked and proportional giant, "some clothes."

"The mule hates you," Dahteste said. "Why go through the trouble of getting it?"

"One, that mule is mine. Or maybe I am hers. Who knows? Second, you and she both hate me so you'll have that in common.

Let's go. With any luck we will get in and out of town before sunrise." Chaim leaned down and whispered in Shlomo's ear. He pointed at piles of earth near the mine entrance.

"Are you serious?"

The golem whispered again.

"No," Shlomo said. "We don't have time,"

"Please Rabbi," the golem pleaded. "He deserves a proper burial."

In obvious annoyance Shlomo went over the rise, retrieved the shovel he had used to bury Beaumont and practically threw it at the Half-Baked Kid. "There," was all the not-so-pious Jew said as the golem happily got to work digging a grave-sized hole with impressive speed. It was only when Chaim started filling the hole with the dirt piled near the cave entrance that Dahteste spoke up, the confusion obvious in her voice.

"He dug a hole," she began.

"Yes," Shlomo answered, the strain of not screaming obvious in his tone. "He certainly did dig a hole, that is true."

"And he is filling the hole dug out of the dirt, with other dirt?" Her confusion was even more obvious.

"Yes, yes he is," Shlomo said pointing at the golem filling the grave with dirt.

"And this is something Chaim the Half-Baked Kid wants to do because it is a part of your customs?"

"Apparently yes, yes it is. We Jews love digging holes out of the dirt to put in different dirt," Shlomo said, not explaining that the dirt was from the previous golem.

Dahteste pondered what she was seeing for a moment before concluding, "You Jews have some very strange customs, Shlomo Jones."

Shlomo turned on the warrior with such a look of frustration and fury on his face that she took an involuntary step back. "Lady," he practically shouted pointing one finger straight up to the starry heavens, "YOU HAVE NO IDEA!"

The End?

Rara Lupus

Julie Frost

"Ladieees and gentlemeeen! Step right up and see a lady werewolf transform right before your horrified eyes!"

My blower's job was to get the marks' attention, and Prentiss was in fine voice standing outside the "Star Attraction" tent. His bright red coat and fancy cane with the gilded skull handle stood in stark contrast to the dusty surroundings, and his waxed mustache and dark eyebrows bristled as he extolled my dubious virtues. He had kind eyes, though most others never got to see that side of him.

I huffed out a sigh and spoke to the doomed sheep tethered beside me inside the wheeled cage. "Do you think he ever gets tired of this? Because I surely do." Of course, the sheep wouldn't have time to get tired of it. Usually we used a chicken, but there was a good crowd tonight, and they'd paid the extra two bits to see me, so they got the added thrill of the sheep.

"Not for the faint of heart or delicate of constitution!" he continued as people from the midsized Eastern Utah mining town and its environs trooped in to fill the seats and stare in aghast fascination, like I was some kind of exotic animal. I supposed I was. I sat demurely in a wooden chair, clad in a tear-away brown gingham pioneer dress with three-quarter length sleeves. My feet were bare beneath the floor-length skirt, and I wore no undergarments, but the audience didn't need to know that.

People in places like this didn't get much entertainment, but the booming mines were a source of vast wealth, giving them money to burn when amusements such as us rolled in. Most of them wore simple homespun or cowboy clothing, with a few gamblers, whores, and dandies sprinkled here and there. A dark-eyed *vaquero* with long black hair on the front row caught my eye—he gazed intently at me, but with none of the revolted curiosity of the others.

He smelled strange. Almost wolfish, but not quite. Other werewolves had a wild and bloody odor about them, untamed fur and fang and claw under a veneer of skin, ready to burst forth at any moment, and especially savage under a full moon. I had that lust myself, always lurking inside, which was why I lived in a cage even when it wasn't showtime. My normal quarters consisted of a trailer much like everyone else's—only barred and reinforced.

This man was different. Restrained. Controlled. Before I could pick it apart, the last seat was occupied, and Prentiss came in and resumed his spiel. "I have here a bottle of liquid wolfsbane." He pointed dramatically at a large and elaborate perfume atomizer, sitting on a table outside the cage. "When I spray our Channie with it, she will triple in mass to a pony-sized wolf."

Several people oohed and ahhed, but there were always scoffers. Someone snorted loudly. Prentiss scooped up the atomizer and held it aloft. "I realize this is hard to accept, but I promise... you *will* believe!"

He squeezed the bulb, and the effect was instantaneous. I doubled over, agony wracking my body, and a tortured groan forced its way from my throat. Bones cracked, muscles and tendons stretched, the dress gave way at the seams. My mind—

My mind shifted, as well. The people in the stands rose to their feet, some shrieking, others holding their kids up to get a better view. My inner wolf saw them all as prey and wanted to slaughter every last one.

All but the *vaquero*. He was one of us. Pack or rival or, dare I suggest... mate? But definitely not prey. He was the only one still seated, his hands clenching and unclenching on his knees, brow furrowed, teeth gritted.

"You. Will. Believe!" The sheep picked that inopportune moment to bleat. I whipped around to face it, catching my reflection—normally-blue eyes gone to amber, usually-pert nose lengthened, ears furring and shifting to the top of my head—in its terrified eyes.

And knew nothing more.

☆   ☆   ☆

I awakened covered in blood amid sheep parts; wool stuck between my human teeth. Just like always. The cage included a blanket, and I reached for it first thing to cover my nakedness from the prying eyes of Eberhart McQuincy, the circus owner, who stared unashamedly. Just like always.

"We're going to have to get us a bigger tent," he said. He'd pulled one of the spectator chairs beside the cage, but not too close. Balding, bushy browed, and broad across his belly, he gave me a toothy grin through his walrus mustache. "You've become quite the celebrity, Miss Channie." One of the troop's capuchin monkey-clowns—used as comic relief in the center ring—sat on his shoulder, makeup smeared and pantaloons grubby. She chittered a "Hello" at me, and I flipped her a tired wave.

I was exhausted, sore, and heartsick, in no mood for Eb's fatuous case of smug. "Just kill me and be done, Eb. You know you'll have to anyhow, sooner or later." I asked him to kill me every time.

And he refused every time. "Well, let's just make it later, all right, honey?"

"You're a son of a bitch, Eb."

"That may be, but I'm a son of a bitch who keeps the law off you *and* your wealthy family's reputation from being sullied back East. Don't you ever forget that." He continued, "Prentiss will be around directly to take you to your trailer. Will you require a meal, or are you still full from your... repast of mutton?"

I grimaced and used a fingernail to pry a bit of fleece from between my teeth. "Really not hungry, but a bottle of whiskey would go down nicely." Maybe it would help me forget what I was for an hour or so.

He hrmphed. "I'll see what I can do." No, he wouldn't. Jolee took off with a screech. She, at least, was on it. Eb hauled himself to his feet. "Sleep well, Channie."

I never slept well, but he knew that.

Prentiss hitched a horse to my cage and wheeled me to my trailer. The horse didn't much like it, snorting and dancing with its front feet, and Prentiss shook its halter rope and spoke soothingly, which didn't really do much to calm it. Horses did not like me. For good reason, I supposed, still prying wool from between my teeth.

Prentiss slid the doors aside. I walked wearily into the place I called "home" on good days and "prison" on bad ones. He promised to hose the cage out. "Are you sure you don't need anything else?" he asked, concern pulling his mouth down at the corners. He didn't particularly like what he had to do to me, but I didn't hold it against him. We all had our roles, and he was kinder than most. By nature, a circus had freaks—and I was by far the freakiest.

"That's all right, Prentiss," I said. "I'll get by tonight."

"Okay. I'll bring you breakfast in the morning, then." He tipped his bowler hat and took his leave, leading the horse with the bloody cage beside him.

I cleaned myself and put a nightdress on. Jolee came swinging up to my window a few minutes later with a nearly full bottle of fairly decent whiskey. She chittered, and I shook my head. "Jolee, you know as well as everyone that turning me loose isn't an option. Remember what happened last time?" Last time, we'd buried three roustabouts in the desert. I didn't leave the cage at all, anymore, and no one teased me through the bars. My entire life had turned into a trap I couldn't escape. The monkey-clowns didn't understand, because they effortlessly broke out of every cage they were put in.

She knew better than to come all the way into the trailer, so I splashed a dram into a little glass for her, and she drank it down and whooped her thanks.

Then she suddenly screeched and took off, which wasn't like her at all. A second after that, the wind brought me a familiar scent, and the wolfish *vaquero* from the front row stepped out of the shadows. I stiffened. It was one thing for him to come watch me at work. It was quite another for him to stalk me to my home. But proprieties didn't mean as much to werewolves as they did to most other folks.

"That was quite a thing you did, Miss Channie," he said with a slight Spanish accent. He wore Levi's and a red bib-front shirt with mother-of-pearl snap fasteners, and a .45 Colt with a walnut stock holstered on his leg. A black flat-topped wide-brimmed hat and brown fancy-stitched cowboy boots with small-roweled spurs rounded out his ensemble.

I bristled at the familiarity. "Come back tomorrow, and you can watch me do it again," I answered, a bit frostily, mind you. "You have the advantage of me, sir."

"Ramon Lanahan. I work at the Wolfe Ranch." I guffawed, and white teeth flashed in his tanned face. That smile was certainly easy on the eyes. "Yeah, yeah. But I'm the only wolf that works there, and it's the biggest outfit in the territory right now."

"Do they know about you? Doesn't your horse have conniptions because of what you are?"

"Well, they know my ma was Mexican, but that don't much matt—oh." He shook his head slightly. "No, they don't know about the wolf thing. I raise my string of horses from when they're foals, before they know they should be afraid." He took a breath. "Not to make too bold with you, *mamacita*, but you should leave this damned circus and run away with me."

I gaped at him. "I should do what now?"

"You live in a *cage*," he said furiously. "That isn't a right thing for anyone, let alone a lovely woman such as yourself. McQuincy is not your alpha. You don't have to be under his thumb."

"You don't know a thing about me," I shot back. "Last time I left this cage, two good men died." And a third not-so-good man, who probably deserved what he'd gotten, but the other two most certainly had not warranted being half-eaten by a wild animal. "I'm in here for people's safety, as well as my own. What do you think would happen if the law got wind of what I am and what I've done? They don't hang women very often, and I'm not sure it would kill me in any case, but it for sure would not be pleasant." I turned to go to my bedroom. "Good evening, sir."

"I control myself, and know who I am, during my shifts. Even on moon nights."

His words dropped on my head like a bombshell filled with silver shrapnel. I froze. "How?" I choked. The full moon was in two days. I dreaded it.

"The local Indians, the ones who carved the rock art hereabouts and then disappeared?" We'd all seen that art, and it was the subject of much discussion. A lot of the pictographs were obviously people and local wildlife, but others had humanlike bodies and horns or antlers, and I'd seen one or two with bizarre big-headed creatures with spindly bodies and huge eyes.

"Turns out they were carving their life stories." He stepped closer to the window. "And those creatures have the power to make it so you're still yourself as a wolf." He held his hand out in entreaty. "They helped me, Miss Channie. Let them help you."

I raised my chin, skeptical. "And why should I trust you? You smell almighty strange, but that doesn't necessarily signify you're telling me the truth."

"Point taken." Ramon touched the brim of his hat. "I'll be right back." He stepped away into the shadows. A minute or so later, I heard a wet-sheet-tearing sound as his muscles and bones stretched and snapped into new configurations, along with a pained grunt, and his scent intensified on the breeze. Then he padded back into view—on all fours.

I stared, a bit openmouthed, as he reared up on his hind legs and rested his forefeet on my window ledge. Wolf-Ramon was black, shaggy, and splendid, the size of a large pony, with the same warm brown eyes he had as a human. His tail waved gently, and his tongue snaked out and gave my hand a careful lick. He was completely under control.

To not be a murderous, raging monster... My breath caught. I wanted that more than *anything*.

When I let my breath escape, it came with a sob. It was too good to be true. I lived in a circus, and I'd heard all about deals of that nature. They were generally made at a crossroads with con-tracts signed in blood. My soul was already stained by the things I'd done with the wolf in charge; I didn't need to further blacken it by walking into a situation like this with my eyes wide open.

Ramon drooped his ears and tilted his head. I reached out and petted his broad forehead, and his tail sped its tempo. *See?* he asked. I could understand him as well as I understood Jolee. I wondered if he could talk to his horses. *Perfectly safe now.*

"And you can change back when you want?"

In answer, he dropped down and trotted off to the shadows where he'd left his clothing. After a few minutes, he came back, dressed as before. "Except during the full moon, I can change at will. You have lovely hands and a kind touch, Miss Channie."

Dangerous hope kindled in my chest. Maybe it wouldn't be so bad. I couldn't help but ask, though. "What's the catch? What's it cost?"

He shrugged with one shoulder. "Far as I can tell, it doesn't cost anything. They said something about feeling responsible, some kind of experiment gone bad, and wanting to fix it." His teeth gleamed in the nearly full moonlight. "Then one of them bapped the other one upside the head and called him an idiot."

That didn't sound like normal demons, at any rate. "And what if it doesn't work?"

"Then I'll take you wherever you want to go. Even back here, if here is where you truly want to be."

I thought it over. What did I have to lose, really? "Let me get some actual clothing on." I donned trousers, a long-sleeved blouse, and a pair of knee-length boots, practical for riding in the desert. Back at the window, I let out a shrill whistle. Jolee and the rest of the monkey-clowns came swinging across the roofs of the trailers, hands to feet to tails and back. They stopped chattering when I put my finger to my lips. "Unlock my door, Jolee, please and thank you," I said.

She cocked her head to one side and let out an interrogative cheep, asking if I was sure. When I said I was, she and the others had the door open quicker than it takes to tell it. I stepped into the cool outdoors, free for the first time since I could remember, and shivered a little, rubbing my arms.

Ramon stepped up beside me with his nostrils flaring, and I turned to face him, skittish. I caught his scent again, horse and leather and honest sweat, with the wolf overlaying it all, but serene. It was more soothing than it had a right to be, and I didn't quite trust it, but I was committed now. My heart pounded.

"Where are we going?" I asked, a bit breathless.

"Out into the desert a ways. Freckles can take us." A black appaloosa gelding with a spotted white patch across his hips and a bald face whickered at us from the shadows where he was ground-tied. Ramon led me up to him and introduced us. "This is Miss Channie, Freckles. We're giving her a ride. She won't eat you."

I certainly hoped not. The horse snuffled my blouse and bumped my chest companionably. I'd never had a horse react like that to me before. It was nice. Ramon mounted, then reached down and helped me up behind him.

Freckles had a smooth rocking-horse gait that effortlessly ate miles. I hadn't been outside like this in ages, able to enjoy the stars and the wild scents. It filled me with heady longing. To be able to do this anytime I wanted...

Ramon reined Freckles in, and I realized I'd been daydreaming. I blinked, and my cheeks warmed. "Sorry," I said. "I probably should have tried to hold up a conversation." I slid off the horse's back and looked around.

"That's all right," Ramon said. "I know what it's like to get out of a prison when you've been locked up through no fault of your own."

I decided not to comment on that. It was his story to tell when he felt like it, really. We'd stopped beside a dry wash with a cliff face to our right, surrounded by twisted cedar trees, red and white rocks, Indian paintbrushes, and red-flowering barrel cacti. The desert was stark and beautiful, with the scents of bighorn sheep, deer, coyotes, and ravens wafting through the air. An eddy of breeze rustled through the bushes and bunch grass. A screech owl called.

"I could live here." I hadn't meant to speak aloud, but it was true.

"Well, I surely do like it," Ramon answered.

Before he could say any more, a trio of creatures stepped out of a hole in the cliffside I could've sworn hadn't been there before. I inhaled and took an involuntary step back, because they were like nothing I'd ever seen, except in the local rock art I'd noticed through my window riding past to our camp spot.

One was square and blocky, a good seven feet tall, with enormous hands and horns like a Hereford range bull. The second was shorter and slimmer; his body was broad at the shoulders and narrow at the hips, and he sported a set of antlers that would have put a trophy mule deer to shame. The third was shorter yet, with a bald, bulbous head, spindly body, and huge slanted black eyes. They smelled of juniper and prickly pear, like they'd tried to mask their underlying otherworldly musk with local odors, but had only been partly successful. I decided to call them "Bull," "Antlers," and "Big Eyes" unless they gave me other names to work with. I wondered if I'd be able to pronounce them if they did.

"What are they?" I whispered to Ramon.

I flinched when Big Eyes answered. Its—his—voice was rough, like he gargled rocks for fun, but perfectly understandable. "We were sent here to study your world." He shot what I could have sworn was a glare at Bull. "Not to interfere with it."

Bull's mouth pulled down at the corners. His voice was smoother; maybe he only gargled pebbles. "How many times do I need to apologize? I keep telling you, it seemed like a good idea at the time."

"Well, it wasn't," Big Eyes reprimanded. "We can't just say

'science' and call that acceptable." He waved a hand at me. "Clearly. Why you had to tie it to the lunar cycle and work in a silver allergy is a question for the ages. Not to mention the wolfsbane effect. Really?"

"I published a monograph about it." Bull sounded sulky, of all things. "The humans are better off with wolf blood and accelerated healing."

"Oh, yes, just ask them."

I hadn't expected sarcasm from them, but there it was. It amused me.

"If I could fire you, I would." He turned to me. "My apologies for my colleagues' idiocy. I presume Ramon brought you here to repair what they mishandled."

"That was the idea, yes," I answered cautiously. "He said you can't turn me completely human again, but you could give me the same control he has when he's wolfed."

"It is, unfortunately, the best we can do. But we owe it to you and are more than happy to help."

"It's better than what I have now, isn't it? What do I need to do?"

"Follow us, please." The hole in the cliffside reopened, and they led Ramon and me into the sort of laboratory that our circus magician had only dreamt about in his most demented imaginings. The walls and floor weren't roughhewn from the cliff, as I'd expected, but were smooth and white. Cabinets and tables of shiny metal surrounded us on three sides, with an adjustable chair in the center of the room. Bull waved me into it, and I sat down gingerly. Its comfort surprised me.

Antlers spoke for the first time. Her voice, distinctly feminine, sounded like birds twittering, but I understood just fine. "May we take some of your blood? It may help us arrive at a permanent cure rather than these half measures." She hastened to add, "It won't hurt."

I nodded, a little overwhelmed, and she held some kind of small glass vial against the inside of my elbow. A few seconds later, it was full of my blood. I hadn't felt a thing, and Antlers thanked me.

Meanwhile, Bull retrieved a sort of shiny metal crown-like affair and fitted to my head. Big Eyes affixed a wire harness to that, tightening toggles to it and then flipping switches on a machine with dials that hummed to life. Lights blinked on it, a few of them amber, but most lit red. Antlers made a "hmm" noise, turning knobs and pressing buttons. The crown tingled, and my hands tightened on the armrests of the chair. "Is it supposed to do that?" I asked.

"The problem with what they did was, it skewed your brainwaves in just the wrong way when you turn lupine," Big Eyes explained. "What we're doing here is tipping them back into a correct pattern. It will feel a little odd."

I looked to Ramon for reassurance, and he nodded. "Tingles and buzzing."

"Then it shouldn't hur-*urt*? Ow!" I doubled over as an electric shock of agony speared through my body from head to toes and back again. Then I was too busy trying to breathe to concentrate on anything else except the feeling of fur sprouting, and my bones and tendons stretching in a familiar and horrifying way.

I shifted.

"No..." The word was a tortured groan forcing its way through my lips. My face shoved outward into a snout. Ramon rushed over and laid a hand on my shoulder, and the creatures made "oh shit" noises and moved with urgency. I couldn't see what they were doing, however, because I squeezed my eyes shut as pain ripped through me again and again, while I lost my sense of who I was...

Again.

"Miss Channie. Stay with me," Ramon urged. "I'm right here."

I barely heard him through the roaring in my pointed ears. Panting, I gripped the armrests tight enough to warp them, claws erupting through my nailbeds. My clothing tore, unable to take the stress of my larger body suddenly stretching the seams.

Gradually, the pain eased to an ache and then faded altogether. I blinked a few times, straightening from my doubled-over position and swallowing hard through my still-tight throat. "What. What was that?" I asked.

I couldn't read the creatures' faces, but they stared at me in what I could only describe as a nonplussed fashion. "That wasn't supposed to happen," Bull said as Antlers took the crown off my head.

I blinked some more, and my hands came into focus. Or, rather, my paws came into focus.

I turned them back and forth in front of my face. They

weren't quite paws, either, stuck in some sort of in-between form. I glanced down at my body. It, too, was between wolf and human. A patting of my head with my strange-feeling paw-hands revealed that I had a half-snout and short, furred ears, and human hair its normal length down to the middle of my back. My breasts, nothing to write home about before, had mostly disappeared.

"What did you do to me?" I whispered. My voice was distorted by the changed shape of my face.

A slip of paper spooled out of a slot in a cabinet, and the Big Eyes tore it off and read it. His eyes closed. "You're the first female we've done this with."

"And?" Ramon asked. "I mean, she's beautiful, *hermanos*, but she can't walk around like this."

"Her hormones apparently affect how the procedure works. I'm afraid—" He stopped, and started again, voice lower. "I'm afraid she's permanently stuck like this."

My stomach clenched, and I gritted my fangs. "You mean," I said between them, "that you can't reverse it?"

He stared at the floor. "I'm sorry." The other two wouldn't look at me either.

Ramon's hand squeezed my shoulder, which I realized was bare. I was half again my normal size, and none of my clothing had survived the experience. I kicked my boots off.

"Miss Channie," Ramon said. "You're still yourself."

He was right, but so what? "Is that supposed to make me feel better?" I snapped, spearing him with a steely glare that made him remove his hand and step backward.

"No, *chamaquita*, I suppose not." He lifted a shoulder in a half shrug. "What do you want to do now?"

I wanted to throw myself on the floor and weep bitter tears. But that was a show of weakness I didn't have the luxury of indulging, especially when I realized that Ramon's wolf scent had intensified.

"I reckon I have to go back to the circus. Act might need to change."

I rose heavily to my feet, wobbly until my tail moved instinctively to steady my balance. My new body should have been clumsy, but it moved with deceptive grace. "Thank you for trying," I said to the creatures. "Even if it ended up like...this. I appreciate the effort."

This was a lie. They'd turned me even more monstrous. Any hope of a normal life lay in shattered wreckage on the ground behind me as I left. Grief for what I'd lost bowed my shoulders, and a single sob tore its way from my throat before I controlled myself. No crying. Not now. Maybe not ever again.

Ramon trailed behind me to where he'd ground-tied Freckles. "Back to the circus?" he asked, mounting up and gathering the reins. "Really?"

I gestured at myself. "Like you said. I can't very well walk around towns looking like this. At least at the circus, I'm employed and fed."

"They don't treat you very well."

He wasn't wrong, but what choice did I have?

We started back. I loped effortlessly beside Freckles. The horse, blessedly, was no more bothered by me half-wolfed than full-human. I was hungry, but not excessively so, not like I always felt during a normal shift. My fingers flexed as I ran. "Well. Maybe things will change now that I'm in control."

"I hope so. Otherwise my own wolf might have to have a word with your ringmaster."

I glanced up to see him frowning thunderously, and remembered what he'd said in the laboratory. "You really think I'm beautiful? Even like this?"

"*Mamacita*, if you knew what my wolf wanted to do with you, you'd tear off my cajones and feed them to me." He glanced at me. "It is not a typical beauty, but, yes, I find you very *magnifica*."

"With" me, he had said. Not "to" me. It was a tiny distinction that made an enormous difference. I wasn't pretty even as a human—I knew this about myself, having seen a mirror—and nobody ever spoke to me in such a manner, especially after finding out what I was. It was new and pleasant to have a man notice me that way, though I felt my face warm. Apparently I could still blush, even like this, though no one would know but me. "Thank you, Ramon."

"Someone should say it." And then he clamped his lips shut and said no more until we got back to the circus encampment.

Jolee awaited us at my trailer. She chattered and leaped to my shoulder, and I froze at what she told me. "Ramon, you should go—!" I shouted.

Eb and some of the roustabouts waited in the shadows.

Two of them roped Ramon off of Freckles from either side, yanking him backwards onto the ground. A third bound him in silver chains, leaving him heaving for breath, helpless.

Eb had a silver chain waiting for me as well, and he lassoed it around my shoulders and arms, paralyzing me before I could turn to run. He dragged me to my trailer and locked me to the bars, sneering. "Well, look at you. Did you really think you could leave us that easily, Channie? With this?" He turned and aimed a vicious kick at Ramon's ribs. "You dare to kidnap my star attraction?" More kicks. The roustabouts started getting their licks in, too.

"Stop it!" I struggled against the chain, but the silver held me just as fast as it always had. "Leave him alone, he didn't kidnap me, dammit, Eb! Damn *you*—"

Ramon was paralyzed by the silver too, unable to defend himself at all. His head snapped back with the force of one kick, and the reek of his blood tainted the air. The roustabouts laughed.

My wolf snarled in the background of my mind. She wanted to eat them. I feared, more than almost anything, that she would.

Almost anything. The way they were going at Ramon, I knew they intended to kill him. They'd forgotten me for the moment, and I wrestled with my conscience for all of five seconds before screaming for Jolee. One of Ramon's bones snapped with a nauseating wet-stick crunch.

The monkey-clowns came whooping onto the scene. They knew what to do with chains, and had me free in a matter of moments. I leapt to my feet and charged, hitting my tormentors like a ton of wrathful bricks, scattering the roustabouts. Eb, more adroit than his bulk would have suggested, twisted out of my path. My claws only caught his coat in passing, tearing rents through the expensive fabric.

He faced me, panting a little. "Behave yourself, Channie. You know what happens to bad dogs."

I stalked him in a circle. "Go to Hell and burn there, Eb. I'm not your dog anymore."

"Apparently you're going to be *his* bitch, though." Eb jerked his chin in Ramon's direction. "And that won't do." He'd been ready for us in more ways than one—he pulled an ugly little snub-nosed revolver from his waistband. I could smell that it was loaded with silver, which was bad enough when it just touched a werewolf's skin; breaking through and drawing blood would be a whole other level of unhealthy. Wounds like that were slow to heal, if they ever did. I tensed, hackles rising.

But he didn't point it at me. He aimed it at Ramon. The monkey-clowns hadn't quite finished pulling his chains away, and he was still down and helpless.

Without conscious thought, I launched myself at Eb. The pistol fired at the same moment I slammed into him, and we rolled over and over in the sage and sand. I locked one hand around his wrist, keeping the gun pointed away. Desperation lent me strength, and I landed on top, finally.

As a human, I'd never been in a fight, but the wolf knew what to do. My clawed hand wrapped around Eb's throat.

With my fangs bared an inch from his face, he froze.

"Ramon." My voice was far calmer than it had any right to be, though I spoke between my teeth. "Are you okay." I inflected it more like a statement than a question, and I didn't know what I'd do if the answer was "no."

Ramon took a couple of tries to get up, but the creatures had been right about one thing, at least—healing fast was a definite advantage. He limped over to my side and laid his hand on my shoulder. "I will be. His shot missed . . . thanks to you."

The scent of his blood infuriated me even more. Nose to nose with Eb, I snarled, fangs dripping, hands tightening. He whimpered and tried to shrink away. A bone in his wrist snapped, and he dropped the gun. "I should kill you," I growled.

"I won't tell if you do," Ramon said, wiping blood from his face. His own hand hovered over his .45, but he didn't draw it. "Or I'll do it if you don't wish to dirty your hands. Just say the word."

I'd be wholly justified. Eb was an abusive bastard who ran the circus with an iron fist that brooked no disagreement. More than one of us had been laid up for days at his hands. Prentiss was all right; he'd be a decent boss. We'd all be better off with him in charge.

But . . .

I'd fought my monster, hard, for years. If I gave in to it now that I had control, what would that make me?

I held Eb's life cradled in my paws. All I had to do was rip through that tender, tempting throat, and we'd be shut of him for good. It would be easy.

Too easy. I closed my eyes, breathing hard. I wasn't the monster. I wasn't. He was.

"You leave," I said, still right in his face. My hand tightened just slightly, claws pricking. "You leave and never come back. The circus is under new management. Understand me?"

"*Magnifica*," Ramon whispered, caressing my shoulder. No man had ever touched me that affectionately. I was still naked and half-wolf, and I felt neither shame nor fear.

Finally, I was at ease with what I was. Monstrous, perhaps. But not a monster.

Eb jerked his chin in the tiniest nod possible. "All right," he croaked.

"And take your toadies with you," I said, releasing him. "We don't need them anymore either."

Before I rose fully to my feet, my hand flashed out and left a set of four bleeding slashes across his face. "That," I said, "is to remember me by. I was merciful, this once. I will *not* be so merciful a second time."

He slunk off with his roustabouts. I instructed Jolee and the rest of the monkey-clowns to follow and make sure they left. They swung away after them.

My shoulders slumped. I was exhausted, and hungry—and triumphant. "How are you doing?" I asked Ramon.

"Better all the time," he said. He tilted his head, considering. "It appears you have some job openings in your circus, Miss Channie. Would you consider hiring me on as a roustabout? Maybe a trick rider?"

I gave him a smile and wondered how it looked on my new face. "I believe I would enjoy that, very much."

"No cages?" he asked.

"No cages," I answered. "Never again."

Stealing Thunder from the Gods

Kim May

Anli Wong-McKinnon hung upside down from the steel guardrail for the narrow catwalk that rimmed the "lungs" of her airship, the *Mystique*. A strong gust had ripped the emerald-and-white-striped silk sleeve encasing the massive balloons that kept *Mystique* aloft. Surprisingly, hanging upside down to reach the tear was the easy part. The hard part was holding onto the needle while wearing thick canvas work gloves. The job would be far easier if she took them off, but it was too cold at this elevation to work without them. Everyone thought the Great Plains were hot and dry, however, in the spring *and* at a thousand feet, it got quite chilly.

Her legs ached from clenching the rail so tightly and the metal dug into the back of her knees. She desperately wanted to stretch her legs out and give them a break, but doing that would result in a hundred foot drop to the *Mystique's* deck, and that's assuming that the wind didn't blow her overboard as she fell.

Anli took a deep breath, pushed a loose strand of her ebony hair that blew onto her face, and refocused on stitching the sleeve. One more inch to go. With her left hand she did her best to hold the two pieces together while she worked the needle with the right. Blood pounded in her ears as she worked.

A strong breeze tugged the fabric out of her hand.

"*Tzao gao!*" Anli cursed.

Thank Buddha it wasn't strong enough to do more to her than

ruffle her hair, but the slightest breeze could catch the sleeve. Even though *Mystique* was a dirigible, at times like this, she felt more like the schooner she started life as. She was simply waiting for a magical wind to turn her balloons back into sails.

Anli grabbed the fluttering ends of the sleeve with a white-knuckled grip and stitched faster. She finished just as her feet were starting to tingle from the lack of blood flow. Anli tied the leftover thread into a messy knot, cut off the excess with her teeth, and stuck the needle into her black corset. The stiff fabric would keep it secure until she could put it back in her sewing kit.

Anli pulled herself up and over the guardrail, and sat on the small platform with her legs dangling over the edge. She held onto the guardrail while the blood left her head. Within a minute, she felt at rights again. She stretched her aching legs, extending the stretch all the way down to her toes—or at least as much as her sturdy black leather boots would allow.

"Honey, you almost done?" her husband, Josiah, called from the deck. Perhaps it was blood rush, but he looked more handsome from this height. His patchy brown beard looked smooth and soft from up here, and she couldn't see the crook in his nose from when it had been broken in a bar fight.

"I'll be down soon," she shouted back. "You can fire it up."

Josiah gave her a thumbs up and went back below decks to fire up the burners. The *Mystique* drifted at the moment. Josiah didn't want the burners active while she worked, which was a sensible—if not entirely necessary—safety precaution. Their altitude had dropped a bit. She could tell by how much taller the high plateaus in the distance appeared. At the beginning of her repair they sailed above their summits. Now the stone monoliths loomed down on them. The *Mystique* wasn't in any danger of crashing, but they were still too low for comfort.

Anli stood and grabbed the nearest guide rope. She swung her legs over the guardrail, locked her ankles around the rope, and slid down to the deck, landing with a soft thud. Her work gloves and boots were a little worse for wear from the trip down, but her feet and hands were a little warmer from the friction so it was worth it.

The sound of clapping made her spin around. It was just one of their passengers. Richard Carter and his wife Delphinia had booked passage back East. Josiah liked them, but something about them didn't feel right to her. Perhaps it was the fact that their clothes, while nice, still looked like pale imitations of the fine tailored suits and dresses that people of their supposed social standing actually wore. For instance, today he wore an all-white suit, but while his pants and shirt were true white, his vest was cream colored, and his jacket and shoes were antique white. The Carters were also too quick to compliment and hadn't said a word about their captain having a Chinese wife. If there was one universal truth in America it was that the upper classes could always be depended upon for a disparaging or racist remark. Often both.

Anli also didn't like that the Carters had a very large crate in the cargo hold—a crate whose contents liked to make strange thumping and cooing noises as soon as the sun rose.

"Well done," Mr. Carter said. He smiled, but his joviality never reached his eyes.

"Thank you, Mr. Carter," Anli said only to be polite. "Would you like some assistance returning below deck? If you recall, my husband told you that it is not safe on deck without a safety tether."

"You don't have one."

"I live here," Anli said firmly. "I know how to be safe when a strong gust or an unexpected crosswind comes. You do not."

Mr. Carter chuckled. "Point taken. If you would be so kind as to guide me back?" He proffered his right arm like he was going to escort her to a dance floor. Anli grasped his bicep instead and led him back to the open hatch. He motioned for her to descend first, but one stern look was enough for him to understand that manners weren't going to put him back in her good graces.

Anli waited until he reached the landing before going below herself. A soft rumble of thunder behind her made her turn. The sky to the north was filled with dark gray clouds.

That's strange. The sky was clear in that direction just a few minutes ago. It was too early in the year for twisters, and those never came from the north. Whatever this storm was, judging by the way the shadows beneath the storm progressed, it was headed directly for them and fast.

Another peal of thunder rumbled across the plain. This one was slightly louder. A loud thump and squawk from the hold seemed to answer it.

Anli slid down the brass handrails, letting her weight propel her to the landing. The second her boots hit the floor, she jogged to the bridge at the bow of the ship. Josiah stood at the main console, monitoring their altitude and the boiler pressure gauges.

"The weather is changing," Anli said. "We may have to fly high for a while."

Josiah looked at her over his shoulder. "I heard the thunder. I'll take her up a hundred feet above cruising altitude. We can reassess when it's closer."

Anli nodded. "It seems to be making the cargo restless too."

Josiah nodded. "I heard *and* felt that." He turned back to the console.

Anli walked over to the navigation wheel at the apex of the bow. Two large windows directly in front of the wheel and two smaller windows on the port and starboard sides gave them a clear view of *Mystique*'s flight path. She turned the wheel to starboard and cranked up the speed on the stern propellers to full. Turning *Mystique* south might give them a few more minutes to climb above the storm. Another thunderclap sounded. The answering thud from below was hard enough that it shook the floorboards and rattled the windowpanes.

"If it gets worse I'm dumping it."

"You do that and we won't get paid," Josiah said.

Anli didn't have to turn around to know that he furrowed his brow and that he leaned on the console to help him bear the weight of responsibility on his shoulders. Anli sighed. "I know. But if I don't, we may not have a ship at all."

With the new and much faster railroad going in, finding enough jobs to keep *Mystique* flying became harder and harder. San Francisco and Kansas City had already cancelled their building plans for airship docks in favor of railroad stations. She and Josiah both knew that someday they would have to say farewell to the sky.

But that day would not be today if she had anything to say about it.

The floor shook again, however, not due to their aggravated cargo. The rapidly approaching thunder reverberated through the cabin. A bright flash on the port side drew Anli's attention. The storm grew frighteningly close—only ten miles out. Lighting flashed, but not the single bolt that she expected. Instead, a rapid succession of bolts rained down from the storm—some striking the ground, or scorching the earth. Some laced sideways through the clouds, while others reached upward through the clouds to the heavens. At the center of it all hovered a large black mass.

"What is that?" Anli wondered aloud.

Josiah walked up to the portside window to get a better look. "Pass me the spyglass."

They kept one mounted on the starboard wall, right next to her father's *jian* in its black lacquered scabbard. Anli reached over and passed it to him without taking her eyes off the terrifying storm. She was afraid that, if she took her eyes off it for a second, when she turned back it would be knocking on the window, asking for a cup of tea.

Josiah brought the spyglass up to his eye and focused on the lightning's nexus. The clouds swirled and parted. Anli saw something dark emerge from the clouds, but she couldn't see it well enough to know what it was. Josiah's jaw dropped as quickly as the spyglass fell from his hands. Anli dove and caught the spyglass seconds before it hit the floor. She was about to ask Josiah what it was when he ran back to the console and cranked all the levers to full.

"What are you doing? You're redlining everything! If the boilers don't explode from the pressure, the burners will ignite the balloons!"

Josiah didn't listen. He kept muttering, "Gotta get higher... maybe if we're high enough."

Anli set the spyglass on the floor and darted over to his console. She grabbed his face and forced him to look at her. "Why are you trying to blow us up?"

Josiah stared at her blankly for what felt like forever but was probably only a minute or two. Finally his eyes focused on her, and he stopped muttering. "We're probably dead anyway." His voice wavered. "May as well take that demon with us."

Anli let go of him and staggered back. The man that could watch his wife hang upside down from a handrail, one hundred feet in the air without so much as a shiver in his spine, was afraid. Whatever he saw emerge from the clouds had him so scared he was willing to sacrifice all of them just to take it out.

What the devil was that thing? More importantly, did she have the courage to find out?

Anli took a deep breath and forced herself to walk over to the port window. She picked up the spyglass on the way and pointed it at the creature. It took her a moment to bring it into focus since it continued approaching at breakneck speed. When she could finally see it clearly, Anli understood why Josiah dropped the spyglass.

It was a black bird with a long yellow beak and a wingspan almost as long as the *Mystique*. Its head alone eclipsed the bridge! It didn't really have eyes. Instead, it had two glowing masses of churning silvery light. From those two glowing pits, lightning forked out, striking anything and everything. Bolts danced along the creature's wings and along its beak. All the while the bird kept flapping those massive wings, gaining ground.

Josiah was right. There was no way they could outrun that beast. The best they could hope for was to do as much damage as they could before it took them out.

"Pardon me," Mr. Carter said from the doorway. "I seem to have forgotten...oh, no! It found us!"

Anli and Josiah whipped around to gape at him. Anli's cheeks flushed. She didn't realize that she'd forgotten to close the door behind her. How long had Mr. Carter been standing there? More importantly, how did he learn to walk that silently? She hadn't heard so much as a footfall!

Mr. Carter bolted down the hallway, and Anli followed, tossing the spyglass to Josiah as she passed. He didn't go far, only to his cabin where his wife passed the time.

"Katie, we have to go now!" he said.

"Katie?" Anli said loud enough for both of them to hear from the hallway. "I thought her name was Delphinia?" Anli skidded to a stop just outside the cabin door and glared at the pair of them. "The truth. Now!"

Before they could answer, *Mystique* rocked violently. There was a loud crash below them. "Delphinia" screamed. "Mr. Carter" mostly kept his composure, but his face was noticeably paler than it was a moment before.

Anli growled. "Stay here." She slammed the cabin door shut and ran back to the bridge. It was difficult since the ship still jolted, but she managed. Josiah struggled to turn *Mystique* due south.

"What's the damage?" he asked her.

Anli went to the console and started watching gauges. "Boiler one is holding steady, but the pressure in boiler two is falling." Boiler two was right next to the cargo hold so that didn't surprise her, especially if it was the "cargo" that caused the shift in the first place. "Altitude is holding steady. I'm shutting off the burners."

Josiah nodded. With *Mystique* rocking so violently it might tilt the burners enough to set the silk afire. It destroyed any chance they had of outrunning or even outclimbing that beast and the storm.

"How long till impact?" Anli asked.

Thunder roared all around them and a bolt of lightning zipped past them on the starboard side.

"Still want me to answer?"

Something hit the deck above them. At first she thought that one of the ropes had come loose and hit the deck, but then the sound started moving across the deck. She exchanged concerned looks with Josiah.

"I'll go."

Anli didn't wait for him to approve or pause long enough to give him a goodbye kiss. She simply turned and walked away. There were too many dangers mounting to dedicate any time to that.

"Anli," Josiah called out.

She looked back. Josiah had taken her father's *jian* off the wall and tossed it to her. She caught it one handed.

"Just in case," he said.

Anli tied the scabbard to her belt with a slip knot and left. This time she made sure to secure the door to the bridge behind her. Just in case.

Mystique's swaying had stopped enough that she could climb the stairs without any trouble. She crept up the stairs and paused when she could see the deck so she could find the source of the noise. A brown-skinned man stood on the deck. He had straight black hair that fell to his waist and wore only buffalo-skin pants and moccasins. There was a tattoo of lightning bolts on his chest and his eyes had the same silver glow as the monstrous bird.

This was impossible! How could a man just land on their deck? In the middle of a storm, no less! Was he some sort of Native immortal? One of their gods? More importantly, how could she get rid of him so they could fly out of this mess?

Anli squared her shoulders and climbed the final steps to the deck. The Native man turned to her. His mercurial gaze sent a shiver down her spine.

"How did you get here?" Anli shouted so he could hear her over the storm.

The Native man cocked his head, much like a bird. Anli didn't know if that meant he didn't understand the question or if he was giving a peculiar refusal to answer.

Anli drew her father's sword. The thin, flexible steel blade reflected the light from the man's eyes. Anli pointed the sword's tip at the Native man. "Go back to where you came from."

He opened his mouth and uttered the most unnatural, ear-splitting sound. It was a cross between a shriek and the cry of a hawk.

Well, at least he understands that language.

Anli closed the distance between them, ready to strike, when another crash from the hold made the violent swaying start all over again. Anli widened her stance so she could remain steady. The Native man didn't bother. Black wings sprouted from his back and he merely floated above the deck.

A shapeshifter? Anli cursed under her breath. That was just her luck. The giant storm bird was a shapeshifter this whole time.

The shapeshifter glared at her again and floated over to the hatch. A rope that must have come loose in the storm swung about wildly in the strong wind. It was one of the ropes that supported the balloons from underneath in order to keep them from falling onto the deck if they became deflated. It was still attached at the center so it swung almost the entire width of the ship.

The loose rope nearly hit the shapeshifter in the head before swinging her way. Anli grabbed the rope the second it came within reach and wrapped it around her left arm. She got a running start and leaped off the deck, timing her leap with the swaying of the ship to get the most momentum.

Anli swung on the rope straight for the shapeshifter. He must have heard her steps because he turned moments before she was within striking distance and easily dodged her slash.

Anli used her feet to stop her swing and pivoted around, still clutching the rope. She stood between him and the hatch, sword at the ready. The unarmed shapeshifter didn't look the least bit concerned that she was armed and that made her nervous. The rope bit into her forearm but she paid it no mind. Instead she focused all her attention on the shapeshifter, waiting for him to make his next move. The adrenaline coursing through her veins urged her to go on the attack, but she didn't want to be rash. The shapeshifter knew something that she didn't.

The shapeshifter shrieked at her again. His fingernails lengthened into six-inch curved talons in the span of a few seconds. But Anli didn't have time to gawk. He lashed out with his talons, bringing them downward in an attempt to slash her across her chest. Anli swung to the left on the rope so she could deflect his talons with a single movement. If she had both hands free she could have easily blocked him without moving, but she couldn't possibly do it single-handed. She didn't have the strength.

Anli circled her wrist to bring the blade back around. She slashed him across the ribs. She could tell from the wound that her aim was true, but the wound didn't bleed normally. A clear liquid that looked more like rain than blood seeped from the shifter's chest instead.

The shifter shrieked and pulled his left hand back to slash at her again. Anli kicked the shifter in the stomach with both feet, using the rope for stability. The shifter staggered, clutching his stomach. Anli used the momentum from the rebound to flip upside down. She wrapped her legs around the rope and pulled herself up as she swung away from the shifter. It gave her a much needed moment to unwind her left arm from the rope. Her blouse wouldn't have protected her forearm much longer, the fabric was already torn in two spots, and her muscles were starting to ache.

Unfortunately, this relief came at a cost. She lost sight of the shapeshifter.

Anli used her newly freed hand to pull herself upright so she could support her weight with her legs again. The movement caused her to spin. The apex of the swing coincided with the very moment *Mystique* swayed to port so for one heart-stopping moment she had a clear, unobstructed view of the ground far below. *Perhaps this wasn't the wisest choice?* She used her new leverage to counter some of the spin. It was enough to get a good look at the deck.

Anli scanned the deck, searching for shapeshifter. He wasn't there. Her slower rotation took the view of *Mystique*'s deck away before she could see any movement on the stairs.

Something moved in her periphery. Anli slid down the rope into a sitting position, tucking her legs beneath her so she wouldn't slide any further. She raised her sword into a defensive position and not a moment too soon. The shapeshifter had taken to the air and flew straight for her. Perhaps it was the angle, but his talons looked longer. They struck the *jian* and curled around the blade. It stopped her spin, which was great. However, it also killed any momentum so she was just dead weight hanging in the air. It would be incredibly difficult to attack or defend against her fully mobile opponent.

The shapeshifter pulled the blade toward him. Before he could disarm her, Anli thrust the blade forward. The point pierced the air to his right but the blade's edge was close enough to slice his side, two inches above the first cut. Anli pulled the blade back and applied a little pressure to deepen the cut.

The shapeshifter cried out and, as before, there was an answering ruckus from the hold. This time though, the shapeshifter looked down, as if he could see through the decks to the hold below, and answered back. Instantly the ruckus from the hold stopped.

Anli's jaw dropped. *It couldn't be...*

She decided to take a chance. She pointed to the deck. "You're here for that, aren't you?"

The shapeshifter looked at her. For a moment, she thought he was going to attack again. Instead he simply nodded.

Anli sheathed the *jian* and slid down to the deck. She walked to the stairs, pausing at the top step. She looked up at the shapeshifter who hovered in the air. "Are you coming or not?" The shapeshifter cocked his head in that birdlike way again.

"*Ching-wah tsao duh liou mahng,*" Anli cursed. *He understood what I was saying this entire time!* She was angrier with herself than with the shapeshifter. She hadn't considered that both of her problems were connected.

Anli put her hands on her hips. "I want it off my ship as bad as you do."

The shapeshifter gracefully floated down to the deck. When his feet touched wood, his wings melted into his back. Anli shivered. The memory of that sight would keep her up tonight. She descended the stairs. The shapeshifter's soft plodding behind her was her only clue that he followed. She couldn't feel his presence or his body heat. It sent a chill down her spine.

When she reached the first deck landing she saw the Carters sneaking down the next flight to the cargo deck. "Where are you going?"

They looked up at her, and then at the shapeshifter. Mrs. Carter screamed. Mr. Carter kept most of his composure, but he did urge his wife down the stairs with a firm push. Anli and the shapeshifter pursued them. Anli braced her arms on the handrails on the last flight of stairs and slid down. Mrs. Carter opened the cargo bay door just wide enough for the two of them to slip in.

As Mr. Carter started to slam the door shut behind him, Anli freed the scabbard from her belt and thrust it into the gap. The door hit the scabbard with a sickening crunch. The wood split and flecks of lacquer flitted to the floor. Anli used the fractured scabbard to leverage the door open enough to shoulder her way in. The Carters backed away. Anli left the door open behind her for the shapeshifter.

"I think it is long past time for you to tell me the truth," Anli said.

"Get him away from us first," Mr. Carter demanded.

Anli shook her head. "Talk." She drew the sword to make certain they understood.

Mr. Carter swallowed hard. "We work for Mr. Barnum," he said. "He hired us to acquire oddities and creatures for his museum."

"Museums usually don't have live displays," Anli said sternly.

"This one does," Mrs. Carter said softly.

Anli gestured with the sword to their mysterious crate, which was the size of a mule. It lay on its side and the boards were cracked and split. Black feathers poked out of the gaps. All around it was a mess of smashed fruit, vegetables, and spilled bags of mail. Pretty much anything that was within striking distance of it was wrecked, including the floor and hull, which bore visible cracks.

"What is it, and why is it trying to destroy my ship?"

Mr. Carter's head drooped. After a prolonged silence it was finally Mrs. Carter who spoke. "A thunderbird. It was so calm and docile when we found it. We didn't think for a second that it was dangerous."

The shapeshifter approached the crate. He knelt down, leaned in close, and chirped to it in a tender way. The thunderbird inside bounced around with enough vigor that it widened the cracks. It chirped back to the shapeshifter, which made him smile—an expression that looked odd on such a fierce being.

Anli felt like an idiot for the second time that day when the realization hit her.

That's his child inside.

Anli walked over to the broken crate and used the scabbard as a lever again, this time to widen the gaps enough for the little one to climb out. The little one squawked when she shoved the scabbard in, but after she pried off the first segment the shapeshifter got the idea and helped pull the rest off.

The little one waddled out of the broken crate and instantly nuzzled up to its father. The shapeshifter looked as though the weight of a stone monolith had lifted from his shoulders. The fierce warrior that she met on deck was gone. That fearsome presence was replaced with the joyful presence of a relieved parent.

Anli unlocked the latch on the cargo bay door—which thankfully hadn't been damaged by the little one—and opened it. The storm had calmed, but the skies were still gray and ominous.

"No!" the thieving Carters cried out in unison.

"We have to deliver it! We'll get the sack if we don't!" Mrs. Carter begged.

Anli rolled her eyes at them. The shapeshifter guided his young to the open door and the sky beyond. He gave the little one a gentle nudge. The little one spread its wings and leaped out. It soared on a gentle current and flew in wide circles near the door.

Mr. Carter stomped his foot. "We won't pay you a cent if you let that creature walk away with our property!"

"If I were you," Anli said, "I would be worried about much more important things."

"Such as?" Mr. Carter asked.

Anli looked to the shapeshifter. While her attention was elsewhere he had once more donned the threatening mantle.

"Please forgive me for earlier," Anli said to the shapeshifter. "I should have asked questions first. Would you like a bandage for that?" He shook his head. He then looked to the Carters and raised a questioning eyebrow to her. Anli nodded and walked to the far side of the cargo hold so she would be out of the way.

Mr. Carter looked very confused and as scared as a jackrabbit. "Mrs. McKinnon! What should we be more worried about?"

"Prairie justice."

The shapeshifter changed, losing all pretenses at being human. In two blinks of an eye, he was a black-skinned monstrosity with glowing eyes, sharp talons for feet, and black wings instead of arms. He reached out with those talons and wrapped them around the Carters. Both of them screamed. The shapeshifter flapped his wings and flew out the bay door. By the time he cleared the ship, he had finished his transformation back into the great black bird she and Josiah saw emerge from the storm not so long ago.

Anli shut the bay door and locked it tight. It did little to muffle the sounds of screams and thunder from outside. She left the hold and rejoined Josiah on the bridge. He pulled her into his arms and held her tight.

"What in damnation happened?"

Anli wrapped her arms around him. "I'll tell you over dinner. The Carters won't be joining us. They decided to depart with the cargo."

Josiah pulled back. "Did you hit your head up there? You're not making any sense."

"You'll understand later. For now, let's just say that humans shouldn't steal thunder from the gods."

Kachina

James A. Moore

"What do you see, Mr. Slate?" Despite the atrocities laid out before him, he said the words with unsettling calm. That was the way with Jonathan Crowley. The very worst things a man could witness seemed commonplace in his eyes.

Lucas Slate was not mundane himself; he was not what a soul expected to see when walking in civilized areas, or as they were right then, in areas of pure savagery. Even before his changes, he had been an albino, as pale as snow, with eyes almost the same color. These days, he was worse. His body was longer, taller and leaner. He looked like the corpse of a man nearly seven feet in height. He sported a decent set of clothes, solely because Crowley had been kind enough to purchase the suit he wore for him and to have it tailor-made.

He reflected on all of that as he considered how to answer his benefactor.

The bodies had been torn apart, or hacked into shreds. The sheer violence of the acts had been made worse by the brutal force employed. Not a single body was intact.

"Must be more than fifty dead, Mr. Crowley." His voice resonated barely above a sepulchral whisper, but carried a gentrified southern drawl. "Looks like they are all Indians, with none spared." His voice grew deeper as he suppressed his anger. "There are women and children and all of them slaughtered."

Crowley, astride his horse, nodded. "What else?"

"What else is there?"

159

Crowley stared at him and sighed. "How were they killed? How many of them died here? What caused their deaths? Was sorcery involved?"

"There were weapons. In most cases, at least. I'd say a sword of some sort and a club. Some of the children were ripped limb from limb and the women..." He stopped there. He knew what had been done to the women and had no desire to say it. Crowley nodded his head.

"Well then." Crowley cleared his throat. "One question remains, Mr. Slate. Was there magic?"

Slate looked across the field of dead people and let his vision unfocus. When he used what his father called *Soft Eyes*, to see everything at once and focus on nothing, the power that rested inside him these days showed him more than he'd ever believed possible. In this case, it showed him red threads of power that touched every single corpse, like cobwebs spiraling between bodies.

"Oh, yes, Mr. Crowley. I'm afraid so."

Crowley nodded his head. Not but four hours ago, while in pursuit of a man named Jacobi, they'd encountered a withered old man on the trail. He'd been badly beaten and savaged. He was dying then and gone before they left the area, but he had spoken to Crowley, had asked him for help in stopping the creature that had hurt him and his people alike.

Jonathan Crowley virtually always said yes when someone asked for his help. He claimed not to like it, but also stated that the rules of his existence meant that he had to answer calls for help against unnatural things.

What they were pursuing was unnatural, and so he was obliged to help.

The fact that the old man's ghost now wandered along with them was merely an inconvenience in his eyes and would not have changed his mind about hunting the thing that had killed him.

There were a great number of corpses. The only dead moving among them was the old man. The rest had the good sense to move on to whatever afterlife waited for them.

"You should be gone." Crowley did not speak the words with his mouth, but with his mind. The dead man answered him the same way.

"Why can you see me?"

"It's what I do. I hunt monsters, and I see dead things."

"I can see better now." The old man blinked several times and then pointed toward Slate. "That man should be killed immediately. Before he becomes worse."

Crowley spoke aloud now. He wanted Slate to know what was happening, and he wanted the man to respond. "Your eyes are better because they no longer have physical limitations. Your hearing is probably better, too. As to Mr. Slate, I'm looking into that matter. Haven't made up my mind yet." Crowley's tone brooked no argument.

Lucas Slate stared at Crowley as he could not see the ghost. He knew Crowley wanted more. He knew Crowley expected more. Crowley could see for himself, but he was doing his best to train Slate to see with his new senses and so Slate obliged and suppressed his annoyance. The problem was since he'd begun his changes, his temper tended to be more active than it had been. He did not always like being told what to do.

Slate said, "It looks like a massacre. I don't see any bullet holes. It's all cutting wounds, slashes, and what might be bear claws." He paused a long moment in thought as he rode his horse slightly closer to the body of a woman who had been torn apart. "There are tooth marks, but they came after death. Someone ate this flesh."

Crowley nodded. "No bullet holes. What does that tell us?"

Slate frowned. "Not white men. Possibly other Indians, but I have my doubts."

"Then what else do you suppose it might be?"

"I expect something other than human, and not a bear."

"And why is that again?"

"There are weapons and tooth marks alike." He paused and stared at Crowley. "I am not aware of any cannibals in this area, and even if they existed, those are very large bite marks."

Crowley nodded and offered a very brief smile.

"Look carefully, Mr. Slate. See if there are any survivors."

There were none, and the men moved on, living and dead alike.

"Your horse is not a horse." The old man pointed to make sure his point was clear. "And his horse is dead." The dead man continued pointing things out, and Crowley ignored him as often as not in the hopes that he would go away. He did not, and so Crowley sighed and decided the dead man could continue his rants until they had revenge for his people.

"His horse died, and he brought it back. My horse is...convenient sorcery." Slate shot him a sidewise glance and frowned.

Slate shook his head. "Exactly what are you talking to, Mr. Crowley?"

"There's a dead man walking with us. He thinks our horses are strange and that I should kill you."

"I'd rather you not." For a second the albino's hands moved toward his weapons, and then he settled down.

They rode through hard winds that birthed dust devils and clouds of sand and dirt. Both of them squinted, finding it difficult to follow the trail of something that did not want to be found and was very good at hiding. Crowley's adeptness at stalking after it served them well, just the same.

Jonathan Crowley, for his part, lectured the man he had come to think of as a friend, despite the sure knowledge that he might, at some point, have to take him down.

Lucas Slate listened, occasionally asking questions.

Crowley had been called "the Hunter" in some areas. He was a killer, to be sure, but mostly what he killed were the sorts of creatures that fed on human beings and their suffering.

Sadly, he also found himself called upon for his duties as the Hunter more often than not. He did not like being the Hunter. It was something he simply could not avoid.

While he'd been trying to ignore his calling, again, in the Colorado territories, he'd encountered Lucas Slate. When he first ran across the undertaker, he was alive and well. The second time he'd met him, the man had begun his transformation. He had been tainted by something, a Native American demon, he supposed. Crowley had killed the creature that caused the changes, but could not stop what was happening to Lucas Slate. Exactly what Slate was becoming remained a bit of a mystery. For that reason, they continued on as traveling companions.

Crowley liked Slate just fine. He hoped he wouldn't eventually have to kill the man.

Slate asked, "So, you're saying there are different sorts of creatures that fall into the same categories?"

"Have you seen different types of birds, Mr. Slate?"

"Well, of course."

"There are different types of clouds, too." The old man's ghost kept up with them and would not stop talking. "Doesn't mean they have different purposes. Monsters are monsters and should be killed.

"It's the same sort of thing, really. There are creatures that can become human and humans that can become creatures. They're all shapeshifters." For his part, Slate liked these times the best. Jonathan Crowley was a very intense man, and often spent his time in a brooding silence that felt like a storm gathering on the horizon and threatening the world around them with the risk of lightning, hail and thunder.

Ah, but when the man taught him, he was a different beast. He had a sharp mind, a calmer demeanor, and so very much information to share.

Crowley gestured around them. "I have seen many of the shapeshifters over the years."

"In this country?"

Crowley smiled tolerantly. "Around most of the world, Mr. Slate. I am newer to this land than you are, remember. No, I have seen *Raghosh* and *Naga* in India. The Raghosh—also called a *Rakshasa*—can take on the form of virtually any animal. The Naga are serpents that can take on human form. You have no less than half a dozen different forms of werewolf."

"We have shapeshifters here, too," the ghost said, interrupting Crowley. "They are called by many names. One of those names is Skinwalker. That thing you continue to talk to, he is a Skinwalker. You should kill him."

Crowley continued to ignore the dead man, but made note of the name. He would see what he could learn as time went on, and it was nice to get confirmation about what Slate was becoming.

If he had a chance, he'd talk to the old man's ghost when Slate was not quite so close by.

The old man's ghost sighed. "He's a Skinwalker. He's lying to you."

Crowley frowned and said to the old man, "He's still new at this. I'm trying to help him out. He never wanted this."

"Beg pardon?" Slate was looking Crowley's way again.

"If you can't see the spirit I'm talking with, you need to concentrate on your newer abilities and senses."

Slate nodded his head. "Have you found anything unique to this land, Mr. Crowley?" The albino looked harder, trying to see what Crowley saw.

"You mean aside from your kind?" His smile was dark, and Slate chose not to take offense.

"Obviously." Slate's response was dry. It had taken them time to understand that Slate was a Skinwalker. In this case, that apparently meant a being twisted by magic until he was capable of performing it, as well. He could not change shapes, which, as they had learned, was what some of the native tribes called those who could shift from human to animal form.

"A simple fact for you, Mr. Slate: Humans tend to bring their own sort of supernatural disorders wherever they go. For us to find truly original creatures, it's best to travel where Europeans have not yet tainted the area. That is getting harder and harder as the railroads make their way across the continent."

Slate nodded his head. He had heard the same sort of comment from Crowley before and understood the wisdom of his words.

"The storm's fading."

Crowley's words were a relief to Slate. "Do you suppose we'll find anything new and different out here, Mister Crowley?"

"It's hard to say. I haven't seen any new plants or wildlife in a few weeks." They were traveling in the Southwest, in an area that seemed made up of sand and wind and little else.

Oh, and Indians. There were plenty of the native tribes around the area, and most of them had less than kind thoughts about the Europeans they encountered. They also had a powerful fear of Lucas Slate, who understood that the curse he carried came from this area. That was one of the reasons they were here now. They wanted to better understand what was happening to him. They also wanted to see if there were new plants or animals that Crowley could catalogue.

The hills around them were of layered stone, cut down by wind over the centuries. Crowley had seen them before in different places but here the colors were vivid and vibrant. It was a welcome change from the endless dust that had marked their travel for several days.

"I'm weary of this journey, Mister Crowley."

Crowley nodded his head and paused a moment. "What makes you so weary here?"

Slate took a long while to answer. "If you discover there is no cure for what I am becoming, I have a powerful suspicion I might not leave this vicinity."

"Mr. Slate, when we find Marcus Jacobi, who just might be a vampire, we might be able to take the time for some answers. As you have been with me on his trail for several days, that is a priority. I am also currently hunting down whatever just killed an entire gathering of local Indians. When I am done with those matters we can discuss whether or not I intend to kill you any time soon. Should I decide to kill you, I will make my intentions known before it happens."

"Then you are a fool," replied the ghostly old man. "Skinwalkers should not be trusted and should be killed as quickly as possible. They take a great deal of killing."

"And should I hunt down and kill ghosts because they walk and talk? Should I trust that spirits deceive and plan only harm?" He looked to the dead man as he spoke, and the man looked back, frowning. "In my experience most of the dead who do not rest deserve to be destroyed."

"Are you speaking to me, Mr. Crowley?"

"No. I'm talking to the dead man who thinks I should kill you."

Slate sighed and lowered his head for a moment. When he raised it again his eyes were narrowed and he began to look, to really, truly look, for the specter that walked alongside them.

The winds finally died away revealing the bottom of a canyon of stone and sand with walls that twisted and turned ahead of them.

"Why would anyone live here willingly, I wonder?" Slate's voice was as soft as ever.

The dead man followed with something decidedly rude by the tone, but Crowley did not understand the words. "Maybe they wanted to be left alone? Maybe they found things here that you are not seeing."

The pale giant looked his way. "I would think they'd prefer to find a place with food, Mr. Crowley."

The Hunter laughed. "There's plenty, if you know where to look." He gazed out at the distant mesas and barren landscape. "Also, though I couldn't prove it, there are many places in the world where the land changes. This might have been a very green area once. Now, however, it is different."

"I have my doubts."

"And why is that, Mr. Slate?"

Slate pointed to a wall of stone not far away where someone, likely a very long time ago, had drawn several images on the rock.

A hunchbacked thing danced and played what looked like a flute. Next to it, a massive hairy shape wielded a large club and what might well be a sword. The head of the thing was adorned with horns and oddly shaped ears, and the mouth was filled with jagged fangs. Images that looked like they could be various animals surrounded the two creatures, though one of the petroglyphs—a humanoid shape with antlers—stood out among the collection.

"What tribe did the old man say he was from, Mr. Slate?"

Slate stared at him, eyes narrowed only slightly. "The Hopi, I believe. I could only understand your side of the conversation, Mr. Crowley."

"I'll teach you how to understand other languages in due time." He waved a dismissive hand. "The Hopi. I have read something about them, but I can't honestly remember what it was."

"They are kachinas. Kokopelli is there. And the ogre, Nata-Aska. Over there is a sorcerer." The old man pointed to an image of the gaunt man with antlers. "Further up the way you can find images of the ant people. They are—"

Slate stared at the markings, his eyes drawn again and again to the gaunt figure with antlers. "What do you make of that, Mr. Crowley?"

"Far more importantly, Mr. Slate, what do *you* make of it?"

"I wonder if it's supposed to be a Skinwalker, like me."

"Just as bad if you ask me." The dead man continued to talk, and Crowley pretended not to hear.

"Perhaps we'll find someone who can tell us." Crowley frowned. "Does it make you feel any connection to the area?"

"No. Not precisely. But that song inside me, the one that comes from whatever abides inside my body, it gets stronger when I stare at that shape."

Crowley frowned. "There is no power here. They are only images." He paused. "At least, as far as I can tell."

The old man's spirit laughed. "Then you are a fool. There is great power here." His smile faded.

Crowley repeated the words to Slate.

High, sweet notes echoed from the rock formations around them and reverberated back and forth. Crowley tilted his head to the left and listened, a faint grin playing at his lips.

Slate shivered at the noises.

"I feel, Mr. Crowley, that we might once again have found

a connection to whatever I am becoming. The thing that makes that noise inspired within me a deep discomfort."

"In the natural world and the unnatural alike, most everything has enemies, Mr. Slate. You might be best off preparing your weapons."

"Do you think whatever made that noise is among these images?"

"That is Kokopelli. He plays to offer you luck in your coming battle." The dead man shrugged. "He is not as offended by your Skinwalker, as I am. Perhaps, I have been mistaken."

"I imagine that stranger things have occurred in this world," Crowley said to the ghost, and then said to Slate, "I don't get the same feeling that you do at all. That noise actually makes me feel happy."

"Truly?" Slate looked genuinely surprised.

Crowley took off his hat for a moment and brushed his hair with his fingers. "Nor do I sense anything of the unnatural here." A small lie for the benefit of the dead man.

"How is that possible, Mr. Crowley?"

"Reality is sometimes fluid, Mr. Slate. It is very possible that the thing making that sound, and all of the images on these rocks, are considered perfectly natural in this area of the world. Gods have influence on their people. Perhaps these things are seen as gods. I have no notion beyond that."

From a different direction than the fading notes of music, a deep roar echoed across the faces of the stone barriers marking the landscape. Slate's face scowled and then the albino bared his teeth. Crowley's concern for his companion grew.

The dead man warned, "That is the ogre. He will come to kill you now, as he killed my people."

"Why did he kill your people?"

The old man's wrinkled face twisted in a mask of sorrow. "Normally, the ogres only come to punish, but I do not know why they would punish everyone."

Crowley said nothing of this to Slate, but continued watching the man's reactions.

Slate swallowed hard. "I can feel it. The thing that made that sound, I think it's what killed those Hopi."

Crowley gave Slate a predatory smile. As was often the case when people saw that expression, it sent a shiver down Slate's spine.

"Well then, I believe I have business to attend to. Will you be joining me?"

Truly, there was no question about it. Even if Slate felt a cowardly desire to stay hidden—which he did not—the song that ran through his body ever since he'd been changed would not have tolerated the notion.

Crowley rode forward.

Slate waited only a moment before following Crowley. His skin felt too tight on his body, and his hair wanted to stand on end. Had he not been wearing his top hat, it might well have succeeded.

Crowley rode steadily, but slowly, taking the time to examine everything around him. Not far along their ride, he came to a complete stop and pointed toward the west.

What he pointed at was immediately obvious—buildings up ahead, clearly built directly into and from the local stone. The structures were solid, and had been worn down by the elements over God alone knew how long. Their location—seventy feet off the ground—would be easily defended and very difficult to attack by surprise. A sheer cliff rose above and below the hidden structures, obscuring much of the sunlight that might otherwise have made the area impossibly hot.

Trees grew nearby, making the area greener than its surroundings, and though they could not see it, the men could both smell water in the area. "Well, that is something I did not expect to see this day, Mr. Slate."

The dead man sounded surprised. "I have never seen this before, and I have traveled these canyons many times."

"Once again I fear that whatever is inside me does not like this place, Mr. Crowley."

"You say that as if it is a bad thing, Mr. Slate. I remind you that whatever it is inside of you is not a good thing. It has given you strength, true enough, but we've seen firsthand what others afflicted by the same curse have become." He furrowed his brow. "Why you are not as completely altered remains a mystery that I intend to solve."

Slate nodded.

The roar came again, echoing from the stone village above them.

Crowley frowned and Slate joined him. "Whatever that is,

I expect it wants to discuss with us what we might be doing around its home."

"Do you suppose it built this place, Mr. Crowley?"

"I've my doubts."

The shape that walked out from the stone structures was much too large to qualify as human. It crawled on hands and knees and then rose to stand like a man.

But, it was most decidedly not a man. The legs were too short, the arms too long and the head would never mimic a human skull. Humanlike, but flawed.

It let out another deep roaring noise. There was no doubting where the creature was aimed as it started in their direction with surprising speed for its size.

"I believe you may be right about this beast, Mr. Slate."

"In that it does not bode well for me? I expect I am, indeed, Mr. Crowley." He settled the long rifle usually slung to the side of his saddle up into his arms. The two pistols he wore stayed in their places for the moment as he took careful aim.

From a hundred yards away, the thing challenged them again, and increased its speed. Lucas Slate took his time, exhaled slowly and pulled the trigger on his Sharps .50-90 buffalo rifle. The rifle was designed to take down a buffalo with one shot and, normally, did its job admirably well. Though Slate had seen no reason to date to hunt buffalo, he'd heard plenty of stories about one bullet dropping the creatures that weighed two thousand pounds or more.

What came at them was substantially smaller than a full-grown buffalo. Slate, who was good at estimating the size of the people he'd once made caskets for, guessed the hulking creature came close to a thousand pounds.

The bullet Slate put through its chest staggered the thing.

The ogre came to a stop and teetered for a moment, but kept its feet. The beast had made it closer to them than they hoped, by a good stretch.

Crowley let out a soft whistle as he stared at the hole in the creature. Blood seeped from the front. He could not see where the bullet had left, if in fact, it did exit the body.

Slate very calmly placed his rifle back in its scabbard and drew his Remington Army revolvers.

Before doing anything else, he asked Crowley. "And did you intend to join in this battle, Mr. Crowley?"

Crowley nodded toward the distant shape. When Slate looked again, the ogre had returned to its previous trajectory toward them and continued to pick up speed.

"You should keep your eyes on your enemy, Mr. Slate. Doing otherwise could easily prove fatal."

As the beast charged toward him, it drew weapons of its own seemingly from thin air. In the left hand, it carried a massive club—a curved, wooden affair with several large spines running along one side. The other hand sported an oversized saber, rusted in places and all too well used.

Slate's heels struck the sides of his horse, and he drove forward, his coat fluttering behind him like dark wings.

Crowley said not a word as the two came closer together. There was no one to hear his words, in any event, except the ghost that was watching beside him.

"Why do you not fight?"

"I will if I have to. This is a chance for Mr. Slate to test himself."

The ogre headed for Lucas Slate with powerful, thick legs and a body as wide as a horse's ribcage. The face was a bestial thing, with a wide muzzle filled with overly large, wide teeth surrounded by blackened gums. Its nose was a mass of wrinkles with two broad slits and its eyes were small and half-hidden by a heavy brow. Ramlike horns adorned the forehead, long and curved and as black as midnight. The ears would have baffled many people, but Crowley had long since studied the creatures of the wild and understood that the shape he was looking at most clearly resembled the ears of some bats. Surrounding that oddity of a face was a thick mane of black hair that ran from the head halfway down the torso of the creature. Several stone beads and feathers had been tied into that hair.

It wore clothes—rawhide pants, a rawhide vest, a heavy belt with a scabbard on one side and a loop on the other, and several necklaces adorned with bones and what looked like skulls of different creatures—and carried weapons. It was not without intelligence, though it hardly seemed to merit credit for civility.

It was a simple fact: Lucas Slate was new at handguns and wasn't very good with them. Give him a shotgun and he was dangerous enough. At long range with a rifle, he was decidedly terrifying, but with revolvers? His aim left much to be desired and doubly so when one considered he was riding at a full run on a horse, over uneven terrain.

No one was more surprised than Jonathan Crowley when the bullets hit their target. Still, when one considered the size of the target, the challenge was lessened a bit. Round after round struck the charging creature and staggered it again and again. Any of those shots would surely have killed a man if he'd been struck in the same places, but the bullets had no more effect than the rifle did.

The ogre—Nata-Aska—kept coming, and Lucas Slate urged his horse on until it rammed into the creature with its full weight. Horse, rider, and beast all fell together in a wave of violent force.

Jonathan Crowley dismounted. He would step in if he had to, but one of the reasons he traveled with Slate was to assess what he was becoming and, whatever that something might be, it was offended by the very existence of the creature it now faced off against.

He wanted to help Slate. He did. But first, he had to know if the man could take care of himself.

Slate was taller than most, almost eight inches taller than Crowley himself, who was only average in height. Still, he seemed miniscule when compared to the thing that came for him as he threw his handguns aside.

The beast was as big as four of the albino, taller by a head and shoulders as broad across as three of him. The mouth of the beast opened again and it roared, spittle blowing from that gaping maw and wetting Slate's face.

Had there ever been a time when he thought the pale man looked meek? Surely so, but not just then; there was murder painted on the man's features, his eyes narrowed with fury and his teeth bared in a snarl.

The creature swept its weapons back over its head, preparing to bring ruination down upon Slate. While the pale man watched that massive weapon waving in the air, the thing he was fighting brought its other fist up and smashed it into Slate's chest like an ax into a log.

Lucas Slate, a man who simply did not move if he did not want to, was knocked through the air, bloodied and dazed. When he hit the ground he did not move.

"Well, damn me." Crowley looked at his companion's unmoving

form and felt a nervous flutter in his stomach. He couldn't exactly call Slate a friend, but he hoped the man had survived.

Nata-Aska turned toward Crowley and roared. The sound was loud enough to deafen, and the thing raised its saber and stampeded in his direction, the earth shaking with each footfall the behemoth made.

The blade was big enough to cleave him in two. The ogre tried to ram the point through Crowley's body.

Jonathan Crowley dropped under the saber and rolled himself closer to the charging monster. His leg swept up and the heel of his foot drove into the crotch of his enemy. He felt the testicle on the ogre crunch on impact.

Any thoughts of how loudly the beast had screamed before were erased at the sound that came from Nata-Aska.

Crowley rolled to his feet and stared at the ogre.

The old man's ghost laughed with pure glee.

The ogre turned toward Crowley and threw the sword aside, its hands clenching and unclenching as it, doubtless, considered the best way to rip him into shreds. Crowley moved himself to the side, careful to make sure the beast didn't have a clear line of sight to either the horses or Lucas Slate.

The beast spoke. He had no idea what words were uttered, but the fury in its voice was impossible to miss.

The old man's ghost said, "He intends to kill you now."

"I expected as much."

Crowley stood his ground and prepared. Nata-Aska would come for him. There were many methods of handling the situation. He expected most of them would end with him recovering from several broken bones.

The great beast came for him again, and Crowley considered whether to dodge the beast or topple it.

Instead he watched Lucas Slate come from the side and crash into the ogre, driving an elbow into the thing's eye.

Lucas Slate, the mildest man he'd met in Carson's Point, Colorado, had changed a great deal since they'd first encountered each other, but at that moment Crowley would have been hard pressed to state anything aside from skin color that the undertaker he'd known and the Skinwalker he traveled with had in common.

He could clearly see where Slate had been struck by the ogre.

His chest was broken in that spot, his ribs were in the wrong positions and the whole of his torso was bruising from the force of the blow.

By rights the man should have been as dead as he looked, but he was moving, and screaming and there was a savagery to him that should not have been there. For one moment, only one, his eyes, so pale a blue as to seem nearly white, were the color of midnight.

The ogre gestured and its saber was once again held in its grasp.

Slate stood taller and as Crowley watched the broken bones in the Skinwalker's chest moved back to where they belonged with several wet, cracking sounds.

While Nata-Aska tried to recover from the damage Slate had done to his eye, which was bleeding now, Slate stepped in close and drove his hard fist directly into the thing's throat with as much force as he could muster. The flesh under that furry neck rippled, and the beast did the only thing it could in that situation—it coughed hard trying to breathe. Slate's hand reached out again, grabbing the hand the beast wrapped around the hilt of its weapon. The creature coughed again and leaned forward, hacking and gasping, trying desperately to take in a breath.

Slate wrenched the saber away and, stepping back, clutched the oversized hilt in both of his hands.

Crowley still did nothing.

The ogre had come for Slate, and according to their dead companion, it was the very nightmare that had killed at least fifty people. Those people likely had blood on their hands. He'd seen what Slate either did not see or did not care to mention: He'd seen the box of Confederate gold resting near the bodies of three dead men. The likelihood was that the gold had not been given freely by the soldiers of the Confederate Army. It hardly mattered that the war was over two years past. He did not care that the very dead holding the gold might well have had good reason for taking it. The odds were that they had killed to get it and that made them both human and monsters in his eyes.

They were mortal monsters, however, and so not his concern.

The great beast shook its head and gasped, desperate to breathe.

Lucas Slate slammed the ogre's sword into its breast, the blade erupting from its back.

There was no other sound. The creature dropped to the ground with an audible thud that Crowley felt from twenty paces away.

Slate looked down at the dead creature and panted. For once the man truly seemed focused on his agenda.

"Well done, Mr. Slate. I'm glad to see you actually concentrating on a task."

He looked back at Crowley only for a moment, but while he did so, the great form before him crumbled into a mass of black ash.

Crowley said nothing about that, and instead saw the look of surprise that slipped over Slate's face.

"We should leave this place, Mr. Crowley."

Crowley looked around and saw the ghost was gone, too. Once avenged the old man moved on, which was what he should have done. Still, he found the lack of the old man's voice left a void he did not expect.

"Indeed we should, Mr. Slate. Jacobi is still out there."

Finding Home

Irene Radford

Take me home, Katie. Kormos bit back the bitter taste of using his host's nickname in his telepathic communication. How was a housegod supposed to know who was whom if they didn't use their given name?

When she'd been born, he'd searched the upper world for days, trying to find this girl's true spirit. The quest went poorly. His search, as always, was limited to relatives who had passed above and not below. He'd never revive the spirit of one who had been found guilty of their evil ways. It was bad form to attempt to resurrect one who had been consumed by his mistress. The goddess of the underworld got a bit testy when you tried.

On the other hand, all was not hidden. Ykaterina, Katie's great-great-grandmother, had been an exemplary woman. Her name was worthy of this independent-thinking girl child, hopefully an accurate forecast of Katie's true spirit.

"Shut up. I'm concentrating," Katie Murray snapped at him out loud—she heard his mind speech, but did not reply by the same means—as she ran her hands along the rubber hose that carried the steam condensate back from the powered looms. The rubber was a prototype from a friend trying to make it stronger and more flexible than other rubbers, and if it failed, the whole system could be damaged.

Why do you build this thing of steam and pistons? Kormos asked. *This place can never be home for me, or any of your descendants. We need cold winds and reindeer herds to be complete.*

175

"You've whined and complained about that for nigh on sixty years to one or another of our clan. When are you going to wake up and spit out the vodka? That home doesn't exist anymore. Granny's family was kicked out of Siberia by the tsar's Cossacks. You're lucky she survived to carry you here. Oregon is a great place to live. Besides, if she hadn't come here, she'd never have met Gramps."

She found a man to love. That doesn't complete a home. It takes more, said Kormos, pounding the inside of Ykaterina's mind.

"You can't stand that Granny and Gramps were happy together because you have never loved anyone. *Not even yourself.* Now let me work. This is important."

He stomped his foot within the tiny carved fetish that imprisoned him. *You need me to generate some chaos among you and your two first cousins. If you get angry enough with each other, you'll abandon this thing you are doing. This horrible project that will be the death of me! Then you will know I am right.*

"I could cut my hair," she said, but kept her focus on the myriad pipes and hoses that made up the boiler for the steam-powered loom. She lay under the apparatus fiddling with connections.

No, he gasped, appalled. He couldn't imagine existing without the sacred protection of a braid. Katie's ancestors knew the importance of elaborate plaits and incorporated them into embroidery and carved designs.

"I cut my hair, and you'd wind up living on a shelf. A dusty forgotten souvenir sitting out of sight with nobody to talk to. No contact with anyone in the family." She squeezed the slight bulge in her thick black braid where a carved reindeer horn statuette resided. He'd been trapped inside the ugly representation since... since his people abandoned their hide-and-mud hut and accepted exile in the new world. The carved figure depicted Kormos accurately with bulging eyes and distended tummy. He had a domed head without a single hair, and spindly limbs—a fine figure of a housegod.

Steam can't warm your spirit like a good fire of reindeer dung, he pouted.

"Steam comes from science and makes a much warmer house. And reindeer dung won't power the loom. Besides, our house isn't a one-room hide tent with three generations inside like it was in your day," Katie said.

Your science steals the ability to believe. Would you have me wither away to nothing? The goddess of the underworld would starve for a lack of evil souls to feast upon if that happened. It is my destiny to feed her with what I create.

Katie smirked. The evil that Kormos recorded—or created—was of the petty variety. His goddess would starve if she counted on Kormos, and all the other Siberian housegods, and their version of evil, for food.

Of course, Katie mused, if she didn't find the problem with this hose, she might need reindeer dung to stay warm this winter.

Kormos pressed his hands to his head. The girl was impossible. The current generation of offspring were so good intentioned and impervious to chaos as to be almost saintly. They even attended *church*, without the priest forcing them.

And even worse, the Murray clan, how he hated that name, had diluted their fine Siberian blood by marrying outside the tribes. Their beloved Gramps.

That was how it started. They wouldn't respond to Kormos's need for chaos, for the friction, the heated energy it brought. He thrived on violence. He fed the Goddess with volatile emotions. But now, he was weak. Only Katie could sense him, and she ignored his needs. She was selfish. She did not fear the Goddess, ignoring his pushes into anger and temper tantrums.

Katie had the thick black hair Kormos cherished as a resting place for his fetish. It reminded him of better days. She wore it in two fat plaits that hung below her waist. Without a braid to cradle him, he'd be an invisible spirit drifting aimlessly, the family beyond his calling.

It was no wonder he weakened. No wonder he slept more than he kept vigil. With a weary sigh, he peered into the gloomy interior of the brick building and shuddered with dread at the permanence of the baked clay. Was this his fate? Inert matter, with no soul, for a dwelling? A hide tent carried the soul of the departed reindeer, fulfilling its fate far beyond life.

While Katie twisted and fiddled beneath and around the boiler, only the angle of the sun changed. Even now, Kormos could see the sun, visible through the doorway, two small windows and a ceiling vent. His hostess still lay under the massive metal machine that spelled his doom and theirs. Her new housegod, he mused.

I want to go home!

Katie ignored him.

You needn't worry so much about the machine, he admonished Katie. *The itty-bitty crack in the line will leak tiny amounts of steam. That will make the wood of your wool carding machine, the spinners, and loom wet. They will seek their original form, with unforced curves until they rejoin the cycle of life. What is the harm if the machine falls limp and useless? It would be a blessing. Without this mill to support you and your cousins, you will take me home to Siberia. You would find warmth within the tents made from reindeer hide. You'll learn to love the aroma of meat cooked over a dung fire.* He lost himself in a daydream of the old times.

He wished he could whisper into the minds of the poets and artists and dreamers in the family instead of only the scientist. He blamed it in part on the fact that the magical chain of seven children broke with this generation. Not one of them had more than a single sibling. And all three first cousins working to build this mill looked to have no inclination to marry and breed. Who would care for him then?

I'm doomed, Kormos wailed.

"Seneca, do we have any more rubber hose?" Katie called to the cousin closest to her in age, eighteen months older than herself.

"Let me look." He set down his new repeater rifle—a weapon worthy only of Cossacks as Kormos had pointed out when he bought it—and scrambled through a pile of discarded materials and tools.

"Rubber is expensive," Isolde, older than Ykaterina by only three years, said from her post on the wooden step below the open doorway. "Starting this enterprise was your idea. You enlisted our help. You're the reason Gramps loaned us any money at all."

"We got the land and the remnants of the buildings and the engine for cheap, so we could afford necessities we can't make ourselves, like rubber," Katie grumbled. "That's what Gramps wanted us to do. Use the money wisely."

"We got the land for cheap because no one else wants it after a band of Bigfoot ripped the timber mill apart and killed three of the twenty workers and timberjacks," Seneca reminded them both. The sun was dropping toward the horizon, and his scrutiny of the tree line became wary. He gripped the six-shooter on his hip.

Kormos knew they would run their mill differently, taking

from the surrounding forest only what they needed, using only enough of the younger smaller trees to fuel the mill until they could afford to shift to coal. There would be no destruction of Bigfoot homes, no reason for the Bigfoot to attack.

"We're creating textiles, not sawing and planing wood," Seneca reassured himself, and his cousins. He was the business person, columns of numbers spoke to him more than ancient family lore. He was blond, like Isolde and Gramps, and therefore less of a person to Kormos.

"The rubber was more expensive than the rebuilt boiler," Isolde answered, but kept her gaze moving from clearing to tree line. "We only bought enough rubber to fulfill your specifications, Katie. Gramps isn't going to advance us more money for a steam mill if this one breaks or is broken up by those murdering Bigfoot." She mindlessly dismantled, cleaned, and reloaded her precious Colt six-shooter. Then she started the same procedure with the Henry repeater rifle lying on the stoop beside her. She took after their gramps, a retired fur trader, in restless energy and need for adventure. She was the weaver in this trio, the least likely to have the scientific bent of the other two. She'd make an admirable hostess for Kormos. But she was blonde. *Blonde,* just like the hated tsar and his murdering brood. Kormos had refused her.

Katie, the engineer, was the least likely person to hear and carry Kormos. She, more than the others, had succumbed to the safety and comfort of *civilization*. Kormos loved it when her cousins raised their guns and shot things, even if only targets. Shooting equaled destruction and chaos. If only their hair was not blond, they could bear the burden of his presence.

"Kormos says the engine angers the spirits of the forest." Isolde imitated the sing-song, breathy voice of another cousin who wrote bad poetry and drifted through life in a dreamy haze. "Like we care about his whiny fears. All he really wants is to go back to Siberia."

Kormos pursed his lips and blew a wet raspberry at her.

"No one cares what that fiend thinks," Seneca spat at her. "We need to worry more about the Bigfoot."

None of the family wanted to admit that Kormos, the malevolent housegod, existed. But they had all grown up with Granny's stories; enough to make them believe he was real, if not believe *in him*. They all had witnessed her temper tantrums that were as fierce as any fit when Kormos got his claws into her mind.

"I wish he was imaginary." Katie sighed. She fingered her thick black braids. "And he also says they are Yeti, that's what they are called in Siberia, not a Bigfoot, or Sasquatch. He thinks we should let him out to sow chaos among them so they won't bother us." *Then I might be rid of him once and for all.*

I heard that!

"Gramps should have buried that thing with Granny," Seneca said.

"But that would have released his nasty spirit into the wild to infect everyone with violence and evil at random," Isolde protested. "He's our problem. We keep him confined."

"Gramps told us that the world is safer when Kormos has a custodian." Katie patted the bulge in her thick braid again. Then she flicked the plait over her shoulder, making certain Kormos shook and rattled as his fetish home thumped against her bones.

"Housegods, demons, evil spirits, they're all just an excuse for people to be mean," Seneca scoffed, rising from his search of the pile of discards. "Is this piece of hose long enough?" He held up three feet of the snakelike rubber.

Kormos hissed; he feared snakes more than the outraged Yeti he heard thrashing through the underbrush about a mile distant. Of course, the monster came with a purpose. It came to destroy this mechanical monster that threatened its home.

Ice and snow! Kormos cursed. *Does that make the Yeti akin to me? And my humans akin to the murdering Cossacks?*

Katie eyed the hose. "Just long enough." Quickly she disconnected the imperfect bit of rubber and substituted the new piece. But first she let her sensitive fingertips examine every inch of it. No splits, bulges, or rough nubs.

Kormos's heart sank. One step closer to completion. The Yeti must know that their doom was imminent. Closer than Kormos's own demise. They would strike when the Murrays were vulnerable.

"Any sign of our friends out there?" Seneca asked.

"Not yet," said Isolde and patted her Henry repeater. "They'll come." She cast nervous eyes into the greenery beyond the windows and door.

Katie completed her inspection of the boiler and nodded satisfaction. A crank of a spigot sent water from the creek through a series of pipes and pumps into the boiler. The level rose slowly but significantly. "Time to fire her up."

"How will you know if it works if it's not connected to anything?" Isolde asked.

"It is connected to the gear shaft in the long shed, if not the spinners and the loom. We need someone watching over there to make sure the shaft moves, and the gears turn. Then we connect," Katie replied. She'd only had to explain the workings and the plan six dozen times.

"I think we're ready. Who volunteers to go watch the gears? I need to stay here and monitor the engine," Katie said. The boiler was more than half full, so she slowed the water intake to a mere trickle.

"Never, not me," Seneca mumbled. "I'm not going anywhere alone this close to sunset. Nor are we leaving any one of us alone."

"Ready as we'll ever be. Light her up. We'll hear the gears. They're only a dozen paces away." Isolde stood and propped the Henry repeater on the windowsill, pointed toward the thickest patch of mixed Douglas fir and cedar trees that ringed their property.

Seneca struck a lucifer against the rough brick wall, igniting a tiny flame. Then he held the match until it lit the kindling in the firebox beneath the boiler. Flames licked the dry wood, hungry for food.

Katie watched in fascination at how the fire caught a bit of dry bark, flared, and curled the fuel then leapt to the next bigger piece of wood. The sweet smell warmed her all the way to her toes. "Your reindeer dung fire doesn't smell so sweet," she admonished Kormos.

Kormos had to agree that this fire carried a pleasant odor. Without fire, humans would not have ascended above primitive animal forms and learned right from wrong. Fire gave him a family to guard . . . or condemn. Knowing right from wrong gave his mistress in the underworld a purpose: judging the deeds of each life and weighing the balance between good and bad. Without those developments his mistress would have starved to death eons ago.

"At last we have a chance to prove to Gramps that we're not idiots just idly waiting for his money," Katie continued. She slammed shut the iron hatch to the firebox. Her English great-grandfather, Gramps's father, a lord of some sort, had turned losing money to drink and gaming into an artform. Gramps made sure none of his offspring had enough money to develop the same bad habits.

Isolde turned back to her vigil of the forest beyond the mill clearing. "Something big is thrashing through the underbrush," she whispered. She didn't need to tell them to take up their guns.

Kormos cringed within Katie's plait. He knew that the Yeti were coming. The first one had stopped to gather reinforcements along the way. Short sharp raps of stout sticks slammed against tree trunks reverberated through the forest.

The Murray cousins stopped their pacing abruptly and turned to listen. "Why? Why are they attacking us? We aren't disturbing them. Not like the timber guys," Katie wondered.

Kormos pulled the carved reindeer bone tighter around him, shutting off most of his awareness of the outside world. He wished he could fall into a deep and dreamless sleep until fate had decided the outcome of this battle.

No! He had to stay awake, be with Katie until the end.

Twilight crept up on them, fading into darkness so slowly that it wasn't until the long shadows of the trees blended into the general landscape that Katie became aware of the loss of light. Her alarm sent jolts of fear through Kormos.

The boiler continued to build up steam. The crank and jerk of tight gears beginning to turn in the adjacent shed rivaled the noise of the tree knocks coming from the depth of the forest.

Battle cries.

And then they ceased, leaving only the grind and chug of gears. It rumbled in the night. A call to the enemy.

A tree knock reverberated, closer. A crack as loud as a rifle shot echoed from tree trunk to tree trunk. This must be a Sasquatch, then. The Yeti of Siberia didn't have trees big enough to make so much noise. The beast whacked a hollow forest giant with a broken branch within feet of the intense shadows of the forest. One knock. Then other raps circled the Mill. They were surrounded.

Katie flinched and ducked, retreating to stand before the boiler. She cocked her rifle, the sound a direct challenge to the tree knocks.

Isolde brought her rifle to bear at the same time.

Keep it away, Kormos gibbered. *It has no mercy. No mercy. Only anger. We are killing its home. It needs its home.*

Katie's innards froze. "Is that what this is all about?" Home to her meant a solidly built dwelling, fruitful work, family all gathered together. Civilization. This mill, only two hours by horseback away from the homestead where they all grew up, should become a new home for herself and her cousins.

Was the Sasquatch out there only trying to protect its idea of home, even if different than her own?

A mighty roar erupted from the trees, followed by another, and another, and another. They were surrounded by angry creatures. Very large, very angry creatures.

Isolde pulled the trigger five times before pausing to assess any damage she might have inflicted.

Then Seneca loosed five more shots from his Remington.

Reluctantly Katie counted the bullets in her bandolier, reluctant to fire a single one until she had to. She knew now that the boiler was the prime target of their enemies.

Resolutely, she took a position and began shooting at shadows, timing her volleys between her cousins' so that whatever was out there, that had wrecked the previous timber mill, never had a lull in the gun fire.

"Got one!" Isolde chortled, reloading her magazine. As she spoke, a dark shape among the dark but tall tree trunks stumbled forward and fell prone on the ground halfway between the brick boiler house and the forest.

"My God!" Katie held her breath, waiting for movement or other signs of life. "The brute must be eight feet tall."

Isolde and Seneca kept firing, without pause.

Katie wanted to vomit.

A wail went up all around them. Each of the Sasquatch mourned their fallen comrade loudly.

Another dark form stumbled forward and fell flat beside its giant mate. This one was smaller with lighter fur. Maybe only seven feet tall. Its eyes remained open, staring at the humans in accusation.

Katie, and therefore Kormos, knew that gaze had held intelligence.

Neither creature had screamed in pain or clutched the wounds that leaked red blood. Blood as red as any human's. They just appeared and fell.

The hairs on the back of Katie's neck stood up in response to the eerie sounds of grief.

Then silence. The absence of sound hurt Kormos's ears as much as the noise.

"Are they gone for good?" Seneca asked.

"Doubtful," Isolde said. "I wouldn't give up a fight so easily."

"They'll regroup, find weapons. Make a plan," Katie said quietly on a long exhale.

My thoughts exactly, Kormos echoed her words.

"What do we do now?" Seneca asked, turning a circle and examining their simple shelter. "The mortar between the bricks is still wet. They could push down the walls if they get close enough."

"We sleep in turns and don't let them get close," Isolde said, cocking her six-shooter.

Biting her lip, Katie kept her own counsel. She knew what they had to do. If they made it out alive.

Here they come again! Kormos yelled at Katie.

She roused from her doze, preparing her rifle as she came to her feet.

"Yee haw!" Isolde shouted. Three shots exploded from her rifle in rapid succession.

A dark form ran forward, one arm raised. It threw a rock almost as big as Katie's head. The knapped edges broke through the wooden door, shattering the planks.

Katie jumped aside. Her chin trembled, and her back teeth chattered in fright.

Do something! Kormos yelled at her.

"Why don't you do something?" she yelled back at him as she shot blindly through the hole in the sagging door.

But I... But I...

Three more rocks flew into the shed through the unglazed windows and the doorway. The few remaining planks crumbled in the next onslaught.

"They're coming closer. I can't see them to shoot at until they are nearly upon us," Isolde said, her voice shaky and uncertain for the first time in her life.

"They...they've learned to aim," Seneca choked out. He kicked aside the next rock that landed at his feet. It wobbled as it rolled, revealing sharp planes on two sides. "And they know how to knap the rocks, like spear points."

Katie fired her rifle at a suggestion of movement.

"Waaah waah!" A smaller furred creature darted out from the tree line. "Waaah waah," it wailed as it knelt by a fallen form. The younger version laid its head on the back of its...mother? Pounding the ground, it lifted its flat face to the rising moon and screamed again.

Katie held her fire, choking on her appalling actions.

Seneca stopped shooting. "We're murdering them," he whispered.

"Them or us, cousin." Isolde gripped his shoulder and squeezed. "We're all just trying to make a home and survive."

"This isn't civilized. Our grandparents, and parents labored in the wilderness for years trying to carve out a bit of civilization. And we are reverting to the primitive violence of our ancestors," Katie moaned.

"They attacked first," Isolde protested.

"Because we invaded their home. This place belongs to them, not us." Katie wanted to cry at the useless deaths.

Kormos had no words of comfort for her. Only accusations. He should be salivating at the thought of being able to report their evil deeds to his mistress in the underworld.

The perpetual hunger gnawing at his belly eased.

Tears he didn't know he could shed dripped from his eyes at the thought of watching Katie die at the hands of the big brutes outside.

"It's *our* land. We bought it!" Seneca protested feebly.

"But they don't recognize our rights to their land, as the Cossacks didn't recognize the rights of our ancestors to grazing land for their reindeer herds." Katie repeated Kormos's thoughts.

"And we don't recognize their right to our land!" Isolde added. But she didn't fire her gun. She didn't even raise it from her side to take aim.

Kormos gibbered in fear at the thought of losing Katie. Losing Katie and her cousins. His family.

"Can you do anything to protect *your* family, Kormos?" Katie whispered.

He gulped. *I'm just a housegod. I watch. I record your deeds. What else am I supposed to do?*

"You are a supernatural being who communicates with the spirit world. Communicate with them!" She pointed out the vacant window.

A large shape stepped free of the shadows but stayed within a single (but very long) step of safety behind a tree. It raised a broken branch above its head, shook it hard, roaring in defiance of the bullets that had taken two of its family.

The single figure stood tall and silent, defiant, challenging the humans to murder him too.

They shouldn't have to watch the destruction of their home as I did, Kormos thought, not caring if Katie heard him or not. To her, he said, *Stand at the window and say as loudly as you can...* He uttered a series of guttural grunts.

Katie shrugged and did as he told her. But she had to stop in the middle of the chain of untranslatable sounds to swallow past a dry lump in her throat.

Kormos knew that a human throat wasn't meant to make such bizarre noises. Still, he prodded her to continue with a stab of pain to the back of her eyes.

"What did I say?" she whispered.

The big Sasquatch stood silent.

You promised that you and your kin would leave this clearing, taking with you every trace of human intrusion into their home, if they will back off for the space of a quarter moon's passage.

The Sasquatch ducked away, thrashing a wide swath of destruction through the undergrowth. Isolde raised her rifle, then lowered it again without pulling the trigger.

"At least the mortar is still moist. We can dismantle this place, remove all evidence of it ever being here, every chunk of baked clay, bent nail, and scrap of wood. We'll settle elsewhere," Katie said. She wasn't sure how or why she, as the youngest of the lot, had taken on the job of making decisions for all of them. "I'll start working on cooling the boiler and taking it apart. That's the most crucial piece of equipment."

"I think I like the idea of setting up our mill someplace more civilized," Seneca said softly. His hands shook as he holstered his pistol. "Somewhere I can have a quiet office and tote up numbers that mean something."

"Someplace where there's a saloon close by, but far enough away from home that Gramps won't come and supervise," Isolde said.

"We need to go east, upriver, where there isn't enough timber, water, or game for the Sasquatch," Katie said decisively. Suddenly it was important to her, and to Kormos, to give the creature its proper name, the name that belonged to this land, not to its cousins in Siberia, or the one imposed by the human invaders from the East.

"I heard that Marshall's Station up Umatilla way has just been renamed Pendleton. Got a railhead and access to river transportation. They even have a post office. And a lot of sheep in the surrounding hills that need shearing every year," Isolde said.

A month later Seneca stopped his wagon loaded with bricks in front of a ramshackle shed in the middle of a goodly piece of land within sight of the rail line in Pendleton. Isolde with the loom and spinners wrapped in blankets and Katie with the boiler, stopped their own wagons behind him.

"Looks good," Katie called.

"And it's civilized!" Isolde smiled hugely as she eyed the wooden sidewalks above the packed earth of the street.

Katie wasn't so sure about the civilization part. But this land wouldn't support another Sasquatch clan.

"Three saloons," Seneca added. "I'm more than ready for a long pull of beer to wash trail dust from my mouth."

A train whistle screamed in the distance, at the same time a steam barge blasted the dock with three short, sharp wails. People on the pier shouted with enthusiasm.

"Ah, civilization," Isolde sighed. "At least we know the dangers here."

Gun shots shattered the window of the first saloon, from the inside. Two wrestling men tumbled out through the jagged glass remnants, trying to pummel each other to death. A gaudily dressed madame stayed behind, taking bets. A horse reared, nearly overturning another cargo wagon. Dogs barked. Women screamed. Dynamite exploded at the back of the bank, nearly deafening them. More shots were fired.

"Chaos," Seneca shook his head.

Home, Kormos whispered. *For me and my family. Home.*

The Murder of the Rag Doll Kid

David Boop

Arizona Territory
1890

The Rag Doll Kid stared at the rapidly cooling *body* on the floor. Pacing, he circled it; his curiosity piqued. He took in the face from different angles. No matter which way he cocked his head, he couldn't deny the fact the dead man looked exactly like him.

He bumped the toe of his boot against the man's blooded scalp. It was spongy under the dirt-water-color hair. He walked around to the front again, crouched and examined a hole just about an inch above the left eye. It still leaked a bit, looking no less like a scarlet worm crawling down a flesh-colored apple. The worm extended its reach across the dead man's nose and over his moss-like mustache to pool on the floorboards. It slunk through the gap between the planks and dripped the twelve or so inches to the Arizona dust.

"Yep. No doubt about it. That's me."

The Kid's voice sounded funny to his own ears, like he was talking in a cave. He guessed that's how ghosts were supposed to sound, anyway. Least, that's the way his pappy had made them sound, when he was young, as they sat around the fire and told stories about wolf spirits and ghost wagons. He shook his head, trying to accept the notion of being known as the Ghost of the Rag Doll Kid from now on.

Would he haunt this cabin forever? He shuddered at the

thought. Once the town folk found his rotting corpse, they'd most likely burn the place down. Then where would he be? Out near the trail into Drowned Horse, haunting that cactus people always peed on when the wagon train stopped? Wouldn't that be worse than being stuck here?

He took one more look at the body.

"God, hope I don't stink too bad when I'm found."

The image of his once friends and neighbors gathered outside the cabin, each battling to be the one to put the torch to the walls, leapt to mind. Maybe the preacher man would say a few words, using his Christian name.

"Lord, commit the body of our fallen brother, William Matthew Ragsdale, to your eternal embrace, or at least have pity on his wretched soul before Satan's foul minions drag it to the fiery pits of hell. Amen."

Children would dance around, singing that dang-blasted rhyme he tried not to hear in his sleep.

Women folk, say goodbye to yer men.
The Rag Doll Kid has come agin'
Oh, mama, keep your boy in tow.
The Rag Doll kid will kill him so.

The men would all head for the saloon to toast their good fortune. Few people liked to have their mistakes shoved in their face, yet those mistakes were painfully clear when they'd seen the rag doll hanging on Will's belt.

Will tried to leave "the Kid" stuff behind him. Heck, it'd been nearly twenty years. He didn't bother nobody. He stayed at home as much as possible, stepping outside occasionally to see what a red-dust-filled sky would do to the sunset. He was rarely disappointed in the view.

Why had someone chosen now to kill him? And who? He'd sent all the ones that'd have a grudge against him to their final judgment, or so he thought.

He checked the window. Had he heard the sound of shattered glass just before the flash of light that put him in this state? Will found a bullet hole there, as he expected. The mystery gunman had to have been waiting for him a long time out in that desert, hoping he'd get just the right angle; one without any chance of missing. The sharpshooter had to know that, if he missed, the Rag Doll Kid would see him dead.

The shooter was good. Will peered through the bullet hole, trying for a guess where he'd been shot from. There were a few spots a man could lay without chance of the sun gleaming off gunmetal. A gulley about three hundred yards out seemed about right. Had the killer set himself up at night and waited through the morning for Will to give him the perfect shot?

Weren't many men could do that. Will actually knew of only one still alive and, if it was him, why'd he chosen now when there'd been so many chances to kill "the Kid" in the past?

'Bout then, Will felt the beginnings of a draw against the back of his shirt. Instinctually, he knew this pull would rip his soul off the mortal Earth. He wanted answers and figured he didn't have all that much time to get them.

Despite his ghostlike state, Will was able to move things around with some effort. The door latch felt slippery as he grasped it and slid it clear. When he walked out into the midday sun, he could still hear his boots against the porch.

He cursed when he couldn't get close to his mare. He'd hoped to untie her and let the old girl carry him into town, but she spooked as he approached. Instead, Will walked out by the yellowed cactus and waited. It only took an hour before the daily stagecoach to town stirred up a dust cloud on the horizon. Like clockwork, it slowed as it approached. Will slid away from the spot that would soon be wet, not just for that reason, but to also be far enough away from the spookable horse team.

No one seemed to see him as he slid around to the back of the carriage. Will even waved in at the passengers, stuck his tongue out, and got no reaction. He climbing up onto the luggage rack and looked at his cabin one last time, knowing that eternity had someplace else waitin' for him.

The town of Drowned Horse was true to its name. A town that nobody ever planned a move to, but they ended up stuck there like a horse carcass in the Cottonwood wash after a big rain in Flagstaff. A passerby would think the whole town was just wood waiting to be burned.

For Will, it was both eerie and refreshing to walk through town and not have people look away from him.

Damn! Never realized that Martha Fenski had such pretty green eyes.

Will considered exploring Drowned Horse in a way he couldn't while alive, check in on the few people he still knew were around. He had no *real* friends left, his actions had seen to that, but it would be nice to look in on a few acquaintances.

Hell, maybe there are other ghosts like me down by the graveyard?

The pull on his shoulders, though, reminded him he had only so much time. Will headed for Nathaniel Chalker's smithy, where resided the only person with the skill and reasons to kill him.

The serrano-thin young man was in the back. Chalker had just put something under a tarp. Slick black hair leaked sweat down the back of his sunburnt red neck, like he'd been out in the morning sun awhile. The smith turned around abruptly, like he'd heard—or felt—someone in the shop.

Will stood still, waiting.

Nate surveyed the place with nervous eyes that took in every corner. He moved to the center of the room. Will took that opportunity to slowly walk to the tarp. He picked up the edge. Nate's special rifle lay beneath it. Once, the twentyish man had drunkenly bragged on killing a coyote with it from nigh on four hundred yards.

It had been just good fortune that had placed Will within earshot of that conversation. The Sagebrush's owner still slipped Will supplies out the back door at night when no one would notice him. He was the only man that never judged Will for his actions that day.

The day that earned him that damn nickname.

"Nate?" Will said, as he tested the sound of his voice, "What'd you do, Nate?"

The smith turned around wild-eyed, looking for the voice's owner.

"What? Who's there?"

"Why'd you kill the Rag Doll Kid, Nate?"

Nate dropped to the floor and crossed himself. He rattled off prayers in succession.

"Why'd you kill the Kid?!"

Nate wept now. He said between sobs, "What—what he'd done to all them folk. He—he deserved—to die."

"You know that's not right, Nate. If he was that bad, he would have killed you, like those he hunted down, just to cover his tracks, but he wouldn't harm a child, would he?"

"He killed—he killed—"

"He killed your pa. Yes, he did. But is that any worse than what your daddy done did to him? He and those friends of his let an outlaw kidnap two people, and they did nuthin'. Nothing!"

Nate slipped into a silent torment, guilt unmistakably furrowing his brow. But something didn't set right with the man Will used to be. Call it lawman instincts, but he thought there might've been more to Nate's actions. Someone had convinced the lad to settle accounts last night. The smithy was hotheaded, but not prone to making decisions on his own. Whatever the crowd wanted, Nate followed.

"Nate? Why now? You could have killed him a dozen times since then."

Nothing.

"Nate? Were you drinking last night?"

Nothing.

The former sheriff-*cum*-outlaw reached down and grabbed the scruff of Nate's shirt. It was filthy and sweat stained from the hours he'd spent in the desert lying in wait to kill the Kid. With extreme effort, Will pulled the smith to his feet. Terror rippled young Nate's face.

Nate hollered as invisible hands shook him. "WHAT ARE YOU?"

Nate's shop was far enough on the edge of town, no one could hear him though, and Will considered that another clue that destiny had plans for him.

"Tell me, Nate! Why now?!"

"Th-th-there was th-th-this man. C-c-came in last n-n-night."

"Who?!"

"Idon'tknow!Idon'tknow!Idon'tknow!"

"What did he say?"

"He k-kept buying me whiskey and t-talking about how much he h-hated the Kid and how c-cowardly it was th-that he'd k-killed my pa."

"Where is he?"

"He's st-still at the Sagebrush. He wanted me to c-come over once I'd done the job."

Will tossed his murderer down hard to the wood floor. The Rag Doll Kid spat invisible spit at the cowardly young man's feet. He purposely walked over to the tarp and uncovered the smithy's rifle, took it up, and turned to see the fear in the lad's eyes. To him, it'd appear as his rifle floating in midair aimed at his heart.

"I am a vengeful spirit, Nathaniel Chalker. The same one that claimed your daddy and his friends. Now, I claim you."

When Nate didn't move, the Kid spoke with the voice of the grave.

"Run."

Nate leapt from the ground and fled, but the Kid knew he wasn't too bright and would run straight down the center of Main Street.

Will placed the gun to his ghost shoulder, and let loose a breath that didn't have any air in it. He let Nate Chalker get into the center of town before he fired.

The rifle's trigger was hard to pull and the recoil launched the gun from his nonexistent hands, however, the bullet was true. The gun's echo rang through town.

Carried by the force of the impact, Nate propelled forward and slid across hard-packed earth to lie still.

The citizens of Drowned Horse ran to the fallen smith, splayed out there in the center of Main Street. At one woman's scream, more gawkers poured out from behind the Sagebrush's doors.

By the time Will got there, someone had rolled Nate over and held up his head as he tried to speak. Blood leaked from his mouth. The smithy coughed, spewing forth life juices. Will leaned over the shoulder of a lady in the crowd and locked eyes with Nate as he lay dying.

"Who done this to ya, Nate?" Clint Butcher asked.

"R-rag..." Another cough. "D-doll K-kiii..."

The last words were but a whisper, however, no one there seemed to doubt their sincerity. Angered, men shouted orders to search the town. Others jumped on horses and rode off toward William's cabin.

"Well, looks like they *will* find me before I stink too bad," the Kid's ghost said in a whisper.

One more stop, Will knew, and then his time'd be up.

The Sagebrush was the blackened heart of town. Will knew every face in Drowned Horse, truthfully these days more from profile, but enough to spot a stranger sitting at the bar. As more people funneled out onto the street, lowering the number of patrons inside, Will searched for the most out-of-place person there. He'd narrowed the list down to three when barkers outside announced to the whole town what Will knew already.

"Nate Chalker names the Rag Doll Kid as the one who done him in!"

One of the three prospective strangers, a man who seemed hauntingly familiar, squirmed uncomfortably at this news. His scalp was visible through his tumbleweed hair, and a long scar ran from his ear to a cleft chin. He stared into the two fingers of gin on the counter before him like a Chinese fortuneteller did to a pot of tea.

Maybe he was seeing his future there, Will wondered.

The man slammed the shot and headed up to one of the rooms on the second floor.

The Kid followed, careful to dodge johns and whores as they came down the stairs. His feet felt lighter against the steps, as if that beckoning force was pulling him up by his suspenders. It had grown stronger in the minutes since he'd shot the smith, but, undaunted, the Kid pressed forward. Visions came unbidden now, and he had to grab the rail for support. Scenes from his life flashed in front of him:

William, the child coming across the prairie with his folks.

William, the naive deputy studying under a great teacher, Sheriff Levi Forrest.

William, a young man in love.

The ghost got himself back to his feet and continued pursuit. Each image became harder to take.

Will, the new husband.

Will, the father.

A noise came from the Kid, half-laugh, half-sob, as the next wave subsided.

I thought your life flashed before your eyes at the moment before your death, not a couple hours later.

Will grieving over Forrest's grave.

And if that had not been nearly impossible to rewatch, the worst ones, the gut-wrenching, spasm-causing memories, nearly toppled William over the balcony.

Why? he called to God. *Why make me see that again?* If he could weep, he would have, witnessing his greatest failure. Seeing *them* die, over and over again.

When he'd reached the second-floor landing, what remained of William Matthew Ragsdale had been burned away, and only the Rag Doll Kid remained.

The Kid leaned warily against the open door to the room his prey had entered. The pudgy man had his back to him. He was gathering up articles of clothing, tossing them haphazardly into a bag. The man who'd instigated the Kid's death turned slightly, and his face was reflected in a vanity mirror.

A final vision came, yet caused no pain, just bringing with it a sense of understanding. The Kid poised at the edge of a ravine. A murderer, a madman, with his hand on a holster. Words spoken that ultimately meant nothing now. A movement. A drawing of guns. Flashes of light and blood and a scream as the villain went over the side and down some three hundred feet into the raging waters of a spring-flooded Oak Creek.

No one could have survived that. No one sane. No one human.

"Hello, James."

James Kettle caught an image of his stalker in the mirror, but couldn't find him when he spun and drew. The motion impressed the Kid, that this jiggly man had drawn so quickly from his hip.

"Where are you, Kid? We got us some things to settle."

The former sheriff stepped inside the room and quietly walked past Kettle. He spoke from the other side of the room.

"Oh, I agree. Just not in the way you're thinking."

Again, James spun with a speed that belied his age and shape.

"Not bad, James. Looks like you've managed to keep that arm in shape despite the rest of you going to seed."

James guffawed. "Nineteen years, Kid! Had a lot of time for practice. Never could get the draw on you before, could I?"

The Kid moved to a new spot.

"Nope, just bank guards, drunken gamblers, mostly. Though, you used your gang to kill my friend, Sheriff Levi." He kept stepping around Kettle. "But it was black magic from the depths of hell that took those I loved most, wasn't it? I really shouldn't be surprised you're still alive, with your voodoo dealin's."

"Stop with the tricks, Kid," James demanded, sweat leaking from his pate. He targeted the new place the Kid's voice came from. "I'm guessing the smith gave me up. He was so sure he could kill you. Hard to believe he missed."

"Oh, but James..."

The Kid stepped up to within an inch of James's face. Despite his spirit state, he could smell the whiskey on the breath of his former archenemy.

"He didn't."

The Rag Doll Kid pushed Kettle hard, forcing the outlaw to fall backward onto the bed. Kettle rolled over it and landed on the opposite side, in front of the window. Fear and alarm stood arm and arm with Kettle as he tried to find something to shoot.

"Jimmy Kettle, leader of the Claw Rock Gang, wanted for the rape and murder of Sarah Ragsdale, wife of William Ragsdale, and the murder of Trina Ragsdale, daughter of William Ragsdale. I am a vengeful spirit. I failed to kill you once.

"Now I claim my due."

The Kid picked up the chamber pot from the floor and threw it with all the strength he had available. It flew across the distance and hit Kettle square in the head. The outlaw stumbled backward and through the window. The Kid heard his recognizable cry, the same cry as when he'd gone into the creek twenty years ago, cut short.

When the Kid peered out the shattered remains of the window, he saw the broken body of James Kettle lying prone over a hitching post. Kettle twitched for a moment or two, then died.

The spiritual pull felt like a tornado as the Kid descended the stairs and exited the saloon. He wanted to look on Kettle's body closely, to make sure he'd done his work right this time, but the crowd had grown even thicker since Nate's death.

The sound of horses at full gallop brought everyone's attention around. The men who had ridden off to William's cabin had returned with his body slung over the back of his horse. It wasn't making any sense to anyone.

"The body was cold and stiff," said the town doctor. "He's been dead awhile, maybe late last night or early this morning."

"But then that woulda been before the smithy," said Clint.

Gasps and prayers echoed, as realization struck them.

"If not the Rag Doll Kid, then who?"

An older man called out, "That's Jimmy Kettle, the guy that Sheriff Rags—I mean, the Rag Doll Kid swore he'd killed. Maybe, it was actually Kettle cleaning up some loose ends. Maybe all this was some sorta payback?"

There were murmurs of agreement, and everyone seemed satisfied. They'd write off Kettle's death as an accident, a cosmic justice to an evil soul. Nobody wanted to think too hard on it.

"The Rag Doll Kid is dead, and Jimmy Kettle now is officially dead. The people of Drowned Horse can breathe easy again," pronounced the preacher, who'd come up to give last rites to both.

Hearing his name spoken aloud, the Kid looked to a spot on his belt for the first time since his death.

It wasn't there.

He made his way around to the horse carrying his own dead body, and saw the small stuffed toy on his hip. It'd been his good luck charm since the day he pried it from Trina's cold hands. He'd worn it as he hunted down the gang of outlaws that had kidnapped and killed her and his wife, Sarah. And after the Kid had dispatched them, he continued to wear it as he hunted down and showed no mercy to the dozen men and women who had stood aside that fateful night and let Jimmy Kettle do his devil's work on his family.

The Kid gingerly spirited the doll away from the corpse without anyone's notice and held it to his chest.

The pull was inescapable now.

He let it lift him up.

He passed the rooftops in an instant.

Clouds surrounded him, and he left his burdens there. The release was welcome after so many years of torment, of guilt, of feeling like a failure. He should've stopped Kettle right away before he could murder the ones he loved. The Kid had wanted to kill himself after he'd finished his vigilante crusade, but, for some reason, he'd held on. As the stars guided him, he understood he'd been kept on Earth to dispense one last piece of justice.

Now, the scales were balanced.

As William Ragsdale crossed over eternity, he saw delicate, tiny hands reaching out toward him. He handed them the rag doll and accepted a hug from his wife in exchange.

Hell-Bent

Tex Thompson

In travel, as in life, the first virtue was self-control.

Presently, Holly could not control the blood spattered on his collar, nor the mud slopped over his trousers, nor the crack in his spectacles.

But he could very well fold his sack coat crisply over one arm, keeping a jaunty grip on his carpetbag with the other, and smile as he approached the rustic fellow leading a mule along the rain-swollen road.

"Pleasant morning, sir," Holly said, and would have tipped his hat, had he retained its possession.

The rustic touched his battered straw brim in reply, and stared in open-mouthed amazement at the view beyond Holly's shoulder.

Holly turned to stare with him. The mud-mired wreck was a good quarter mile behind him now, the stagecoach's skyward-facing wheels having long since ceased to spin. "Oh, don't be alarmed," Holly said. "The reinsman and the shotgunner were both thrown clear, and my fellow passengers have enjoyed the grace of God and steel-ribbed corsetry. You see how they've set to drying their skirts on firmer ground, there. We're all just cuts and bruises, nothing worse."

A gunshot split the humid morning air.

"Well, perhaps not the horses." Holly turned back to the rustic, whose expression had deepened its resemblance to a shriveled apple. "It's not far to town, is it?"

Holly could not recall the name—something picturesque like Hobnail or Boot-Hump or Stye—and perhaps the rustic had the same difficulty, as it was a considerable time before he replied.

"...no, not hardly; Hockit ain't but two miles up the road." He crafted a helpful compass of his thumb.

"Splendid," Holly said, as the sun was already making a white-linen swamp of his back and underarms. "Do you know whether they might have a doctor in residence?"

"Oh, sure," the rustic said to the drying blood in Holly's hair. "Doc Fitch's place is cat-a-cornered from the hotel, can't miss it. Just watch out for his boy Lan-Yap. He's one of them hellbenders from the bayou, and you know what-like *they* are."

Holly didn't actually, but that was fine: This was surely rural racialism at its finest, a delicacy as authentic as any that had ever been plated and sold to a world-hungry expeditioner.

He smiled. "Fantastic," he said. "I certainly will. And while we're exchanging confidence, you'll do very well by Miss Hinch-cliff back there if your mule can spare his blanket. We pulled her out by the window, and I'm afraid her crinoline is a lost cause."

His debt thus repaid, Holly took his leave and went on, boots squelching, carpetbag's contents clinking merrily. Here was the true art of the traveler: One had only to retain mastery of one's own person—and hand luggage, where possible—in order to enjoy all the education and entertainment that Nature reserved for the portable man.

And that was before profit even figured into it.

Holly introduced himself to the town's main thoroughfare according to the rustic's instructions: past a livery and the butcher's, deftly avoiding horse piles, mud puddles, and the pious shadow of the church, until the gay green-and-white front of the Hockit Hotel directed him across the intersection. There, on the promenade, waited a shop advertised only by a pair of stoppered glass bottles in the window.

Holly folded and pocketed his cracked spectacles, tugged down the tips of his wine-colored waistcoat, and applied his knuckles with utmost gentility to the door.

"Come in, please!"

Holly was greeted first by the uncommonly pleasant voice, and then, upon admitting himself to the office's dim interior, by a strikingly disagreeable smell.

As his eyes adjusted, Holly had little difficulty in spotting his target: The good doctor and his apprentice were bent over opposite sides of a table near the window, their mutual concern blocked from view by an apothecary's counter.

The apprentice—a small, dark, native fellow—remained fixed on his object, but the doctor straightened. He had a pleasant young face, a gangly frame, and a white surgical smock absolutely saturated with blood.

Holly blanched. "Ah, Dr. . . . Fitch, is it? I'm terribly sorry; I see I've interrupted you. Is there a better time when I might—"

A snort from the apprentice cut him off. "It's no trouble; she's not going to get any deader."

Stricken with horror and a surge of postmortem chivalry, Holly took two further steps into the room . . .

. . . and discovered that the "patient" on the table was a weanling pig, tied down and divested of its innards.

How vulgar.

"That's tremendously gracious of you," Holly said, his voice frosting over, "but I was rather more concerned about the doctor's time. Please, sir," he said, "let me make an appointment, and no further inconvenience."

Dr. Fitch seemed momentarily taken aback, either by the sharpness of Holly's tone or the deplorable state of his trousers. After a moment's silence, the apprentice glanced up from his grim project. "Well, Doctor?"

That seemed to shake the tall blond master surgeon out of his daze: He blinked, and then beamed. "Not at all, not at all," he said to Holly, waving away a particularly enterprising fly. "Please, have a seat at my desk; I'll wash up and be right with you. I could do with a fresh face—God knows I've been looking at this one long enough!"

Holly couldn't have said whether the good doctor was speaking of the apprentice or the pig. Nor could he afford to waste an invitation, no matter what its odor. "Thank you kindly," he said. "I'd be much obliged." He ducked to avoid the hanging nets of dried herbs, his boots stifling their imposition on the dusty floorboards until he had seated himself in the lesser of the desk's two straight-backed satellites.

He shouldn't have let that crude fellow lance his temper like that. Rudeness never profited anyone, and worthy gentlemen did not go about taking a coarse tone with other men's menials.

Even if said menial was a "hellbender" . . . whatever that was.

Well, Holly would make amends for it presently. In the mean-time, he pulled out his abused spectacles to study the framed diploma on the wall. It was difficult to read all the flourishes of penmanship in this light, but the essentials—

Board of Medical Examination and Registration, Province Lebeque—This Certifies—A Graduate in Surgery and Medical Jurisprudence—

—were unambiguously concluded with the name T. B. FITCH, the signature of three presiding scholars, and a date not even two years past.

Perfect.

"A little self-important, isn't it?"

Holly glanced over at the doctor, who was already busying himself at the washbasin.

"Not at all! The University of Eau Doux has a sterling reputa-tion even by northern standards," Holly replied. Though it did explain where he'd picked up his swamp-dwelling apprentice. "I'm a Dutton man, myself."

Because one could legitimately claim to be a "Dutton man" even if he'd only studied there a week, and Holly had persisted all of ten.

Dr. Fitch was duly impressed. "Dutton? Ah, now I have to ask: What terrible business brought you here, Doctor...?"

"Holly," he said, drinking in this magnificent misconception like a tonic for his distressed sensibilities. "Frank Holly. And I'm no doctor—I leave that to my partner, Wilberforce Digby. Do you know his work?"

A rural sawbones like Fitch almost certainly wouldn't, but Holly was happy to imply otherwise. Courtesy always spent.

"Digby... Digby... is he that clever optician with the iris spatula? No?" Receiving nothing but an insouciant shrug from his apprentice, the doctor apologized to Holly with a shake of his head. "May, you'll have to acquaint me—just as soon as we patch you up."

"Oh, not at all," Holly demurred. "There's no need; it's only a—"

"My foot!" the doctor said, drying his hands on the inside of his gore-spattered smock and then reaching for the appropriate liniments. "Can't have all that Dutton education leaking out of your skull; goodness knows you spent enough stuffing it all in there. Sit and be agreeable, Mr. Holly; we'll just clean the cuts and see what's what."

Holly would have felt considerably more agreeable if the doctor would consent to take off that dire apron first...but if there were an inoffensive way to word that particular proposition, the coach wreck had rattled it out of him. "I'd...of course, thank you...and...that is..."

"Now then!" The shadow that fell over Holly's seated frame announced itself with a collegial clap on the shoulder. "Tell me what kind of mess this was."

"Oh, nothing very spectacular," Holly said, his tone endeavoring to soothe his own stomach. "Those storms last night turned the roads to rivers of mud, of course, and everything's pleasantries and polite conversation until someone spots a half-drowned tree fallen across the path, and someone else veers a little too sharply to avoid it, and before you can work out what pleasant impropriety has brought your face to union with Mrs. Mayweather's lap, there's an unholy amount of screaming and sideways-going, and a sharp suspicion that your skull has gotten off to quite a bad start with the corner of the window frame."

From behind him, the doctor snorted. "Go to bed! And you don't consider that spectacular? I hate to think what—"

At that moment, he leaned forward to dip his cloth in the washbowl at the corner of the desk, and the smell of offal enveloped Holly so completely that he spoke in immediate preference to vomiting. "Oh, you see a hundred times worse every day, I'm sure! Mud-caked tourists aside, what tends to ail the good people of Hockit?"

"Complaints?" Undeterred by the interruption, the lanky blond gentleman daubed with professional care at the gash on Holly's scalp. "Oh, nothing special—whooping cough in the winter, malaria in the summer, and worms regardless."

For his part, Holly kept his gaze fixed on the clean, still water in the bowl, and breathed through his mouth only. The sooner he closed the deal, the sooner he could quit this cheerful butchery. "Of course," he said. "Is it very difficult to get bog yams here? I hear they're quite good for sinkworms."

The rhythmic twinges in his scalp paused as Dr. Fitch leaned forward again to refresh the cloth. "Oh, for the larvae, yes—a little purple paste on the foot sores and you can tweeze them right out. But that's no help once they've rented a room in your innards, is it? The potato will kill you before the worm ever gets wind of it. Nasty things. They'll clog up your bowels faster than you can—"

"I'd heard just the same," Holly quickly agreed, struggling to stifle his nausea with a tried-and-true sales pitch, "and that's why I was so surprised when Dr. Digby said he'd found a way around all that. You see, he spent a considerable time among the mereaux down south, and—"

"Oh, the fishmen!" Fitch interrupted, and in a tone of the most childlike glee. "Fascinating folks, aren't they? We got to treat one just this spring...what was his name? Boudin? Bonbon?"

"Bouillon," the apprentice said.

"That's the one! Oh, I wish you'd met him, Mr. Holly. Even your worldly Dr. Digby would have stunned to see him. We talked for better than twenty minutes, as close as the two of us here, and as I live, it wasn't until he opened his mouth for the tooth extraction that I figured him for anything but a perfectly human being. May, this could do with a few stitches."

Adrift in a blizzard of irrelevance, Holly all but tripped over that last sentence.

Certainly not. He'd sew it himself before he let this unfathomable taxidermist pick up a needle in his presence. "Oh—I don't know about that; I'm very quick to heal."

"Are you sure? It's very quick, and I can numb it with—"

"I wouldn't be so much in your debt!" Holly sputtered, starting up to his feet.

Fitch's hand on his shoulder was firm. "Then let's at least have some iodine." Was that disappointment in his voice?

"Thank you kindly," Holly said. He yielded his posterior back to the chair, and struggled to right the conversation. "Anyway, I imagine you must have seen them with fair regularity during your time at school. As I was saying, the mereaux—"

"Oh, now don't take on like that," Fitch admonished him. His paintbrush announced itself like a feather drawn across an open sore. "Nobody on this side of the border will understand you. Call them fishmen if you like, but they've got a far more familiar name around here. Now then, Mr. Holly, to business: Do you have any headache?"

"No," Holly lied. If he hadn't had one when he walked in, he certainly did now.

"Are you sure? No pain at all?" He pressed his cupped hands with relentless inquisition over and around Holly's skull.

Unable to suppress a flinch, Holly struggled to excuse it. "Oh—only a bit, just there."

Far from disapproving, the doctor's voice was positively gleeful. "That's what I thought! Dizziness, disorientation, nausea?" he asked hopefully.

"No!" Holly said, this time with the conviction of an inmate before the parole board. "Nothing of the sort."

"Hmmm." There was a longer pause, time enough for Holly to engender some wild hope of being allowed up from the chair. He desperately needed fresh air.

Fitch stepped around to the front. Holly held his breath. Without his glasses, he could nearly pretend that that was red paint. "Well, let's just try your eyes. Watch, please."

The doctor held up the brush he'd used to paint the cuts. Holly tracked it as the doctor moved it up and down, to the left and right.

From the edge of Holly's periphery, the apprentice pulled something out of the carcass. Holly stared, transfixed, as the apprentice held up a length of intestine, and used his forceps to draw out something long and wet and heavy, like noodles, like shoestrings, like—

"Mr. Holly?"

Holly lunged forward, shoving the doctor violently aside, and had just time to plant his hands on the desk before he was retching into the bowl.

Fitch said something, but Holly heard nothing but the sound of his own disgrace until he'd relieved himself of his stomach contents . . . and his dignity. It didn't take long.

When he finally straightened, the doctor regarded him with his arms folded, one hand cupped sideways under his chin, and an expression somewhere between vindication and disappointment. "You know, Mr. Holly, I'm beginning to think you haven't been honest with me."

Holly finished wiping his face with the cleaner part of the washrag, and tossed it to the desk. It landed with a wet *splotch.* "Honest?" he repeated, incredulous. "Of course I haven't been honest! Any honest caller would have dropped over at the first whiff of this place! What do you do for a confinement? Drape yourself with the sheets from her childbed? Does she give him the afterbirth to play with? And for God's sake, what *is* that?"

From the distant receiving end of Holly's out-flung hand, the apprentice looked up. "A word of advice, sir," he said as he toweled off his intestinal treasure and held it up for his own inspection. The window's dirty afternoon light profoundly deepened the object's resemblance to a necklace—a locket, in fact, on a length of fine chain. "If you ever suffer a broken engagement, resist the urge to do anything terribly literal with your love tokens."

The apprentice glanced at the disemboweled pig on the table, and then over at the doctor. "I think we'll want the carbolic acid before we return this to Miss Miller."

A small, feebly protesting part of Holly's mind wanted his attention. But it had been a hot and tiring walk, his headache was ripening fast, and if he'd just time enough to sit and properly *think* for a minute . . .

"What's that?" Dr. Fitch indicated the vial that Holly had drawn from his pocket.

Holly glanced down at the impressively purple fluid. It was Digby's dubiously dyed wonder-water, and the only remedy he had for the burning in his throat and the bile aftertaste in his mouth. "This?" Having definitively ruined any chance of a sale, Holly suffered no impediment to honesty. "This is what I was coming to sell you." He uncorked the vial and drank it in half a swig, the licorice flavor for once very welcome.

From this calmer remove, Holly began to regret his outburst. Who was he to present himself unannounced and then complain that the premises weren't up to standard? He ought to pay the doctor for his time and care, and to volunteer it before he was asked. What would be considered generous here, assuming one didn't intend to settle in livestock?

"Really?" In spite of everything, Fitch's long face creased in curiosity. "What does it do?"

Whatever you want, Holly thought. But if there was to be any hope of keeping his job after this appalling incident, he'd have to do better. "Oh . . . a great number of things," he said. "As we were discussing earlier, the—er, the fishmen have long cultivated bog yams for a number of medicinal purposes. Dr. Digby's breakthrough was in developing a distillation method that leaches the healthful mineral essence from the root, leaving the toxins behind, so that we can be relieved of a whole host of parasites, dyspepsias, digestive complaints... it's not half bad for a nervous stomach either." This, with a chagrined hand on the area in question.

Actually, Digby's real breakthrough was in packing up the medicine show and employing people like Holly to pitch his panaceas directly to rural doctors. Then there was no risk of getting pinched for selling alcohol and laudanum to natives, harlots, mereaux, or other "morally wanting" clientele. One had only to confirm the doctor's license, and let him accept all liability for his prescriptions.

A good strategy, provided the salesman didn't outrage every notion of decorum in the process.

But *this* doctor had something of the outrageous in him too. He stared at Holly's bag, his young face drawn in scrutiny. "So... you were coming to Hockit just to sell me this medicine? And when your coach turned over, you carried it here and presented yourself, just the same?"

It sounded even more crass and manipulative now than it had then. Holly draped the washrag discreetly over the bowl beside him. "Well... yes, essentially."

The doctor clapped his hands like a gunshot. "Splendid!" he declared. "How much do you have?"

Holly was beginning to feel that disorientation now. "Er... a dozen quart bottles in hand, and substance for four dozen more, if you're not averse to preparing it in-house...?"

"Of course not!" Fitch cast an emphatic, upturned hand at Holly's empty vial. "This is a drug worth suffering for! This is what a man drinks when he's been reduced to honesty! *This* is what we need here!" He left off gesticulating at the window and glanced back at Holly. "Unless it's very expensive?"

It was ten dollars a bottle. And this time, Holly knew exactly what to say. "Oh, not at all. Ordinarily it's twelve-fifty a bottle, but I'm so extraordinarily in your debt—would you accept ten dollars even?"

He would—Holly could see it already—and opened his mouth to say as much.

"If I may..." the apprentice interrupted. He'd put down the necklace and wiped his hands, and now ventured out from behind the gruesome table.

Holly had no grounds for objection as Fitch bent to oblige his assistant's whisper.

There was something wrong with the apprentice, Holly decided. Not his race: Heaven knew he couldn't help his rusty skin or sooty hair or slight frame, nor any of the poor stature they conferred on him. Maybe it was his voice, and its peculiar hint of an accent. Or that faint, irritating asymmetry in his shoulders, like a picture hung five degrees off-center.

Regardless, the only certainty was that the apprentice meant to get even for Holly's rude tone earlier—perhaps by talking his master out of the deal.

Well, let him try. Between the expensively constipated pig and the aborted suturing of his own skull, Holly was beginning to get the idea that this Dr. Fitch was a fellow who liked getting his hands dirty.

By the time the good doctor straightened again, Holly was as prepared as a duelist with first choice of the pistols.

"Ah. Please pardon us, Mr. Holly." A blonde curl flopped over Fitch's ear as he graced Holly with an apologetic smile. "We—I was just wondering, before we put pen to paper, what evidence you have for your miraculous medicine. You know, so that I can recommend it with authority."

In other words, *prove it.* Holly returned the smile, and feigned surprise. "Oh! Well, the active ingredient is patented, so I'm not at liberty to disclose its exact composition, but let me think..." And then, as if struck by a fresh and exciting idea, Holly held up a placating finger and turned to fetch his bag from the desk's foot. "Ah, yes, you see—I've still got a few things that haven't smashed themselves to bits. Would you help me rig up a demonstration?"

"Oh, by all means!" the doctor said. "What do you have? What do you need?"

It required no more than five minutes' preparation. Holly produced the sachet of Digby's patented powder, poured it into his freshly emptied vial, and topped it with ethanol of the doctor's generous provision. Then he stoppered and shook it to clarity as the doctor cut up a bog yam—because as it happened, he had one readily at hand—and dropped the chunks into a clean glass jar.

"Splendid," Holly said. "And now it only needs a bit of chloroform—let me see if I've still got mine..." He rummaged around in the bag, careful not to reveal his own bottled ethanol and withered bog yam. It always worked better when customers thought you did it on the spur of the moment, improvised and especially for them.

"Oh, don't worry about it. Here, how much?"

"A scant tablespoon, poured over the top," Holly said helpfully. "There, and now we just close and shake it, like so—we always want to coat all the root's surface, you see." He handed the vial of clear liquid to the doctor, and indicated the bottle. "Will you do the final honors?"

Fitch was only too glad to oblige: Like a schoolboy at his first experiment with vinegar and saleratus, he poured the one into the other and watched eagerly for a reaction.

The apprentice watched Holly all the while.

"Look!" the doctor cried, jabbing his menial freely at the arm. "Look! Do you see that? Now what do you have to say?"

There in the jar, as timely and reliable as the sunrise, violet tendrils began to seep from the purple flesh of the yam, curling and clouding their chemical bath.

"Lovely, isn't it?" Holly was mindful to keep his face straight and his gaze averted from his foiled nemesis. *What do you think of that, you tedious drudge?*

"It's marvelous!" Fitch agreed. "And is this the final product?"

Holly tipped his head modestly from side to side. "It's the essence of it. You're welcome to keep this batch, if you like: Just strain it tomorrow, then top it up with perhaps a pint of water and something for taste, at your discretion. We generally suggest a tablespoon for adults, a teaspoon for children under twelve, and five drops for infants."

This was the point at which the diligent salesman would ask for the sale, but Holly had no need: He had his success in the declarative slap of the doctor's palms on the desk. "I'll take it all! How do you want the money? And when can I have delivery?"

By then, the blood and flies and ambient pigs-bowel smell had entirely ceased to matter. The cheap narcotics blossoming in his stomach lent an edge to Holly's giddy enthusiasm as he retrieved his battered sales book and spread his papers on the desk. "Well, I have every confidence in the Gideon-Wright Overland Freight Company, but I expect it will be some hours before my inventory catches up with me, and I understand you still have an appointment to keep. Could I call on you tomorrow morning?"

Fitch pushed pen and ink forward for the bill, his gaze fixed on the serenely bleeding yam all the while. "Oh, I think that would be fine...around nine or so? I can have cash for you then."

Holly could hardly believe his great turn of luck—and without a word about installments or interest! He hurried to put the figures to paper. "Smashing! I just need you to sign the transfer of liability—opiates, you understand—and have a second glance at the bill. I've included four dozen of the packets at two dollars each, but I can get you bog yams if you need them, and...oh, pardon my asking: What does 'T.B.' stand for?"

"Tuberculosis."

Still doubling twelves and carrying twos, Holly dropped his mental digits and looked up.

"Consumption, you know," the doctor added absently, his fair brow furrowing as he read through the liability form.

Holly opened his mouth to clarify what he'd meant, and then looked back down at the bill. He filled in the last of the zeroes on *216.00*—which was to say, over *twenty-one dollars'* cash commission, immediately payable to one Dagobert Francis Hollingberry Junior—and prudently forgot bookkeeping protocol as he wrote *T. B. FITCH* in neat letters at the top of the page.

"Ah...thanks very much," Holly said, and returned the pen. The doctor signed with the grand, flourishing scrawl for which his profession was known, and offered his handshake in preference to sealing wax.

Holly had no trouble matching Fitch's glad demeanor, but as soon as he reclaimed his hand and the requisite paperwork, he excused himself with blistering alacrity. By his own wits, he'd survived the doctor and the apprentice both, and escaped their ghastly premises with the year's most lucrative and ludicrously improbable sale.

Evening found Holly well ensconced at the Hockit Hotel, and very kindly inclined toward the porter who arrived with the crate. On prising it open and, finding its straw-packed contents unmolested, Holly busied himself for the next hour with a bottle of glue and a stack of labels. He set aside the clothespinned sets of *Digby's Scrofula Tonic, Digby's Female Remedy,* and *Digby's Neuro-Sanative Elixir,* and christened each naked bottle as *Digby's Digestive Specific.*

☆   ☆   ☆

A knock at the door woke him the next morning. Sluggish and wretched, with a strident headache, Holly pinched his eyes and struggled to recollect himself. Wreck. Rustics. Doctor, blood, nausea, tuberculosis—oh, God! The deal!

Holly sat up at once, the sunlight seeping through the thin muslin curtains suddenly a dire portent. How late had he slept?

The knock came again, soft, perfectly reluctant to impose. "Yes, what is it?" Holly called, his voice still rough from sleep.

The door opened to admit the apprentice. He was cleanly dressed today, plain linen shirt and spotless charcoal vest positively hanging from his spare frame.

But whatever he'd come about would have to defer to Holly's guilty panic. "Oh, I'm terribly sorry... I'm late, aren't I? I can't apologize enough... I'm never a late sleeper, really... but I'll be there just directly with the product, and..." A horrible thought struck him, one too grim to speak directly. "...that is, if it's still all right?"

The apprentice's dark-eyed gaze lingered on him, taking in Holly's bare chest and thoroughly unimpressive physique. "That's fine," he said. He glanced over at the crate near the door. "Shall I take this for you?"

There was the first sensible notion of the day. "That would be grand, thank you. Please let the doctor know I'll be right along." Holly did not bestir his naked frame from the bedclothes as the apprentice lifted the crate onto his mismatched shoulders and excused himself.

Then the door closed. Holly positively hurled himself out of bed, assaulting himself with clothes as fast and fiercely as if he were mopping up a human spill.

He was halfway through his buttons when he realized what he'd just done.

Article 6, Section 7: Be it further enacted that any person vending, distributing, or otherwise furnishing opium or spirituous liquors to any indigenous or non-human person, shall forfeit a sum not exceeding two hundred dollars, or be imprisoned not exceeding six months.

Holly swore aloud. Surely not. *Surely* not. The apprentice had either just robbed Holly blind—or else was plotting to get him arrested.

No, not at all, he told himself as he jammed his feet in his shoes and fairly bolted from the room. The apprentice merely acted on behalf of the doctor, who was a licensed physician and the buyer of record. Holly swore again and about-faced to retrieve the bag containing his sales book and papers. No right-thinking person could suppose otherwise.

Outside, the few people out on the streets might have marveled at the sight of a sloppily dressed dandy stuffing in his shirttails as he ran across the road, but Holly saw only his memory of the apprentice's baleful stare.

Someone had left the door open. Holly all but threw himself over the threshold, already knowing he wouldn't find the apprentice there.

Fitch sat at his desk, swirling the thoroughly purpled contents of the demonstration jar. Across from him, in the chair Holly had so reluctantly occupied, a portly gentleman of perhaps fifty looked up at Holly's uncouth arrival.

"Terribly sorry…please excuse me," Holly said breathlessly. "By any chance, have you seen…" Damn it, what was the fellow's name? An-Lap? Yan-Ap?

True to form, the doctor interrupted. "Oh, Mr. Holly! Good morning! How did you sleep? Do you still have that headache? You thought I'd forgotten, didn't you?"

Bloody hell. There was no telling how far or fast the little bastard had absconded, and—

A wooden creak sounded to his left. There in the corner, at yesterday's dissection table, the apprentice pried another nail from the crate.

Holly's stomach sagged at the sight.

Of course there was nothing wrong here. He'd been fool to think otherwise. Holly drew a deep, calming breath, squashing the urge to laugh at his own paranoia.

"Frank Holly?"

The portly gentleman stood up. He cut a respectable figure with his chalk-striped coat and trimmed silver beard, and would not have been out of place even on a northern city street.

Holly stepped further inside, wishing he had a hat to remove. This was probably an officer of the bank, here to oversee the transaction. "At your service, sir. To whom do I owe the pleasure?"

The gentleman's tone promised no pleasure at all. "Magistrate Linas Comstock. I'm here to arrest you for violation of the Commercial Intercourse Act."

Holly's nerves hit the floor and shattered.

"On what evidence?" he demanded. "I've entered into a lawful transaction with a licensed medical professional, and I've got papers to prove it. I gave the product to this man as a good-faith representative of the doctor, and you can see he's conveyed it here intact, so what possible cause do you have to imply otherwise?"

The magistrate didn't seem so much moved by Holly's impassioned defense as wearied by the sound of his voice. He pinched the bridge of his nose. "Doc, shut the door."

Fitch paused in fishing pieces of bog yam from the demonstration jar, but it was the apprentice who moved to oblige.

The apprentice's name had two syllables—Holly remembered that much—but neither had sounded like *Doc*.

An awful, creeping suspicion wormed through his gut.

Holly spoke slowly and clearly, not trusting his reason, and pointed at the apprentice. "Do you mean to tell me that *he's* your doctor?"

The magistrate arched an eyebrow at Holly's rudely outpointed finger, and matched it with a thumb jerked back toward the man at the desk. "You mean to tell *me* that you thought this harebrained hellbender was anything like it?"

From the receiving end of the magistrate's gesture, the lanky blond fellow—the "doctor"—had just popped a piece of bog yam into his mouth. He stopped chewing and flashed Holly a guilty, sharp-toothed smile.

Mereau. By the Sibyl's swollen teats, they'd duped Holly into selling to a God-damned fishman.

And he wasn't about to stand for it. "I did, because he presented himself as exactly that, which means he's committed criminal impersonation in the first degree."

The mereau looked guiltier still, wilting faintly under his golden wig. "Please, Madge, I didn't mean it that way. He was just so sure I was the doctor, and we didn't want to embarrass him—"

The magistrate held up a hand for silence, his steely gaze evened with Holly's all the while. "You got any evidence for that?"

"Certainly," Holly said. If these backcountry jakes thought they'd get him on the paperwork, they deserved every bit of their dim reputation. "He forged the doctor's signature." He found the folded paper by touch, and handed it over.

The magistrate unfolded the transfer of liability. He snorted.

"Boy, if you're too dumb to read, you are sure as hell too dumb to be selling medicine."

"What?" Holly snatched the page back and took his first proper look at the elegantly scrawled name.

Lagniappe

Holly's gaze drifted back to the small, dark, slightly bent fellow in the corner, the page wilting in his hands.

Then it crumpled in his fist. "And since when do you let 'indigenous persons' work as doctors?" he demanded, his voice channeling the unspoken slur.

The magistrate's face reddened. "Since right after they started graduating from doctor school!"

The indigenous person in question said nothing, but Holly was aware in his dimmest extremity of a slight up-tilt in the native fellow's fine-boned chin, a promissory glint in his dark eyes.

Article 6, Section 8: Be it further enacted that Article 6, Section 7, may be suspended in individual cases by order of federally-recognized military authority, or recommendation of any provincially licensed medical board.

Holly could not read the diploma's three signatures from this distance . . . but then, he hardly needed to. He had sold opiates to a mereau—a fishman, a "hellbender," whatever they called those false-faced egg-suckers out here—and now the doctor, this licensed and practicing indigenous God-damned person, was going to have him strung up to dry.

The magistrate advanced on him, his country twang flattening to pass formal sentence. "I find you guilty of violating the Commercial Intercourse Act, and fine you two hundred dollars for the offense." He pulled a pair of handcuffs from his pocket. "And you don't look worth more'n twenty."

Holly backed up and ran a hand through his hair, his outrage melting into desperation. "No—I mean, just wait a minute, can you? Look there, you see, I've got valuable medicine and a bill showing its agreed value at $216, and since I haven't received payment yet, it's still my property. That's far more valuable than a man in a cell, isn't it?" And then Holly could mark the product lost in the accident, and let Digby go barking at the Gideon-Wright Overland Freight Company for compensation, and then—

The magistrate turned to the appr—to Dr. Tuberculosis Fitch, Hockit's diminutive and highly irregular physician of record, who had since finished prising the top from the crate. "What do you reckon, Doc? Two hundred plus?"

The doctor hefted out one of the bottles, uncorked it, and took a whiff. "Unlikely. It seems to rely on chloroform and alcohol to react with an aniline dye. An entertaining presentation, but I wouldn't drink it."

The magistrate looked back at Holly, his anger now sanded down into smooth malice. "Well, partner, it looks like you picked the wrong place to peddle your juice. Got any other entertainments for us?"

Why, certainly: If they thought the bog yam demonstration was diverting, they'd be positively thrilled when Holly made a break for the door.

"If I may, sir..." Dr. Fitch's slender brown fingers picked idly at a loose corner of the bottle's label. "This Mr. Holly came to us yesterday bleeding from a head wound. My apprentice and I observed headache, nausea, vomiting, and emotional excess, to which I might today add some irregularity of sleep. It's my opinion that he's suffered a concussive brain injury. If that's so, he can't be held legally liable for his actions while his judgment is so afflicted."

Holly stared at him, struggling to grasp the idea. Did this mean he was off the hook?

The magistrate folded his arms, his tone verging on annoyance. "What're you saying, Doc?"

Fitch put down the bottle. "A concussion persists for days or weeks, sir...you remember what Asa Burroughs was like after that horse kicked him. It would be irresponsible of us to turn Mr. Holly out of town until he's fully recovered his faculties." This, with a serious demeanor and a perfectly straight face.

The magistrate's moustache did a poor job of hiding his smile as he finally caught on. "Irresponsible, yes. Can't have it. All right then, Mr. Holly: I hereby remand you to the doctor's custody 'til further notice. You can have your juice back when he says you're free to go." And he started for the door.

Holly stood still, stunned to utter impotence. The magistrate stopped beside him, and pulled him in to whispering range. "And if I catch you makin' a run for it, or selling your swill here ever again, I will pour it down your throat 'til you piss purple. Got it?"

He smelled of aftershave and gunpowder.

Holly nodded.

"Y'all have a nice day, now." The magistrate clapped him on the shoulder and ambled on out.

The daylight at Holly's feet faded with the closing of the door. There was some silence after that.

Finally, the mereau spoke up. "What do we do now?"

Fitch tipped his head, left and right. "Well, he's your patient, Lagniappe. What do you think we should do?"

The lanky blond apprentice brightened at this grand responsibility. "Oh! I so wanted to give him those stitches, you know, because it'd be such a shame if the cut festered...but it'll have all scabbed over by now."

Fitch smiled. "I think that's a fine idea. Why don't you fetch the needle and suture? It's high time I showed you how to debride a wound."

Lagniappe positively leapt to his feet at the suggestion. "Yes, doctor! Oh, and we've got to make him comfortable. Come along, Mr. Holly, come sit down, and I'll just take your bag. Don't worry a bit, now; you'll feel so much better for having it properly seen to. And after we're done, I'll have a look at your teeth! You have to care for your teeth, and with the wonderful new fillings we have nowadays, there's no reason not to have them done while you're here..."

Holly was dimly aware of being led back to that hated chair, felt himself seated in preparation for something truly awful.

No, he decided, travel was really quite a splendid business: If you were hell bound regardless, you might as well get there on your own initiative.

Ghost Men of Sunrise Mesa

Jonathan Maberry

– 1 –

"They say you're a bit strange."

That's what the man said to him. The first thing. Before hello. Before introductions. Just that. That was yesterday morning and now it was well into a hot afternoon, and those words followed him out of town and into the hills like a pack of dogs.

They say you're a bit strange.

Red MacGill hated when people said those kinds of things. Even though it was true. He was strange. Always was. Always would be.

That's why people hired him. A strange man for strange jobs.

Like this one. Like hunting ghosts out here in the Kansas hills.

– 2 –

It was hot as hell out there. Desert hot, with the hardpan and rocks taking the heat like a frying pan, with every plant, tree, and animal cooking in their own juices. Sweat ran down inside Red's clothes and glistened on the neck and flanks of his big horse, Nightmare. He cut covert looks at the man who hired him, a thin stick of a farmer named Mathew Hollister, but he seemed unaffected by the burning sun. Probably because all of the life had already been cooked out of him.

"How far?" asked Red.

Hollister squinted into the glare ahead. "Few more miles."

Ahead of them the ground sloped very gradually toward a cluster of broken hills surrounding a lopsided mesa. On maps it was called Sunrise Mesa because it faced east, but everyone around here called it Ghost Mesa. Though, it did not look particularly ominous. Well, except for the buzzards swirling in big, slow circles. Above them the sky was so hard a blue you could scratch a kitchen match on it. Not a goddamn cloud anywhere, nothing to provide shade.

Even so, he brushed his fingertips along the walnut grips of his pistol and loosened the Winchester in its scabbard. Touching the guns was a ritual for him. The barrels of each were covered with sacred symbols—not just of his mother's people or his father's faith, but of dozens of religions around the world. The weight of the bowie knife strapped to his left leg was a comfort.

He had planned on leaving Kansas and heading out toward California and the blue Pacific, or possibly heading down to Mexico. The trip out here had been frustrating and a rare failure for him. He'd been hired by a rich man who was more than a little crazy. The man believed that either bands of Arapaho had somehow managed to steal three complete freight trains—engines, caboose and all; or the *demons* the Arapaho prayed to had done it. Red, who more or less believed in demons, thought the old bastard was plain crazy, and thought it more likely that bands of white men had ambushed and robbed the trains. But that had proved a dead end. No one he talked to—white or red—had a clue, and none of the cargo, which was raw and processed metals, industrial crystals, machine parts, and tools had turned up in the hands of the people who traded in stolen goods. Red wasted several weeks of his time and a lot of the old man's money and ended up getting fired for being useless. Fair enough. But now he was broke and needed a stake to finance his trip out of this part of the country. He was down to his last dollar when Mathew Hollister found him in the town saloon.

"Tell it to me again," Red said.

Hollister looked at him. "I done told it four times."

"This will make five, then."

Hollister licked dry lips and glanced away. First toward Ghost Mesa, then up at the uninformative sky, then down at his own hands folded over his pommel.

"Like I said, Reverend Kit Smoke was through here last spring," said the farmer. "He told us all a lot of tales."

That part made sense. Reverend Smoke was, like him, half breed. Red was white and Comanche, while the reverend was black and Apache. But Smoke was a good man most days, though he was mad as the moon. Red had been of some use to the good reverend a few years back and now the preacher was wont to tell anyone, who would stand still long enough to hear about it, the full story. And, from what Red picked up, that story had grown considerably in the telling so that now it bore no resemblance to anything that ever happened. Stories were like that, and Red seldom bothered to set people straight. The real story was strange enough, and the fiction brought in good business.

His business was that of a "sorter of problems." Not wolf packs or cattle thieves. Stranger problems. It was not a crowded profession, and it brought people like Hollister to him.

"Reverend Smoke said you knew how to deal with unnatural stuff," continued Hollister. "Ghosts and suchlike."

"That's the part I don't quite follow," said Red. "Do ghosts *need* settling? Seems to me they mostly leave people alone."

"Not these ghosts," declared Hollister and now, as before, there were tears in his eyes that broke and rolled down his weathered cheeks. "These spooks have been slaughtering wild animals and cattle, and now I think they've gone and killed my brother."

– 3 –

Mathew Hollister owned a medium-sized farm out by Sunrise Mesa where he grew wheat and rye and some other crops. He and his brother, Jack, who was a lawyer in town, amused themselves by doing a bit of prospecting. Red had laughed at that, because there was a very short list of people who'd pulled gold from this part of the Great Plains. When Hollister showed him the map, Red shook his head. It was like a thousand he'd seen—printed on parchment paper and boiled in tea. Sold for a dime, which meant that it wasn't even worth the weight of the silver it cost to buy it.

They rode on, watching the buzzards. They were closer now, and Red could see that there were more of them than he thought.

"Um," began Hollister, "about those stories the reverend told us . . . they was all pretty wild. Campfire stories, I guess. Like you'd tell a kid to get him to eat all his peas so the boogeyman didn't come for him."

Red said nothing. He'd had this same conversation fifty different ways over the years.

"I mean," continued the farmer, "that was mostly Reverend Smoke *being* Reverend Smoke, if you follow me."

Red said nothing.

"But . . . he said some things that plum made the hair stand up on the back of my neck. Like about the screaming woman people see on farm roads down near the Rio Grande. The one they say's looking for the baby she drowned. And those two brothers in Albuquerque who turned into wolves. I mean, they didn't really turn into wolves, did they? They couldn't, right?"

Red said nothing.

They rode on with Hollister staring at him. Red tried not to laugh, though not all of it was funny. Reverend Smoke was one of several people who seemed compelled to tell stories about the half-breed problem sorter. Sometimes it got good business, and more than once it got Red ushered out of town by deputies and townsfolk who didn't want his kind around. And in those cases that had nothing to do with Red's Comanche mother.

As for the individual stories . . . even Reverend Smoke did not know all of them. Or even all the details of the ones he told. Like the two brothers in Albuquerque. Hell, it was only the younger one that was the problem, and a silver bullet sorted him out right quick.

"Tell me again what you saw," he said. "The ghost, or whatever it was. Tell that part again."

Despite the heat, Hollister shivered. "I only caught that one glimpse. Jack and I were supposed to meet out here and work a big cave we found. Sure, we knew that it was probably only going to be more fool's gold—iron pyrite—but we had fun up there. Talking old times and shootin' the breeze. With his lawyering and my farm, it's the only time we ever get to talk."

Red made an impatient twirling motion with his finger.

"Well, I saw Big Al—that's Jack's horse—wandering free on this slope that goes straight up to the cave mouth. I called out, but not too loud. Didn't want to spook Big Al. But Jack didn't answer. So I tied my own horse to a tree and went up on foot, slow-like, trying to calm Big Al, but he suddenly bolted and ran across the slope past the cave and began climbing a rocky path. I ran to follow, afraid the fool horse would break a leg in all those rocks, but just as I passed the cave I saw it."

"'It,'" echoed Red. "Tell me exactly what you saw."

Hollister let his horse walk a dozen paces before he answered.

"I saw its skin first," he said in a hushed voice. "Just inside the cave mouth, lying over a flat rock. It was like some animal, some great lizard, had shed its skin. But the more I looked the more I realized that the skin was not lizard shaped. It was *man* shaped! I picked it up and it was heavier than I thought it should be. A lizard or snake skin is thin when it's shed. This wasn't, nor was it kind of see-through, like a shed snake skin. This was more like a garment, like overalls, but it wasn't any kind of denim of anything else I ever touched before. It fair made my skin crawl to handle it, and the smell! God above, there was a stink rising from that skin like whatever shed it was sick and dying. I flung it away from me and then...well...that's when I saw *it*."

"Ah," said Red, leaning forward with interest.

"Well, now...remember when I told you about that orange monkey I saw in the zoo? It was like that. A bit like that, anyway, but it didn't walk about on its knuckles and feet. This thing stood erect, and it wore some kind of garment, like a long breechcloth an Indian would..." He let the rest trail off and looked away in obvious embarrassment. Red wanted to laugh. White men were so funny at times.

"Like a breechcloth..." he prompted. "Tell me about the ghost."

Hollister cleared his throat again and continued. His voice trembled as he described the monster in the cave. "Well, I'm not completely sure it was a ghost, but I don't know what else to call it. It weren't natural, I can tell you that. It was shorter than me, but broad at the shoulders and covered all over with pale hair. Not blonde, not like my wife's, nor the pure white of an albino, like the farrier's eldest son. No, this thing's hair was dead-looking, as if all the color was somehow plum sucked out of it. Its skin was as pale and gray and mottled as a mushroom, like some foul thing that grew in the dark. The face was no monkey's face, nor anything worn by a man. Maybe Judas has a face like that when he burns in hell—you can ask the Reverend Smoke next time you see him. Let me tell you, though, that face will haunt my nightmares the rest of my life. No chin to speak of, and a wide mouth full of crooked teeth that were smeared with blood. I kept trying not to believe it was my brother, Jack's, blood. God a'mighty! But, let me tell you—it was the eyes that were the worst. Big and round like a fish's, but gray and red, like blood mixed with river mud. It was horrible—*horrible* I tell you."

"And you just turned around and ran?" asked Red.

Hollister stared at him. "Wouldn't you?"

Red said nothing.

In fact, he wasn't at all sure he would have stood his ground. Not because he thought it really was a ghost, but because what Hollister claimed to have seen reminded Red of a monster from his mother's people, the *Mu Pitz*—the wild cannibal men of Comanche legend. It was a persistent monster that appeared in a number of ways in the stories of other native peoples. It was the *Manito* to the Obinwa, the *Nun' Yunu' Wi* to the Cherokee, the *Shampe* to the Choctaw. There were so many monster legends, and Red had stopped believing that all of them were superstitious nonsense. He'd left that prejudice behind a long time ago because experience was an effective, though cruel, teacher.

They rounded a bend in the trail and Red could see the black mouth of the cave where Hollister had seen his ghost. Or whatever it was.

"We're there," said Mathew Hollister. "It's just up the..."

His words died in the hot, still air.

Halfway up the slope was a congregation of vultures. Not flying, but clustered tightly around something that lay red and lumpen on the rocky ground. Flies in their thousands buzzed with frantic determination to take their portion of the grisly feast and lay their eggs for the maggots waiting to be born.

Nightmare juddered to a stop and gave a low, frightened whinny, but Red was already swinging out of the saddle. He snatched the rifle and levered a round into the chamber before his boots touched down. Red ran up the slope, scattering buzzards before him. They screeched in outrage and protest as they flapped into the air. Red skidded to a stop, the stock socketed into his shoulder.

But his finger still lay outside the trigger guard. There was no one and nothing to shoot. The buzzards weren't worth the bullets, and the thing on the ground was beyond killing.

It was a horse. A big one. Part Percheron and part Appaloosa. Or, it had been.

Now it was meat, baking in the sun, writhing with maggots and beetles. The tough hide had been peeled back to expose yellow fat and marbled red flesh, with edges of white bone sticking out like knives. He heard a gagging sound and turned to see Mathew Hollister standing a few feet behind him, one hand over his mouth. In the other the farmer held a pistol that was pointed almost at Red.

"Stay there," Red said, but he reached back and gently pushed the barrel away.

"That's . . . Big Al."

"Yeah," said Red, "I figured it was."

With his rifle in both hands he moved in a slow arc around the dead horse and up a rocky slope toward the mouth of a cave. There were bloody footprints all around. Most were birds and rodents and other scavengers, but beneath these, nearly obscured, were stranger prints. Red knelt down and studied them carefully. The shape was unusual. Long and narrow at the arch, blunt and round at the heel, and with a flare across the ball of each foot to accommodate those ungainly toes. The big toe hooked around at an unnatural angle, but it was still a toe—the pressure marks showed that. That toe looked more like a thumb, but Red didn't believe it was a creature walking on its hands. This thing walked upright like a man.

But he was certain it was *not* a man. He'd hunted people more than animals, and Red was sure he'd only ever seen something like these prints once.

Six years ago Red had gone East, all the way to Chicago, hunting for a person he thought was a monster, but who turned out to merely be mad. A peculiar kind of madman who skinned his victims alive and wore their skin like a suit. Red ended that man and was injured in the process. During his slow recovery, he spent many days walking the paths of the Lincoln Park Zoo, and there, in a big cage, he'd seen a creature who left prints similar to this. It was a kind of ape he'd never heard of before—covered in coarse orange hair and with a face like a sleepy drunk. An orangutan. But as he studied the prints, matching them against memory, he did not think apes had escaped a zoo or carnival and come out to these hills on a murder spree.

No. And the gait was wrong. Orangutans had a curiously light rolling walk, but the impressions here—formed by dry blood—were of something that plodded heavily.

"Not a ghost," he murmured.

"What's that?" asked Hollister nervously. "What's that you say?"

Red stood and turned in a slow circle with the rifle. Everything around him was still except for the flies and buzzards. He faced the cave again, which was a black nothing.

"I said it wasn't a ghost."

"How can you tell?"

"Never heard of a ghost leaving footprints like that," he said. "And, besides, why would a ghost kill a horse, skin it, and cut steaks out of it?"

Hollister blinked at him in astonishment, then gaped down at the dead animal. Red pointed with the rifle barrel to where sections of the hide had been pulled away rather that torn through with beaks.

"There's knife marks on the sides there," he said, "and on the flanks. And see those big missing sections. You're a farmer, man, you want to tell me you never seen a cow butchered before? Or a horse, for that matter. No...something's up here, that's for sure, and it's hungry and it uses tools. We're not looking for any ghost."

"Then...then...what *are* we looking for? And where's my brother Jack?"

Red chose not to answer that because there didn't seem to be anything to say that wouldn't hurt. The farmer was a simple man—uncomplicated and honest. Red regretted ever agreeing to let him come along.

"I'm going to check out the cave," he said. "Stay here."

"But—"

"Watch the horses. If something gets to them, we'll never make it back to town." He paused and looked Hollister in the eye. The man was terrified and on the verge of tears again. "I need to you to guard the horses and watch my back. If you see or hear anything—anything at all—you call out. You got that?"

Hollister nodded, but Red pressed him.

"I need you to say it, Mr. Hollister. I need you to tell me that you can do this."

The farmer took a breath, let it out, and then straightened. "Yes," he said. "I can do it."

"Good man. Eyes and ears," said Red. "Eyes and ears."

He turned and faced the black mouth of the cave. The slope rose sharply, and he carried the rifle at port arms, ready to tuck the stock into his shoulder and fire. The Marlin Hollister used was a .22; Red's rifle was a good deal more powerful and, on the ride here, he had taken each round and used a silver knife to cut tiny symbols into the soft lead noses of every bullet. Protection symbols he'd learned about from his mother and uncles. Comanche and Celtic magic that was generations old. Sometimes that sort of thing helped. Sometimes a bullet was only a bullet. He wouldn't know what would work here. If hot lead didn't slow them down, then he had other tricks up his sleeve. His thrice-blessed knife, the herbs in the leather pouch hung from his belt, the tattoos drilled into his skin. The last years had taught him all kinds of techniques.

Above him, the mouth of the cave yawned wide. The sun was slightly to the west and, from that angle, it chased the shadows deep inside the opening. Only, they retreated just so far and then coalesced into an impenetrable wall of utter blackness.

As he raised his rifle, and took his first step toward that place of darkness, pain and mystery, everything changed.

The shape of the day.

The structure of the world.

Everything.

– 4 –

At that moment, the screaming started.

It exploded into the air like the shrieks of ten thousand seagulls. A piercing sound pitched so high that Red cried out, dropped his rifle, and staggered backward as if he had been punched in the head. The vultures flapped away with such terror that two of them flew into the edge of the big tumble of rocks and fell broken to the unforgiving ground.

Blood erupted from Red's nose and his knees buckled. He curled up into a tight ball on the ground, helpless as a stillborn baby. His own scream was lost inside that sound. No steam engine, no cannon, nor the gunfire of a thunderstorm could match that noise. It seemed to go on and on and tear the sky.

Then it stopped.

Bang. Like that.

The abrupt end of the noise was, in its own way, equally jarring. It tore a gasp from him like a man on the terrible edge of drowning suddenly rising to the surface of water. The first inhalation of air burned. The second was like ice.

Red fought to uncurl his body, to roll onto hands and knees. It was like trying to raise a buckboard with his bare hands. His muscles were locked and moving them felt like tearing the fibers. He forced his arms and legs to straight, his back to move. One hand flopped out and fumbled for his fallen rifle. He blinked and worked his jaw and wasn't at all sure if he could hear. Had the sound blown out his eardrums? There was no sound at all, so he could not be sure.

He turned his head, which seemed to take more effort than bending a horseshoe barehanded.

"H-Hollister..." he groaned, but Mathew Hollister lay sprawled in the dirt at the bottom of the slope. Red had to stare at him a long time to be sure the man's chest rose and fell, but the fellow was out. Maybe the sound had done something to him, or maybe he'd fallen and hit his head.

The world itself was silent as a tomb. Not a fly buzzed, not a bird sang. There was no sound at all.

Until there *was* a sound.

Not a shriek this time, but a kind of whirling sound, like the vanes on a windmill turning in a storm breeze. A *fast* sound, and buried within it was a thin, high whistle that did not sound in any way natural. There were clicks wrapped round the whistle, and he had the bizarre mental image of a breeze blowing through the gears of a tower clock in windy Chicago.

He raised his head to look.

And very nearly died because of it.

Something big and pale shot past him, over him, beyond him, passing so close that it slapped the hat from his head and sent it bumping and tumbling in its wake. Red cried out as he flattened, and then rolled over, his cramps forgotten as he stared in shock at the thing that had narrowly avoided decapitating him. He blinked, trying to clear his eyes because the thing they saw could not be real. Must be some kind of hallucination, the result of brain damage from that sound. A trick of the light.

Blinking did not change a thing.

The thing moved past him and hit the midpoint of the rocky slope. It skidded all the way down to finally collide with the bones of Big Al.

It was a sled, he thought, like something drawn through snow by a horse on a winter's day in Montana. As it skidded and slewed to a stop, Red wondered how such a fragile-looking thing had not immediately smashed to pieces.

It had a metal frame like the kind of sled horses pulled through winter snow. It was constructed of steel struts and brass tubes and coils of copper. There was ivory in there, and many crystals of exotic kinds and colors, some of which were opaque while others were as transparent as glass. He saw gears, too, like those in a clock and knew that he had not been far wrong in understanding the sound of the thing as it hurtled overhead. As much as it looked like a sled it also looked like a carriage from some fairy-tale story, with filigree that ran in lines of gold and silver. A cloud of dust rose up around it, conjured by the machine's long skid and from some internal working that appeared to be in distress.

All of this was amazing to him, appearing as it had from nowhere and flying over his head with the force of a cannonball. Gravity clawed it down and the sled slammed down onto the hard rock of the slope and immediately began to swerve and fishtail out of control. Showers of sparks flew up from its metal runners and the whole contraption wobbled so violently that it threatened to turn a slide into a deadly sideways roll. Red stared in horror because as it landed he could see that there was a person inside the thing. It was not a ghost or an ape-footed creature, nor even the *Mu Pitz* monster of his mother's people.

It was a woman.

She was a tiny thing, though. Frail looking and slender as a willow wand, with masses of pale hair hanging loose around her shoulders. Red cried out for fear that she would be crushed or torn to pieces. Her hands seemed to dart and move everywhere, clutching at knobs and levers and dials as if there was something she could do to stop the mad careening of the machine. For machine it had to be, though its design was totally alien to him and its purpose beyond his understanding.

The sled skidded down the hill and to his horror Red saw that Mathew Hollister lay in its path. The farmer's doom seemed certain, but suddenly the woman wrenched a long lever hard to one side causing some of the crystals to suddenly pulse. The sled seemed to jump sideways somehow, as if vanishing and instantly reappearing a few feet to the left. It was surely a trick of the light, but Red could have sworn the whole thing disappeared and reappeared out of the path of Hollister's certain death.

The sled slithered down the far side of the slope and then jolted to a stop against a pile of rocks. The woman was jerked violently forward and back, but did not hit the metal frame. As Red hurried down after her, he could see why. There were straps holding her suspended like a spider in a web, each one fastened with such balance that they kept her from striking the metal or being hurled out. Even so, the force of the stop winded her, and she sat there for a moment, gasping and dazed.

Red slowed and stopped a few yards away, glancing at Hollister, who was showing faint signs of returning to consciousness, and at the bizarre and improbable contraption. How had such a ponderous device been flung with such violent force—and from where? It seemed to come from the direction of the cave, but . . . how?

The woman, groaning and gasping, released some control and the straps fell away. She sagged for a moment, then with a small cry of anger, pulled herself out of the machine and stood swaying on the slope.

Her clothes were strange. She wore a simple tunic of some lavender material that shimmered like fine silk, girdled at the waist with an ornate belt of leather upon which many pouches and pockets were affixed. A small knife hung at her hip and, on her left side, she wore a kind of holster that Red thought held some kind of pistol, though it seemed to be made from green glass or porcelain.

The woman's face was flushed as if in fear or from exertion, but her eyes were clear and steady. Her full-lipped mouth set firm. The woman stared up at him with an expression of surprise that likely matched his own, before giving a small cry and frantically fumbling with the brass levers. If there was some purpose to this Red could not see it for nothing at all happened. Her alarm was immediate and obvious and enormous. The next cry that escaped her lips carried with it notes of terror.

Red staggered.

"Who are you?" gasped Red, steady on his feet, but not at all sure the world followed suit. "And what is all this?"

She stared at him and replied in a string of words so alien to him that, at first, they did not appear to be any language at all. It was more like a song, the words flowing like musical notes. It would have been quite lovely had threads of panic not been so obviously sewn through the fabric of what she said.

"I...I don't..." he began, and then faltered as a scuffle of noise made them both turn. Mathew Hollister was awake and stood shakily on his feet, blood painting one half of his face and his eyes glazed. He blinked several times as he looked from the woman to the machine to Red and back again.

"What is all this?" he asked, and it came out in a thoroughly reasonable tone, as if someone on the street had merely ask what time it was o'clock. He stumbled over to stand by Red, still blinking and confused. "What's happening? What is that thing? Who's this young gal?"

The woman opened her mouth as if about to answer, but then she froze and stared at them. A sound was torn from her. Not a word but a cry of mingled horror, revulsion and naked fury.

And then the woman drew her strange pistol and fired at them.

- 5 -

The draw was so fast that her hand seemed to blur. No Dodge City gunman could ever hope to match the speed of that draw. No rowdy or tough or badman from the rough country could have outshot her. One moment her hand was empty, and then she held the crystal handgun out.

The weapon had no visible cylinder, nor even a proper barrel. Instead three brass prongs were set into the snubby business end of the gun, and there was a hollow *TOK!* By then Red had an arm hooked around Hollister and dove for safety. They fell hard and rolled down toward the butchered horse.

Red did not hear the whine of a bullet but instead the air above them flashed with intense light and heat. He scrambled to his knees, bringing his rifle up, ready to shoot this strange madwoman, but stopped short, the trigger half-pulled because her gun was not pointed his way. Red turned to follow her line of sight and saw a scene out of some nightmare of hell. But *who's* hell was beyond knowing.

The mouth of the cave was suddenly on fire—not only the

dried weeds that grew round it, but for a moment even the rocks seemed to blaze. The blast of that crystal gun had done something, projected heat in a way totally outside of Red's understanding. As if hellfire was its bullet. Pieces of charred rock flew through the air, raining down all around. A second blast struck the wall and nearly half of the cave's opening cracked apart and fell with a thunderous *whump*, belching gas and dust into the hot air. The debris piled high, blocking more than half of the entrance.

That was not the strangest part, though.

Standing to one side of the cave mouth were three of the strangest figures Red MacGill had ever seen, and he had seen spirits and demons in the dark. The figures were pale and covered in loose skin that sagged from arms and groin and legs but which was tight across sloping and muscular shoulders. Although the skin was smooth and hairless, the hides of each monster was splashed with blood and filth, and Red knew without question what had happened to the rest of Big Al, and likely the remains of Jack Hollister.

The heads of these monsters were not the apelike visages described by Hollister but were smooth and featureless except for a single eye that was like a bar of green glass across the upper third of their faces. These creatures—for Red could not call them men—shied back from the fire, but still held their ground. Instead, they raised weapons of their own that were similar in design to the one the woman held, however, while hers was formed from green crystal, they aimed a crude conglomeration of metals.

"It's them!" cried Hollister. He was on his back and scuttled away on hands and heels. It's the ghost men! Jesus save my soul..."

Red had never seen anything like these things. They were not like any man he had ever seen or read about in books. Frankly, he had no idea what they even *could* be, and that in itself was terrifying. Ghosts were something he understood—or thought he understood—and men were men. These things were... *what*? Demons of some kind?

The creatures disregarded Red as if he was of no consequence, and instead aimed their weapons to fire at the woman, who took cover behind the metal sled. They hesitated, though, as if for some inexplicable reason she frightened them as much as they clearly did her. Maybe even more, because they cowered back into the cave mouth.

The woman pointed her gun, but did not yet fire, clearly torn between conflicting thoughts the nature of which Red could not begin to guess.

But then he thought he *did* understand. As impossible as it seemed, given the nature of her sled, the thing had come from that cave. Now most of the entrance was choked by the debris torn from the ceiling by her strange gun. Was it, he wondered, that she needed to keep that cave mouth open? Did she need to return? Or was there something inside that mattered to her? Perhaps something stolen or guarded by the strange brutes?

The monsters hesitated also and, in a flash of insight, Red thought that they either needed to take her alive, or they had a concern of damaging her carriage.

All of this made sense at least—the motives behind the standoff—even if nothing else held a shred of sanity. And that forced Red to make a decision. He could run, because the combatants were so thoroughly fixated on one another that they seemed to disregard him. Or he could pick a side.

Then Mathew Hollister shattered the standoff by standing up, brandishing his rifle and roaring at them. "Where's my brother, you sons of Judas? Where's Jack? What have you done with him, you—"

The closest of the creatures spun toward him and fired his strange weapon.

TOK!

Mathew Hollister had time for a single earsplitting shriek of total agony and then he was gone. His body seemed to explode from within, becoming an intense ball of white-hot fire. The fireball plucked Red off the ground and hurled him twenty feet away. He slammed into the withered arms of a sunbaked tree. He tucked his chin to protect his head, but the trunk punched him between the shoulder blades and drove all the air from his lungs. Red slid to his knees, losing his rifle, and fell forward onto his palms. Sick, winded, but not out. Not gone. Not yet.

Even as pain burned through his back and lungs, he pawed the Colt from its holster, raised it in two hands to keep it steady, and fired and fired. The first bullet missed the bastard who killed Hollister. The second did not, catching the thing as it turned its hellish weapon on him. The big lead slug did not pass through as if encountering spectral vapors. It struck meat and bone and when it did pass through, the bullet exploded out the other side and sprayed blood on the rocks. Bright red blood. Real blood.

The screams were real, too.

Not human, but no ghostly wails. Cries of agony. A death cry, he hoped.

The other brutes shrank back, and Red chased them with his last four rounds, missing twice, hitting one in the hip and catching another in the shoulder. The uninjured creatures fired back, but they did it while running, while dragging their wounded comrades back into the cave. Then one of them exploded in the same way Hollister had, and Red realized that the woman had fired her gun at them. Red shoved his pistol into the holster and snatched up his fallen rifle. He fired from the hip, but by now the remaining creatures were gone, swallowed by the darkness of the cage.

Gasping with pain and all but biting chunks of the air to fill his tortured lungs, Red scuttled behind a boulder and fumbled to reload his rifle and pistol. Even dazed and hurt he did it fast, but there was no one left to shoot. The creatures were gone, leaving only blood and death and mystery behind.

He turned toward the woman who was still crouching behind the machine. She was fiddling with something on the confounded thing and finally pulled away with a gleaming quartz rod in her hand.

There were sounds coming from the cave and Red thought he saw many of the lumbering shapes milling around just inside there. He was in no shape for a fight—he was flash burned, plastered with Mathew Hollister's scorched blood, and the world was spinning so harshly that even walking took all of his strength. The woman seemed to realize that. She grabbed him by the arm and pulled him away. Red did not want to flee. He wanted to fight, but now was not a time for fighting. Now was a time for dying or running, and so he ran.

Later, though...Oh yes, later there would be a time for fighting. For killing.

They ran.

– 6 –

The woman led him away quickly, but it was clear she did not know where she was going. Red forced himself to think and act with sense, and in turn guided her to where Nightmare and

Hollister's horse were tethered. The woman shied back, wary of the big creatures, but Red told her it was okay. She allowed him—with great reluctance—to help her mount. Red put her on his own horse, whom he knew and trusted, and then climbed onto the farmer's threadbare mount.

They turned and rode away from the haunted mesa, riding toward another cluster of tall rocks that rose above a stand of trees. It was a few miles' ride, and they went hard, the woman clutching on for dear life. She stayed in the saddle, though, and continually watched Red as if studying what he did to control his mount. By the time they reached safety, she was managing a fair imitation of handling the reins. It impressed Red, and he found that her intelligence—as well as her obvious courage—made him like her.

They circled the rocks and dismounted. Red climbed to the top of one and used a small pocket telescope to study the terrain. Then he slid back down to the ground.

"They're not following," he said.

"No," she said, and it was the first word of English she'd spoke. "They do not like the sun. Even with their protective garments."

She had a soft voice and an accent that sounded vaguely British, but as if British was overlaying something else that he could not identify.

"I just need to rest up for a spell," said Red. "Then I'm going back."

"Yes. I need to go back, too."

"Oh, hell," Red said sternly. "You're staying here where it's safe. This is man's work..."

He stopped talking because the look she gave him all but shriveled the skin from his hide.

"'*Man's work*'?" she echoed coldly. "Are you really that kind of shortsighted fool? You could go charging back there, and they'd skin you alive. Literally. Together we might have a chance."

Before Red could reply there was a strange, piercing cry from the mountains they'd just left. It rose like some tortured seabird, climbing high into the sky and echoing across the plans, battering into one cluster of rocks after another before being shredded by the wind. Red did not have to ask what unnatural throat uttered that plaintive, horrific sound. His hand fell to the holster Colt, but there was only the faintest cold comfort there. When he glanced at the woman he saw a glittering steel hardness in her eyes and he knew that she was right and he, despite his understanding of the world, was wrong.

"We need to get to shelter," she said. "They hate the sun, but once it's down they will be hunting us."

Red led her into the trees and they found a tiny spring seeping sluggishly from a cleft in the stone. Both of them drank greedily, and the cool water did him a power of good. It chased much of the dizziness away, though his back still hurt and the burns on his skin were painful. He watered the horses, then set about filling the two saddle canteens. While he did that, the woman sat down on a rock and watched him with large, almost luminous eyes.

She pointed to his pistol and held out a hand, palm up. Red hesitated, shrugged, and then handed it over, butt first. The woman examined it, her lips pursed like a jeweler appraising an antique watch.

"Bullets...?" she said, offering the word as a question.

"Yes."

"Crude," she concluded and handed it back.

Red could see her in more detail now, and he found himself awed by how exotically beautiful she was. Like a woman in a painting from one of the islands, though far paler. Or a fairy in an old book of poems.

"Who are you?" he asked. "And what in the hell is going on?"

The woman considered him, and his questions, for long seconds. "Tell me... your name," she said.

"Manfred MacGill," he said. "People call me Red."

"Like the color."

"Yes."

"Like your hair."

"Yes."

She touched her own chest. "Oona."

"Ah. A pleasure, Miss Oona."

"Just Oona."

"Okay, Oona... now just what in the hell was all that about back there? Who are you? What was that machine, and where did it come from? And what on *earth* were those... those... things?"

She considered his questions, almost smiling as if they were somehow naïve; and maybe they were, because nothing of the last half hour seemed to fit into any version of the world as he understood it. Not even of what his mother called the "larger world," where spirits and monsters and demons lurked at the fringes of reality. The other strange things he'd encountered as a sorter of problems all seemed to fit with a degree of practical rightness into that larger world. These things, though, were different, and he'd sorted through the difference on the ride here. The creatures, the woman, their odd weapons, and that mechanical sled, as bizarre as they were, had a sense of undeniable reality to them. Ghosts and other monsters seemed to always live on the other side of a thin veil, as if they were part of a dream that was slipping through a crack into the real world. Not the things he saw today. Everything about them was real, and that made them that much more impossible.

She licked her lips and with a small snarl of intense distaste said, "Those creatures are called Morlocks."

- 7 -

"*Morlock*?" he asked, confused. She spoke as if it was the most horrible word a person could utter, but it meant nothing to him. "Are they men? Where do they come from? And for all that, where do *you* come from?"

Oona studied him, chewing a full lower lip for a moment. "Tell me, Red MacGill, are you a good man?"

The question startled him, but her eyes spoke the earnest need for truth.

"I believe that I am," he said. "I'll do no harm to him as has done none to me. I don't steal, I don't cheat at cards, and when I give my word, it has meaning. You can count on it." He paused. "Is that what you wanted to know?"

She nodded. "My father was a good man. He was like you. Like this..." She waved to indicate the land behind them, which made no obvious sense to him. "He came from here. Not here in this desert, but from here. He came to where I live. Where my mother lived. Before he came to us we were very primitive. As helpless and uneducated as little children. Then my father came and brought so many things with him—science and fire and learning. He taught my mother how to read. He taught her friends how to fight, even though we never understood what we fought for."

Red didn't understand, either, but did not say so.

"He came once and then went away and came back," said Oona. "He came a long, long way. When he came back again he brought books, and a gun like yours, and many things. He stayed that time. Settled there. Had children." She paused as a shadow drifted across her face. "The Morlocks killed him. Killed my mother, my brothers and sisters. They killed everyone but me, but I survived because I was away. I came back to find them all dead."

A single tear, delicate as a jewel, glistened on her cheek.

"When you say your father 'came,'" began Red, "came from where to where?"

Oona paused. "My father said that when he told his friends about his journeys none of them believed him. He said he stopped trying to convince people that what he said was true."

"Try me," said Red. "I've come to believe in all sorts of things lately."

Oona gave him a strange look. "My father was a time traveler," she said.

Red couldn't help but smile. "A time...?"

"See, he was right, people from your time don't believe."

"From my time?"

"My father was from a land called England. From this *time* in England. He told me stories about it. A great island shrouded in fog. It is the heart of the greatest empire of this age, but it began to slide into decline. On his travels he saw it fall, as all empires fall. He saw many others rise all around the world. He saw the rise of this country—your country—as an even greater empire."

"America?" laughed Red. "An empire? Well...okay, I can understand that. They've conquered so many nations to build what they have. They've slaughtered uncounted millions. My mother's people among them."

She nodded. "America rose in power because of the richness of the land and the development of machines of war. Flying machines. Bombs that can destroy whole cities. Diseases used as weapons, and other things that even I, my father's best pupil, do not understand." She touched his arm. "But the American Empire did not last, either. Nothing lasts. As the centuries were consumed by millennia, everything made by man—no matter how strong—falters and falls. Rotted from within, destroyed by conflict, or eroded by entropy. He even went to the very end of

Earth itself and beheld its final hours as a world whose vitality had been spent, whose potential to renew itself had been finally exhausted. Even the stars themselves will eventually swell and collapse and die. The greatest glory for a time traveler is to see the wonders of a changing world; but the greatest tragedy is that nothing lasts except time. Maybe, in the very end, time itself will end, but who could travel that far to know?"

"If your old man was from England and is still alive right now? Can't you get him to help with this?"

"He is...but it is the wrong time. He launched his machine in 1895, which means right now it isn't built or even conceived. To contact him now would be to create a paradox that might prevent him from building his machine in the first place. Besides, how could I ever convince him that I was his daughter when he had not yet met my mother? Such a thing might drive him mad."

"Might be doing that very thing to me, truth to tell," admitted Red. He looked back the way they'd come. "And that sled you were on? What is that...?"

"It is my time machine," said Oona, nodding. "Not my father's original machine, for that was stolen. No, this is my own, built with my father's help while he was alive, and completed after the Morlocks..." She stopped and shook her head, unable to give words to a memory that was clearly too horrible to recount.

Red's heart went out to her. He could never fully describe to another person the atrocities committed upon his mother's helpless body by white men who wore the uniforms of soldiers.

"Once my father began fighting them in defense of the Eloi, my people, the Morlocks needed to be able to hunt us in the open."

"'Hunt,'" echoed Red, nodding. "They slaughtered a local man and ate him, and his horse. They provided for the Eloi, keeping you fed. Why? Were your people...*food* to them? Were you their cattle?"

She shivered and nodded. "My father changed that. It took a long time, and he sometimes had to be brutal with us, but he taught us to fight. It was not a concept we understood. Violence, aggression, the very concept of *self*-defense had been bred out of us, and my father forced it back into our experience. Perhaps some philosophers of the future will label him a monster because the Eloi were happy, but that will be unfair. We were happy because we were too stupid to understand our purpose in life.

We were only food. We had no other purpose. We made nothing, created nothing, thought nothing of depth. We were cattle, as I understand that concept. My father used that word a lot. Cattle, sheep, lambs."

"You're different," said Red. "You don't act like a sheep."

Oona gave him a faint smile. "I was born his daughter. My father raised me to be different. To think, and to know, and to continue the fight should he fall. As he did." She took a breath. "My father took us to war against the Morlocks. He burned many of their underground cities and drove thousands into the light, where they starved and died. He armed the Eloi. He traveled back in time over and over again to bring us weapons. He scoured the abandoned cities of my world to find other weapons, like these microwave pulse pistols." She touched the strange pistol at her hip. "To help us be free, he turned us into killers. He became the Devil to the Morlocks. A concept no one in our world understood. The Morlocks learned of it firsthand, to them, he was the soul of evil, just as they had finally become true evil to us."

Oona rose and walked a few paces deeper into the mouth of the cave.

"The Morlocks did more than murder my father," she said. "They stole his original time machine. They took it and over years tore the secrets from what my father had built. They had never lost their understanding of science, of engineering and manufacture."

Another plaintive cry tore through the air. He glanced in that direction and, through the skeletal arms of the tree saw the sky darkening beyond the rocks where the Morlocks hid.

"We can't do anything until the sun goes down," she said.

"Why? If they can hunt us at night..."

"They will, but it means many of them will leave the cave, and we must go back there. By now, they'll have taken my machine. Theirs will be in the cave as well. I need to reclaim my own and destroy theirs."

"I have a man to find," said Red. "The brother of the poor fellow who the Morlock killed. He went missing yesterday. It was his horse they'd butchered."

Oona shook her head. "If they killed his horse they probably killed him, too. The Morlocks are carnivores, and worse...they are cannibals."

"That doesn't surprise me all that much," said Red. "I have to find Jack Hollister though. Alive or dead."

"Why?" she asked. "What is this man to you?"

"A stranger. His brother paid me to help him find Jack, and I keep my word."

"Even if both of them are dead?"

Red looked at her. "You are fighting your father's fight, and he's dead."

They sat for a while with that hanging in the air between them. Finally Oona nodded and continued with her strange narrative.

"Tell me more about these Morlock fellows? What in tarnation are they?"

"They are monsters from what is the future of your world and the present of mine," said Oona. "They were servants and laborers, once upon a time. People who worked in the factories and underground workshops of the world's great cities. Over the years they provided so much for the entitled, who lived up in the sunlight, that it caused a split in evolution. The entitled became so reliant on these luxuries that they lost the ability to provide for themselves. They grew frail and weak and stupid, while the laborers grew stronger and cunning." She paused and her cheeks colored. "My people—the Eloi—are what the entitled became by the time my father arrived. Stupid and innocent and naïve, and totally dependent on the Morlocks for our food and clothing. Meanwhile the Morlocks, who lived too many thousands of years in the dark, became monsters like this one."

Red's lip curled in horror and disgust at the very thought that a monster like the one he killed was a cousin to this beautiful woman, which made him kin to Red himself. It was an appalling story, even in the shorthand version she told because there was no time for a fuller tale. His mind, as it was wont to do, grabbed at the disparate pieces of the puzzle and found that they fit together easily, though the picture they made was ugly.

She cut him a look. "You only saw them in their protective garments, but you did not see them as they are. They lived all those years in the shadows and cannot abide the sunlight. Beneath those false skins, they are more hideous than I can describe, and more so for having once been part of the same human race from which my people sprang. They are our brothers." She shuddered at the thought. "They are the face of the sins of our ancestors."

"But they're nothing more than flesh and blood," said Red, nodding, once more touching the handle of his pistol.

"They are more than that," she said quickly. "They are monsters, yes, but they are sly and cunning. They build machines and understand them. They stole my father's time machine and used it to come here. To the past, to your world."

"Why? Just to hunt?"

"No," she said, "to conquer."

– 8 –

"Conquer?" laughed Red. "How? There can't be many of them in the cave."

"There aren't," agreed Oona. "A dozen at the most."

"Then..."

"By comparison, how many white men came to this country? A few hundred at first? And there were many millions here."

"They had guns, and we, my people, had stone axes and bows, and every year more and more ships arrived."

"The Morlocks have microwave pistols and a time machine," Oona countered. "The time machine can carry four on each trip. With one machine, it will take many trips to bring more, but they can keep making trip after trip. And the reason they chose *this* age is that there is everything they need. Machinery, manufacturing plants, processed materials. This is the earliest point in human history where industry will suit their needs, and where opposition is limited to primitive weapons. They came here, to this remote place, in order to establish a foothold." Her expression darkened and she looked sick. "Now they have my machine, as well. Soon, they will double their efforts. They'll have enough of them here to form an army. They'll raid your towns, take over and repurpose your factories."

She stopped and shook her head, fraught with the horror and the plausibility of their plans.

More howls filled the night. Red could see the swollen sun hanging on the edge of the world, ready to fall.

"There is one hope," said Oona. She dug a hand into her pocket and removed the crystal rod Red had seen her take from her sled. "This is a control rod, and it is very difficult to manufacture. With this, they could use my machine—without it, the machine is useful only as a blueprint to help them build more. It will take them many weeks to find this kind of crystal and fashion a replacement rod."

Red nodded to the rod. "That's why they're going to come hunting for us, isn't it? You didn't just take it to keep them from using your machine, it's bait to clear them out of the cave. Am I right?"

She smiled. She hadn't smiled before now, and it changed her face from one of unmarked innocence to something else entirely. There was a feral, predatory cast to it, and the gleam in her eyes was dangerous and sly.

"My father once told me guile and its many uses," she said. "It was unknown to the Eloi, and it saddened him that it was one of the gifts he brought to my people. However... it's useful. The Morlocks are devious and evil and tricky, and to fight them one must sometimes *become* like them. Does it shock you, Red MacGill?"

His answer was a bitter laugh. "I'm half red man. White men slaughtered most of my people, including my mother. They are the Morlocks of my world, and I have learned to walk within their world. Because my father was white, I have not gone to war with all of them; but when I need to hunt one, I do so without hesitation or mercy. Tell me, Oona, does that shock *you*?"

"Not in the least."

"Good."

A chorus of howls filled the darkening sky. The horses stamped and tossed their heads in fear.

"Do you have any kind of plan?" asked Red.

"I do, but it's not a complicated one."

"Try me."

"And it may be suicidal."

"You should have been with me in Albuquerque."

She did not ask why but clearly took his meaning. "Do you have any god you pray to?" she asked.

"I pray to the ghosts of my mother's ancestors."

Oona considered that. "I suppose I'm like that, too. The Eloi have no religion, and on my travels through time I found that religion as a concept burned itself out of the human consciousness tens of thousands of years before I was born. But... I tell my father what I'm going to do and ask him to watch over me."

"That'll do," said Red. He drew his pistol and showed her the barrel, then handed her the rifle. "These are symbols of protection from religions all over the world. Some of those faiths have also died out."

"And yet you carve their symbols onto your weapons?"

"Sure," he said. "Why not? Just because no one else believes in the old gods, it doesn't mean that they don't exist. There might be whole planets of other people who still believe in them. Or . . . maybe believing in them doesn't matter a damn. What *does* matter is that it comforts me to go into a fight thinking that maybe these sigils and symbols might give me a little bit of an edge."

"And if that's just self-delusion?"

"If it is and I die, I'll never know, will I?"

She laughed, a strange and musical sound. "I like you, Red MacGill."

He looked away, slightly embarrassed. The howls were closer now.

Oona stood and drew her porcelain pistol, frowned at it, then took a small knife from a pouch of her belt. She held the weapon into the spill of moonlight and used the edge to carve a name on it. Red stood close by and watched.

"Your father's name?" he asked, and Oona nodded.

– 9 –

They mounted the horses and rode away. They rode long and far and in a big circle, and came up on the hills and the cave from the far side.

The moon was still down, but there were ten billion stars to show them the way. They tied the horses to a dead tree a mile from their destination and went in on foot. Low and fast and very quiet. It was reasonable to think that any Morlocks hunting them would have followed their path of escape toward the other rocks. The howls had been going that way, and even now they could hear more of the ghostly cries far off in that direction.

When they reached the edge of the slope, Oona stiffened and uttered a tiny cry, for her sled—her time machine—was gone. Long scrapes along the surface of the slope told the story of the machine being dragged into the heart of the mountain. Red also noticed that there was much less of the horse now, with most of what had been left cut away with brutal precision. He knew for sure now that Jack Hollister was not waiting to be rescued. Maybe Mathew had been luckier than his brother, because he had died instantly in that fireball, while his brother's death was likely more painful and grisly. Poor bastard.

Oona suddenly clutched his arm and pulled him down. Ahead of them a piece of shadow seemed to detach itself from a bigger patch of darkness. As it moved away from the side of a towering piece of rock, Red saw what it was and a thrill of terror spiked through his heart. His blood turned to rivers of ice.

From its size and shape and the lumbering gait he knew it was a Morlock, but it no longer wore the protective garment. It stood there, hideous and terrible. Mathew Hollister had not exaggerated in his description. This was a monster, and its wide mouth full of crooked teeth that were smeared with blood. But *whose* blood, Red did not want to guess.

Worst of all was the expression in those eyes and carved into every evil line of its face. Despite the lineage of this creature, there was no trace of humanity left. There was intelligence and cunning and naked hunger, but beyond that, overshadowing it all, was a vile and obvious pleasure in this thing being what it was. Here was avarice and rapaciousness and gluttony and greed and malice combined into a focus of mind and a nature of being that viewed everything as either food or opportunity. There could be no willingness to bargain or reason with such a creature. You were its food or its enemy, but nothing else.

Oona made a soft sound of disgust as she raised her pistol, but Red touched her arm and when she looked at him in confusion, he shook his head. He used one finger to draw a circle indicating the landscape around him then touched that finger to his lips. She understood. It was too soon for noise. Then he silently drew his knife. Like pistol and rifle, it too was carved with holy symbols and had been blessed by medicine men from three nations—Comanche, Apache, and Cheyenne. Three warrior nations. The thrice-blessed knife was his favorite weapon, the one he trusted most.

He stood his rifle against a rock and moved off, relying on every trick of silence and hunting he had ever learned. He made no sound at all.

It is human, he told himself as he moved. *It bleeds. It can die.*

The Morlock walked along the perimeter of the hill with the cave in it, clearly posted as a sentry. He kept his head down, though, as if unwilling—or more likely unable—to bear the bright starlight.

Although the Morlock looked powerful and dangerous, that weakness cost him.

Red came up behind him and clapped a hand across the creature's broad mouth, pinching his nostrils shut with thumb and forefinger. As he did that, he kicked the Morlock in the back of the knee, canting him backward against Red's chest while the blade bit deep into the monster's throat. Red turned the Morlock's head from right to left as he drew the blade from left to right. The thrice-blessed blade cut deep, and Red twisted the dying beast to one side so that the spray of blood struck the ground rather than shoot into the air. The whole movement was precise and very fast and it did not allow the Morlock to make any sound. One moment it was alive—an alien and impossibly terrifying thing—and the next it was empty meat sagging toward the ground.

Red settled it down and crouched over it, looking down at the dead face. The stamp of horror was still there on the features, but there was no intent left as the muscles grew slack. Red was not winded. The killing was a simple thing, and something he had done before on white throats, red throats, and brown throats. Fast, easy, and silent as the grave.

He rose and turned and found Oona standing there. If he expected to see disgust or shock on her features, he was once more wrong about her. There was look of competent appraisal in her eyes. She nodded approval, and as she drew close said, very quietly, "You'll have to teach me that."

Then she moved past him toward the cave, pausing only long enough to spit on the corpse. Red smiled. He really liked this woman. He wiped the knife clean on the Morlock's fur, sheathed it, picked up his rifle and followed.

They crept close to the slope but did not step onto it because its entire length was exposed. So, instead they circled around until they found a pile of broken rock that offered the right blend of useful handholds and flat sections where they could make a stand and shoot if they were spotted. It was a hard climb, though, and there was no way to do it while carrying the rifle. Red was loath to leave it behind because it had range and more stopping power than his Colt, but needs must when the devil drives. Or so Red's dad often quoted.

They climbed and with them climbed the moon, leering over the edge of the mountains and then showing its scarred face as evening became night. Red wished he'd asked if it was brightness or actual sunlight that hurt the Morlocks. If the latter, then the moon might be a weapon because its light was merely reflected from the sun over the horizon. But he discarded that hope. The Morlocks were abroad at night, and they had to know what sunlight was. Then he realized that in his fear he was grasping at straws. A foolish practice for a warrior going into battle.

They reached the top of the rock pile and it was only a long step over to the top edge of the slope. He went first and then pulled her over. They paused to catch their breath and listen for sounds from within.

There was a noise and it confused Red, because it was not at all what he expected. It was an almost impossible sound. There were clangs as if hammers were beating on metal, and strange exhalations as if from the throats of dragons. There were metallic thumping and whooshings that sound like freight trains running fast along a track, but they were many miles from any rail line. There was the *tink-tink-tink* of tools on metal and rock and something that sounded like glass. And the coarse and guttural sound of deep voices speaking in a language he could not begin to understand.

When he turned to Oona, her face had gone white as milk—paler even than the moonlight. She touched her throat in fear, yet bent to listen more closely. He leaned toward her and mouthed the words *"What is it? What are they doing in there?"*

Oona shook her head and drew her pistol.

He drew his, too, and also drew his knife, keeping that in his left.

There was no plan beyond coming to this moment. They nodded to each other, each drawing in breath, and then rounded the corner before charging into the cave.

– **10** –

There was darkness at the mouth of the cave, but there was light further along. Pale light, from shielded lanterns. Light to work by, but mindful of the weak eyes of these underground abominations.

Enough light to hunt by.

There was one guard inside the tunnel, but no way to kill him with the absolute silence as the other one. Even so, Red took him before the creature could scream, driving the big knife blade into the socket of the thing's throat and giving the blade a vicious quarter turn. The throat exploded in blood, but the windpipe was destroyed and the Morlock dropped to its knees, its pistol falling with a clatter to the stone. Oona snatched it up and now had a pair of nearly identical weapons. She grinned like a wolf.

They moved forward, following a sharp downward curve of the cave as it dropped into the earth and then broadened into a large cavern. Work lanterns were strung everywhere, casting the whole space in a dirty yellow glow. Oona and Red froze, shocked to absolute stillness by what they saw.

There—impossibly there—in the heart of the cavern, were three massive freight trains. Each bore the seal and logo of the crazy old man who'd hired him to come to Kansas. Not stolen by Arapaho demons or white men thieves. Somehow the Morlocks had stolen them. By what means, and how they transported all those hundreds of thousands of tons of metal and cargo here was something Red never learned. Even Oona, who knew so much of the Morlock's science, was dumbfounded. And yet here it was. Or, what was left of it.

The boxcars had each been dismantled and their contents removed. Some of the cars were stripped down to steel skeletons, and of these none were whole. Beyond the line of cars was a massive cauldron in which the steel was being melted down and poured into molds. The engines had been torn apart and reassembled into some fantastical new shapes that were more like the factories Red had seen in Chicago for stamping out shaped metal for building and manufacturing. Stacks of newly made parts stood in rows. The massive cylinders and pistons chugged and worked, spitting out new parts with every minute. The engines glowed with heat, as if the need for the Morlocks to finish their work was pushing them to the limits of their potential. He saw them shudder and tremble; steam rose from tortured metal, and yet they clanged and chugged and belched smoke and spat out their infernal devices.

"No!" gasped Oona, but when Red glanced at her she was not looking at the factory but at something that stood near one of the walls. It was her sled, her time machine, and a Morlock mechanic was busy working on it. Some of the crystals inside the machine glowed and pulsed with strange lights. Oona pulled Red down behind a stack of crates and bent close to whisper in his ear, her words masked by the thunder of this strange factory.

"They have my time machine *working*," she cried. "That's impossible. I took the crystal controller."

They saw at once why it was more than possible. The Morlock dug into a canvas bag slung around his chest and removed a handful of crystals identical to the one Red knew Oona had in her pouch. He selected one and screwed it into place. The glow of the time machine grew brighter still, and although the Morlock winced at the light, he was smiling a broad and evil smile of pure triumph.

Oona began to say something to Red, but her words faltered as she looked past her machine. Her mouth fell open and Red turned to look, too. It took him a moment to make sense of it.

There was another time machine a few feet away.

It was not as battered as Oona's, and looked quite new, though the design was somehow cruder. Blockier and far less elegant.

Beyond that was another.

And another.

Red stared through the yellow gloom. There were many more. *Rows and rows of them.*

And now he understood.

The Morlocks had come here for more reasons than one. Somehow their bizarre perspective of looking backward through time had allowed them to know about the transportation of tools and equipment on those trains, and they'd come back to this time to set up their factory. With all of these resources and a remote, secret place to work, they had toiled like hungry vermin in the bowels of the earth. Building time machines. Building a fleet of vessels that would allow them to conquer all of this world. Of Red's world. They would be like a plague of locusts swarming through time itself. Maybe even ravaging other worlds. Red did not understand the science, but the implications were like icy daggers in his heart. He was witnessing the end of the world. Of all worlds and all times.

The Morlocks worked like fiends. There were not a dozen of them, as Oona had thought. There were scores of them. Perhaps hundreds. Milling, white as maggots, all over their machines, running their factory, preparing for a war that could not be won by anyone but them.

Unless there was some way to stop them.

He felt like a fool for even thinking that. It was a thought born of hubris; like the challenge of a mouse preparing to wage war in a house of cats.

No. Not like that.

It was like his ancestors must have thought when they first heard the crack of a musket and saw the bad medicine of a bullet kill a red man beyond the range of bowshot. Like the Comanche and Apache and Cheyenne and the other nations felt when they rode in packs toward a line of cavalry who stood behind rows of nine-pounder cannons. Such a thought was perhaps noble—or would be in a song, if anyone was left to write songs—but it was nothing when measured against the Morlocks and their fleet and their monstrous factory. He might as well have stood on a New England rock and hurled stones at the *Mayflower*.

Oona seemed to deflate beside him, and he knew that her own bravado was being ground beneath the wheels of reality. She looked down at the two pistols she had and shook her head, clearly measuring their meager power against the might of the Morlock army. She bowed her head and then sagged back and sat hard on the ground. The two porcelain pistols fell from her fingers, and she buried her face in her hands.

"I'm sorry, Father," she said in a voice so broken it tore at Red's heart. "I tried...Please forgive me, but I tried."

She wept as the machines thundered and the smoke curled like storm clouds against the ceiling of the cave. Red felt so bad for her that a fiery rage burned in his chest. He wished he had the power of the demons his mother prayed to. He wanted to reach up and pull the ceiling down and bury these monsters and their factory in ten million tons of rock.

But he was only a man, with a man's strength, and this was the end of the world.

Then...

He looked up again. At the machines. At the glowing hot metal of the train engines as they struggled to match the insatiable demands of the Morlocks. He looked at the steam shooting from the vents. Urgent, angry.

He looked down at Oona, this small, strong, brave, time-lost woman. He looked at her strange hair and clothes. So alien to him. He looked at her weapons, discarded on the ground.

And Red MacGill smiled.

It was not a nice smile. Although he could not see it, he felt it, and when he'd smiled like that before, his enemies had recoiled. Maybe Comanche demons glared out through his eyes when he smiled like that. Or maybe the Celtic gods of his father's people. Or, perhaps it was simply a level of madness entirely his own.

He bent and picked up one of the pistols.

"Tell me," he said with an odd gentleness in his voice, "how does this work?"

Oona shook her head and turned away. "What does it matter? We can kill ten, twenty, a hundred of them, but they can bring back whole armies. We've lost."

"How does it work?"

"Why bother?" she snapped. "We can't kill them all."

Red touched her chin with one finger and turned her head. She resisted at first, but then she allowed it. He didn't turn her to face him—and not because he did not want her to see that smile on his face—he turned her toward the laboring machines. Her brow furrowed in confusion.

"How does this gun work?" he asked again.

The confusion melted like wax and ran from her face, leaving her brow clear. Then she did look at him, and her smile was every bit as wild as his own; every bit as insane.

She picked up the other pistol. "You turn this dial. Lowest setting will kill a man."

"And the highest setting?"

Her answer was a demon's grin.

They both turned the dials all the way up.

"It will bring down the whole mountain," she said.

"Yes," said Red.

"We'll die, too."

"Sure," he said, "but not alone."

Oona got to her feet. She stood on her toes to reach his mouth with hers, and kissed him.

"You're a good man, Red MacGill," she said, meaning it in a different way than before. "My father would have liked you."

"Your father would be proud of you," said Red.

They raised their guns.

A Morlock saw them and shouted a warning. A dozen of them pulled their own pistols.

Oona took Red's free hand in hers.

They fired.

– 11 –

It was a sultry night on Coronado Bay in San Diego.

The man with the burned face sat on a chair that was tilted back on two legs. His booted feet were on the rail of the small cabin, a glass of beer resting on his belly. There was music on the wind. Spanish guitar. Laughter, too.

Beside him was a woman with bandages on both arms and shadows in her eyes.

They watched the moon's reflection on the ocean, a river of silver light that stretched from the beach to the horizon.

The man's face itched where the burn scabs were healing. The woman told him not to pick at it. He did anyway. He drank some of the beer.

They said very little. There was time for talk, for sharing of her world and his. This wasn't that time. In the three months since they crawled out of the smoking mouth of hell, they had talked and talked. But on nights like this they often lapsed into silence. The world turned on its slow axis and spun through the blackness of space. On the face of the world, children played and babies cried, people loved and hated and fought and died and were born. Nations strove one against the other, masterpiece paintings were wrought, books were written, dances were danced. It was not a calm world, and often not a nice one, but maybe people would learn to get along. Maybe.

There was time for that.

There was plenty of time.

Red drank his beer. Oona stared up at the stars. Sometimes they smiled at each other.

There would be plenty of time for everything.

About the Contributors

About the Editor

David Boop is a Denver-based speculative fiction author and editor. He's also an award-winning essayist, and screenwriter. Before turning to fiction, David worked as a DJ, film critic, journalist, and actor. As Editor-in-Chief at *IntraDenver.net*, David's team was on the ground at Columbine making them the first *internet-only* newspaper to cover such an event. That year, they won an award for excellence from the Colorado Press Association for their design and coverage.

David's debut novel, the sci-fi/noir *She Murdered Me with Science*, returned to print in 2017 from WordFire Press. (Simultaneously, he self-published a prequel novella, *A Whisper to a Scheme*.) His second novel, *The Soul Changers*, is a serialized Victorian horror novel set in Pinnacle Entertainment's world of *Rippers Resurrected*.

David edited the bestselling weird Western anthology, *Straight Outta Tombstone*, for Baen, and has followed with *Straight Outta Deadwood* and *Straight Outta Dodge City*. David is prolific in short fiction with many short stories and two short films to his credit. Additionally, he does a flash-fiction mystery series on Gumshoereview.com called *The Trace Walker Temporary Mysteries* (the first collection is available now). He's published across several genres including media tie-ins for *Predator* (nominated for the 2018 Scribe Award), *The Green Hornet*, *The Black Bat* and *Veronica Mars*.

David works in game design, as well. He's written for the Savage Worlds RPG for their *Flash Gordon* and *Deadlands: Noir* titles.

Currently, he's relaunching a classic RPG, *Bureau 13: Stalking the Night Fantastic*, as a Savage Worlds title, complete with tie-in novel.

His third go at a "real" degree landed him Summa Cum Laude in the Creative Writing program at UC-Denver. He also is part-time temp worker and believer. His hobbies include film noir, anime, the Blues and Mayan History. You can find out more at Davidboop.com, Facebook.com/dboop.updates or Twitter @david_boop.

About the Authors

Joe R. Lansdale is the author of forty-five novels and four hundred shorter works, including stories, essays, reviews, film and TV scripts, introductions and magazine articles.

His work has been made into films, *Bubba Hotep* and *Cold in July*, as well as the acclaimed Sundance TV show, *Hap and Leonard*. He has also had works adapted to *Masters of Horror* on Showtime, and wrote scripts for *Batman: The Animated Series* and *Superman: The Animated Series*. He scripted a special Jonah Hex animated short, as well as the animated Batman film, *Son of Batman*. He has also written scripts for John Irvin, John Wells, and Ridley Scott, as well as the TV show based on *Hap and Leonard*.

His works have been optioned for film multiple times, and many continue to be under option at the moment.

He has received numerous recognitions for his work. Among them the Edgar, for his crime novel *The Bottoms*, the Spur, for his historical Western *Paradise Sky*, as well as ten Bram Stokers for his horror works. He has also received the Grandmaster Award and the Lifetime Achievement Award from the Horror Writers Association. He has been recognized for his contributions to comics with the Inkpot Life Achievement Award, and has received the British Fantasy Award, and has had two *New York Times* Notable Books. He has been honored with the Italian Grinzane Cavour Prize, the Sugar Pulp prize for fiction, and the Raymond Chandler Lifetime Achievement Award. *The Edge of Dark Water* was listed by *Booklist* as an Editor's Choice, and the American Library Association chose *The Thicket* for Adult Books for Young Adults. *Library Journal* voted *The Thicket* as one of the Best Historical Novels of the Year.

He has also received an American Mystery Award, the Horror Critics Award, and the Shot in the Dark International Crime

Writer's Award. He was recognized for his contributions to the legacy of Edgar Rice Burroughs with the Golden Lion Award. He is a member of the Texas Institute Of Literature and has been inducted into the Texas Literary Hall of Fame and is Writer in Residence at Stephen F. Austin State University.

His work has also been nominated multiple times for the World Fantasy Award, and numerous Bram Stoker Awards, the Macavity Award, as well as the Dashiell Hammett Award, and others.

He has been inducted into the International Martial Arts Hall of Fame, as well as the United States Martial Arts Hall of Fame and is the founder of the Shen Chuan martial arts system.

His books and stories have been translated into a number of languages.

He lives in Nacogdoches, Texas, with his wife, Karen, as well as a pit bull and a cranky cat.

Mercedes Lackey was born in Chicago, Illinois, on June 24, 1950. The very next day, the Korean War was declared. It is hoped that there is no connection between the two events.

In 1985 her first book was published. In 1990 she met artist Larry Dixon at a small science fiction convention in Meridian, Mississippi, on a television interview organized by the convention.

They moved to their current home, the "second weirdest house in Oklahoma" in 1992. She has many pet parrots and "the house is never quiet." She has over 135 books in print, with four being published in 2019 alone, and some of her foreign editions can be found in Russian, German, Czech, Polish, French, Italian, Turkish, and Japanese.

Mercedes Lackey has written and published 135 books in many series, including the Secret World Chronicles, Hunter, Valdemar, Elemental Masters, SERRAted Edge, Elvenbane, and Obsidian Mountain series from Hyperion, DAW, Baen, Tor and many others.

James Van Pelt is a full-time writer in western Colorado. His work has appeared in many science fiction and fantasy magazines and anthologies. He's been a finalist for a Nebula Award and been reprinted in many year's best collections. His first Young Adult novel, *Pandora's Gun,* was released from Fairwood Press in August of 2015. His latest collection, *The Experience Arcade* *and Other Stories* was released at the World Fantasy Convention in 2017. James blogs at www.jamesvanpelt.com and he can be found on Facebook.

Ava Morgan writes steampunk and fantasy. In a distant parallel universe, she studied to be a lawyer and once worked in the legal field behind a desk. However, one trip to a sci-fi convention years ago cemented her desire to pursue her true calling: writing stories that were just a little bit different. She still works behind a desk. However, at the very least, she gets to deal with unique settings and diverse, quirky characters. Maybe being a writer isn't that different from her former profession after all...

Ava's bestselling steampunk adventure series Curiosity Chronicles is still going strong with the recent release of *The Scarborough Affair*. When she's not writing, Ava can be found bicycling with her husband under a Texas sunset, raising two rambunctious children, and wearing vintage fashion. Visit her site at www.avamorgan.com for the latest updates.

Harry Turtledove earned a PhD in Byzantine history after flunking out of Caltech at the end of his freshman year. (Want fries with that?) When he couldn't land a teaching job, he scammed the beginnings of an sf/f-writing career into a tech-writing job, which he kept for eleven and a half years. After quitting it to write full time, he has made a poor but none too honest living turning out tales of alternate history, other sf, fantasy (much of it historically based), and, when he can get away with it, historical fiction. He has won a Hugo, lost two more, lost a couple of Nebulas, and pilfered three Sidewise Awards and a Dragon Award for alternate history. His latest novel is *Through Darkest Europe*, an alternate history; forthcoming is a new historical, *Salamis*.

He is married to fellow writer and Broadway maven Laura Frankos. They have three daughters and two granddaughters, and live in a not-quite-big-enough house with three overprivileged cats. If you like, he can annoy you on Twitter @HNTurtledove. He tries not to take life too seriously.

Samantha Lee Howe began her professional writing career in 2007 and has been working as a freelance writer for small, medium and large publishers, predominately writing horror and fantasy under the pen name *Sam Stone*. This body of work includes thirteen novels, five novellas, three collections, over forty short stories, an audio drama and a *Doctor Who* spin-off drama that went to DVD.

Samantha's breakaway debut thriller, *The Stranger in Our Bed*, was bought by HarperCollins and will be released under their One More Chapter imprint on 14 February 2020 (digital) and 16 April 2020 (paperback).

A former high school English and Drama teacher, Samantha has a BA (Hons) in English and Writing for Performance, an MA in Creative Writing and a PGCE in English.

Samantha lives in Lincolnshire with her husband, David, and their two cats, Leeloo and Skye. She is the proud mother of a lovely daughter called Linzi.

Eytan Kollin has written the successful and award-winning Unincorporated series with his brother, Dani. The first book in the series, *The Unincorporated Man* won the Prometheus Award (with two of the three other books in the series nominated, as well). Eytan and Dani have also published a book of short stories called *Grim Tales of the Brothers Kollin* through WordFire Press. Baen will publish *Caller of Lightning*, a Benjamin Franklin historical fantasy that Eytan coauthored with Peter J. Wacks, in June 2020. He has also sold the rights for his first solo novel, *Balancers*, to Automatic Publishing; release date to be determined.

The writing of "The Adventures of Rabbi Shlomo Jones and the Half-Baked Kid" started as a simple conversation about how almost any cultural background could find its way into the Wild West. Thus, the story of a golem was suggested. Eytan wrote another Shlomo Jones adventure with his father, Rabbi Gilbert Kollin, a man whose knowledge of Judaism and the Wild West proved of great benefit to both the first and second stories.

Julie Frost grew up an Army brat, traveling the globe. She thought she might settle down after she finished school, but then married a pilot and moved six times in seven years. She's finally put down roots in Utah with her family—a herd of guinea pigs, three humans, a tripod calico cat, and a "kitten" who thinks she's a warrior princess—and a collection of anteaters and Oaxacan carvings, some of which intersect. She enjoys birding and nature photography, which also intersect. Utilizing her degree in biology, she writes werewolf fiction while completely ignoring the physics of a protagonist who triples in mass. Her short fiction has appeared in too many venues to count, including *Writers of the Future 32* and *The Monster Hunter Files*. Her werewolf private eye novel series, *Pack Dynamics*, is published by WordFire Press. She whines about writing, a lot, at agilebrit.livejournal.com.

Kim May has always been a storyteller—just ask her mother. On second thought don't. She knows too much. Kim writes fantasy, sci-fi, thrillers, YA, historical fiction, steampunk, and a bit of poetry because she collects genres like a crazy cat lady collects strays.

Kim's debut novel, *The Moonflower*, was a 2017 Whitney Award nominee. She also won first place in the Named Lands Poetry Contest with a haiku. Kim's short stories can be found in *The Monster Hunter Files, Eclipse Phase: After the Fall, Put Your Shoulder to the Wheel*, and several issues of *Fiction River.*

Kim lives in Oregon where she works at an independent bookstore and watches a lot of anime. She's a retired stage actor and has a penchant for fast cars, high heels, and loose screws. You can follow her on Facebook, Twitter, and at ninjakeyboard. blogspot.com.

James A. Moore is the bestselling and award-winning author of over forty-five novels, thrillers, dark fantasy and horror alike, including the critically acclaimed *Fireworks*, the Seven Forges series, *Blood Red*, the Serenity Falls trilogy (featuring his recurring antihero, Jonathan Crowley) and his most recent novels, the Tides of War series (*The Last Sacrifice, Fallen Gods* and *Gates of the Dead*), *Boomtown*, and *Avengers: Infinity*. In addition to writing multiple short stories, he has also edited, with Christopher Golden and Tim Lebbon, the *British Invasion* anthology for Cemetery Dance Publications. Along with Christopher Golden and Jonathan Maberry he is cohost of the *Three Guys With Beards* podcast. More information about the author can be found at his website: jamesamoorebooks.com.

Irene Radford has been writing stories ever since she figured out what a pencil was for. Editing, as Phyllis Irene Radford, grew out of her love of the craft of writing. History has been a part of her life from earliest childhood and led to her BA from Lewis and Clark College.

Mostly she writes fantasy and historical fantasy including the bestselling Dragon Nimbus series and the masterwork Merlin's Descendants series. Look for her in December of 2019 writing historical tales as Rachel Atwood. In other lifetimes she writes urban fantasy as P. R. Frost or Phyllis Ames, and space opera as C. F. Bentley. Lately she ventured into steampunk as Julia Verne St. John.

If you wish information on the latest releases from Ms. Radford, under any of her pen names, you can subscribe to her newsletter: www.ireneradford.net. Or you can follow her on Facebook as Phyllis Irene Radford, or on twitter @radford_irene25.

Arianne "Tex" Thompson was once described as "an explosion of fifty-two enthusiastic kittens latching onto everything at once." After earning a bachelor's degree in history and a master's in literature, she channeled her passion for exciting, innovative, and inclusive fiction into *Children of the Drought*—an internationally-published epic fantasy Western series from Solaris.

Since then, she's become an international raconteur, most recently keynoting for GIFcon at the University of Glasgow and ruckus-raising from Boise to Bulgaria. A passionate instructor for LitReactor and Writing Workshops Dallas, Tex regularly presents for writers far and wide, once preaching the page-turning gospel over nine cities and two thousand miles in a single two-week "Tornado Alley Tour."

At home, Tex is the founder and "chief instigator" for WORD (Writers Organizations 'Round Dallas)—a coalition of North Texas writers groups and an aspiring "literary cartel." Now a 501(c)3 nonprofit organization, WORD regularly brings over four hundred writers together for WORDfest and Writers in the Field (which still boasts a stunning 0% mortality rate in spite of the tornado).

On the page and on the stage, Tex is proud to bring her particular brand of "red-penthusiasm" to conferences, conventions, and workshops all over the country—as an egregiously enthusiastic, endlessly energetic one-woman stampede. Find her online at www.TheTexFiles.com!

Jonathan Maberry is a *New York Times* bestselling author, five-time Bram Stoker Award–winner, and comic book writer. His vampire apocalypse book series, V-Wars, is in production as a Netflix original series, starring Ian Somerhalder (*Lost, Vampire Diaries*) and will debut in 2019. He writes in multiple genres including suspense, thriller, horror, science fiction, fantasy, and action; and he writes for adults, teens and middle grade. His works include the Joe Ledger thrillers, *Glimpse*, the Rot & Ruin series, the Dead of Night series, *The Wolfman, X-Files Origins: Devil's Advocate, Mars One*, and many others. Several of his works are in development for film and TV. He is the editor of high-profile anthologies including *The X-Files, Aliens: Bug Hunt, Out of Tune, New Scary Stories to Tell in the Dark, Baker Street Irregulars, Nights of the Living Dead*, and others. His comics include *Black Panther: DoomWar, The Punisher: Naked Kills* and *Bad Blood*. His Rot & Ruin books are being produced as webcomics. He is a board member of the Horror Writers Association and the president of the International Association of Media Tie-in Writers. He lives in Del Mar, California. Find him online at www.jonathanmaberry.com.